MIST ON THE SALTINGS
HENRY WADE

MIST ON THE SALTINGS
HENRY WADE

PERENNIAL LIBRARY
Harper & Row, Publishers
New York, Cambridge, Philadelphia, San Francisco
London, Mexico City, São Paulo, Singapore, Sydney

First PERENNIAL LIBRARY edition published 1985.

Library of Congress Cataloging in Publication Data

Wade, Henry, 1887–1969.
  Mist on the saltings.

  "Perennial Library."
  Originally published: London : Constable, 1933.
  I. Title.
PR6001.U3M5   1985   823'.912   84-48630
ISBN 0-06-080754-7 (pbk.)

85 86 87 88 89 10 9 8 7 6 5 4 3 2 1

CONTENTS

CONTENTS

MIST ON THE SALTINGS

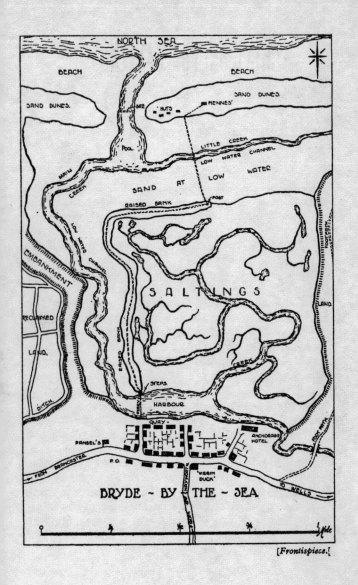

BRYDE ~ BY ~ THE ~ SEA

[Frontispiece.]

MIST ON THE SALTINGS

CHAPTER I

BRYDE-BY-THE-SEA

HILARY PANSEL straightened her back and
stretched her arms in an attempt to get rid of the
little gnawing pain that always attacked the middle
of her spine when she was washing up or ironing—
anything that involved bending for more than ten
minutes at a time. It was nothing that mattered,
of course—only one more small addition to the
burden of single-handed domestic drudgery.

It had seemed such fun when she and her big,
adorable John had bought the little cottage at
Bryde-by-the-Sea, and started on their venture of
living and becoming famous entirely by their own
efforts—no rich relations, no staff of hired servants,
practically no money, to help them on their way.
They would do it all themselves, quietly, with no
advertising ; there would be hard times, of course ;
they would have to ' go without ' while the founda-
tions were being laid, but that would be all part of
the fun. It was John, of course, who was to be
famous, was to make, in time, the fortune that
would compensate them for the quietness and
simplicity of their start, but she, Hilary, was to
have an equal share in the building up of his fame,
by feeding him and nursing him and keeping him

happy and cheerful so that no worries or silly little
domestic troubles should interfere with his work.
It would be John's name that would be famous, but
people who *knew* would say : ' Ah, he would never
have done it without her. She has been his inspira-
tion—his good angel. Their life together has been
so idyllic that he could hardly help becoming a great
artist.' Then they would sigh and wish that they
had done as much for *their* husbands—for it would
be women, of course, who talked like that—men
were too unimaginative to think of it.

It would take a little time, of course ; they had
realised that from the first. There was not much
money in painting till you *were* famous, or at any
rate till some art gallery had taken you up. John
would have to be content with fifteen or twenty
guineas for canvases that in a few years' time would
be changing hands at three-figure prices—for other
people. But by then he would be earning big money
himself. Vayle was getting three hundred for his
oils and forty or fifty for the smallest water-colours—
mere scraps of paper with a few quick, inspired
strokes of the brush dashed on to them. " Vayle ",
some wag had said, " has only to blow his nose on a
handkerchief and frame it and there's forty guineas ".
Of course that was an exaggeration, and not very
kind, but it was a great compliment in a way—that
people should be willing to pay such prices for what
were (to Hilary) little more than suggestions of
pictures. There were painters, of course, who got
even bigger prices—a thousand guineas was not
unheard of, even for a landscape—but they were
mostly men who caught the popular fancy with
work which (John said) would be out of fashion

2

and dead in a generation. John would not be like that—his work would last and become greater and more admired long after he was dead—as was the case with all great artists.

It was not only the money that mattered, of course ; that would be nice for what it would enable them to do. What would be so lovely would be meeting celebrated and brilliant people, not only painters but artists of every kind and actors and authors and everybody worth meeting—people who had made their names and their fortunes by their own talents and not by just inheriting what other people had done for them—the ' parasites ', as Hilary in her healthy young scorn had called them. Hilary was herself the daughter of a younger son of an obscurer—and poorer—branch of a good family, and the sting of being neglected by the higher branches of the family tree had left its mark upon her young and sensitive spirit. So that it was with enthusiasm not unmixed with bravado that, at the age of twenty two, she had married John Pansel, eight years older than herself and of no family at all—just a painter who had got badly hurt in the war and whom she had nursed back to health in the hospital which Lady Waterley—one of the ' higher branches '— had established, with lavish display of patriotism and womanly feeling, in the ancestral home at Glynde Park. Hilary was welcome enough then ; she was young, enthusiastic, and didn't mind what, or how much, hard work she did, and was quite ready to attend to the obscurer patients while Lady Waterley and her plain daughters fussed round the ones whose mothers might be useful ' after the war '.

And ' after the war ' Hilary had been dropped

like a hot potato; she was far too attractive to have at Glynde while her plain cousins were trying to harvest the seeds that had been sown in those grim years. Hilary had received a photograph of the group taken when the Queen had visited Glynde, with Lady Waterley in flowing coif and two medals on her right, and Sir Patrick Boynton, the great consultant, on her left, framed—the photograph was—in silver, together with an autograph letter of thanks and a vague invitation to ' come and see us again at Glynde some day '. That had been the end of it for Hilary, but the beginning of her real love for big, good-tempered John Pansel, who had laughed at her anger and shown her what real life was like and drawn for her visons of a future of which the little cottage at Bryde was to be but the first stage.

The very name of the place had fascinated her—Bryde-by-the-Sea. It was so deliciously appropriate to their honeymoon—for they spent their honeymoon in preparing the little house that was to be their home till fame came to John. It was bound to come, because John's reputation as a painter had been firmly established before the war came to smash everything that was beautiful and of good repute in the world. He had won a travelling scholarship at the Lambeth Art School, that wonderful training ground for the real working artist which one of the great City Companies had established and endowed. The scholarship had taken him to Paris and Rome and in 1914 he had won the Prix du Louvre, second only in importance to the Prix de Rome. Sir Otto Geisberg, the great collector, had sent for him and encouraged and advised him,

4

offered to finance him for a further two years of study in Rome. The ball had been at John Pansel's feet, fame beckoned to him with golden finger, the glory and wonder of his art and his opportunity dazzled him—and a group of young firebrands in Sarajevo threw a bomb which shattered the whole firmament of creation into a million fragments and turned all the thoughts and efforts of men for years to destruction, destruction, destruction ∴ . .

For a year after the war John Pansel's spirit had remained in a state of torpor—stunned by the shock and horror of its experience. The agony and beastliness of his wound—a severe abdominal laceration— had hurt more than his body ; the years of merciless destruction had killed—so he thought—the power, even the desire, to create ; the possession of money, his war gratuity, encouraged the evil lethargy which was stifling him. A war friend had lent him a small cottage in a drab part of Essex, where no beauty of scenery or surrounding beckoned to his dormant muse ; he was content to lounge through the days, smoking his pipe, feeding a few stupid chickens, digging the stiff, grudging soil of a rectangular patch of garden. No doubt it was good for his body, this absolute rest after the years of strain, but his spirit might well have sunk for ever into obscurity.

Then a chance meeting at an Oxford Street tea-shop, on one of his rare visits to London for a Medical Board, had revived his acquaintance with the attractive young nurse whom he had been too ill and tired to do more than like and be grateful to at Glynde. To his surprise, John Pansel had felt, during this short half-hour's talk, a stirring of youth and interest. He was thirty now and had come to

think of himself as a middle-aged man. Women
and the thought of marriage had not entered his
mind during the last five years ; even before that
he had been too deeply immersed in his budding
career to do more than play with the lighter fringes
of love. Now, as he travelled back to his lonely
Essex hovel, he found himself thinking with eager
affection of Nurse Keston, who had been kind to
him in that hellish hospital—Glynde, to him, was
a nightmare of draining-tubes and ether—and who,
this afternoon, had smiled and talked to him as if
he were a human being and not a ' case ' whom the
Medical Board had that afternoon scheduled as
' cured '.

That had been the first of many meetings, half-
surreptitious at first on the part of John, almost
shame-faced at the idea of having anything to do
with a girl. Gradually Hilary's vigorous enthusiasm
and healthy scorn had stirred a response in John's
dormant spirit ; he had begun to talk of his ambitions, his early life—a hard, bitter struggle till the
beneficent City Company had given him his chance,
but a life which taught Hilary the smallness of her
own angers and ambitions. Spurred on by Hilary—
no longer now ' Nurse Keston '—John had dug his
' outfit ' and his old canvases out of the studio in
which he had been allowed to store them during the
war, had taken a small studio for himself in the
purlieus of Hammersmith, had sold his chickens and
thanked his Essex friend, and established himself
with a bed and a gas stove and a frying pan under
the north light that of itself stirred the spirit of his
genius back into eager life.

But that life, though eager, was at first but a

feeble flame. John got easily tired and easily depressed. Hilary saw that, if his revival was to be permanent and progressive, she must be constantly at his side to help and encourage him. That meant marriage, because John was far too conservative and respectable, for all his early life, even to think of any less permanent arrangement, and in any case there was no reason why they should not marry. Hilary was entirely her own mistress now; after the war she had been unable—after a brief and unhappy experiment—to settle down in the dull little provincial town where Dr. and Mrs. Keston divided their time between routine work and little parties and 'the wireless'. Hilary, with a hundred a year of her own, left to her by a thoughtful and accommodating aunt, had struck out for herself and found work as a receptionist to a Brook Street milliner. She had no training but she was nice to look at and had a friendly manner that made customers think that they were really welcome in the shop and not mere tiresome intruders, as was the curious custom in most millinery establishments.

But after a year the work had begun to pall and Madame Vertigot, to whom at her engagement Hilary had rashly mentioned the name of Lady Waterley, had for some time been complaining that she did not bring enough custom to the shop. It had dawned on her that she was expected to tout round among her friends, and *that* she was emphatically not going to do—even if she had had the friends who could afford Madame Vertigot's prices.

So marriage would be a solution for her as well as for John and as John was temperamentally incapable of suggesting it, Hilary had proposed to him herself, and—after an interval of astonishment amounting almost to consternation on John's part—had been rapturously and gratefully accepted and they had been married at a registry office because John certainly could not have afforded the clothes for the sort of wedding that Mrs. Keston would have insisted on if it had been in church.

They had intended at first to live in the Hammersmith studio, under the north light and with the help of the gas stove and the frying pan, but London—even the humblest part of Hammersmith—was desperately expensive to live in—lettuces cost five-pence and Hilary couldn't live without lettuces if she was to do her own housekeeping, which would consist of them and bread and butter and eggs and oranges—so they had begun to talk about living in the country until John's name had become established and his work was selling steadily. Then they would move to Chelsea, or at any rate Earl's Court, and have a small garden with a frame for their own lettuces and a little car to run them out into the country when they felt inclined, for Hilary loved the country and John at that time loved everything that Hilary loved—and even everything she touched.

And then another war friend of John's had told them about the fascinating little village on the Norfolk coast which he had found on a walking tour, and especially about its wonderful lights—he was by way of being a painter himself in an amateur way—its greys and mauves, and pale yellows and quiet greens. And food there—the friend had said—cost nothing ; a flounder was a penny—even if you didn't catch it yourself, which you easily could with a thing called a butt-prick, something like Britannia's

8

trident, only a net was easier, though more expensive to buy. So Hilary and John had rushed down to Bryde-by-the-Sea on a week-end excursion ticket and fallen in love with it and found exactly the right little house with a bedroom with a skylight on the sea-ward side that provided the right light for painting, though a lot of draught as well, and Hilary and John could sleep in the other two bedrooms which were smaller but would do quite well till they could afford to build on a wing or go back to London.

So they had spent the last two hundred odd pounds of John's war gratuity in buying the little house—it was a cottage really—and had spent their honeymoon getting it ready, because they hadn't been able to afford a honeymoon when they were married—and then they had got rid of the Hammersmith lease for quite a good premium, sold their sticks of furniture which were not worth the cost of moving, and transplanted themselves to Bryde with two trunks and a suit case and John's big easel and canvases.

For the first three months Bryde-by-the-Sea had given them a happiness that had seemed almost impossible except in a book by Gene Stratton-Porter. Then the winter and the storms and the cold and the perpetual wind had come and they had still been ideally happy but not quite so comfortable, and single-handed domestic life had seemed to Hilary not *quite* such fun as at first. But things were going pretty well and before long they would be able to afford a woman to come in and do the rougher work and give Hilary more time for amusement. John's early patron, Sir Otto Geisberg, had died during the war—died in an internment camp, of unhappiness

9

and horrible food and loneliness and the ugly side
of a life that till then had been, for him, nearly all
beauty.   But one or two galleries had remembered
about the Prix du Louvre and had taken some of
John's work and sold it and asked for more and John
had suggested twenty-five guineas this time without
being snubbed.

Then—in about 1921 or '22—had come the slump,
which at first had seemed to be about shipping and
steel and had even made the cost of living in Bryde
cheaper than ever and seemed to be very good for
John and Hilary Pansel, if not for shareholders and
people who had money.   But then the galleries had
begun to write letters about it—generally with a
capital S—and it seemed that if things weren't so
good for the people who had money they couldn't be
so good for the people who hadn't it—people like
painters and the other kind of painters, because the
people who had money hadn't got money any longer
—at least, not enough to buy pictures and have their
drawing-rooms redecorated on a new scheme every
six months.   And taxes that were to have come down
didn't come down.   Not that taxes affected John
and Hilary much because they only had Hilary's
hundred a year and what John earned with his
brush and he got something off for that because he
had earned it and when he didn't earn it any longer
he hadn't got it to pay taxes on.   But it affected the
people who had money so that more than ever they
hadn't got money with which to buy pictures and
so on.

But Austen Chamberlain had said that if only the
country could stand the high taxes he was asking for
for another three years it would reap the benefit

afterwards and prosperity would come and people with money would be able to have their drawing-rooms redecorated on a new scheme every six months or even oftener, and so on. And now, twelve years later or more, another Chamberlain was saying exactly the same thing, but as he didn't wear an eyeglass, or even an orchid, perhaps he was more reliable.

Hilary—thirty-four-year-old-now Hilary—sighed heavily and wriggled her back to get rid of the pain and looked out of the window at the greys and mauves and pale yellows and quiet greens—the same window that she had been looking out of when Austen had said it—and dried the same plates, only not so many of them. They had bought a dozen when they married, because they would have little parties occasionally—to celebrate, perhaps, the sale of some picture at a new high-level price. That had actually happened once or twice and been very thrilling though not the people, because, except during August, the possible guests were a dull lot and even in August, when the Anchorage Hotel was full, you could hardly go down there and look through the visitors' list and pick out the names you had heard of or that sounded nice and invite them up to dine with you—complete strangers—because the Old Masters Gallery had sold a painting for you at thirty two and a half instead of thirty. And in any case the occasion had only arisen twice, and that was ten years ago or more ; now you would be lucky if you didn't have everything thrown back at you, with a bill for carriage.

Ten years ! It seemed a lifetime. It *was* a life-time. Hilary had been young ten years ago and full of hope and spirits and ambition—and love. Now she was old. Or, at any rate, her youth had gone, and with it her hope and her ambition and her . . . no, that wasn't true. She did still love John, of course, tremendously ; he was everything in the world to her—but it was in a different way. She didn't any longer feel a thrill each time she saw him, or tremble when he touched her. She was tremendously fond of him, and worried horribly if he got ill and would miss him unbearably if . . . oh, but that simply couldn't be thought about. But . . . perhaps it just was that he didn't any longer feel like that about *her ;* his eyes didn't light up as they used to and he never now picked her up in his arms and dumped her down in his lap in their one big chair and hugged her till she couldn't breathe. Of course it was silly to expect him to. You couldn't expect a man to go on loving the same woman like that for ever—men weren't monogamous by instinct as women were supposed to be (but were they ?). And of course that must make a difference to what one felt oneself.

But perhaps they *would* both have gone on feeling like that if life hadn't turned out to be so different— and so hard. If they had been able to get back to London, or at any rate to build on or buy a better house, or at least have a maid so that she, Hilary, had not had to become a complete drudge and spoil her hands and lose her looks and get tired and cross. And if poor John could have had a little success to cheer him up and make him take a pride in himself again and have a little fun—even if it was only a fortnight in Italy or Germany every year—how different everything would have been.

But they had not had a penny to do anything with. After the first year John's pictures had stopped selling, except very occasionally and at very poor prices, hardly enough—he said—to pay for the canvas and the paints and the carriage and the gallery fees. They had lived almost entirely on her hundred a year. John had absolutely refused to allow her to realise one penny of the capital. She had wanted to realise some and live on it as income till times got better and his work became established and his pictures sold properly. But he had put his foot down on that, and lucky that he had, because times had got no better—worse, if anything, and if they had lived on capital there would have been no hundred a year now. But it had been, naturally, a bitter blow to John, to have to live on his wife's money. He had become very touchy about it, even morbid, and that hadn't made things any happier between them.

They were lucky, of course—in a way—not to have had any children. They simply couldn't have afforded them. They had decided at the very beginning not to have any until their income had risen to a thousand a year and they could afford a nurse. (How shocked Hilary's mother and father would have been if they had known of that decision—a 'judgment', they would have said all the subsequent troubles were.) Hilary would have loved to have a child—a daughter ; John, of course, wanted a son. But as things had turned out, it would of course have been madness—the end of everything. Sometimes, even now, Hilary regretted it. A child would have given them something to think of, to talk about, besides just money and the sale or nonsale of pictures and domestic worries. They might even have gone on loving each other properly if . . . but it was no good thinking about it, it was utterly impossible.

They must just go struggling on till something happened. Things must get better some day ; everyone said that. But when ? Thank God, they couldn't get worse for Hilary and John Pansel. Income Tax didn't affect them. It was inconceivable that the Funding Loan should pass a dividend. The cost of living was going down—that seemed to be a bad thing in some mysterious way—the fall in prices. No, things couldn't get worse ; they would almost certainly get better, but oh, it was dull, dreary work, waiting. Dull, dull, dull . . .

CHAPTER II

As she looked out of her kitchen-scullery window, Hilary Pansel could see practically the whole setting that had so fascinated her and John at their first sight of this remote corner of England. *Bryde-by-the-Sea, though nominally a harbour, lies nearly a mile back from the ocean which surges invisibly against the line of low sand dunes limiting the northern horizon. In between lies a wide expanse of weed-grown mud, intersected by a maze of channels which at high tide are full to the brim of salt water and at low are mere trenches of black and treacherous ooze. These are the Saltings ; the home of a hundred varieties of sea-birds, of countless sea-plants, of insects, reptiles, fishes, animals—according to the state of the tides and the time of year ; at one time a silvery dazzle of southernwood, at another green with samphire, at another brown with sea-churned mud, and sometimes—at the highest of the ' springs '—completely submerged under the smooth, swirling waters of the flowing tide. Dreary and desolate though they are, the Saltings have for those who love them a fascination which no written word can describe, a beauty which defies the most skilful brush.

So, at least, thought John Pansel as he sat on a three-legged stool at the mouth of the creek, by which the tide crept in twice in the twenty-four hours

* See Frontispiece.

to fill the inland harbour, and tried to commit to cartridge paper the utterly baffling and illusive colours of a scene which never changed but, to his artist's eye, was never twice the same.   The silvery-yellow of the sands, the green and lavender of the saltings, the grey and purple of the skies, all these, if you studied them, became flat and colourless, but if you shut your eyes a minute and then opened them you were dazzled by the beauty of their tones, bewildered by their changing values ; you dashed for your brush and palette, mixed up your colour wash, looked again—and behold, the sand had become grey, the saltings yellow, the sea purple ; it was baffling, humiliating, impossible—and utterly fascinating.   Only with water-colours could you hope to catch the fleeting effects ; with breathless speed you might convey to paper your impression of the morning's light—an impression which might be transferred later, at your studio leisure, to the richer medium of oil or tempera.

It was waste of time, of course ; not once, in all his hundred and more attempts, had John Pansel produced a painting which satisfied himself, which reproduced, even measurably, the beauty that his eyes saw ; as for the public, the art-fanciers, not one in another hundred was attracted by pictures of a scene which, on paper or canvas, was either desolate, featureless, and flat, or impossibly garish, exaggerated, unbelievable.   And yet the urge to try again was irresistible ; it drew the artist like a magnet.   And after all, what did it matter ?   If he stayed at home and worked on some model—' the old long-shoreman ', ' the fisher-lass ', or constructed new groupings of the picturesque old flint and pantile cottages, would anyone buy them ? Better do work that gave one pleasure, however profitless it might be.

So Pansel sat patiently on his little stool and washed in the heavy thunder-clouds that were beginning to appear on the south-western horizon ; they would be right over him in another hour, perhaps less, and would completely change the values of his intended picture, but he might be able to get what he wanted before then. *He was sitting at the mouth of the creek, where the bar—a squat breakwater—forced the water at low tide into a narrow, swirling channel ; now the tide was beginning to flow and the breakwater was just covered, the stream broadening out at once to fill the pool formed by the ends of the two sandhills that guarded the mouth. From that point the creek followed a winding course round one side of the saltings, hugging the high embankment that had been built, nearly two hundred years ago, to keep the sea away from the reclaimed land—land which had been saltings but now was rich meadow-land on which a bullock could be fattened. After a passage of some three-quarters of a mile, the creek reached the village, broadened out slightly into a rough harbour, turned parallel with the coast line and then curled out again into the saltings, among which it wound and writhed until it died away to nothing not far from the point at which it had started.

At this moment, early flow, the water in the creek beyond the pool was only a few inches deep and died away into mud a hundred yards beyond the village ; no boat could navigate it, unless it was completely flat and empty, propelled by its owner paddling in

* See Frontispiece.

the stream and pulling or pushing. Even then navigation was only possible to someone who knew the channel, for the ' deep water ' of six inches switched from side to side of a bed that otherwise was no deeper than three or two or one. Directly the tide crossed the bar at the mouth, however, the creek would begin rapidly to fill and a boat would float of its own accord up to the village and beyond.

Pansel bent over his painting-block. He must hurry if he was to catch the effect he wanted, which was governed not only by the thunder-clouds but by the winding silver ribbon of the low-water channel. Quickly his brush swept over the paper. It was coming this time ; in another ten minutes he would have fixed it. . . .

" Ahoy ! Mr. Pansel ! "

At the shrill call the painter involuntarily raised his head. A small sailing boat was sliding towards the barely submerged line of the breakwater. Two boys of about thirteen and fourteen were in it, the sons of Vaughan Cadnall, proprietor of the ' Anchorage '.

" Morning, George ! Morning, Frank. Mind you don't go aground on the bar."

" Oh, she'll do it. We've got the centre-board up."

" Then take care you don't turn over ; the wind's puffy. Better let it down now."

The little boat was safely over the obstacle and slipping across the pool.

" Matter of fact we can't. The beastly thing's always sticking if one pulls it up. She'll be all right up the crik ; we shan't have to tack with this wind."

The last words were almost inaudible as the boat

disappeared round the bend. John Pansel bent over his pad again, mechanically raised his brush, looked up—and cursed.

" Blast ! it's gone again ! "

In the two minutes that the little conversation had lasted the light had completely changed. The silver line of the creek had become leaden, sea-green had changed to olive, pink of the distant roofs to brown. John threw his brush back into the open box and rose to his feet. It had happened so often, this frustration on the threshold of success ; he should have been accustomed to it by now, and yet each fresh time he felt the same sense of anger, of personal affront, as if some malign spite was aimed at him. In the early months of his life at Bryde it had been a joke ; he and Hilary had laughed at it together, but gradually a bitter note had crept into John's laughter and now, with ten years of disappointment and ill-health behind him, the painter made no attempt to check the growing sullenness of his temper.

Ill-health, of course, was at the bottom of his mood. Officially, ' cured ' and pensionless, John Pansel's digestion had been ruined by the jagged sliver of shell-case, the ripping knives, the draining-tubes, the cat-gut, and all the pains and paraphernalia of healing. If his subsequent life had been easy and carefree, if he had been happy and successful and carefully fed, John might have weathered the storm ; as it was, with the best will in the world but no experience and a minimum of money, Hilary could not provide him with the delicacies, the subtle cooking, the appetite-nursing that he needed. His digestion became steadily worse and with it his health—and his temper. One good turn poverty did for him ; it kept him from drink. A man could not—a man like Pansel could not—soak on his wife's money ; pride kept him from that. Two pints of beer he had a week ; Hilary insisted on that ; it took him among his fellow men and cheered him up, but the money for it came out of a special box into which he put the earnings from pencil-sketches of visitors at the hotel—work which he loathed and yet which enabled him to have small luxuries such as this and tobacco without drawing on the house-keeping funds.

John kicked over his camp-stool and looked about him. It was too early to go back—lunch would not be ready for another hour and a half. Besides, he did not want the bother of walking if he could get a lift. A boat was sure to come along as the tide rose ; there was always an odd fisherman working home from sea with his nets and meagre catch, or a pleasure-seeker slipping down to the bar and back in motor-launch or sailing-boat for the sake of the run. Half-way along the pool a dark figure was bending over what was probably a boat hidden by the curve of the beach. John walked towards it, and as he approached saw that it was a fisherman in blue jersey and black thigh boots, filling a heavy, flat-bottomed boat with shingle.

" Good-morning, Polly ", he said. " Going to mix some concrete ? "

Without start or hurry, the fisherman straightened up and turned towards him.

" Good-morning, Mr. Pansel ", he said, gravely. " Yes, I'm taking a load up for Mr. Martin's ; he's putting on a new scullery and a bath-room."

" You building it for him ? "

" Yes. He's in no hurry and I can work at it between times."

The sharp cackle of the Norfolk fisher-folk cannot be reproduced on paper without an exaggeration that would be misleading. They speak, as a rule, in a staccato shout, but their English is as pure as another man's. The men, especially, are well educated and well-read, besides being extremely intelligent and capable with their hands. Most of them have some second trade or side-line with which to supplement the meagre earnings of the dwindling fishing industry. Christian Madgek, to whom John was now speaking, was a skilled builder and plumber, and though he worked in his own good time and refused to be hurried his services were in considerable demand among the few inhabitants of Bryde who could ever consider the luxury of building. Nor was that Madgek's only sideline. It was common knowledge that many a hare and wild duck that appeared on the menu of ' The Anchorage ', or on the table of less important dwellings, had fallen to his skilful snare or gun, though this he would flatly have denied.

" I wish I could do something useful ", said John Pansel, gloomily eyeing the shining heap of gravel in the clumsy-looking boat.

" I'm sure what you do gives great pleasure to people, sir ", replied Madgek politely. His private opinion was that picture-making was pure waste of time and good paint, but nothing would have induced him to hurt the artist's feelings by saying so.

" It's as well you've got your building to fall back on ", continued John. " With these big trawlers covering a wider field every year it must be getting harder than ever for local fishermen to find a market. Science and machinery are more of a curse than a blessing to a place like Bryde."

" Oh, I wouldn't say that, sir ", replied Madgek, folding his arms and leaning back against the rising wind. " The fishing's maybe gone, but motor cars bring holiday folk and trippers who'd never have got here without them. They like their bit of a sail or a run in the motor-boat and there's as much money in that as ever there was in fish. We've little to complain of."

Madgek, one of the village capitalists, owned a large motor-boat in which, during holiday weather, he ran parties of visitors down the creek to the bar and back for sixpence a head. On the way he picked up many an odd half-crown by towing rash or inexpert sailers off the sandbanks on which the falling tide had stranded them.

" You're a bit of a philosopher, Polly. But I daresay it's easy to be that when you've got something in the bank and no one dependent on you." There was a touch of bitterness in Pansel's tone which his companion either did not notice or ignored.

" I know little enough about philosophy, sir ", he said, " but I see no sense in complaining of what can't be cured. The steam trawlers have come to stay—till something better comes along to turn them out."

John Pansel cast an eye over the pool.

" Tide's coming in quick now ", he said. " Hadn't you better get on with your loading if you want to get up with the flood ? "

Madgek had been thinking this for the last ten

minutes, but his manners were far too good to let him break off his conversation with Pansel as long as the latter wanted to continue it. Now he quietly picked up his shovel, spat on his huge, horny hands, and with slow, deliberate strokes began to scoop up shovelfuls of glittering shingle and throw them into the boat. The artist watched for a minute ; then, as the first drops of the approaching storm smacked down on the water he frowned and said impatiently :

" Here, let me have a go. You'll never get done at that rate."

Madgek handed over the shovel without a word and, slowly lighting his pipe, stood watching while John, with a terrific burst of energy, sent the shingle flying on to the growing heap. Pansel was a big man, with naturally strong muscles, and for a quarter of an hour he could keep up that pace, but the fisherman knew what the difference would be if his companion had to continue working at manual labour throughout the day. However, it got his boat filled and he was the last person to criticise gratuitously.

" She'll just take us both now, sir. If you'll bring along your traps I'll be getting up the anchor."

Madgek had judged to a nicety the weight of his load ; when the two men were on board about four inches of free-board appeared above the water. John Pansel perched himself on the heap of shingle, while the fisherman stood upright and steered with an oar over the stern. No propulsion was needed to send the boat along ; the ' race ' was coming in now and the heavy vessel slipped up the creek at an astonishing speed. But though no strength was needed, the trip was only possible to a man with intimate knowledge of the channel and long experience with a steering-oar. The slightest deviation from the true course would have sent the heavily-laden boat aground on a submerged sandbank or crashing against one of the groins now covered by the tide ; and to do either with that deep draught would have been almost certainly to capsize.

But Madgek had handled a boat on this creek for thirty out of the thirty-five years of his life. He knew every inch of it, every trick of tide, every eddy of backwater. With effortless grace he steered his clumsy craft up the half mile of channel, dodged between the anchored craft in the little harbour, then with a sudden swirl of the oar swung her out of the stream into a small bay of slack water, turned her just as she appeared on the point of running aground and allowed her to drift slowly sideways against the sloping bank of sand and shingle.

" If you'll step ashore now, Mr. Pansel, I'll run her a yard up the bank."

John put one foot on the gunwale and sprang lightly to the bank. He knew enough by now not to thrust downward on the gunwale and force it under the water. As soon as he was ashore Madgek swung the boat round again till her nose was to the shore, then slipped over the stern and gave a quick push so that the nose drove into the sand. Wading leisurely ashore, he seized the prow on each side of the painter ring, and with a series of short, sharp heaves dragged the heavy vessel a foot or two up the bank.

" That'll keep her from floating till I've got my cart," he explained. " You never know what these boys'll do with a floating boat if they get the chance."

John had watched the final operation with mingled admiration and envy. He knew well enough that he could not himself have heaved that tremendous dead weight one foot up the bank, but Madgek, a considerably smaller man than himself, did it with apparent ease. It was knack, of course ; the fisherman knew just where and when and how to exert his strength ; but the strength must be formidable, for all that. Christian Madgek was certainly a fine-looking man. Standing about five feet ten, with broad shoulders and long arms, he gave a first impression of superfluous fat, but probably that was provided by nature to protect him against the exposure to bitter cold which his calling demanded. Unlike most of the ruddy, brown-haired fisherfolk of Bryde, Madgek was black, his hair rather long and curly, his complexion sallow, his eyes steel grey, the lashes of a curling thickness which any woman would have given her soul for. It was a face of great interest, one which John Pansel had often painted ; a face liable to arouse passions, either of love or hate, but one which no man or woman could regard with indifference.

John had often wondered what was the explanation of this unique strain among a people who, without being in-bred, adhered rigidly to type. The simple answer would appear to be gipsy blood, but though the darkness and the curls might be explained by that it would hardly account for the pallor or the peculiar quality of the eyes. The man's parents were of the common type, as had been their parents before them ; Christian must be a throw-back to a distant age and John liked to imagine that it was some Spanish grandee—no common sailor this—

wrecked in a straggler of the Armada, whose blood had descended in a subterranean flow until it burst to the surface three and a half centuries later in the person of this handsome young fisherman.

The nickname, Polly, so utterly unsuitable to the man's appearance, had originated with some visitor at the hotel, who, mindful of his Bunyan, had in conversation among other visitors, changed the man's name from Christian to Apollyon, a name appropriate enough to that saturnine appearance. The nickname had spread but had soon proved too cumbersome and had been abbreviated by profane youth to its present familiar form. Not, however, to his face, except by the privileged few, of whom John Pansel was one ; to his fellow-fishermen he was ' Madgek ' or, more rarely, ' Christian ' ; to one girl only he was ' Chris.'

With a short word of farewell to Pansel, Madgek climbed the beach and moved off towards the village with the slow, rolling gait of his kind. Everything that Madgek did was deliberate and dignified, giving an impression of grace and strength in natural harmony. To the artist it was a constant joy to look at him, but to John Pansel, the man, there came often a twinge of jealous anger as he watched the confident, carefree air with which Madgek strolled through life. Why should this humble jack-of-all-trades, some of them none too reputable, carry himself as if the world was at his toe, captain of his fate, master of his soul, while he, John Pansel, better bred, better educated, the winner of a great prize, a man with an established reputation in the world of art, a man with a dress-suit and a name in print, dragged himself about this same obscure little

corner of the world with his head down and a gnawing
sense of bitterness, of discontent, of failure, always
in his heart ?

With a shrug of the shoulders John picked up his
bundle of painting things, gave a quick, appraising
look round at the familiar scene, richly coloured now
under the rolling cloud-bank, and trudged off across
the beach towards the end of the village where his
cottage stood. The sudden rain-storm, which he and
Madgek on the bosom of the waters had scarcely
noticed, had driven indoors or away the usual
groups of idlers, and, save for an occasional fisherman or errand-boy going about his business, the
artist had the place to himself. It was so that he
liked it best. The red-tiled roofs, the flint walls of
the little squat houses glistened in the rain, the grass
and shrubs in the little scraps of garden looked fresh
and vigorous, while the downfall had not been
long or heavy enough to crush the pretty summer
flowers. Occasional blue jerseys and sou-westers
fitted into the scene, unspoilt by the hideous holiday
attire of middle-class visitors. Pansel had seen it
so a hundred times, but once again there leapt to
his quick artist's eye the framework of yet another
picture ; he stopped in his stride and narrowed his
eyes ; that group of cottages—Banyatt's and
Horling's—on the right, balanced by the stunted,
wind-swept ilex, the road curving away towards his
own little house and the figure of a woman, her
skirts kilted . . .

The picture vanished from the artist's mind ; he
frowned unconsciously. A figure had appeared in
the doorway of the little house that had been the
keynote of the middle-distance of his picture ; now

it had detached itself from the house and was in the road. Even at this distance he could see that it was that tiresome fellow Fiennes. He was always in and out, imagining himself welcome, even conferring a favour by his presence. Some men were like that ; it never seemed to enter their heads that they might not be wanted. Writers—novelists— seemed to be the worst of the lot, thinking themselves so clever and amusing, eaten up by conceit really. Well, thank goodness he had turned down towards the beach—going across the saltings to his hut on the sand dunes, probably. Why couldn't he stay there and do some work ?

John strode on down the empty village street. Everyone was indoors now, having their mid-day dinner—those of them who had not got it with them in a can at their work. It was after half-past twelve. No doubt Fiennes had turned up with the idea of cadging a free meal—a man who could well afford to keep the whole population of Bryde in free meals for a year without noticing it ; Hilary had very properly packed him off empty, though of course she would do it so gently that a thick-hided fellow like that wouldn't realise that he was being snubbed.

John Pansel turned in at the low gate of his minute garden and, walking round the house, entered it by the back-door. Mud and sand were not welcome all over the house if you had to do your own cleaning. The living-room, a good-sized room with windows to south and west, was empty. John could hear a clatter of plates in the kitchen down the passage—a matter of a few yards.

He kicked off his gum-boots and pushed his feet into a pair of broken-down felt slippers which, when he wasn't wearing them, always lived by the back-door.

"What was that fellow after?" he called. "Free food?"

A quick step crossed the kitchen and Hilary appeared in the doorway, a sparkle of pleasure in her eyes.

"Oh, John, such fun!" she exclaimed. "Mr. Fiennes has got seats for 'The Yeomen of the Guard' next Tuesday—there's a touring company in Hunstanton—and he wants us to go with him."

John Pansel stared at his wife.

"My good girl; how on earth can we afford to go to the theatre?" he asked.

"Oh, but he's taking us! We're to be his guests."

"Not if I know it!" John's voice was gruff with annoyance. "We're not going to be beholden to that fellow."

Hilary stared at her husband in blank astonishment. Then the light faded out of her eyes, the corners of her mouth drooped and she turned slowly back into her dreary kitchen.

CHAPTER III

THE HAPPY AUTHOR

DALLAS FIENNES was smiling as he walked away
from the Pansels' cottage. He had come to Bryde
for the summer months to work ; the solitude of
the place was admirably suited for that purpose.
London, where he had lived nearly all his life, had
become increasingly difficult as a place to work in.
When he was obscure and friendless it had been
easy enough ; you can be as solitary in a London
boarding-house as on a desert island ; but now that
his reputation was established and he had a host of
friends and acquaintances it was difficult to make
them realise that at least twelve hours in the twenty-
four must be his own. The men were all right—
they had their work to do ; but women seemed to
be at a loose end at all hours of the day and night,
and it was not only as a novelist that Dallas Fiennes
had made a name. So he had looked about for a
summer cottage and had found one in Kent and it
had been just the one place of all others in which
his women friends adored to spend a week-end, or
a week, or sometimes longer. Then he had tried
Dartmoor ; that had thinned them out, but the
faithful few had stuck. So last year he had found
a hut on the sand-dunes at Bryde-by-the-Sea, and
after the name had simply fascinated them and they
had come down and inspected the hut with its sand
and its draughts and its inaccessibility and had tried
the ' Anchorage ' hotel for a night or two and been

bored absolutely to tears by the desolation of the place, they had gone away and Dallas had settled down and written a novel which had completely restored a reputation that excess of friends had caused to sag, and had gone back to London for the winter and been received with rapturous welcomes and had spent in riotous living nearly a quarter of the royalties earned at Bryde during the summer.

So now he had come back to Bryde to earn some more. He had had some doubts about coming back. Last summer had given him exactly what he wanted, but it was a somewhat grim experience. To a man accustomed to live in great comfort, as for the last five or six years Dallas Fiennes had done, life in a hut on a desolate sand-hill, even in the summer, was no joke. But apart from discomfort, the boredom of the life had almost shattered him. He had worked hard, spending whole days at a stretch at his writing-table, but he could not work all the time. He must have some air and some recreation, otherwise his brain would become clogged. The air was easy enough, it was incomparable, but the recreation was appalling. The fishermen were pleasant fellows ; for a time he enjoyed their leisurely talk, their simple philosophy, but that soon palled. Apart from them, there were a few professional men who came down for an occasional week-end, a few visitors at the ' Anchorage,' that sullen painting fellow Pansel and his dully demure wife. One or two of the village girls were good-lookers and not too reluctant, but that form of amusement carried no great kick.

Now, however, Dallas Fiennes was smiling. He had been back at Bryde for a week or more and had determined to provide himself with amusement at

any cost. To hunt for it would add to the zest.
Hilary Pansel was the obvious quarry ; there was
nothing wrong with her looks ; it was her obvious
simplicity that had put him off last year ; he had
not tried to look below the surface. This year he
was determined to explore. Whatever the result—
whatever degree of success might crown his endea-
vours—the enterprise would provide him with
sufficient recreation to keep his mind in good order
for his work.

Fiennes had seen John Pansel's approach up the
village street and was glad to be able to turn down
the little alley which provided a short cut to the
ferry and his path home. The man was a plain bore.
Conceited, stupid, heavy—not even a gentleman.
His wife was far too good for him—wasted on him,
wilting away in this poverty-stricken wilderness.
Well, he would provide her, as well as himself, with
some fun. It would brighten her drab life ; would
be a good deed really ; it was seldom that Fiennes'
amusements could be described as that, even by
himself.

He had to be more or less civil to Pansel, otherwise
the pitch would be queered. The oaf was quite
capable of ' forbidding him the house ' and Hilary
was, Fiennes thought, sufficiently Victorian to obey
her husband if there was anything in the shape of a
veto. That would spoil his plan and must be
avoided. A semblance of politeness must be maintained, but there was no need to court a meeting.
So down the alley Fiennes turned and within a
couple of minutes was at the ferry.

The ferry consisted of a patriarch named Giles
Banyatt and his equally ancient tub. The old man

earned a few pence a day by ferrying occasional fares across to the raised bank which separated the saltings from the main creek. The bank had been constructed, no doubt, to prevent the creek from spreading into the saltings, and so to ensure a sufficiently deep channel to allow the fishing boats to get up to the inland harbour.

" Morning, Giles. Am I disturbing your dinner ? "

Fiennes had a cheerful, familiar way of talking to people that made him generally popular, but he would never be accepted as a friend by the natives as John Pansel was.

Old Giles touched his forelock, deliberately scraped the few remaining morsels of potato from the bottom of his can, tucked the can away in the bows of his boat and held the latter steady while Fiennes climbed in over the stern. Shipping the small anchor, Giles himself climbed in, giving the boat a skilful shove with his hind leg as he did so. Then, standing up in the stern with an oar in the notch he gently propelled the boat across the few yards of water to the rough wooden steps at the end of the bank.

" Thank you, Giles. I shan't bother you again to-day."

The old man touched his forelock again and without a word started on his return journey. No money passed ; Fiennes had compounded with the ferryman for a pound for the season, this sum to provide free portage for himself and for the woman who came twice a week to clean up his hut. The previous year Fiennes had for a short time had a manservant living in the hut with him, but the fellow had made such heavy weather of the discomforts and inconvenience of the life that Fiennes had thought him more trouble than he was worth and had packed him off to London. Since then he had done his own cooking and housemaiding—which did not amount to much—whilst twice a week a widow woman named Barle came over and 'put the place to rights'. As Fiennes would not allow the table at which he worked to be touched this did not amount to much either, but it kept the worst of the sand out of his bed and his cooking utensils.

*The bank to which Fiennes mounted ran along the western edge of the saltings and at the north-west corner turned east for half the northern face of the marsh. Here it stopped abruptly, presumably because it was no longer needed as a bastion for the main creek. The remainder of the northern edge of the saltings consisted of a natural, not a constructed, mud bank, high enough to keep the sea out of the saltings at normal times, but it was over this part that the invasion came at the spring tides, when the whole face of the saltings was covered, save the raised bank. A path had been worn along this bank by the feet of people making for the huts on the sand-dunes, or of those intrepid adventurers who, exploring the channels which wound among the saltings when the sea was up, had been marooned when the tide fell and forced to leave their boats on the mud and scramble somehow to firm land. This was not always an easy or even a safe undertaking, for some of the pools were filled with a viscous, slimy substance that could hold you very tight indeed.

Fiennes' way took him to the very end of the raised bank, where, to a wooden post, his own boat

* See Frontispiece.

was moored. It was high tide now and a broad
expanse of water stretched between him and the
sand-dunes. At low tide this would be dry, save for
the little creek which was shallow and could be
forded by anyone with calf-high gum-boots, or bare
legs and kilted skirts, as Fiennes' charwoman crossed
it. To live on those sand-dunes, however, required
a certain amount of calculation ; if one did not think
out one's movements and times beforehand, one was
liable to find at high tide that the boat was at the
wrong side of it. This necessitated a long detour by
the footpath which left the main road some way
beyond the eastern end of the village, crossed the
dry land which bordered the eastern edge of the
saltings, and joined the sand-dunes at some considerable distance from the huts.

Dallas Fiennes, however, did not make mistakes
of this kind. For a man of letters he had his wits
remarkably well under control. The small boat
took him across the flood to the sand-dunes in a very
few minutes. His own hut stood rather removed
from the main colony and was of superior construction. Most of the others were only used
during the day, though a few hardy spirits camped
out in them for a week or so at a time. Fiennes
alone lived there throughout the summer. His hut
had been built by a consumptive who saw no reason
to pay a sanatorium ten guineas a week for fresh air.
It had a broad covered balcony running the whole
way round the house, which allowed of a pursuit of
the sun and a change of scene, but had the dis-
advantage of darkening the interior. It was reason-
ably wind- and sand-proof and was furnished rather
well. Fiennes had bought it when the owner

decided to die in comfort rather than live in draughty solitude.

On this sunny morning—for the storm that had driven John Pansel from his work had quickly passed away—the hut looked cheerful enough. As Fiennes unlocked the front door, which opened direct into the living-room, a patch of brilliant sunlight illuminated the saxe blue carpet which the novelist had imported to create what he considered a suitable atmosphere for his particular genius. Curtains of primrose repp and cushions of more riotous hue on the big divan under the window added their notes of cheer, though they might have raised doubts in the mind of Mr. Fiennes' more sensitive admirers.

But Fiennes was not at present concerned with colour schemes. Throwing his hat into a chair, he went into the little kitchen-scullery, opened a cupboard, and drew out the remains of a tongue, a bottle of O.K., and a loaf of bread. It was a meal from which, fifteen months ago, his fastidious appetite would have revolted ; on his first arrival in Bryde last year he had begun by cooking himself exquisite little meals with chafing dishes, herbs, sauces, Boulestin recipes, but the labour of it had soon exhausted his first enthusiasm, especially as the enthusiasm of his week-end guests began to wane at the same time. There followed a period of weekly cases from Fortnum & Mason, but the expense of these was formidable, even to a bachelor best-seller, and by degrees he had slipped into the local grocery and scrambled egg habit with which he was now well content.

Putting his food on the living-room table—the process could hardly be dignified by the term

' laying '—Fiennes crossed again to the front door
and opened the flap of the letter-box. That letter-
box was his only structural alteration to the consumptive's home. It had its drawbacks and Mrs.
Barle cursed it both publicly and in private. When
the wind blew, as it frequently did on that bleak
coast, the flap of the letter-box admitted more than
it was designed for ; the late owner had been at great
pains to procure doors and windows designed to
exclude sand from his modest home ; the novelist
had gone out of his way to provide an entry.

But the novelist must have his post. It was
awkward enough living at this distance from his
public and his publisher and—more important still—
his literary agent. So far as the postal authorities
were concerned it would have been prohibitively
inconvenient ; dwellers on the sand-dunes were not
provided with an official delivery ; but Fiennes had
come to a friendly arrangement with the husband of
the local postmistress, himself only a part-time
employee of the Service, whereby that gentleman
undertook in his spare time to deliver the novelist's
mail once a day at the hut and, if Fiennes were at
home at the time, to collect any letters for the outgoing mail. It meant a delivery of varied time,
depending on the state of the tide at Little Creek,
which without a boat could not be crossed for two
hours each side of high tide, and the post office being
at the west end of the village, Jude Tasson could not
be persuaded to take the long way round by the
footpath east of the saltings. Not that Fiennes
minded about the irregularity. If he was working
he lost all sense of time ; if he was not he would
almost certainly be going to the village himself, his

boat making him independent of tides, and would
call at the post office himself and collect any mail
that might be awaiting delivery. In the same way,
if he had any outgoing letter of importance, he could
quite well take it to the post himself.

On this particular morning, when he called at the
post office he found that Jude had already delivered
his mail at low tide while he was himself tinkering
with the car which he kept at the hotel garage. It
was a post of normal size, about a dozen letters, some
circulars, and a tiny bundle of press-cuttings.
Fiennes threw the lot on the table, sat down to his
meal, and with the first mouthful began to sort out
his catch. With the feminine instinct that had given
his work so wide a popularity, he turned at once to
the plums. The buff wrapper was slit from the little
green bunch of press-cuttings and the long slips
unfolded. Fiennes' last book had been out long
enough for the first rush of reviews to have subsided ;
these three were from provincial papers which, he
knew from experience, often provided the most
thoughtful and intelligent criticism. His anticipation proved to be right ; as he munched his bread
and tongue Dallas read, with a glow of naive pleasure
of which all his success had not robbed him, that
" Mr. Fiennes is one of the small band of popular
novelists who still think it worth while to take
trouble with their writing—to give of their best.
There was a moment when he wavered from his own
high standard ; now, in ' Jesting Angels ', he has
returned to his true form. This is work of which
any writer might be proud."

That was satisfactory enough, and would re-kindle
sales which—his publishers had warned him—had

begun to show signs of waning in that particular corner of England. The other two reviews were only less satisfactory to the author because they had not noticed the falling-off of which he himself had been conscious—which was, in fact, the cause of his self-banishment to Bryde-by-the-Sea. It was comforting to be confirmed in his judgment of the advisability of a rather drastic and uncomfortable move.

Putting aside the clippings, Fiennes picked up a large square envelope, addressed in neat typescript, which he had recognised at once as coming from his literary agent. In his early days, that typescript had appeared all too often upon bulky envelopes containing, besides his own MS., a note of polite regret for ' inability to place '. The acceptance of ' Wise Hypocrite ' by the new publishing house of Verity, and the instant success of the book under their vigorous management, had put an end to that first period of trial and disappointment ; thenceforward the square envelopes had borne nothing but good tidings—foreign rights, serial rights, film rights, all the extras that flow so easily, so automatically to the successful, but which to the struggling author hover like will o' the wisps always just out of reach.

" DEAR MR. FIENNES ", wrote Vincent Hanserd,

" I am happy to be able to tell you that I have disposed of the second serial rights of ' The Case of Mrs. Chaston ' to Northern Newspapers Limited for Two Hundred and Fifty Pounds (£250). You will remember instructing me that you would accept £200 for these rights and under the circumstances I think we may regard the figure now agreed upon as quite satisfactory.

" I have not yet heard from Central European Publications, Ltd., about the Czecho-Slovakian rights of ' Sigh no More ', but I have little doubt that I shall be able to arrange matters with them on suitable terms.

" I hear from Verity that ' Jesting Angels ' continues to move very nicely.   They expect to order a further printing within a week or two.

" I hope that you are enjoying pleasant weather upon the coast of Norfolk and that your new book is developing to your satisfaction.

Yours sincerely,
VINCENT HANSERD."

That, too, was all that could be desired.   It was comfortable to have an established reputation, a faithful public, assured sales.   Life really was very pleasant to an author ; it was difficult to believe that he had once had difficulties, doubts, had known poverty and even despair.   Going to a cupboard, the happy author extracted a bottle and poured himself out a glass of excellent light port.   As he sipped it he slit open an envelope, the writing on which he did not recognise.

" DEAR MR. FIENNES,

If you could see the eagerness with which the working men and women of this small town clamour for books in our little library I am sure your heart would glow with sympathy.   Unfortunately we have no endowment with which to purchase fresh supplies and so keep up-to-date and meet the ever-increasing demand.   We are compelled to rely upon the generosity of our friends and of authors who, like yourself, have met with well deserved success and are willing to give our members the opportunity to read books which would otherwise be beyond their reach.

"May I hope that you will respond to my appeal and send us a copy of your wonderful ' Jesting Angels ' and indeed of any of your books of which you may happen to have copies to spare.

"Thanking you in anticipation,

I am,

ANNIE SWILLS,

Honorary Librarian.

P.S.—Do *please* help ! "

Dallas Fiennes tossed the letter aside with a grunt of annoyance. To what limits of impertinence some people were willing to go in their urge to get something for nothing. How was an author expected to live if he was to give away free copies of his books ?

The next letter received even brusquer treatment.

" DEAR MR. FIENNES,

You who are yourself so successful can hardly turn a deaf ear to a struggling and unfortunate writer whose work meets only with barren esteem. A sick wife and . . ."

Fiennes ripped the letter across and flung it into the waste-paper-basket. A more generous sip of port barely smoothed the furrow from his brow. This mail was tending to irritation. And it might become worse. One letter still unopened he recognised only too well ; it bore possibilities of considerable annoyance. Leaving it to the last, Fiennes opened one which bore a local postmark. It was, he saw, from Frank Helliott, a young local squire whom he met fairly often in the neighbourhood but with whom he had not previously had any correspondence. The boy wrote from Brulcote Manor, the old house in which Helliotts had lived for several hundred years, which had seen the rise of the family to ownership of a big estate and its gradual decay to its present condition, Frank Helliott, the last of his line, owning and farming a few hundred starved acres, barely able to find means to keep himself and his sister from the workhouse. With knowledge of these facts Fiennes read the letter with misgiving.

" DEAR MR. FIENNES,

Can I have a talk with you sometime ? I don't mean in front of a lot of other people but somewhere where we can talk in private. I could come to your hut or perhaps we could have a walk.

Yours,

FRANK HELLIOTT."

It was significant, Fiennes feared, that he was not invited to Brulcote, where Helliott's sister might be one of the people in front of whom he did not want to talk. It was with an uneasy feeling that Fiennes put the letter in his pocket and picked up the one which he had left to the last. It was from Norah Beldart, and three years ago Dallas would have opened it, first of all his letters, with eager delight. Now he dreaded its contents.

" Dallas, you *must* send me some money " (it ran). " I'm simply desperate. Jane is so ill that I can't leave her to look for work. We've got nothing to eat and hardly any clothes. You were very good to me once and I'm very grateful, but I was good to you, Dallas, when you wanted me. Doesn't it mean anything to you to think of me like this? I know you say that you've done all you can, but have you? You're so rich now; you could so easily help us, Dallas. You must; you must. I'm getting desperate, Dallas. I don't want to do anything dreadful but you know I've got those letters of yours; don't force me to use them! We've been here three weeks but I don't know how much longer we shall be able to stay. The landlady is becoming very difficult. Write to me here quickly before anything happens.

You must, Dallas, you must!

NORAH.

Garth is dead. Did you know?"

The minutes dragged on in the silent hut. At his littered table the happy author sat, pulling moodily at his lower lip.

CHAPTER IV

THE sunny afternoon had a salutary effect upon John Pansel's spirits. He had made a satisfactory drawing of the group of cottages—Banyatt's and Horling's—which had caught his eye in the morning ; it would, he thought, compose into a really effective picture. The indifferent lunch which his ill-humour had constrained him to eat now contributed to a really healthy appetite for supper. This meal was a combination of tea and dinner, partly in the interests of economy and partly to save washing up ; it was timed for a vague seven o'clock and consisted of tea, sardines, an egg if one wanted it, jam, and fruit if there was any. To-night John put an egg in the saucepan for himself and persuaded Hilary to have one too. Watching them boil, he began his apology.

" Sorry I was disagreeable about the ' Yeomen ' ", he muttered into the lid of the saucepan. John Pansel had always found apology a difficult matter.

" Oh, it doesn't matter ", replied his wife, to whom the disappointment still mattered a good deal.

John realised that he must do better than this. Replacing the lid he went up to his wife, who was cutting bread, and slipped his arm round her waist.

" It matters that I should be an ill-tempered brute with you ", he said. " I'm sorry, Hilary ; please forgive me."

Hilary twisted round and put her arms round his neck.

"Darling, of course I forgive you. It doesn't matter in the least about the 'Yeomen'. I *was* a little bit upset at your growling at me. Were you feeling rotten, darling?"

John gave a wry smile.

"Women always think one's got a pain in one's stomach if one's cross", he said. "I'm perfectly all right. I just don't like Fiennes."

"Why don't you, dear?"

"Too damn pleased with himself. Thinks every woman's going to fall down and worship him."

Hilary laughed.

"What nonsense you talk, John. Well, I'm not going to, anyhow. How long are you going to boil those eggs?"

"Good lord; I'd forgotten them!"

John took a step towards the stove, but Hilary's arms were still round his neck.

"Kiss me first, darling", she whispered.

John's arms tightened round her slim body and he pressed his lips against hers.

"Make me nicer, Hilary", he muttered. "I don't like myself."

Hilary's answer was to cover his face with kisses, release his neck, and push him towards the stove.

"Go and attend to your duty", she said, gaily. With his back to her, John did not see the sparkle of tears in his wife's eyes.

The eggs were hard-boiled but their freshness was beyond suspicion—a quality of major importance to anyone who has lived long in a town. Hilary opened a fresh jar of John's favourite home-made marmalade.

" You'll go to the ' Yeomen ', won't you, Hilary ", said John as he lit his after-supper pipe.

" If you will, darling."

John frowned.

" I'd honestly rather not, but I'd like you to go."

" I won't unless you do."

" Then I shall think you're still cross with me."

Hilary's brow puckered in a frown of thought. Men were very difficult.

" All right ", she said. " If you really mean it. I'd enjoy it much more if you came too."

" Fiennes will enjoy it much more if I don't ", replied her husband, collecting the plates.

The frown deepened.

" Don't spoil everything, John."

" No. All right. Sorry. I'll put these in the tub."

After washing-up, husband and wife went for a stroll together onto the high ground at the back of the village. The evening was clear and still, the world at peace. They talked of their early days together in London and no more was said about Dallas Fiennes.

On the following morning Hilary sent the novelist a note by Mrs. Barle, whose bi-weekly charring-day it was. She wrote that John didn't care for Gilbert and Sullivan but that she herself would love to hear the ' Yeomen of the Guard ' if Mr. Fiennes would get someone else in John's place. Of course he might well prefer to find a couple, in which case she would quite understand. In any case she thanked him very much.

Fiennes' first reaction to this note was delight at

the prospect of a tête-à-tête. It almost looked as
though the girl was meeting him half-way. These
demure women were often . . . but second thought
intervened. Fiennes was a sound judge of women ;
he felt quite certain that Hilary Pansel was as naive
as she looked. He was also a clever tactician. He
felt sure that if he was to get what he wanted he
must first win Hilary's confidence ; then he would
be able to play on the obvious strings of her loneliness—how dull a life she lived—how he would like to
make things brighter, happier for her—the usual
stuff. Sending a note back by Mrs. Barle, he replied
that he was delighted that Mrs. Pansel would
accompany him to the opera and that the third seat
was at her disposal if she cared to ask anyone else,
though for his own part he would be very happy
to leave it a party of two. This was permissible
gallantry which any woman would expect. If she
wanted a tête-à-tête she could have it ; at the same
time she could not think he was forcing himself upon
her. Fiennes settled down to his work with a smile
of satisfaction.

The manœuvre met with the success it deserved.
Hilary at once told her husband that Mr. Fiennes
had asked her to invite someone else in his place ;
that showed how unjust his (John's) remark had
been. She did not show him the note.

John grunted. He was moderately impressed.

" Who'll you ask ? " he said.

Hilary thought for a minute.

" I think I'll ask Beryl Helliott. She's musical
and she doesn't have much fun."

" Good lord. Fiennes won't thank you, will he ?
She's hardly his line."

" She's a very nice girl. I don't know what you mean by ' his line '."

" Sorry. I just thought he didn't care for plain women. But of course it's the music he'll be thinking of."

Hilary opened her mouth to retort, but thought better of it. A cantankerous man was best left alone.

Beryl Helliott was the elder sister of Frank, the squire of Brulcote. She was twenty-nine, was short-sighted, and was too depressed with poverty and dullness to take any trouble about her appearance, which in any case was homely. Hilary had called her a nice girl, which meant that she was sorry for her and could not under any conceivable circumstances feel jealous of her. Beryl passed her life in keeping the wolf from the doors—front, back and side—of Brulcote Manor, and trying to make her brother remember that he was a gentleman before he became a farmer. Her one source of happiness was her piano, an old Broadwood grand, to keep which tuned she sacrificed half her meagre dress allowance.

Beryl was at home when Hilary walked over on Sunday afternoon. She was always at home unless she was shopping in Bryde, or once a month in Wells. Occasionally when she was in Bryde she looked in on Hilary for half-an-hour ; otherwise she went straight home and worked in the house or the garden. Anyone who saw her eyes light up as she greeted Hilary would have realised what this one friendship meant to Beryl Helliott.

" How lovely to see you, Hilary ", she said. " You'll stay to tea, won't you ? "

" I'd love to. May I see your irises ? "

" Of course, but they're nothing much. I haven't time to divide them."

" I'm sure they're lovely. I do envy you your garden, Beryl. Our cabbage-patch doesn't run to anything more ambitious than wall-flowers and forget-me-nots."

" You wouldn't change with me, Hilary."

Hilary flushed. This was one of those conversational gambits, typical of a lonely spinster, to which it is so difficult to reply.

" We've neither of us got everything we've dreamed of, Beryl ", she answered gently. " But I've got a treat for us both ", she added more briskly. " At least, I hope you'll make it one. Mr. Fiennes wants us to go to the ' Yeomen of the Guard ' with him in Hunstanton on Tuesday evening."

Beryl Helliott flushed.

" Oh, I couldn't ! " she exclaimed.

" Why not ? "

" I don't know him."

" That doesn't matter."

" But you said he wanted me—us—to go with him."

Caught again.

" He asked me to ask someone else. Do come, Beryl."

But Beryl was stubborn.

" Why doesn't your husband go ? "

" He doesn't like Gilbert and Sullivan."

" But I heard him whistling ' Is life a boon ? ' only last week when I came to see you."

Again.

"Well, he says he doesn't—tired of it, or something. Anyhow, he won't come."

Beryl remained silent.

"Do come, Beryl. I can't very well go by myself."

"I see."

Hilary frowned, then laughed.

"Beryl, I shall shake you in a minute! Do come. I want you to. You know I do."

Beryl's set face relaxed.

"I'd like to, Hilary, but I'm frightened of Mr. Fiennes. He's so . . . such a . . ."

"Such a man of the world? And we're such country mice? We're both in the same boat there, Beryl. I don't suppose he thinks anything about that. I think he wants to be friendly. It must be pretty lonely for him down here—away from all his friends."

"I suppose it must, rather", said Beryl reluctantly.

"Then you'll come?"

"But I've got nothing to wear."

Beryl was in the woman's Last Ditch.

"Nor have I. I shall wear my last year's summer frock."

"I didn't have one last summer. Or the summer before."

"I'm sure you've got something, Beryl. Can't we go and hunt through the family wardrobe? I do so want you to come."

The girl's face softened.

"Do you really, Hilary? I can't think why you should, but it's very sweet of you. I'd love to come."

Hilary gave her friend's arm a squeeze.

" Good. That's splendid. Oh, there are the irises—aren't they heavenly. What are those tall brown and yellow ones ? "

" They're just irises. I don't know anything about names. How shall we get there, Hilary ? "

" Mr. Fiennes will take us in his car. Will you come and have something to eat with us first ? About half-past six ? "

" I'd love to. I adore the ' Yeomen '. What fun it'll be."

The girl had forgotten her first reluctance. Her repressions often melted away before Hilary's sunny friendliness. They chattered through the afternoon, picked some flowers, dug out an old-fashioned but pretty silk frock for Beryl, and walked together half the way back to Bryde.

Nothing more was said about the outing by John until Tuesday evening when, having forgotten that supper was half-an-hour earlier than usual, he arrived late and was annoyed with Hilary and anything but nice to Beryl Helliott. Politely they sat on at the table while he began his supper and were rewarded by being asked whether a man couldn't eat without being stared at. As there was a guest, supper was laid in the living room instead of, as usual, on the kitchen table. The two women were only able to move into two other chairs in the same room, while John munched on in sullen silence. It was a relief when the hoot of a motor horn outside presaged the arrival of Dallas Fiennes.

The novelist wore a dark blue, double-breasted flannel suit, a silk shirt and bow tie, with a yellow carnation in his buttonhole. Though nearly fifty and distinctly grey about the temples, he was an attractive-looking man, if one did not mind a slight suggestion of fleshiness. His appearance and turn-out made John Pansel seem by comparison dirty and uncouth ; for the first time in her life Hilary felt slightly ashamed of her husband. The latter's behaviour was not calculated to remove that feeling. He remained sitting at the supper table when Fiennes entered, greeting him with a curt nod, and taking no part in the polite introduction and conversation which followed.

" Lovely evening. Almost a pity to sit in a stuffy theatre ", said Fiennes breezily. " Sure you wouldn't rather go for a run in the car, Mrs. Pansel ?"

" Oh, but we want to hear Sullivan ! Miss Helliott's very musical ! " exclaimed Hilary.

" Then of course you shall ", said Fiennes with a bow. " How charming you both look ; I shall be proud of my party. What a pity you aren't coming, Pansel ; we should have made a neat *parti carré*."

The remark was well calculated to stress the difference between John Pansel's appearance and that of the three theatre-goers.

Hilary flushed uneasily as she saw the scowl on her husband's face.

" Oughtn't we to be going ? " she asked, hurriedly.

" Perhaps we had better. Sure you won't change your mind, Pansel ? There's room in the dickey. We could probably raise a seat for you somewhere in the theatre."

" Very good of you, but I've got the washing up to do ", replied John with ponderous sarcasm.

" Well, come on then, ladies. We shall have to pack a bit tight but it'll keep us from rattling. Don't sit up for us, Pansel ; we shall probably have a look at Ely Cathedral by moonlight after the show."

As they walked to the car, Fiennes' high-pitched voice must have carried half-way down the village. John Pansel slammed the door of his house and flung himself angrily into a chair. With an empty pipe in his mouth he sat staring at the no less empty grate.

In the meantime Fiennes' luxurious coupé swung easily along the narrow, winding road that led to Brancaster and Hunstanton. It took the three of them abreast quite comfortably, though, as its owner had said, there was certainly no rattling. His only regret was that the shoulder and thigh which pressed against his own were those of Beryl Helliott and not of Hilary Pansel. However, by keeping his eyes on the road in front, a man of imagination could get some pleasure out of even that situation. By skilful ushering of his party the courteous host was able to arrange matters more to his satisfaction in the theatre, Miss Helliott going in first, Mrs. Pansel second and himself last.

It was a warm evening and the theatre was already unpleasantly stuffy, but Dame Carruthers' rich contralto soon carried Hilary, and at any rate one of her companions, away to the cool shade of the Tower walls, the dappled foliage of its plane trees. For an hour or more she listened, enchanted, to the delicious music of Sullivan, the sparkling wit of Gilbert, and it was with a sigh of regret that she watched the curtain roll down upon the grim figure of the executioner, standing alone, cheated of his victim, beside the dreadful block. . . .

Beryl Helliott had sat motionless throughout the

act, her plain face charmed by the twin wizards into a glow of happiness that was almost beauty. She turned to Hilary with an enchanted smile.

" Isn't it heavenly ? " she whispered.

Dallas Fiennes was more practical.

" Hellishly hot in here ", he said.   " Shall we go and get a breath of fresh air ? "

" It would be rather nice ", said Hilary. " Coming, Beryl ? "

The girl made a movement to rise, but the instinct of self-effacement was quick to re-assert itself. The others, she thought, would much rather be without her ; two was company . . .

" I'll stay here. I like watching the people. You go ", she said.

Hilary hesitated, but it really was stuffy and, the enchantment over, she found that her head was aching ; fresh air would probably put that right. She followed Dallas out into the cool night.

The night was not only cool, by comparison with the theatre, but starlit. As Dallas said, ' Ely was indicated '.   Hilary, however, was not going to miss the Second Act ; she would stroll down to the sea front for five minutes, then they must get back.

They strolled in silence. Dallas saw that his companion was still in a state of semi-enchantment. He was wise enough not to break it by talk. They reached the promenade above the pier and leaning upon a railing looked down upon the sea. The tide was up but the air was so still that not a fleck of foam broke from the waves as they rolled lazily, almost silently, up the beach. The moon was almost new but the stars were bright enough to show Fiennes his companion's face. Innocent of make-up, in that dim light, with the look of enchantment still in her eyes, Hilary's beauty thrilled Dallas. It was all he could do not to make instant love to her. But his self-control was just strong enough to obey the dictates of his scheming brain.

" Delicious, isn't it ? " he murmured, looking at her fair loveliness.

" Heavenly ", whispered Hilary, her eyes upon the star-lit sea.

Another silence. Then :

" I am so grateful to you for coming this evening, Mrs. Pansel."

Hilary turned her eyes upon her companion's face. The dim light gave it a false air of refinement. There was a look of appeal in the grey eyes.

" Are you ? I am grateful to you for bringing us."

" You can hardly realise, I suppose, how lonely a man's life can be."

" Lonely ? But you've got swarms of friends."

" Friends ? " Fiennes gave a bitter little laugh. " I thought so once."

" Oh ! " Hilary felt a little flutter of interest. " Aren't they . . . ? Don't you . . . ? "

Dallas drew himself up. His voice took a firmer note.

" Mrs. Pansel, I'm not going to whine to you. I deserve what I've got—my loneliness now. I've been a fool—perhaps worse—and I've got to pay for it." The repentant sinner was, Dallas knew, almost irresistible to a good woman. " I'm not asking for pity, but if you can bring yourself to give me your friendship Bryde will be a very different place for me."

Hilary's innocent heart glowed.

"Why, of course, Mr. Fiennes. John and I will be only too glad . . ."

"Ah, John knows me too well, Mrs. Pansel. He won't make a friend of me, and he will be right."

"Oh, but of course he will, if I . . . But you mustn't tease him, Mr. Fiennes."

"No, of course not. It's so typical of me to be a cad when I want to. . . . I think it's really jealousy, Mrs. Pansel . . ." said Dallas, with his most effective little note of bitter regret. But Hilary wasn't listening.

"Oh ! " she exclaimed. "What are we thinking of ? We've been ages. The second act must have begun long ago ! "

Fiennes cursed under his breath, but, like a great general, he knew when to give ground—*reculer pour mieux sauter*.

"I'm so sorry. It's my silly fault—selfish as ever. We haven't really been very long. We shan't have missed much."

They hurried back and, amid scowls and stares, pushed into their seats as Jack Point and Wilfred Shadbolt skipped off the stage, together at the conclusion of their famous song and dance.

CHAPTER V

For some time after the others had left him John
Pansel sat staring at the empty fireplace. He was
furious with Fiennes, disgusted with himself. The
man, of course, was a cad, a smooth-tongued, oily
cad, who thought he had only got to flatter a woman
and she would fall into his arms ; an offensive cad,
too, who thought it was funny to be rude to men
with a less glib tongue than his own. He himself
was a cad, an ill-mannered, sullen brute who could
not be decently polite to his wife's guests, a selfish,
jealous brute who didn't care how much he hurt
the one person in the world whom he loved if he
could flatter his own vanity, appease his own injured
feelings, by doing so.

The trouble was that John Pansel had seen that
look on his wife's face, that look of reluctant dis-
paragement as she compared her sullen, untidy
husband with the dapper appearance and polished
manners of the novelist. This was the first time
that it had ever crossed John's mind that his wife
might regard him as anything but perfect and the
realisation was an unpleasant shock. The fact that
he was himself conscious of his imperfection did
not improve matters ; it added to his disgust with
himself without removing the grievance against his
wife.

With a shrug of the shoulders John heaved himself

out of his chair and, carrying the supper things into
the kitchen, began to wash up. It was a job that
he detested, messy, back-aching, menial. He did
not mind helping Hilary, drying while she washed ;
there was a sense of magnanimity to be got out of
helping one's wife—one's very attractive wife ; but
to do the work all alone, while she went off and
amused herself with another man, was a very
different story. John knew perfectly well that this
was grossly unjust, that he was only doing these
things because, in spite of all her entreaties, he had
refused to go with her on this jaunt, but in his
present mood it gave him a savage pleasure to be
unjust.

Having at the moment no work on hand that
could be done by artificial light, John tried to read
a book, but the library was limited ; he had read
most of it five times over and the unread were, to
his taste, unreadable. He was not fond of the wireless and in the absence of Hilary he felt at a completely loose end. The only thing to do was to go
and gossip at ' The Virgin Duck '. This quaintly
named inn was situated in the centre of the village
and its tap-room was the meeting place of those
inhabitants of Bryde-by-the-Sea who considered
themselves its upper class. It was a picturesque
old building, dating from early Tudor times, and
the tap-room itself was oak-panelled and warmed
by a large open hearth on which, summer and
winter, a few logs or many were always burning.
There was also a private bar—a ' parlour ' which
the landlord, Sam Pete, tried his best to make the
gentry adopt for their own use, but they would have
none of its grained and plush stuffiness, with the

result that Sam's native patrons gradually dropped away, awed by the presence of the great, and took their custom to the rival ' Fisherman's Arms ' nearer the harbour. It was a serious loss to Pete, but he did not know how to remedy it, and in any case he got the ' through ' custom of lorry-drivers and occasional charabancs.

The origin of its name was lost in mystery. One theory was that ' Duck ' was a perversion of ' Duke ' and, originally ' The Virgin's Duke ', referred to some ducal member of the court of the Virgin Queen.

Dallas Fiennes, however, pointing out that Earls had played a more prominent part than Dukes in that monarch's life, suggested that the name was correct as it stood and, with the lewd impertinence of the period, suggested an intimacy between the Queen and her great admiral, Drake. For neither theory was there any historical foundation, but John Pansel had amused himself and pleased his host by painting a new signboard with Elizabeth on one side and a mallard duck on the other.

This evening there were two other ' regulars ' in the bar when Pansel arrived : Guy Vessle, a singer with T.B. tendencies who spent all his ' resting ' time on the coast, and Boyton Sarne, an engineer who had built himself a week-end cottage in Bryde and who now, owing to the depression in the engineering trade, found his week-ends extending into three days on each side of Sunday. Vessle was an amiable, friendly little fellow, tiresomely fussy about his health and of limited intellect ; Sarne, on the other hand, was shrewd enough, but had a bitter, cynical tongue which grated upon John Pansel, and indeed upon anyone who had to put up with it for long. Still, on an occasion like the present, any company, John thought, was better than his own.

" Hullo, Pansel ", exclaimed Sarne, as John entered. " Third time this week. You'll break up the happy home."

John greeted this sally with a wry smile and ordered a pint of half and half.

" Have you another exhibition coming on soon ? " enquired Vessle, who always pretended a polite ignorance of the difficulties and misfortunes of others.

" Exhibition ? What a hope ! " growled the artist. " The galleries won't look at me now. Nothing more risky than Seaton or Fox Wellard for them ! "

" Indeed ? I'm sorry to hear that." Vessle's diction was as prim and careful as his light tenor voice. " Your work should meet with the success it merits."

" At least you can make your own work, if you can't sell it ", said Sarne. " We poor bloody engineers have to sit and twiddle our thumbs while the Government and the local authorities cut out all the works they ever intended to do."

" Indeed that applies to my profession too, in a different sense ", said the singer. " Nobody but the B.B.C. dare organise a concert, and opera is dead unless you were born in Germany or Italy."

" Yes, we encourage our enemy aliens and put our own heroes on the dole ", snarled Sarne with the bitterness of an ex-serviceman who had built roads in back areas.

" You can hardly call Italy an enemy ", suggested Pansel.

" She soon will be if little Benito has his way. That lad's blowing up for trouble."

" I'm not sure another war wouldn't be rather a pleasant change ", said John, who had reason enough to hate the last one.

" Heaven forbid ", exclaimed Vessle, who had not left England but disliked bombs.

" Oh, you needn't lie awake o' nights, Caruso. We may not be too proud to fight, but we're too damn poor."

" As a nation, do you mean ? Or as individuals ? " asked Vessle.

" Both, of course. Who's got any money now ? "

" I fancy our friend Fiennes has ", replied the singer who, for all his primness, could not conceal his jealousy of the successful novelist.

" Ah, yes, Master Dallas. The public will always waste money on trash ", replied the engineer, who would have applied the same word to the art of both his companions.

" I suppose he's working to-night." There was a pathetic note of envy in the unemployed singer's voice.

" Not he ", answered Sarne. " He's poodle-faking as usual. I saw him all dressed up to kill. Some girl's going to be lucky to-night."

John Pansel felt a surge of blood rush to his face. He clenched his fists but managed to keep his mouth shut.

' Some girl ' ! His wife. ' Poodle-faking ' ! Disgusting, vulgar brutes, all of them. Why had he let her go ? . . . let her expose herself to Sarne's filthy tongue, Vessle's dirty little snigger ?

" Wonderful what he manages to pick up in a

61

God-forsaken hole like this ", Sarne was continuing.
" He can't be very particular."

" Some men seem to have an obsession for that
sort of thing. They seem to have no discrimination."
Vessle's prim voice suggested that he was above
such things but that, should he feel inclined, he had
but to pick and choose.

" That's about it. Since his London bitches
deserted him he has to take what he can get and be
thankful for it."

John writhed in his chair. A knotted vein was
throbbing in his forehead but the others were
too much engaged in their pretty talk to notice
him.

" Well, I wish him joy. He'll be lucky if he
doesn't . . . Hullo, Farmer Giles ; how are the
mangold wurzels ? "

The door had opened to admit a young man of
about twenty-six. He was dressed in flannel
trousers and an old norfolk jacket ; his hands, none
too clean, looked hard and muscular, in contrast to
a face which, though pleasant enough, gave an
impression of weakness. He responded to Sarne's
greeting with a nervous smile.

" Good-evening everybody. I'm afraid the rabbits
are getting most of my roots. They're simply
swarming this year."

" You'd better get Polly Madgek to trap them for
you ", suggested John. " If rumour speaks true,
he's an artist at that job."

Frank Helliott smiled. He liked John Pansel,
who always treated him as a man and not a joke.

" I fancy he has as many of them as he wants as
it is ", he said. " I wish I could swap jobs with

him ; fishing, building and poaching are more profitable than farming."

" Yes, we all want to swap jobs with the other fellow ", said Sarne, " but as a matter of fact every man's as big a beggar as his neighbour nowadays."

" Except Fiennes ", said Vessle, who liked to dwell on a favourite note.

Helliott looked at him quickly.

" He is rather rich, isn't he ? " he asked.

" Rolling. Baths in champagne, a wife in every village." Sarne, too, had his favourite note. A psychologist would have diagnosed his trouble in ten minutes.

" Is he . . . is he coming in to-night, does anyone know ? " asked Helliott, whose sister had only told him that she was going to a concert with Hilary Pansel.

" He is not. He is gazing at the lovely stars with some fair damsel ; I expect about now . . ."

John Pansel sprang to his feet.

" For God's sake stop it ", he cried, and flung out of the house.

The others stared at the still shaking door.

" What on earth's biting that fellow ? " asked Sarne.

" He seems to be upset about something ", said Vessle.

" Upset ? " The engineer stared at him. " Good lord ! You don't think . . . ? It isn't . . . ? " He lay back in his chair and shouted with laughter.

" What on earth's the joke ? "

" Why, don't you see ? It's . . . my hat, what a joke ! It's our demure little Hilary who's stepped

into the breach. That's why he's here to-night.
That's why . . . Oh lord, ha, ha, ha, ha . . ."

Vessle joined in with a sycophantic titter, though
he didn't appear quite to understand the joke.
Frank Helliott sat silent.

" Don't look so glum, Squire Hayseed," exclaimed
Sarne breaking off his laughter. " Haven't shocked
you, have we ? "

Frank murmured something about getting home,
took a drink from his tankard, and walked out of the
room. Outside he stopped to relight his pipe. A
fisherman, passing, wished him good-night, and
Frank returned the greeting automatically. Then
he walked down to the edge of the saltings and sat
on a boat listening to the faint noises of the waterfowl. When he got home, more than an hour later,
he found his sister waiting up for him. Beryl never
trusted her brother to lock up, though there was
little enough to tempt a thief. Frank flung himself
down into a dilapidated armchair and sucked at his
empty pipe.

" I wish you wouldn't do that, Frank ; it sounds
horrible ", said Beryl.

Frank took no notice.

" You like those Pansels, don't you, Beryl ? " he
asked after a pause.

" Yes, dear ; why ? "

" Well, I like him. He's always been ripping to
me, but he does seem to have got rather a foul
temper—all of a sudden, I mean."

" He's not at all well you know, Frank. He was
terribly wounded in the war and isn't really right
now. I'm sure he's awfully nice really. Hilary
loves him. Why do you ask about him ? "

" There was something odd going on at the
' Duck ' to-night. That fellow Sarne was chaffing
Pansel and he—Pansel, I mean—flew into a temper
and stumped out of the bar. I couldn't make out
what it was all about but Sarne said something—
after Pansel had gone—about ' our little Hilary '.
Dashed cheek, I thought it."

Beryl had flushed at the mention of her friend ;
she seemed uneasy.

" I don't think he's a very nice man, Frank. I
shouldn't pay any attention to what he says."

" Oh, I don't, but he makes me feel rather sick.
I mean, I'm not a prig, far from it, but I think all
this *talking* about women . . . and that sort of
thing . . . well, it's all rather beastly."

Beryl got up from her chair and leaning over her
brother kissed him tenderly.

" Darling Frank ", she said ; " I do love you.
Come on up now ; I'm rather tired."

Frank sprang up from his chair.

" Oh, I say ; what a pig I am ", he said. " I
forgot you'd been out. And that dress looks
ripping. Did you enjoy yourself ? "

" The music was lovely ", said Beryl.

CHAPTER VI

CHRISTIAN OCCASIONS

WHILE Hilary Pansel was enjoying herself in Hunstanton and John her husband was seeking, but not finding, consolation under the wing of the ' Virgin Duck ', Christian Madgek was about one of his more lawful occasions. He was, at this period, engaged in courting one Elsie Dallington, daughter of the most prosperous publican in the neighbouring market town of Great Hayworth. Christian was well aware that a fisherman, even if he owned a motor-boat and had a side-line in bricks and mortar, was no match for the only child and heiress of Sam Dallington ; Elsie was also aware of this fact, but she could not resist the dark curls and magnetic grey eyes of her handsome suitor. Christian's awareness of his ineligibility did not cause him to despair ; it merely caused him to exercise more guile and spend more money over his courting than was the common habit of the Norfolk fishermen. His plan was to wind himself so closely round the heart of the susceptible Elsie that her indulgent father would find it impossible to resist her pleading, while at the same time he, Christian, withheld those ultimate delights for which she yearned until her person and dowry were equally well secured to him. He was, in fact, reversing the usual process, allotting to her the rôle of suppliant, himself assuming for the nonce an air of wayward modesty which should have been the girl's.

At the same time, he thought it diplomatic to give an impression of wealth and generosity sufficient to impress the girl, though if her father chose to investigate his position at all closely, Christian knew only too well that it would prove to be considerably less water-tight than his boats. It was Elsie's passion and her estimate of his worth that must win him through. The plan of campaign demanded a considerable amount of self-control, for he wanted Elsie as well as her fortune ; it necessitated, too, an expenditure of money far beyond what he could afford, but this he regarded as ground bait—bread upon the waters which would attract a rich haul.

While Hilary Pansel watched the starlit waves lapping upon the beach at Hunstanton, the while her gallant escort watched her own starry eyes, Christian sat with his Elsie upon a fallen tree-trunk in a secluded lane half-way between Great Hayworth and Bryde-by-the-Sea, and played his own subtle but less ignoble game. Withdrawing his arm from Elsie's clinging embrace, he slipped a hand into the pocket of his reefer and pulled out a small parcel. Unwrapping its paper covering with tantalising slowness, he disclosed a small velvet-covered case.

" I've brought ye a little gift, my girl ", he said, turning it over in his fingers.

Elsie's own fingers itched to open it but she restrained herself.

" Oh, Chris, what is it ? " she asked eagerly.

" 'Tis what I would gladly see you wear in my house, Elsie, but I fear you and they are too fine for a fisherman."

" Oh, Chris, I'm sure we're not. Do let me see."

Slowly, almost reluctantly, Christian surrendered

his gift.   Pressing the catch, Elsie exposed to view a
necklace of aquamarine and brilliants, a choice which
did credit to Christian's taste as well as bearing false
witness to his wealth.

Elsie gasped and stared at them in delight.   In
the starlight her eyes sparkled as brightly as the
gems—as brightly as did Hilary Pansel's above the
waves at Hunstanton.

" Oh, Chris, how lovely ! Oh, but you mustn't
give me such wonderful presents ; I know you can't
afford it."

" Oh, but I can ", said Christian quickly. " That's
nothing—nothing at all."

The girl looked at him doubtfully.   She was no
fool, she knew something about the state of the
fishing industry and of trade generally ; she knew,
too, that truthfulness is not one of the standard
qualities of the fisherfolk ; but Christian returned
her gaze with absolute steadiness ; there was such a
look of simple candour, of trustworthiness, in his
grey eyes that she could not doubt him.   Surely her
father could not either ; he *must* let her marry
Chris ; he would as soon as she could make up her
mind to tackle him.

Impulsively she laid her soft hand upon Christian's
hard, horny fist.

" I don't care whether you can afford it or not ",
she said ; " it's absolutely sweet of you to give it to
me. I shall always wear it, Chris, and " (her eyes
dropped modestly) " I hope soon in your house . . .
with you always."

That sounded all right, but she had said this—or
something like it—before, and still she did not open
the siege that was to break down her father's

resistance. Christian knew well enough that time was not unlimited ; her passion for him might fade, another suitor—more eligible—might appear and win her favour as well as her father's ; he could not possibly find the money to buy her another gift of this calibre ; it was the last shot in his locker.

" Won't you put it on, Else ? " he asked diffidently.

Lifting the necklace from its case she raised her hands and deftly fastened the clasp behind her neck.

" Does it look nice ? " she asked.

Christian raised his own hand and lifted the necklace as if to examine it more closely. As he did so he allowed his fingers to brush against the smooth skin of the girl's neck where it disappeared in soft curves behind her low-cut shirt. Instantly he felt her quiver in response to his touch ; the colour rushed into her cheeks.

" Oh, Chris ! Chris ! I haven't thanked you. I . . . I . . ."

She flung her arms round his neck and pressed her face against his. Christian felt her soft breath fanning his cheek, her lips seeking his own. He folded his arms round her and pressed her body against him, pressed his lips against hers ; for a moment he would respond, give her kiss for kiss, enflame her ardour, then he would . . . but in his scheming Christian had rated his own self-control too high ; as Elsie's soft, moist lips clung to his own her passion kindled a response in him that suddenly shook his whole body with desire ; the blood surged in his ears, his senses reeled.

" Elsie ! Elsie ! "

" Chris ! Oh, Chris ! "

The girl pressed herself more closely against him ; her being seemed to flow into his. Blindly Christian's hands wandered over her soft body, his fingers tore at the flimsy shirt. . . . With a tremendous effort he rose to his feet, flung the girl from him, staggered away, his hands pressed to his forehead. Elsie lay on the ground where she had fallen, her body shaken with dry sobs.

For five minutes there was silence, as Christian slowly regained control of his senses ; then he went back and knelt down beside his sweetheart.

" Elsie ", he muttered. " I'm sorry. I oughtn't to have done that. I'm sorry, girl."

Elsie did not move, but her sobbing ceased.

" I oughtn't to have treated you like that, Elsie ", Christian blundered on. " I know I oughtn't. I lost control of myself. It was wrong. When we're married, we . . ."

A low groan forced itself through the girl's lips.

" What is it, Else ? Can't you forgive me ? "

" Go away. Oh, go away ! "

Though the words were hardly audible the force behind them was unmistakable. Christian rose slowly to his feet and stood looking down at the crumpled body.

" I'm sorry, Else. I'd . . . perhaps I'd better go."

There was no response. Christian turned away and slowly trudged towards the metalled road that crossed the bottom of the lane. For ten minutes or more the girl lay still, then slowly rose, first to her knees, then to her feet. Her sobs had ceased, but her face was white and drawn. Mechanically she patted her hair, pulled her shirt together ; as she did so her fingers touched the necklace, clung to it. Then she too moved forlornly down the grass ride, reached the road, and turned towards her own village.

In the meantime, Christian Madgek was making his way back to Bryde. He was still feeling dazed by the sudden burst of passion which had taken him completely by surprise. He had always been fond of Elsie, even attracted by her, but had imagined himself to be master of his own feelings—had felt contempt for the lack of control which he had seen in others. This sudden flaring up of unimagined forces had shaken his faith in himself, had almost wrecked the carefully calculated plan of campaign which was to carry him and Elsie together to the altar, was to bring him not only a comely wife but a comfortable fortune. If, contrary to his ' proposing', the course of love in those intoxicating minutes had rushed on to ' its right true end ', he would have fallen from the pedestal upon which stand only the unattainable ; it would have been impossible to prevent its happening again ; Elsie would have been satisfied in her eager desire—perhaps sated—and would in time sufficiently recover her senses to realise the folly of her *liaison* with a man whom her family and friends would consider beneath her both in fortune and station.

It was true that ' the right true end ' had *not* been achieved ; Christian *had* recovered control of himself in time. But he was shaken, he was slightly less unattainable than before, he could no longer trust himself. Even now, as he remembered that passionate moment, as he felt again Elsie's breath upon his eyes and cheek, her eager lips seeking for his, her soft body pressing against his own, Christian felt the desire for her rise up again within him ; he was tempted to turn back, to find her again, to . . . Savagely he struck his face with his own clenched fist, the pain, angering, sobered him, and he tramped on at a greater pace than before.

Gradually he calmed down and by the time he had reached the outskirts of Bryde he had been able to persuade himself that all had turned out for the best, that the nearness of attainment would only arouse Elsie's ardour to greater heights, that her passion for him would now compel her to go to her father and force him to consent to the marriage. With complacent satisfaction Christian pictured to himself a visit from Mr. Sam Dallington, sullen but suppliant, his own indifference—even antipathy—to the match, his eventual, reluctant agreement to a settlement—a settlement which even in imagination made Christian's mouth water.

Just short of the village Christian stopped and, leaning on a gate, looked out over the flats and the marshy saltings towards the sea. The air was still and sound travelled far and clearly to his trained poacher's ears. The plop of a fish turning over in the water, the pipe of some sea-bird, the sudden scurry of an animal's feet—each told its tale of love, of hunger, of tragedy, to Christian. But he hardly heeded them ; his conscious mind was bent upon his own affairs, and he soon resumed his walk and passed through the silent village towards his own little house on the far side. It was an extremely small house, consisting of a kitchen and one bedroom, but that was all the bachelor Madgek required, and it had the supreme advantage of detachment, with a small yard for his building materials and a not much larger garden for his vegetables. It was a snug little home and would do well enough until the bride and her dowry demanded, and made possible, a richer setting.

Christian pushed open the door and bent his head to enter. Nobody in Bryde-by-the-Sea ever locks up his house or his cottage ; to do so would be considered an insult to one's neighbours. So that it was no shock to the fisherman to see the figure of a man seated in the one armchair which the room contained.

" 'Evening ", he said, and without more ado proceeded to light the oil lamp which stood upon the table. Its first feeble light revealed a small, shabby-looking man in a dark nondescript suit, with a stubble of black hair on his face and a mouthful of broken, discoloured teeth. Only his eyes relieved him from suspicion of being a tramp ; they were too keen, too full of life for that.

" It's you, Sim Fardell ? "

" It's me, Christian Madgek."

" You'll take a cup or a drop of something ? "

Hospitality precedes curiosity on the Norfolk coast—but not much else does.

" I'd welcome a drop."

Christian went to a cupboard in the corner and brought out a black bottle and two small glasses, into which he poured a careful measure of dark golden spirit.

Simeon Fardell's eyes glittered as he watched.

" Trade on the road ", said the fisherman, raising his glass.

" Harvest from the sea ", responded the pedlar.

Two quick jerks of the wrist and the tingling brandy shot down the throats of the toast-givers. Fardell's eyes turned eagerly to the bottle, which Madgek calmly picked up and put away in the cupboard. Hospitality was satisfied, at any rate till curiosity, and perhaps business, had had their turn.

" You wanted to see me ? "

The fisherman's staccato, querulous voice made the question sound like an accusation. The pedlar, more cosmopolitan in his speech, as in his life, nodded.

" It's time we came to an arrangement, Christian", he said.

" Oh ? How's that ? "

" You've paid nothing the last two months."

" Trade's bad."

" I know that well enough. That's why I want my money."

" You'll get it all right."

" When ? "

Madgek hesitated. Should he tell his creditor the truth ? explain the foundation upon which his expectation of wealth was based ? That surely would satisfy him—keep him quiet. But the habit of a lifetime—more, of generations—was against truth. Some natural secretiveness, some ingrained fear of giving anything away, restrained Christian.

" Soon enough. It can't be long."

" How am I to know that ? " asked the pedlar, with not unreasonable suspicion. " You've told me that before. I must have my money."

" You must wait then."

" I want it now."

" You can't have it now—that's straight enough."

Fardell's little eyes glittered angrily.

" Then I'll summons you."

This, as it happened, was an empty threat. The money-lending pedlar would no more have dreamed of putting his head inside a court of law, even a County Court, than he would of foregoing interest on his loans. Not only had he an inborn dread of the law but any such action would have ruined his reputation with his clients. Still, Christian Madgek could not know this. He dared not risk even the remotest possibility of such action—or even the threat of it. If it became known to Elsie and her father—and a word to any neighbour would mean, in due course, a word to them—that his presents to the girl were bought, not with his own earnings nor even from accumulated capital, but with money borrowed from this itinerant Shylock, his chance of marriage to the heiress would vanish into thin air.

" It'll do you no good to summons me, Sim Fardell ", he said doggedly. " The money'll come to you in time. I'm paying you good interest."

But Fardell was no less dogged.

" Times are bad. I want my capital ", he barked. " You can sell your motor-boat."

Madgek winced.

" If I did that I'd be a ruined man, Sim Fardell ; you know that. There's nothing in the fishing now. You don't want to ruin me. Where'd be the sense ? "

" I don't want to ruin myself. I'll give you one more month, Christian Madgek, and then if I don't get my money the boat'll have to go."

He rose to his feet. He was a small man, little more than five feet in height and thin-boned at that. Christian Madgek could have broken him with his

two hands. But it was common belief that Simeon
Fardell carried a revolver and no one on the coast
doubted that he would use it if anyone offered
violence to him.

" I've been generous to you, Madgek ; you know
that ", he said.

Christian nodded. Within his limits Fardell was
a fair man ; the fishermen knew it and respected
him for it. The pedlar remained standing but his
eyes wandered to the cupboard in the corner.
Christian hesitated ; it went against the grain to
waste so much good, duty-free brandy on a little
squirt like this ; still, the spirit had done him a
good turn already—got him a month's grace. He
fetched the bottle and poured out two more measures.
He did not want another himself but it would be
considered inhospitable not to drink glass for glass
with his guest.

" Fair winds."

" Kind walking."

The two glasses rose and fell. The bottle was
returned, despite all Fardell's eye-play, to the cupboard. The pedlar tripped across to the door. On
the threshold he turned.

" This day four weeks, Christian Madgek ", he
said, then pattered away up the road, his short legs
moving so quickly as to be almost running.

With a scowl Christian turned back into his
cottage and shut the door.

CHAPTER VII

JOHN PANSEL waited up until his wife's return from Hunstanton. He opened the door to her, said a curt good-night to Dallas Fiennes and lit the bedroom candlestick. Hilary saw at once that he was out of temper but was both too happy herself and too tired to go even a quarter way towards the quarrel that he appeared to want. She had enjoyed every minute of her evening. The opera had been delightful, Dallas Fiennes had been entertaining and, above all, had made her feel that she was still an attractive woman and not just a housewife buried by the sea-shore. She felt years younger and more cheerful than she had for ages—but she was definitely tired and she was going to bed.

John's sullen anger could not penetrate the elusive lightness of her defence ; she hardly seemed to notice him and his mood, but at the same time she chattered away to him through the connecting door of their bedrooms as she was undressing and gave him a more than usually affectionate hug when she said good-night. John still retained grace enough to respect her mood and made no further attempt to intrude his own.

In the morning he felt better—even ashamed of himself for the fury of anger that had driven him from the ' Virgin Duck ' and kept him tramping the roads until his wife's return. However justified he might be in his suspicion and dislike of Fiennes there was no reason why he should vent his anger upon his wife, who could not possibly realise the baseness of the fellow's intentions and only accepted them as a sign of friendship. No breath of suspicion, John very well knew, could possibly touch Hilary ; she was purity and simplicity personified. It was his, John's, duty to protect her, but not to be angry with her. The feeling of magnanimity which these noble sentiments engendered did the painter good and gave him an appetite for his breakfast.

Hilary was delighted to see her husband's change of mood, but unfortunately she misread it. Thinking that he was regretting his rudeness to Dallas Fiennes she began to praise the man, explaining to John that beneath the other's flamboyant manner there was a genuine sympathy and friendliness that were worthy of return. As he listened to this pæon John's spirit began to cloud again, dark thoughts to arise in the background of his mind. Fortunately breakfast was not a protracted meal and the subsequent washing-up broke off the unwelcome subject, so that by the time he had got out his painting things and begun work upon the picture which he had sketched in the day before, he was actually so forgetful of his doubts and troubles as to begin whistling.

Hilary's own spirit responded to the cheerful sound. The past evening had opened before her a vista of long-forgotten hopes, hopes of the happy life she and John were to have led, the pleasures, simple perhaps but real, that awaited them. Sullivan's music and even more, though this she did not realise, Fiennes' expert manipulation, had re-awakened feelings and aspirations long dormant in her mind. Life, after all, was good, full of pleasure, full of hope ; people were very kind, very willing to create happiness even in her quiet world ; Beryl Helliott had been sweet to her—so grateful and friendly ; Dallas Fiennes had been charming—only too anxious to make her life happier and more cheerful. She would persuade John to like him ; then they could all be such friends together and have a lovely time.

So thought Hilary Pansel, and in the fulness of her heart took her mending up to the little studio on the first floor so as to be with her husband for a time while he worked. John, still full of magnanimity, was glad to see her and the cheerful sound continued.

" You're very musical this morning, John ", said Hilary, lifting a pile of canvases from the only chair.

" Good tune, isn't it ? " replied her husband, mixing flake white and Payne's grey, with a dash of Naples yellow.

" I expect so. What is it ? "

" What it it ? What an insult ! It's ' Tell a tale of cock and bull '."

" It sounds a bit hearty. What is it ? Some music-hall ditty of your salad days ? "

" Music-hall ditty ? "

John stared at his wife.

" D'you mean to say you don't recognise it ? "

" Never heard it in my life, so far as I know."

John's expression had gradually changed from surprise to suspicion.

" What opera did you go to last night ? "

" ' The Yeomen of the Guard '—I told you. Why ? "

"Only because that song which you've never heard comes out of it."

"Oh!"

The expression on Hilary's face was not calculated to set her husband's doubts at rest. John put down his brush and palette and came across to her.

"Where *did* you go last night, Hilary?" he asked in an ominously quiet voice.

"What do you mean? You know where we went."

"I know one place you didn't go to, and that's to wherever the 'Yeomen of the Guard' was being performed last night. You're not going to tell me that you could go to an opera and forget all about one of the best songs in it."

Hilary, constitutionally incapable of guile, contrived to look as guilty as if she had a deliberate intrigue on her conscience.

"Don't be silly, John", she said, in a nervous, high-pitched voice. "We must have just missed that song."

"Did you arrive late?"

"No; we were there in plenty of time. We heard the whole of the first act."

"It's in the second. You didn't stay for that, perhaps."

"Yes we did. Only we were a little late in going in after the interval. It was very stuffy inside and we strolled down to the pier."

"All three of you?"

Hilary shifted restlessly in her chair.

"I don't know why you're cross-examining me like this", she said. "It's absurd. As a matter of fact

Beryl didn't come ; she said she wanted to watch the people."

" How tactful of her. So you and the seductive Fiennes had a nice little stroll in the moonlight by the sad sea waves ? "

" Oh, do stop, John. You're being odious . . . and . . . and stupid."

But John was inexorable. His face was hard and set.

" I certainly have been stupid. So this wonderful music you were raving to me about last night couldn't compete with the soft words of the charmer."

" I tell you we only went down to the sea for a few minutes to get some fresh air. Surely there's nothing in that to make all this fuss about. We were only a few minutes late."

" In fact, you only missed half the act."

This was grossly unjust. A quarter of an hour at the outside had elapsed before Hilary's return to the theatre, but without previous knowledge of the opera she could not be certain how much or how little she had missed. She rose to her feet.

" I'm not going to stay and be talked to like that, John ", she said, with a greater show of dignity. " You're being perfectly absurd and I can only suppose that you've eaten something that's disagreed with you."

Without waiting for an answer she walked out of the room and down to the kitchen. With a good deal of unnecessary noise she began tidying things that did not need to be tidied. She was very angry —angrier than she could ever remember to have been before. She was unaccustomed to jealousy, had not thought it possible that John and she could ever have such feelings about each other. She was completely innocent of any disloyal thought and John had treated her as if she was a . . . an unfaithful wife. It was disgusting.

With an ungraceful snort of indignation Hilary picked up her shopping basket and walked off towards the village grocery. John, from his bedroom window, watched her go. He was miserable ; furious with himself, indignant with Hilary ; how could she so demean herself as to flirt with this low-class novelist ? A middle-aged, conceited braggart— a notorious seducer of women. The thought of Fiennes turned John's anger into a cold rage of hatred. Free from temptation himself, John regarded such men as Fiennes, unscrupulous indulgers of their senses, as the lowest grade of humanity, unfit to live with decent men and women, unfit to live at all. Until now this feeling had been abstract ; he had merely disliked, despised them. Now one of them had crawled into his own life, was threatening with his slime the one creature in the world whom John loved. In his heart John adored Hilary, worshipped her ; the disappointment and dullness of his life had buried his feelings beneath the surface, but they were there, the stronger for being hidden, ready to burst forth into vigorous, even rank, growth should something happen to disturb them. Now something was happening.

John returned to his studio and picking up a piece of charcoal dabbed vaguely at his half-empty canvas. The attempt to work was not convincing and he soon gave it up and sat staring in front of him. How was he to deal with this problem that had suddenly arisen ? He had never before been faced by any

problem of psychology. It would be easy enough
to smash this dirty little worm, but what effect
would that have upon Hilary ? Women were (so he
had read) funny creatures ; violence might drive
her into the man's arms. He could refuse to have
Fiennes in the house, forbid Hilary to see him ; but
might that not have the effect of driving her to him ?
John groaned at the very thought of it, clenched his
fists and ached for violence. He was, poor fellow,
hopelessly at sea.

After half an hour of fruitless thought he took his
stick and went for a tramp over the hills behind the
village. He had not gone far when he saw a tall,
lanky figure approaching him down the narrow lane.
His first inclination was to turn aside, but it would
have been too unmistakable an avoidance and Hugh
Fallaran was the last man whose feelings John would
hurt. Fallaran was a barrister who had built up a
considerable practice at the Probate and Divorce
Bar ; his career had been interrupted by the war, in
which he took an honourable part, and it had taken
him a few years to recover ground lost to men who
had stayed behind, but all was going well with him
again when he had suddenly begun to grow deaf.
For a year he struggled against the severe handicap
which this affliction imposed upon him ; his colleagues and the Bench had been more than kind—
had told him that it was his brain and tongue and
not his ears that mattered, but Hugh soon discovered
that neither a quick brain nor a ready tongue could
play their part effectively unless they were ' fed ' by
receptive ears ; one day he overheard—the irony of
that word—a junior complaining to a colleague of
the tedious business which shouting at Fallaran

entailed ; within a month Hugh had finished his last case and retired to the depths of the country.

The shock had been terrific ; to an ambitious man the sudden ending of a brilliant career was a blow that literally staggered his reason ; for several dark weeks he actually contemplated suicide, but decided to fight it out, hoping to achieve by his pen something at least of what his tongue could no longer do. Having no relatives he retired to the depths of the country to write the life of a distinguished barrister, but it was a slow and wearisome business and the medium was unfamiliar to him. He had always lived nearly up to his income, though a large part of it had gone in open-handed charity ; now he was poor and alone, cutting himself off deliberately from his friends in unreasonable fear that his disability would be a burden to them. He lived in a small cottage half a mile out of Bryde and when he was not working spent much of his time walking on the shore, where the sound of the waves drowned for a time the surging, whistling tumult in his head. He was really happy there and was already beginning to recover his health and mental balance, though the look of strain quickly returned to his face if he had to speak to anyone. John and Hilary Pansel saw a good deal of him and he enjoyed talking to them— had come to believe that they liked talking to him ; that was why John could not risk appearing to shun him now.

" John Pansel, well met ", exclaimed Fallaran, slipping his arm through the painter's. " I'm feeling rather out of the world ; whisper the latest gossip in my ear. Up here a good healthy shout will pass for a whisper."

John smiled.

"I don't mind who hears my gossip", he said. "I'll tell the world I think the little hamlet of Bryde holds four of the nastiest fellows you'd find in a day's march."

"Good heavens; what an indictment. Am I one?"

"You're the only Christian. I'm talking of that conceited pimp Fiennes, that sneering dirty-minded fellow Sarne, that oily, sniggering little fool Vessle, and a surly, ill-tempered brute called John Pansel."

Hugh Fallaran gave his companion a shrewd glance.

"Some of them I don't care for myself", he said. "I don't know the last fellow, but I shouldn't bother my head about the rest.

John shook his head.

"The last's the worst of them", he said. "I hate the fellow."

They walked on for a minute in silence, the barrister too well-trained to risk a leading question.

"Fallaran", said John at last; "why did you never marry?"

His companion laughed.

"My dear chap—with my practice? Half a dozen divorce cases a week. Was it likely?"

That question had often been asked, though not always to his face. Hugh Fallaran had attracted and been attracted by many women, and though his answer was always what he had given John his real reason was that he loved women so much that he doubted his own ability to be faithful to any one of them.

"I know what you're thinking", he added. "A

wife would be a wonderful help to me now—a
wonderful companion. In many ways, Pansel, I
envy you more than I can say. If I was to marry
it would have to be someone very like Mrs. John
Pansel—lovely to look at, brave, cheerful, unspoilt,
sweet and innocent in the only real sense of those
much-abused words. I don't mind your knowing
what I think of your Hilary—because I'm as celibate
now as any monk. The more I cared for a woman,
the less could I bear to tie her life to mine now that
I'm crippled. I should always feel that I was a drag
on her happiness."

As Fallaran spoke a hot flush spread over John
Pansel's face, but the deaf man did not notice it.
He was looking out over the sea, an expression of
almost sublime sadness on his face. Suddenly he
pulled himself together.

" I've had a very happy life, you know, Pansel.
I've nothing to complain about at all."

" And I do nothing but complain. And I've
got . . . so much. I told you I was a surly brute."

Fallaran laughed and pressed his companion's arm.

" What you want is a more congenial companion
in your toping ", he said. " Leave that indifferent
lot at the ' Virgin Duck ' and come and drink a
modest Bass with me when you feel inclined. Here's
my turning ; I must go and pore over the windy
platitudes of m' learned friend."

The talk with Hugh Fallaran, though at one
moment it touched him on the raw, had done John
good. He felt no less angry with himself but he
knew that the barrister's estimate of Hilary was
right. Whatever had happened she was not to
blame ; he must not be angry with her. As he

walked his mind became clearer on that point. He
must be gentle with Hilary, sympathetic, tactful.
As to the other fellow, he must wait for the spur of
the moment to decide ; he simply did not know
what his attitude should be—still less whether he
would be able to observe any 'attitude' that he
might decide on. He would keep his eyes open and
try to steer things clear of trouble. In the meantime
he would apologise to Hilary for his behaviour after
breakfast.

But John did not apologise to Hilary. Hilary
herself had been thinking—or trying to think—a
rather different thing. Her thinking had really
amounted to giving her senses free rein, her sense of
indignation, her sense of dignity, of injured innocence. All these had boiled up and temporarily
overwhelmed her very real love for John. His
behaviour had been absolutely unjustified, ground-
less, inexcusable, abominable. Each time she
reached that point she stamped her foot—literally
or metaphorically according as she was situated at
the moment. When she got home she was still
indignant and rather nervous. John was out. Why
couldn't he have stayed in till she got back ? She
was not going to let him see that she was upset,
that she cared, however idiotic he might be. She
became more nervous and, when he came back,
was casual and insincere. She had bought a 'Tatler'
from a travelling newsagent and sat, swinging her
leg, on the dining table, commenting in an affected
way on the people who had been at Ascot or at
Lord's, or some such Society function. John felt
his mind cloud with annoyance, unreasonable but
obstinate. He stifled it.

"Hilary, I want to say . . . about this morning. . . ."

"My dear man, surely we've had quite enough about this morning. Let's have a little peace."

Hilary could hardly believe her own ears. Was it she who had said that ? in that silly affected voice ? What on earth was she doing ? John flushed with anger and turned abruptly away. He did not apologise.

And so the little rift widened, as little rifts will if they are not instantly bridged. Hilary was deeply hurt at John's mistrust of her. She would forgive him readily enough when he said he was sorry, but in the meantime it was not for her to make the first move. The unlucky thing was that at this time John was suffering more than usual from his war-damaged digestion. In an attempt to provide variety to their simple diet, Hilary had rashly ventured on a crab caught by one of the fishermen and the result had been disastrous. Indigestion will disturb the temper of the mildest of men—and John was not that. He woke up every morning feeling ill and he became more difficult and unreasonable as the day progressed. It was inevitable that this distemper should react upon his wife, so that the seeds of quarrel fell upon soil only too well prepared to yield a harvest of disaster.

CHAPTER VIII

EVIL CHANCES

IN a cottage it is extremely difficult for two people to ignore each other's existence—each other's mood. Unless they are clods they must be on either good terms or bad. For two days Hilary maintained her air of casual indifference ; John, having missed his chance of apologising at once, found it always more difficult to bring himself to the point. He, too, tried to appear indifferent, and only succeeded in appearing sulky. On the third morning she had made up her mind that the whole thing was too silly to continue ; if John wasn't man enough to say he was sorry (as she felt sure he was), she would herself take the initiative, tell him what she thought of him, have—if necessary—a blazing row, and so clear the air for a return to their normal relations. She would do it after breakfast ; men were always crochety before.

The post, usually confined to bills and circulars—for Hilary and John, with few relations or friends, were in any case bad correspondents—brought to Hilary an envelope, the handwriting on which she recognised as that of an old school friend living in Norwich, whom she had seen occasionally in the last few years. She tore open the envelope and began to read the letter, her face lighting up with pleasure as she did so.

" Oh, John ", she exclaimed, forgetting all about the situation, " Gwen Farnes wants us to go and

stay with her next week and go on the Broads !
How lovely it'll be."

There was no answer and she looked across at
her husband, who was himself reading a letter, a
scowl on his face. It was from one of the galleries,
the one which was most successful in selling his
work ; recognizing the typescript he had opened
it with pleasurable anticipation and now read it
with angry surprise. His obedient servant, Raphael
Stein, manager, regretted that in his opinion the one
oil-colour and two water-colour paintings which
Mr. Pansel had recently sent him were not suitable
for inclusion in his August exhibition and he was
returning them that day by the East Coast Road
Service which undertook to deliver within forty-
eight hours.

This was a stunning blow to John Pansel. The
oil-colour which he had sent up was, in his opinion,
the best which he had done for some years. He
had counted on getting at least thirty, perhaps forty,
guineas for it. The loss of the money was serious
enough, but that his pictures should ' not be considered suitable ' for exhibition in a gallery which
in the past had made a very good thing out of its
commission on his pictures was a blow to his pride
which infuriated him beyond all reason. It was an
unfortunate letter to arrive on that particular
morning.

" John, dear, did you hear what I said ? "

" Eh, what's that ? "

John looked up, the scowl still on his face.

" Gwen Farnes has asked us to stay with her next
week."

" Hang Gwen Farnes ! "

John turned his eyes back to his letter, which he had already read three times.

" John ! "

There was an ominous ring in Hilary's voice, quietly though she spoke. It penetrated through John's ill-temper, which he controlled sufficiently to ask, in no very agreeable voice, what Gwen Farnes wanted them to stay for.

" I told you—if you'd only listen. She's making up a party for a sailing-trip on the Broads—four days ; she wants us to go."

John Pansel had never been socially inclined ; in the last few years he had gone nowhere ; in the last few weeks he had felt too ill and too upset to want to do anything but snarl ; on that particular morning—with that particular letter in his hand— he loathed the very thought of his fellow men and women.

" What a ghastly idea ", he said gruffly.

" Oh, John, I should love it ! " Hilary was too upset to remember that she was by way of being dignified.

" Well, I shouldn't. I should hate it."

" Oh, how selfish you are ! Can't I ever do anything that's amusing ? Surely you can think of me for once in a way."

" Well, you'd better go, then. I'm damned if I will."

" But I can't go without you ", exclaimed Hilary tearfully, " she wants a man to help with the boat. You might come, John."

" My dear girl, how can I go joy-riding all over Norfolk in a boat. I've got my work to do."

" Your work ! " Hilary was too much disappointed and hurt to think what she was saying or how she said it. " You could go joy-riding all over Europe for the rest of the year for all the good your work does ! "

It was a cruel thing to say, doubly cruel on top of the letter in John's hand, though that Hilary could not know. The moment it was out she regretted it, opened her mouth to retract . . . but it was too late. John sprang to his feet, his face black with anger, hurt to the depth of his being.

" If you want a man, you'd better take your friend Fiennes. No doubt a successful novelist is better company than a penniless painter."

John Pansel flung himself at the door, but forgetting to duck his head, struck his forehead against the lintel. Savage with pain and anger he crashed his fist against the door, the flimsy panel cracking under the blow. A second later the back door slammed and steps crunched down the path.

For five minutes or more Hilary sat at the breakfast table, on the brink of tears. She had never been a crying woman ; even the disappointments of the last ten years she had faced with a philosophic calm and a sense of humour which reduced them to bearable proportions. But this sudden storm which had burst upon her—really it was only the first rumble of approach—was something quite new to her. It was so unexpected, so unjust. At this point her sense of indignation came to her rescue. She pushed back her chair, brushed her hand across her eyes, and began to clear away the breakfast things. The work of washing-up was scamped that morning ; so was the bedmaking and dusting. Usually Hilary took a pride, even a pleasure, in keeping her house neat and spotless ; this morning she wanted to get away from it as quickly as possible.

By eleven o'clock she had finished and, taking a soft straw hat in her hand she set out for a walk on the high ground behind the village, following very much the same course that John had taken two days previously. It was a glorious morning ; the sun shone brightly but a pleasant breeze from the sea tempered its heat. Already the fields of corn showed a tendency to ripen, a glint of gold in the green. Their gentle swaying before the breeze had an irresistibly soothing effect upon the most jangled nerves. Above in the clear sky larks hung poised, carolling their song of joy to all who were not too physically or mentally deaf to hear it. Hilary heard it and her naturally happy disposition began to throw off the evil humour of the morning. If she could have finished her walk under the same conditions, all would probably have been well ; she would have realised that John's ill-health and his disappointment about his work must be humoured, that she must herself take the first step towards a reconciliation which, at this early stage, should have been easily achieved.

But the evil spirit that had already been at work that morning, in sending John Pansel the ill-timed letter from his Gallery, was now ready to play its second trick.

Dallas Fiennes had unexpectedly come to an end of his scribbling paper. He bought large quantities of it at a time, in blocks, and each time said to himself : ' There, that'll last me for months '. It was never till the last block was reached that he realised that his stock was nearly exhausted. He

was an untidy scribbler and now that he was trying
to cure himself of the trick of careless writing into
which he had fallen he frequently tore up work with
which he was not satisfied. So the paper disappeared at an incalculable rate. He had, of course,
his fad about what paper he could write on and what
he couldn't; his blocks came from a particular
stationer in London and to-day was Friday, so that
there was a good chance of his fresh supply not
arriving before Monday or even Tuesday; and he
was in full swing and wanted to work right through
the week-end. If he was not to have the flow
interrupted he must get a supply locally and the only
stationer he had so far discovered who kept even
approximately what he required was in Fakenham,
twelve miles south of Bryde.

With a good deal of grumbling Fiennes got himself
into some tidy clothes and set out across the saltings
to collect his car from the 'Anchorage' hotel.
When working at his hut or messing about the
shore or on the creeks in his boat Fiennes wore any
clothes that were comfortable at the moment—grey
flannel trousers and an open shirt in the summer, a
jersey in winter; but when he went abroad—anywhere outside Bryde—he was always carefully
dressed. His principle was always to be prepared—
fully prepared—for anything that might turn up.
This morning he wore a light grey flannel suit, a silk
shirt and bow tie, a pair of suède shoes, and a soft
hat; the effect was pleasant—he looked cool, comfortable and attractive. Not that he had any
immediate object for attraction in his mind's eye.
He had not seen Hilary Pansel since the evening in
Hunstanton, partly because he thought he would be

more successful if he did not make himself too cheap
and partly because a talk with Boyton Sarne had
slightly disquieted him. Meeting Fiennes on the
morning after the performance of ' The Yeomen of
the Guard ', the engineer had described with
malicious gusto the ill-humour of John Pansel at
the ' Virgin Duck ' on the previous evening. Sarne
had not hesitated to adopt as the truth his own
guess that Hilary Pansel had been the novelist's
companion on the previous ' evening on the tiles ' ;
he had rallied Fiennes—who enjoyed being considered a rake—and then warned him to mind what
he was up to—John Pansel was a hot-tempered
fellow with, for all his digestive troubles, a formidable pair of arms—and feet ; Sarne thought he
would not hesitate to use them if really roused.
This aspect of the matter had not previously struck
Fiennes ; during his career as a philanderer he had,
of course, aroused jealousy from time to time but he
had so far escaped violence. John Pansel would
certainly not be a pleasant person to scrap with. He
decided to go warily—not, certainly, to give up his
pursuit of Hilary, but not, on the other hand, to ask
for trouble.

It was an admirable morning resolution but when
he saw Hilary's slim figure, in its sleeveless summer
frock, in the lane in front of him as his car climbed
to the ridge behind Bryde, Fiennes' overwhelming
passion for the chase swept all other considerations
from his mind. Declutching, he let his car run
quietly up beside her.

" Well met, fair lady ", he said, taking off his hat.
His short, dark hair, with its touch of grey at the
temples, was one of his best features and he generally

kept his head uncovered when he wanted to attract a woman.

Hilary's start of surprise was in part due to the fact that she had not heard the car until it pulled up beside her, but it was accentuated when she realised the identity of the driver.   Dallas Fiennes had been too much in her mind of late for his presence to leave her quite unmoved, and her slight embarrassment gave rise to a blush which the novelist at once interpreted to his own advantage—and encouragement.

" Can I persuade you to drive with me to Fakenham ? " he asked.

Hilary had not quite collected her wits and found herself asking, rather stupidly :

" Why Fakenham ? "

" My immediate object is purely commercial—the business of my trade—but you have but to say the word and for Fakenham we will read Eldorado."

Hilary gave a self-conscious laugh.

" That sounds rather a chilly spot, from what I remember of the poem ", she said.

Fiennes pricked up his ears but took no apparent notice of the opening.   Pushing open the left-hand door he patted the seat beside him.

" Come on ", he said, " it's much cooler driving than walking."

Hilary hesitated.

" But shall we be home in time for lunch ? " she asked.

Fiennes laughed.

" Good heavens, no.   Why lunch at home every day ? "

" But I've got to get John's lunch ready."

" Isn't there a tin of sardines or something he can open for himself ? "

" Oh, yes, I suppose so ", replied Hilary vaguely.

" Then come along, Mrs. John Pansel, and forget you're Mrs. John Pansel for one morning. Are you never to have any change ? any amusement ? Must you live by routine every day of your life ? "

Put like that, it was rather absurd. After all, thought Hilary, she had an existence of her own ; she was not only a wife. In any case, a motor drive was a harmless amusement. She was still sufficiently under the influence of her indignation with John to be slightly rebellious. Another half hour of the lark-and-waving-cornfield treatment and she would probably have returned to her customary docile state of mind, but Dallas Fiennes had come before the process was complete.

Hilary stepped into the car.

" All right ", she said. " It will be very jolly."

It was very jolly. Dallas, when he set himself to the task, could be a very entertaining talker. Hilary soon found herself in an almost continuous chuckle of delight. They were soon in Fakenham, the small ' trade business ' effected, and a few minutes later, almost without comment, were running smoothly, their bonnet still pointed southward, on the road to Castle Acre and ' a little restaurant ' that Dallas knew, where a really good, simple lunch could be obtained. Hilary's early doubts were quickly set at rest ; the man was obviously not trying to make love to her—only to amuse her, to give her a good time. It was perfectly true, as he had said, that she lived an unnecessarily dull life and a little harmless pleasure like this would do her good. Already

her ill-humour, her quarrel with John, had passed
out of her mind ; in fact—ominous sign—she had
practically forgotten him.

The ' little restaurant ' lived up to its reputation.
It was, in fact, little more than an old farmhouse,
cleverly transformed, with tables under the trees of a
shady and smooth-grassed orchard.   Already it was
beginning to achieve a reputation among intelligent
motorists but it was not yet overcrowded or spoilt.
The luncheon consisted of a fish salad, made with
fresh, crisp lettuces, followed by a tender chicken
and new peas, finished with delicious strawberries
and cream.   It was years since Hilary had enjoyed
a meal like this, simple as it was.   The actual
physical sense of well-being that it induced had an
extraordinary effect upon her mental outlook ; she
felt happy, care-free, younger than she had done
since the early days of her marriage.   She tilted
her chair back and smoked one of Dallas' slender
cigarettes, letting the smoke trickle luxuriously down
her nostrils and fanning it away with a laugh of
happiness when it stung her eyes.

Dallas watched her carefully.   This was the right
beginning ; happiness and confidence must first be
engendered.   But it was not enough ; there was no
note of sentiment here ; that must wait for a riper
occasion.

The cool of the shady orchard was too tempting to
allow much scope to any activity on the part of
Hilary's conscience and it was not till after a light
and early tea that the Baroda's nose was turned
north again.   For a time they drove in silence,
Hilary sleepy and Dallas thoughtful.   It was
difficult to spend a whole day with—so close to—this

attractive woman and keep one's mind entirely upon
tactics. Her bare shoulder, from time to time
touching his arm as he drove, now, in his shirt-
sleeves, sent a thrill of excitement through Dallas.
The breeze continually blew the light skirt back
from her knees and, after one or two attempts,
Hilary had become too sleepy or careless to bother
about it ; the beauty of her slim legs, even in the
cheap, imitation silk stockings, was almost too much
for Dallas' self-control.

As they approached the high ground above Bryde,
the sun suddenly disappeared ; unnoticed, a heavy
cloud had crept up to obscure it. Hilary shivered
and for a moment leant deliberately, if half-con-
sciously, against her companion. Instantly Dallas
slipped his arm round her and at the same moment
skilfully brought the car to a standstill at the side
of the secluded lane along which they had been
running. Gently Dallas increased the pressure of
his arm.

" Been happy, Hilary ? " he murmured.

For a moment Hilary remained motionless, then
raised her eyes to his, eyes with a glint of tears in
them, and nodded. The look stirred something in
Dallas' heart—something different to the sensual
condition to which he was accustomed. He pressed
his cheek against the girl's soft hair.

" I want you to be happy. I terribly want you to
be happy ", he whispered.

Taken by surprise—surprise at herself rather than
her companion—Hilary made no attempt to release
herself from his embrace. She felt giddy, breathless,
thrilled. Not for years had any man spoken to her,
touched her, like this. She had imagined that such

things ended with marriage, and she had not consciously wished them to continue. But now, after twelve years of placidity, her senses suddenly awoke in a flame of excitement, the blood surged in her temples, drummed in her ears. She tried to conjure the feelings of outrage, of propriety, of ordinary wisdom, that she knew to be appropriate to the occasion, but they simply would not respond. She simply did not feel shocked—not even at herself, only thrilled—and intensely, almost impersonally curious. Lying back against Dallas' arm she closed her eyes, trying to steady her whirling senses. She felt his breath against her cheek, heard his eager whisper: ' Hilary, Hilary ! ', and when his lips pressed against hers she responded, blindly, passionately, to his kisses.

CHAPTER IX

HILARY PANSEL'S only feeling, as she walked up the little garden path to her house, was one of surprise—surprise that she felt so little, that she was so calm, that she was not wondering what to say to John in explanation of her absence. She was as unmoved as if nothing had happened outside the ordinary routine of her life, was in fact much calmer than when she had left the house that morning ; she was astonished at her own self-possession.

The house was empty and she quietly set about the preparation of supper. When John came in ten minutes later her heart did not even quicken its pace. Though she did not kiss him, as she usually did when he returned from a day's work she realised that he had been drinking, not beer, whiskey—which was quite foreign to his custom ; she was conscious of a slight feeling of contempt, but nothing more. Their supper was eaten in silence, but Hilary noticed that her husband's usually steady hands were trembling, as if with suppressed emotion. His eyes were slightly bloodshot and moved restlessly from side to side, from his plate to her face, from her face to the window. When they had finished Hilary rose to her feet, but John remained seated, staring at his empty plate ; when she removed it she saw him stiffen and his hand, which was on the table, clenched. With detached curiosity she watched the knuckles go white ; there was a patch of ' madder ' paint on

101

one, which made it look comic next to its neighbours. Usually John cleaned his hands very carefully with turpentine. It looked as if . . .

" Where have you been ? "

John's voice, husky and constrained, startled
her.

" What ? Oh, to-day ? I've been to Fakenham."

Hilary's voice was pitched higher than usual, but
it was quite calm.

John was not looking at her. He sat staring
at the window. Only a muscle in his cheek
moved.

Why didn't he ask her anything more ? It seemed
rather silly just to say : " I've been to Fakenham."

" Mr. Fiennes took me in his car. We had lunch
near Swaffham."

Still John sat silent. He had jumped to the conclusion, of course, that she had *arranged* to go for a
drive with Dallas. Well, let him. If he asked her,
she would tell him how it had really happened, but
she wasn't going to volunteer a long explanation,
just as if she had got a guilty conscience. Curiously
enough, the fact that she had not arranged to go for
the drive seemed to Hilary to clear her of all blame
for what had subsequently happened. That had just
happened. She picked up her tray and carried it out
of the room.

While she washed up, the events of the afternoon
slowly unrolled themselves in Hilary's mind, almost
as if they were a cinema film of which some other
woman was the heroine. At first she felt a curiously
detached interest in the story, but when it reached
the point where she (most unaccountably, she felt)
had leaned against Dallas and he had put his arms

round her and made love to her, she suddenly found that her heart was beating fast and that a smile of almost childish happiness had spread over her face. She tried calmly to analyse her feelings. Surely she couldn't have fallen in love with a man whom she hardly knew ? She, who had always regarded herself as a woman who could never love anyone but her husband ? She thought of John, whom she loved. Oh, yes, certainly she loved him. But she wasn't much interested in him. She was very fond of him, but after all these years . . . She found herself smiling again ; her mind had slipped away from John, back to the events of the afternoon.

Putting away the last plate, Hilary slipped on a light jumper and went out into the starry night. The air was absolutely still, the sky cloudless now. She walked down to the harbour and watched the tide creeping in. It always fascinated her to see the creeks gradually filling, especially at night when the moon or the stars made the water look like quicksilver slowly creeping into the winding maze of the saltings. When she got home an hour later Hilary's mind was in exactly the same vague condition ; she felt ridiculously happy and rather excited, but could not understand why. John was still sitting where she had left him ; he did not seem to have been either reading or smoking. She took a book and told him she was going to bed. He did not appear to hear. An hour later, curled up in bed, she heard him come upstairs ; he did not come in to say good-night to her. She blew out her candle and, with a little sigh of happiness, fell asleep.

In the meantime, Dallas Fiennes, having dropped

Hilary on the outskirts of Bryde, had turned his car round and driven along the coast towards Cromer. He did not feel inclined for the rather witless humour of the little coterie at the ' Virgin Duck ' ; he certainly could not work. He was feeling slightly bewildered. The ease and rapidity with which the coveted prize had fallen into his arms was almost disconcerting. He felt like a general who, having planned and prepared for a long and arduous siege, suddenly found the enemy's defences crumbling away almost before he had opened fire. It was true that only the outer defences so far had fallen into his hands, but the alacrity of their surrender did not suggest that the defence of the citadel would be anything more than a brief formality.

As he slid along the narrow, winding coast-road, Dallas wondered whether he had all along been mistaken in his judgment of Hilary Pansel, whether she, whom he had imagined so prim, had in reality been waiting impatiently upon his laggard overtures. The idea was a shock to his self-conceit ; he, a novelist, had always prided himself upon his knowledge of human nature, his judgment of women. There was, too, the slight feeling of disappointment over a prize too easily won. He would almost have preferred a long siege, a frightened, fleeing maiden, a relentless, ultimately successful, chase. His short experience of deer-stalking had taught him that it is the spying of the quarry, the long difficult stalk, the final crawl to position, that provide the zest of the sport, not the ultimate shot.

But mingled with this slight feeling of disappointment Dallas was aware of another, much more pleasant sensation. If he regretted the ease of his

capture, he was more than delighted with the prize
itself. Hilary had been so sweet, so simple, so devoid
of the affected coyness which, in previous triumphs
had so often grated upon his artist's finer feelings.
She seemed to him now little more than a girl
awakening to the first call of love ; he himself—
strange experience—actually felt that his heart was
stirred, that he wanted Hilary for herself, that he
actually loved her. He laughed aloud at himself
and even as he did so was aware of a slightly
hysterical note of happiness in the sound. And with
that feeling of happiness came the realisation that
Hilary could not be the forward, a-moral minx that
he had begun to think her ; her sudden surrender
was due to the fact that she was ripe for surrender,
starving for love ; how could she be else, living
with a sullen uncouth boor like John Pansel ? Dallas
congratulated himself that it was he and no one else
who had come forward to awaken, to claim, her love,
though he felt, without undue conceit, that it was
his own personality and attraction that had largely
been the cause of the awakening. Having got so far,
it was not long before he was not only not regretting
the shortness of the chase, but actually welcoming it
as a sign that Hilary had succumbed, not to a carefully conducted scheme, but to the passion which
he himself had aroused. When a man is fifty he has
far less difficulty in fooling himself in affairs of the
heart than he had before he reached years of discretion.

Almost before he realised it, Dallas was in Cromer.
He enjoyed a leisurely dinner at the Belgravia,
smoked a cigar on the pier, and drove back in the
star-light to Bryde-by-the-Sea. Stabling his car at

the ' Anchorage ', he walked to the far end of the harbour, which he reached about half an hour after Hilary had left it. The tide was nearly high, and as Giles Banyatt was long since in bed he borrowed the old man's boat and ferried himself across to the steps leading up to the path over the saltings. Driving the anchor firmly into the bank he set out across the flat, desolate expanse of mud and water. The moon had risen now and he had no difficulty in following the path. On a dark night it would have been folly for anyone but a native to go that way without a powerful torch, for the path turned sharply in one or two places and it would have been a simple matter to wander from it into one of the holes with which the saltings were covered, or even to fall into one of the winding branches of the creek itself. That, whether it were filled with water, or empty of all save mud, would have been no pleasant experience.

To-night, however, the way was clear enough and Dallas strolled along, oblivious either to the eeriness or the beauty of the surroundings. The soft quack of duck, the twitter and trill of marsh birds, the plash of rising fish, the lapping of the tide, fell upon deaf ears ; the novelist's senses were still absorbed with the thrill of this new experience, this awakening in his ageing heart of an emotion which he had again and again so glibly described, but had never before known. Automatically he untied his boat from the post at the end of the path and paddled himself across to the sand dunes, pulled the boat up a foot or two on to the beach, anchored it, and strolled up the slope towards his hut. He was within ten yards of it and was automatically feeling for the latchkey on his chain when suddenly his heart stood still; his body followed suit. From the gloom of the verandah a blacker shadow had detached itself.

Dallas Fiennes was not a nervous man, otherwise he could not have lived for months by himself upon that lonely shore. But he knew that none of the other huts were at present occupied at night and it flashed across his mind that out here, a mile from the nearest house and surrounded, almost, by water, he would be singularly at the mercy of any ill-intentioned person.

"Who's that?" he asked, in a voice that was creditably firm.

"It's only me", came the reply in a pleasant, youthful voice.

Fiennes felt his blood begin to circulate again.

"Me being Frank Helliott," he said cheerfully. "You gave me quite a start."

"I'm sorry. I ought to have whistled or something. I forgot you couldn't see me as clearly as I could see you."

"It doesn't matter. What's up? Come for a drink?"

"I wanted to talk to you, Mr. Fiennes. You haven't been at the 'Virgin' the last night or two and I thought I should find you here. It's rather urgent. I . . . I want to ask you something."

"Yes. I remember you wrote to me. I ought to have answered. Come along in and we'll have a glass of sherry—unless you prefer something else."

Helliott mumbled some reply and Fiennes, fitting his key into the lock, pushed open the door.

"Half a mo' till I light the lamp", he said.

In a minute the room was comfortably illuminated by a well-shaded lamp. Fiennes pushed a box of cigarettes towards his guest and walked across to his cupboard.

"Sit down, Frank", he said, producing a bottle of sherry and two glasses. "There you are. Now, what can I do for you? A bit of advice from the man of the world?"

Dallas Fiennes liked calling people by their Christian names. It was noticeable that this familiarity was seldom reciprocated by men. Frank Helliott, of course, was not much more than a boy. Actually he was twenty-six but he had had a narrow upbringing and had never been out in the world, so that he was *naïf* and young for his age. He was good-looking in a simple way, but had a sullen expression that was no doubt partly due to the dull life he led. Though he often sat with the others in the bar of the 'Virgin Duck' he did not talk much and appeared to have no facility for expressing himself. The warm glow of the sherry, however, seemed to loosen his tongue.

"I'm afraid you'll think I'm an awful nuisance—perhaps something worse", he said, "but I'm in an awful hole and there's absolutely no one I can go to for help."

He hesitated and looked enquiringly at his companion as if for encouragement. Dallas blew a cloud of smoke down his nostrils.

"Fire ahead then", he said, stifling a yawn.

"It's awfully good of you, Mr. Fiennes. I don't know . . ."

"There's no need to call me 'Mr.'. I'm not so venerable as all that."

Frank Helliott blushed.

"Oh . . . er . . . all right. Thanks very much . . . er . . . Fiennes. Well, you see, it's like this."

Fiennes shuddered. When would the youth of England be taught to express itself intelligibly ?

"There's a girl", continued Helliott, in a nervous, hurried voice. "And I'm afraid . . . that's to say, she's had a baby and she's got no money at all and I've scraped up everything I can and we haven't got any either and I'm at my wits' end to know how to send her any more."

He paused for breath and Fiennes tried his best to conceal his amusement.

"Do I understand", he asked, "that this baby is also your baby ? "

"Yes. Yes, I'm afraid it is."

The young man, for all his twenty-six years, was actually blushing.

"Is there a Bastardy Order against you ? "

"Oh, no. No, rather not. She wouldn't do that. It's quite . . . voluntary "

"I see. Moral obligation ? "

"Yes ; of course. She's . . . well, she's a lady and . . . I want to marry her but she won't. She says there's little enough money as it is and if we married we should have more children and as it is she earns a bit in a shop in London. But the baby's been ill and she's had to spend an awful lot on doctors and chemists and special foods, and she's got behind with the rent and the landlady's threatening to turn her out and keep all her clothes and things and she hasn't the least idea where to go or anything."

Fiennes felt himself growing sleepier and sleepier.
The story was so hackneyed, so featureless. He
could have told it himself, sentence by sentence—
and told it a damn sight better.

" Hasn't she got any relations ? " he asked.

" Yes. That's almost the worst of it. She's got
an invalid mother and a father who's frightfully
strict. He . . ."

" Oh, of course. Angry father—parson—Metho-
dist minister. We know all that ", thought Fiennes.

" He sends her a little money but never goes to
see her. She goes home occasionally. Of course she
hasn't told them. She daren't. She's terrified of
him."

" I'm beginning to wonder whether this young
lady's such a fool as she sounds ", thought Fiennes.
" I believe she's telling the tale. No doubt she
doesn't *want* to bury herself down here and have
more babies. Well ", he added aloud ; " it's an
awkward business. It looks as if you'll have to sell
something."

" But that's just it ; I can't. Everything at
Brulcote's mortgaged. My solicitor can't raise
another penny . . . and he won't lend me any
either."

Fiennes woke up with a start.

" You're not suggesting that *I* should ? " he asked
sharply.

A dark flush spread over Frank Helliott's face.
This was ghastly—worse than he had expected. But
he simply must do it, for Kitty's sake.

" I . . . yes, I was going to ask you if you would.
I know it's an extraordinary thing to do, because of
course there's absolutely no reason why you should

lend me money, but there's absolutely no one else I can think of who might help me—no one rich, I mean—and at any rate you know all about me—about Brulcote and all that. I mean, I shouldn't just disappear when you'd lent it me."

Fiennes gave an impatient laugh.

"My dear boy, you've just told me that everything at Brulcote is mortgaged and that you can't raise anything on it, so what's the use of quoting it as a security?"

Helliott flushed.

"It's only a security in the sense that it holds me there. I'm not likely to run away from my home. I'd be able to pay you back in time—a pound or two every month. I'm only asking for fifty pounds."

"Fifty pounds! *Only* fifty pounds! What on earth do you take me for? I suppose you've been reading an article on 'best sellers' by some Fleet Street hack who's never sold anything for more than a couple of guineas in his life. Let me tell you, young fellow, that authors have to work damn hard for their living. They *don't* make fortunes; on the contrary, at the present time they're suffering from trade depression just like every other business man. You talk about my being rich; I'm not rich, and even if I was I shouldn't lend money right and left to every young idiot who gets a girl into trouble and then comes whining to me to pay for it. You'd better do a job of work yourself and shoulder your own worries."

As Frank Helliott listened to this tirade he felt the blood ebbing from his face until it seemed to be actually cold and stiff. Disappointment and anger mingled into a kind of cold despair, that made it impossible for him to speak—almost impossible for him to move. Slowly he dragged himself out of his chair and, without a word to his host, opened the door and stumbled out into the night.

Fiennes watched him go, first with surprise and then with a slight feeling of compunction—even disquiet. The stricken look on the young man's face touched a chord of sympathy in his heart. Although entirely self-centred, Dallas Fiennes had imagination ; he could realise that this rebuff to his hopes must be a severe blow to Frank Helliott ; he had, perhaps, been unnecessarily severe in his manner of declining the loan. Rising from his own chair he went to the door and looked out. The night had, unexpectedly, clouded over ; it was quite dark and there was a feeling of oppression in the air. How was the boy going to get back to Bryde ? Was he going the long way round by the footpath ; surely he would never find his way in this thick blackness ? Or was he going by water ? How ? Was he taking his—Fiennes'—boat ? without asking his leave ? What damned impertinence !

Instantly the novelist's mind, which for a few minutes had been concerned with someone else's worries, switched back to his own interests. It might be damned inconvenient to have his boat the wrong side of the creek to-morrow ; tide would be coming in again soon after he was up ; he might want . . .

" Frank ! " he called. " Where are you ? How are you going back ? "

There was no answer. No footsteps, no sound of oar, or crunch of shingle.

" Frank !   Helliott ! !   Helliott ! ! ! "

Not a sound.   Only the muffled beat of the waves on the far side of the sand-dunes.   With a shrug of the shoulders Fiennes went back into his hut and locked the door.

CHAPTER X

IN the days that followed, Hilary was surprised to
find that John's behaviour, both towards herself and
towards Dallas Fiennes, had improved. He was not
his normal self—he was too polite for that ; but he
no longer sulked or snarled when Dallas' name was
mentioned and he even went so far as to speak to
him in a friendly way when they happened to meet.
But though Hilary was mildly surprised at this
improvement she was far more surprised to find how
mild was her interest in her husband's attitude. It
was much pleasanter not to have to live in an
atmosphere of sulk or snarl, but she realised that her
pleasure was purely selfish and that she was not
thinking at all about John's feelings in the matter ;
she hardly bothered to wonder whether he was
behaving more pleasantly because he was happier or
whether it was out of consideration for her—or what
was the cause of it. If Hilary had thought about
her husband at all at this time she could hardly have
failed to notice that when he was not actively trying
to be normal and good-tempered he was very far
from being either one or the other ; that when he
thought he was alone or was off his guard for a
moment his face fell into the drawn, haggard lines
of a man who is very sick, either in body or in mind.

But Hilary's thoughts were entirely with herself
and her own emotions—emotions which were very

pleasant, very absorbing, very exciting. Quite
suddenly she had come to life ! After twelve years
of hum-drum married existence, in which she had
gradually slipped into middle-age, accepting without
question the placid, almost sexless rôle of house-wife,
her eyes had suddenly been opened to the fact that
she was still young, still attractive, still . . .
desirable. To a woman of thirty-four, a wife of
twelve years, that realisation was inevitably, un-
deniably pleasant ; to one who, in addition, had
hardly spoken to a man, other than her husband, in
all those years, it was extremely exciting.

It would have been a shock to Dallas Fiennes had
he known how small a part he himself played in
Hilary's emotional life at this time. She was
definitely not in love with him. Love, to a woman
like Hilary, meant something very much finer, more
enduring, than this stirring of the emotions. She
was in love, rather, with the idea of love, thrilled by
the unwonted courtship ; she was very much
attracted by Dallas, she liked—even enjoyed—his
making love to her, as he did now at every possible
opportunity. They took all reasonable precautions
against their meetings being seen, and both were
sublimely content to believe that these efforts were
successful, that their love-making was unnoticed,
unobserved.

John Pansel himself appeared to be painting very
little at this time ; he had developed a sudden
passion for sailing, in which he was encouraged by
George and Frank Cadnall, the sons of the proprietor of the ' Anchorage '. The Grammar School
at which they boarded had been closed owing to an
outbreak of scarlet fever and the two boys were

revelling in the unaccustomed midsummer holiday. John Pansel had always been a good friend to the two boys. He treated them as equals, not as rather tiresome children as did their father, or as a species of animal to be petted or teased as did people like Boyton Sarne and 'that writing fellow', Dallas Fiennes. They were delighted to have John as a companion in their sailing trips and did their best to teach him the art and craft of managing a small boat in the narrow, winding channel, on a racing tide or a few inches of slack, in the pool at the creek mouth or on the ocean itself, in a catchy wind, half a gale, or—as it seemed to John—a dead, breathless calm. It was no easy task that they had undertaken, for John had none of the instincts of a sailor ; he was a landlubber and seemed to the boys curiously stupid and clumsy where a boat was concerned.

Nor was the boat itself an easy one to handle. Vaughan Cadnall had bought it second-hand at a sale, without mast or rigging. These he had added as and when he picked them up—an odd lot, a shade too heavy for the boat. Finally, the centre-board had an awkward habit of sticking when it had been drawn up ; it required a combination of knack and strength to get it down again. That was one reason why the boys were glad of John's company ; he supplied the strength without which their knowledge was not always able to cope with the awkward tackle ; John, for his part, for all his strength, seemed unable to master the knack of the thing, and until he did so the boys refused to allow him to go out by himself.

Before they went back to school, however, George and Frank formally passed John Pansel as proficient and awarded him a certificate to that effect—a certificate drawn up by themselves with much loving care and gaudy illumination. The final test consisted of crossing the bar with centre-board raised, dropping it in the pool, and tacking home against an off-shore breeze ; John passed it successfully but only he knew how desperately near to capsizing the boat came when the gusty wind caught him in the pool while he was still struggling with the refractory centre-board.

Two days after the boys went back John was making down the creek in the *Happy Pilgrim*, of which they had persuaded their rather reluctant father to give him free use, when he saw Dallas Fiennes standing on the sand-dunes below his hut. With a clumsily skilful jerk at tiller and sheet John brought his boat in to land close to where Fiennes was standing.

" Coming for a sail ? " he called cheerfully.

Fiennes stared at him in almost genuine surprise, then glanced from his own neat flannel suit to John's stained trousers and jersey.

" I'm afraid I'm not dressed for the part", he said. " I'm going in to Hunstanton."

The corner of John's mouth twitched but he kept back the sneer that had sprung to his lips.

" Then let me run you up the creek ", he said. " It rained pretty heavily last night ; there'll be mud on the path . . . might spoil your shoes."

Fiennes sensed the veiled insolence behind the harmless words but he too kept a check on his tongue ; it was no part of his plan now to irritate the painter.

" You're sure you won't upset me ? " he asked,

with a laugh. " I'm very delicate and . . . you *are* safe, are you ? I hadn't realised you were a sailor."

" I've just taken it up. I'm told that all men of art and letters should have a hobby. Mine is going to be . . . well, I'll show you if you'll honour me. I promise to land you in safety at the harbour in ten minutes."

Fiennes scrutinised the rather heavy face of the painter. It was surely impossible that the fellow was ' getting at him ' in some way ? He was a fine painter but Fiennes had never credited him with any brains. In any case, it would please Hilary if he was friendly with her husband—women had such odd ideas about that sort of thing—and would do away with any awkwardness there might be in going to the house of a man with whom he was not on speaking terms.

" I'll risk it, then ", he said with a laugh, and stepped carefully into the boat. John pushed off, hoisted his sail, and swung the boat's head round towards the village. The wind was almost straight across his course and it only needed an occasional tack to get him back up the creek. Well within the scheduled ten minutes they were running into the little inland harbour.

Two men in flannels stood on the tumbledown quay, idly watching the slow movements of some fishermen pushing a heavy boat down the shingled bank into the water. As the sailing boat rounded the last corner they turned dull eyes upon it ; then the taller of the two suddenly came to life.

" Good lord ! " he exclaimed ; " look at that ! Fiennes and John Pansel in the same boat ! "

" The lion and the lamb ", murmured his companion.

A malicious grin spread over Boyton Sarne's face.

" You've got it wrong ", he said.

Vessle sniggered.

" Say rather : ' The raven and the hornéd owl ' ", he suggested.

The singer prided himself on a poetic tendency.

" What on earth have you fellows been up to ? " called Sarne as the *Happy Pilgrim* glided past. It was simpler to land on the beach than on the rotting quay. John Pansel took no notice of the speaker ; his attention was apparently fixed upon his task. Fiennes looked up with a smile.

" Pansel's been displaying unsuspected talents ", he said.

" Ah, there's a lot goes on in the world that we don't know about ", remarked Vessle sententiously.

" Yes, but not in Bryde-by-the-mud ", replied his companion.

The two men strolled along the beach to the spot where Pansel had run the nose of his boat into the shingle. Fiennes was on the point of jumping ashore.

" Wait a minute and we'll carry you ", called Sarne ; " you mustn't spoil those pretty yachting shoes."

" That was just what Pansel said ", replied the novelist. " He said there was mud on the path over the saltings. I thought it very considerate of him."

" Amazing."

The engineer looked curiously at John, who was preparing to push his boat off again.

"Is the fellow blind or just complacent?" he muttered.

It was impossible that John Pansel could have heard, but he turned at that moment and looked at the two newcomers with eyes that had a disquieteningly searching stare.

"Would either of you care for a sail?" he asked.

"Not much. We value our skins."

Sarne was usually the spokesman when he was about with Vessle, as he often was.

"Fiennes will give me a character", replied the artist.

"Oh, yes, he's safe enough. Well, I must be off. Thank you again, Pansel; see you this evening perhaps." He turned up the beach, followed by the two cronies.

"Where are you off to in all that finery? Giving someone a treat?"

"I've got some shopping to do in Hunstanton. Do my clothes annoy you?"

The novelist was often irritated by Sarne's sense of humour. But the latter's skin was impervious.

"I just love them", he said, and broke into song :—

"She asked me to buy her a bunch of blue ribbons
"To tie up her bonny *gold* hair."

Dallas Fiennes felt a flush of annoyance creep over him. At one time he had rather enjoyed posing as a rip in front of these seedy professionals, but now—with Hilary as the object of their smirks—he hated them. Still, it was difficult to shake the fellows off if they chose to hang on to him, at any rate as far as the garage. He walked on in dignified silence, while

Sarne and Vessle sharpened their wits on him in a contest of humorous innuendo. Fortunately, the garage of the 'Anchorage', where he kept his car, was only a few hundred yards from the beach. Without wasting time over water, oil, or petrol, Dallas started up his Baroda. Sarne made a tentative remark about wanting to find some technical paper in Hunstanton, but the novelist paid no attention to it and drove out of the garage with a violence of acceleration that made the wheels skid.

The object of his journey, as a matter of fact, was neither what he had stated nor what Sarne had guessed. He was going to his bank. For the last few days he had been feeling uncomfortable about his interview with Frank Helliott. He could, of course, quite well help the boy out of his difficulties without any inconvenience to himself, even if he never saw the money again. He liked Frank and certainly had no moral scruples about helping him ; had he not been in very much the same boat himself, though without the complication of financial stringency ? Why, then, had he refused to help him— and refused in such a churlish manner ? Dallas found it difficult to answer the question himself. There had been, of course, a certain naive confidence about the request that had irritated him, and of course it would not do to let it get about that he was prepared to lend money. But Dallas knew well enough that the first objection was trivial and that the second could be circumvented without much difficulty. The real trouble, he had to confess, was that there was a streak of meanness, or at least of selfishness, in his make-up. He had earned the money by the sweat of his brow ; why should some-

one else have it ? That was all. It *was* selfish,
mean, to have that feeling but it was quite real.

For a day or two Fiennes left it at that. Then he
found that the slight grating in his conscience, the
irritation of his own complacency, of his self-esteem,
was interrupting his work. His mind would slip
back into an argument with some mythical accuser
(*qui s'excuse?*) and he would waste five minutes in
justifying his action. It wasn't worth the bother,
the interruption. Besides, he was a very lucky
fellow himself ; his affair with Hilary was going with
unexpected smoothness ; he would celebrate his
good-fortune by making somebody else happy too.
And while he was in the mood he might as well do
the thing properly and make it a gift rather than
a loan ; it would come to the same thing, anyhow.

So Dallas was on his way to his bank in Hunstanton. He was not going to send Frank Helliott a
cheque ; the young ass would probably cash it at
the village shop and there would at once be talk,
speculation, gossip. He would send him the money
in notes, and, what was more, he would send them
anonymously. Then there would be no risk of this
momentary weakness on his part being taken as a
precedent. Frank himself might—probably would
—guess whom they came from, but he could always
deny it, and the boy would have his money and be
able to flounder out of his immediate problem. But
there must be no more of it ; Fiennes was quite
determined on that.

The road to Hunstanton was narrow and winding
but the surface was excellent, and Fiennes' Baroda
did the journey in less than half an hour. He

endorsed his cheque and asked for fifty £1 notes.
Being himself a romantic novelist he did not read
' detective trash ' and so had not in his mind the
risk of his gift being traced by the numbers, but he
had an idea that a girl in impoverished circumstances
might have difficulty, even arouse suspicion, in
trying to change notes of large denomination. The
sight of the thick bundle, however, alarmed Dallas
for his figure—in a pocket-book they would bulge
any coat out of shape ; so he returned twenty of
them and had four fivers instead. Even so the
pocket-book was a bulky and heavy article.

Driving out of the town Dallas passed the theatre
at which his campaign against Hilary's wifely
fidelity had begun. The sight of it brought his
thoughts back to her with a rush of quickened
pulses ; his eyes which, while money was uppermost
in his mind, had borne a coldly calculating look, now
lit up with a glow of real happiness, an emotion more
genuine and at the same time more unselfish than
any he had experienced for many years. Although
even now he hardly realised it, Dallas Fiennes was
in love.

He was not going to see Hilary again before the
evening. He had planned to work all the afternoon.
So, not without an effort of will, he drove straight
past the Pansel's cottage, through the village,
garaged his car at the ' Anchorage ' and walked back
to the harbour. He remembered now that, as he
had come up the creek in Pansel's sailing boat, his
own boat would be on the wrong side of Little
Creek ; as the tide was still up he would not be able
to get across to his hut on the sand-dunes—not, that
is to say, unless he took off shoes and trousers and

waded, or else went round by the long route, both of which courses he disliked.

He was just cursing his luck—or rather, his lack of forethought—when he saw that Christian Madgek was on the point of starting from the quay with a boat-load of trippers. Here indeed was a piece of luck ; Madgek could run him down the creek and drop him at the pool at its mouth.

" Hold hard a minute, Polly ", he called. " I'm coming with you."

Christian's mouth tightened on the instant into a hard line. Dallas Fiennes was not one of the people whom he liked to call him by that name. Still, sixpence was sixpence, always to a Norfolk fisherman and especially to one so hard-pressed for money as Christian was at that moment. Without looking at Dallas he nodded to a vacant place in the bows.

The novelist did not hurry himself, but stopped to say a word to old Giles, who was standing on the quay, sucking an empty clay pipe. The old man had noticed Madgek's look when Fiennes hailed him and watched the little comedy that followed with inward amusement. Having finished his ' few words ' with Giles, Dallas walked to the edge of the quay and put one foot on to the gunwale of the boat ; as he moved his other foot forward to step down on to the bottom, Madgek let in his clutch and the boat moved quietly forward. It was beautifully timed ; the movement was almost imperceptible, but at that exact moment it was enough to throw the novelist off his balance ; he swayed a moment, clutched at a boy's head to steady himself ; the boy naturally ducked and Fiennes toppled forward on to his knees and hands with a crash.

All the trippers burst into high-pitched laughter, which infuriated Dallas even more than the pain he was suffering. He staggered to his feet and turned upon the boatman with a face of fury.

" What the hell . . . " he began, though Madgek was looking at his engine and did not seem even to have noticed what had happened.

" Hi, mister, you'd better not leave that on the floor."

One of his fellow-passengers broke into the stream of his invective.

Fiennes stopped and, looking down, saw his pocket-book lying on the bottom of the boat. The fall had evidently jerked the bulky thing out of his pocket. It lay open, but the notes, which had been tucked into the flaps, had not escaped. Fiennes picked it up and with a muttered word of thanks, stowed it away in his pocket and sat down on a thwart. Christian Madgek, his engine now running smoothly, kept his keen eyes fixed upon the winding creek before him.

CHAPTER XI

ON the Wednesday following Hilary's momentous motor drive, Jude Tasson was late in delivering the morning mail. It arrived half-way through breakfast and Hilary's alacrity in accepting the single letter which constituted it was not far removed from an impatient snatch. Having snatched it, however, she dropped it carelessly on the table and concentrated her attention on the bronzed kipper that represented her breakfast on three days in every week. Then, with an air of casual indifference that might have deceived a small boy—but not his little sister—she opened the letter and read it. At once a flush of colour spread over her cheek and there was a tremor of excitement in her voice as she exclaimed :

" Oh, what fun ! Gwen wants me to go after all. I told her you couldn't come but she's got another man instead. She wants me to go on Friday. You won't mind, will you ? "

John remained silent, his eyes fixed on the cup of tea which he was slowly stirring. He had seen the flush of colour in his wife's face and had felt at the same moment the blood ebb from his own. He had not the smallest shadow of doubt as to what that blush implied.

" Like to see it ? " Hilary held out the letter.

John gave no sign of noticing either the word or

126

the movement ; indeed he was hardly conscious of them. He was feeling physically faint with misery and despair. His world—the quiet world that he had taken so much for granted, was tumbling about his ears and he did not know how to steady—to restore it. Blind anger shook him ; his eyes hardened, his mouth set in a bitter line.

Hilary saw the look and, with a shrug of the shoulders, withdrew the letter. She rose from her chair and began collecting the breakfast things to wash up. John did not, as was his custom, help her. Presently he too got up and went out into the sunshine. Although it was still early in the morning there was a hard brilliance in the light that hurt his eyes ; mechanically he went back for his hat and as he reached it from its peg he heard Hilary singing happily in the kitchen. The sound was like a stab in his heart.

John Pansel had had very little experience of women. His mother had been a simple, unimaginative creature, quietly happy in her married life ; the idea of infidelity had never entered her head nor that of her husband, so that the subject had never touched John's life while he lived at home. Later, when he was studying art and beginning his career as a painter, he was too deeply immersed in and thrilled by his work to take any notice of women ; they were either fellow-students or models—nothing more. It was not till he met Hilary after the war that the idea of love had entered his mind ; even then, though he imagined himself deeply in love, it had been a very unimaginative, selfish emotion. After he was married to Hilary it had never even crossed his mind that she might cease to love him,

still less that she might fall in love with someone
else.   He had taken her fidelity—and equally his
own—absolutely for granted.

Now, however, that his illusion had been shattered,
now that the maggot of doubt, of suspicion, had
crept into his soul, he swung to the opposite extreme.
He was ready to believe the worst on the smallest
provocation ; he doubted if Hilary had ever loved
him, wondered whether he had been blind for years
to other infidelities, searched his memory for hints
and signs that he might have missed, applied evil
constructions to the most harmless incidents.   In a
few days his whole being changed ; from a slow,
easy-going, unimaginative simpleton, he developed
into a sullen, suspicious, evil-minded schemer, with
hatred and murder in his heart.

It is not difficult to find excuses for him.   The
shock must have been terrific ; although unimaginative he was highly sensitive, and once his suspicion
had been aroused it was inevitable that it should
flare up into a scorching flame.   Hilary made little
attempt to help him or to understand the misery
which her behaviour was causing him.   When she
was innocent she had naturally been angered by his
doubt of her, but now that his doubts were justified
she appeared not to realise any difference in the
situation.   She too had lost her balance ; she was
excited, entirely self-centred, and made no real
attempt either to leave the dangerous path that she
was treading or to set her husband's doubts at rest.
Her ignorance of life was hardly less abysmal than
his, and she had not the faintest realisation of the
terrible danger into which her behaviour was guiding
their joint destiny.

The two days before Hilary's trip on the Broads was due to begin passed in uneasy avoidance of reality. John Pansel was almost silent, Hilary pretended to ignore his mood. They only met at meals and such intercourse as they had was entirely artificial. It was a relief to them both when Friday morning arrived. The train for Norwich, where Hilary was to join Gwen Farnes, left Great Hayworth at 9.40 a.m. With laboured politeness John offered to carry her bag to the station and see her off ; Hilary would much have preferred to go alone in a taxi but her conscience would not allow her such an extravagance under such circumstances—a typical example of the feminine conscience that strains at a gnat while swallowing a camel. So she and John tramped solemnly along the two miles of dusty, gritty lane that leads to Great Hayworth, exchanging occasional remarks of profound banality and each intensely wishing that the ordeal was over.

At the station John bought Hilary's ticket to Norwich and an illustrated paper, put her suit-case on the rack over her corner of the third-class carriage, and shifted from foot to foot, cursing under his breath the loquacity of guard and stationmaster, while the train lingered interminably at the platform. Over the buying of the ticket a problem of stubborn difficulty had suddenly presented itself to his labouring mind : should he buy her a single or return ? If a return, it would look as if he counted on her coming back, whereas he was not at all sure that she was going to. If, after such an assumption, she did not return, he would suffer a rebuff which would gall him horribly. On the other hand, to present her with a single ticket might appear mean—

as if he meant to spend as little on her holiday as
he could. Hilary had declared her intention of
paying for it herself, but her husband had for once
displayed a determination that defeated her. From
all of which it will appear that John Pansel's ' pride '
was of no less illogical a character than his wife's
conscience.

Eventually John had evolved a compromise in
the shape of a single ticket and money with which
to buy a return. At the last moment he had thrown
in an explanation—the single ticket was ' in case
she happened to get a lift home '; whereupon
Hilary had flushed and John's worst fears had
received further confirmation.

But the longest agony must end and at last the
guard, having finished his account of what he had
seen on Sunday night, waved his green flag and the
train rumbled off towards Fakenham. As it turned
inland from the coast, so Hilary's mind turned from
the difficulties and problems of her married life to
the unknown perils and excitements of the adventure
that lay ahead of her. It was extraordinarily difficult
to realise what was happening, to believe that this
woman sitting in the corner of a railway carriage,
with a single ticket to Norwich in her purse and a
smuggled crêpe-de-chine nightgown in her suit-case,
was Hilary Pansel, wife of John Pansel the well-
known painter, had once been Hilary Keston, the
mouse-like daughter of Dr. and Mrs. Albert Clarence
Keston, pillars of a provincial Anglican community.
It couldn't be real ; it was a dream. She would
wake up presently and find herself back in the
cottage at Bryde-by-the-Sea, washing up plates or
darning a pair of socks that had little of the original

wool remaining. How often had she not had the same feeling before—on her way, with her mother, to the dreaded dentist to have a childish tooth ' drawn ' ; waiting, years later, in the visitors' room at a hospital to hear the result of an operation on that same beloved mother ; waiting, even, for John Pansel to make up his mind to accept her own offer of marriage. The last memory brought a hot flush to Hilary's cheek ; it was so very sacred, so very dear. Was it possible that she was . . .

With a harsh grinding of brakes the ancient train pulled up at Fakenham station and there on the platform was the neat grey figure of Dallas Fiennes, hurrying from carriage to carriage, peering inside each one in turn, till Hilary put her head out of her window, and in a half-nervous, half-excited voice called " Dallas ! " At once Dallas looked towards her, his face lighting up with eager pleasure.

" Hilary ! " he cried, hurrying to her door and flinging it open. " Hilary ! I can't drive to Norwich all by myself. Get out here and come with me. Is that all your luggage ? No one knows us here ; it's perfectly safe. Quick, it's just going to start ! "

Seizing the suit-case, he swung it out of the carriage and Hilary obediently followed, leaving John's illustrated paper lying forlorn, un-opened, upon the carriage-floor. As the train steamed slowly away, Dallas slipped his free hand under Hilary's arm and squeezed it.

" Darling ! " he whispered. " Isn't it wonderful ! Are you happy ? "

She looked at him and the adoration in his eyes drove from her mind the last cloud of doubt. Smiling, she squeezed his hand against her body.

" It's wonderful, Dallas. I'm terribly, terribly happy."

They reached the gate into the station-yard and as she surrendered the bit of paste-board that had caused John such anxious heart-searching, Hilary's curious conscience gave one final flicker of life—and flickered out.

* * * * *

All through the long week-end John Pansel wandered about Bryde like a lost soul. His passion for sailing had apparently deserted him ; he did not put foot inside the *Happy Pilgrim*. On the other hand, the sea itself seemed to draw him as if it were magnetized. Each morning after breakfast, each afternoon after his scrappy lunch—if he ate one at all—his feet led him down to the harbour and thence across the saltings, if the tide were low, or round by the footpath to the dunes and the desolate sea-shore. On more than one of these occasions he saw the lanky figure of Hugh Fallaran in the distance, striding along the beach or standing at the edge of the tide, gazing out to sea. As a rule John felt too miserable for company and chose to turn aside before he had been recognized, but once he did join the barrister in his walk and the two compared notes of their love of that desolate coast.

" I haven't seen your wife in her garden lately, Pansel ", said Fallaran after a time ; " not ill, I hope ? "

John struggled hard to control his expression.

" No ", he answered, " no. She's gone to the Broads for a few days—staying with a friend."

" Then we're both lonely men. Come up and share my solitary supper to-night ? "

" That's very good of you." John hesitated, but only for a second. " I'd like to. I *am* feeling rather . . . lost. First time we've been separated since we married."

" Lucky people ; I should have starved if there'd been many like you."

After supper, Hugh Fallaran showed John some of the material for his book—letters, notes, reports— much of it too intimate for publication. The two men talked of their work and for an hour or more John forgot his troubles in the interest of this communion with another man of his own type. When recollection of his tragedy did return to him he was for a moment tempted to unburden himself to a friend who had shown so much understanding, but the effort of expression was too great ; his early training had been one of self-reliance and self-control ; he had never unburdened himself to another man—to Hilary alone had he been able to do that. He went home with the black horseman still upon his back.

So the long walks continued ; for miles he tramped along the deserted beach, returning exhausted and footsore but as restless and forlorn as ever. Several times he passed Dallas Fiennes' hut and on Saturday evening, after dusk had set in, he prowled round it for an hour or more like a hungry but cautious wolf. There was not a sign of life in the place. He had heard that Fiennes had announced to his cronies at the ' Virgin Duck ' that he was going to London for the week-end, and the news, though it was only what he expected, had made him writhe with misery and anger. It might have been imagination, but it had seemed to him that Vessle, who imparted the

information, watched his reception of it with
lascivious interest ; John had turned away quickly
to hide the agony that he felt must be visible on his
face.

The suspicion that other people knew and were
enjoying his shame added a hundred-fold to his
misery. Gradually that one question loomed larger
and larger, as such things do to a fevered body and
mind. Did they know ? Were they talking about
it ? Laughing at him ? John writhed and clenched
his fists, gritted his teeth and ground his heel into
the unresponsive sand. As the dry sand slipped
back into the hole his heel had made, so the problem
slipped and slithered in his mind. At last, on
Sunday night, he could stand the doubt no longer.
He must find out, once and for all. At that hour,
nine o'clock, Sarne and Vessle would almost certainly be at the ' Virgin Duck ', possibly Frank
Helliott too, though John did not remember having
seen that solemn young man for some days. With
the curious self-torture that urges a sufferer to probe
an aching tooth, the painter made his way, slowly,
reluctantly, but doggedly, to the little inn where he
might expect to learn the worst.

It was a hot, still night. Even the birds and fishes
seemed to feel the oppression, as there were few of the
usual sounds from the saltings. The heat, though
he was not consciously aware of it, contributed to
the physical and mental congestion which played
so large a part in John's tragic mood. As he stalked
down the village street his face was dark and swollen
and a knotted vein stood out upon each side of his
forehead above the temples. A knot of idlers
lounging against a corner house watched him with

idle curiosity and two among them, young fishermen,
wished him good-evening. John strode past without
apparently noticing them and this unusual dis-
courtesy on his part, together with his appearance,
were sufficient to start their tongues wagging ; there
are not too many subjects for speculation in a
fishing-village and a fertile imagination can work up
quite a pretty crop of rumour out of soil less
promising than this.

Although it was still daylight out of doors, the
' Virgin Duck ' had ' lit up ' to the extent of two
oil lamps in the bar, so that a gleam of cheerful light
under the door greeted John as he turned into the
dark passage. For a moment he hesitated, dreading
the ordeal of meeting those leering faces ; there
was still time to turn back ; what was the point of
torturing himself ? He knew already all that he
could learn from . . . A sudden shout of laughter
from the tap-room checked him just as he was
turning away. Involuntarily he strained his ears to
try and catch what was being said, trying—and yet
dreading—to hear his own name, or worse still,
Hilary's. He could hear a voice, talking in a high-
pitched, excited tone. He did not at first recognize
it ; then some familiar inflection caught his ear and
he stiffened suddenly. Was it possible ? Surely
that was Fiennes' voice ? And yet, what was he
doing here when Hilary was still . . . ?

His brain reeling with the shock—the sudden
blinding flash of hope, John stood stock-still in the
passage, trying to collect his wits, to work out the
meaning of this thing. Could he have been mistaken ? Was it possible that after all Hilary had
not been with Fiennes ? Was it conceivable that

all his dreadful suspicions, his foul imaginings, were wrong ? Dizzy with hope, John staggered out into the fresh air, then, as a cold douche of doubt struck him, stopped again. *Was* it Fiennes' voice that he had heard ? At first he had thought that he did not recognize the voice ; it was only as a second impression that he had judged it to be Fiennes'. Had his first impression been right ? With a quick movement John spun round on his heel, strode down the passage and flung open the door of the taproom.

The cackle of conversation and laughter stopped on the instant as John entered. His appearance had been so sudden that everybody in the room had turned to look at the intruder. Two strangers in a corner, seeing nothing to interest them, at once dropped their eyes back to the draught-board that lay between them, and Sam Pete behind the bar only nodded a greeting and returned to his task of washing glasses. But upon the larger group in the window the effect of John's appearance was more lasting. At a solid oak table sat three men, Boyton Sarne, Vessle, and a friend of Sarne's who occasionally came down to stay with him for a week-end ; on the end of the table itself, with one foot on the floor and one on a chair, was perched Dallas Fiennes. A bottle of sherry stood on the table beside him and wineglasses in front of each of the group contained varying quantities of amber wine ; on the window-sill behind Vessle stood an empty bottle. On three of the four faces there was a look of startled amusement, which increased as John continued to stand in the doorway staring at Fiennes as if he saw a ghost.

The latter was the first to break the strained silence. Pushing forward with his foot the vacant chair, he lifted the bottle of sherry.

"Come along, my merry P . . . Pansel", he exclaimed. "Join us in a loving-cup. Sam, another goblet!"

With a start, John collected his wits. Surprised as he was to see Fiennes there, he was still more surprised to realise that the novelist was drunk. He did not know how to interpret either the man's presence or his condition, but a growing sense of hope began slowly to flood his being. At whatever cost he must find out the truth, once and for all; not here, of course, in front of these prying busy-bodies, but if he humoured Fiennes he might be able to lure him out of doors—perhaps walk home with him. In the open air, away from the village, they could talk in safety and he would get the truth, if he had to force it out of the man's throat.

Sam put an extra wine-glass on the table and Fiennes pushed the bottle of sherry towards it.

"Help yourself", he said, "and if it's empty there's more where that came from. Sam keeps a special bin for me, don't you, my genial host."

"That's right, sir," said the innkeeper, running a superfluous cloth over his immaculate counter.

With a hand which he tried hard to keep steady John Pansel poured himself out a small quantity of sherry and raised the glass to his lips.

"Cheerioh", he said huskily. The word seemed to stick in his throat, but he forced it out; at all costs he must be genial—till he knew.

"Funny your coming in just then", continued Fiennes with careful deliberation. "We were just

talk . . . talking about you.   That's so, isn't it,
Sarne ? "

The engineer grinned broadly.

" Funny is the exact word ", he said.

Vessle gave a shrill cackle of laughter and took a
sip of his sherry.   It was his third glass and he felt
delicious ;   everything was funny, everyone a jolly
good fellow—even that conceited bounder Fiennes
and that boorish dog Pansel.   He would say something funny himself in a minute, something that
would make them all laugh and think what a witty
fellow he was.   There were lots of funny things to
say ;   the only trouble was that by the time he had
thought of them the conversation always seemed to
have turned to a different subject.   What were
they talking about now ?   Why was it funny that
the painter fellow had just come in ?   What had
they been talking about when he came in ?   Something funny . . . damn funny. . . .

" Very hot to-night ", said Pansel awkwardly,
running his handkerchief round his neck, which
was moist outside and dry as tinder within.

" Not so hot as . . . oh, well, let that pass ",
returned Fiennes, his face solemn as a judge's.

John could see that Sarne was watching him, the
corner of his mouth lifting sardonically.

What was he to say ?   How could he be genial in
front of these sneering, drunken hypocrites ?   What
was there to say ?

" Had a good time in London ? "

Why had he asked that ?   Why in God's name
had he asked that ?   Of all the . . .

" London ? "

Fiennes' handsome eyebrows were raised.   Sarne

was staring. The stranger, Sarne's friend, was looking puzzled—and uncomfortable. Vessle . . .

A burst of laughter, shriller than before, startled everybody in the room. The little tenor, cackling with delight, struck the table with the palm of his chubby hand.

" I'll sing you a song ! " he exclaimed. " Jolly good song. Jolly good fellows. Most ap . . . apt."

He rose to his feet, set one of them on the chair, and raised his glass. His tremulous tenor voice rang clearly through the room and out into the night.

> *" What shall he have that killed the deer ?*
> *His leather hide and horns to wear.*
> La diddy umpty dee
> *Take thou no scorn to wear the horn ;*
> *It was a crest ere thou wast born :*
> *Thy father's father wore it*
> *And something something bore it ;*
> *The horn, the horn, the lusty horn*
> *Is not a thing to laugh to scorn."*

Guy Vessle tilted his glass, smacked his lips, and looked round at the astonished faces of his audience.

" Shakespeare, gentlemen ", he said solemnly, and subsided into his chair.

For a moment there was silence, then Boyton Sarne burst into a roar of laughter.

" *In vino veritas* ", he exclaimed in gasps. " By God, Vessle, you've said it. Now you'll get your ruddy little neck wrung."

Dallas Fiennes, his quick wit dulled for the nonce by drink, had remained staring uncomprehendingly at the singer, but at Sarne's words he seemed to wake up ; slowly a broad smile spread over his face as he turned to see the effect of the satire upon its unconscious object.

They were laughing at him ! Yes, at him ! What was it ? What had that fat little fool been singing ? He had not listened ; he had been thinking about his idiotic question. What had it been ? Something about a deer, he had heard, and horns . . .

John's head reeled. The faces of the men round him seemed to swell into great masks—masks of hideous, Gargantuan laughter.

" Do they fit, my dear Pansel ? "

Through the surging of his own blood he heard the words but could not tell who had spoken them. With a groan of agony he reeled to the door, tore it open, and stumbled out into the night.

CHAPTER XII

PARTY

FOR three or four days after that Sunday evening at the ' Virgin Duck ' Dallas Fiennes was at considerable pains to avoid meeting John Pansel. The situation, in view of his relations with the artist's wife, had been delicate enough before, though highly entertaining ; now that the man had been openly insulted it had become positively dangerous. Dallas realised that a physical assault by Pansel would be no joke, and he cursed the second bottle of sherry that had dissipated his own discretion and loosened that little idiot Vessle's tongue. He even contemplated leaving Bryde, but to beat an open retreat would be damnably ignominious—Dallas could see the sneer on Boyton Sarne's face and hear the singer's cackle of malicious mirth ; besides, ' Butterfly Kiss ' was going well and the novelist hated changing quarters in the middle of a book—it broke the continuity of thought and atmosphere. At least he would come to no decision till he learnt a bit more about Pansel's mood ; Sarne would be able to tell him about that. In the meantime he would lie low.

But in a small place like Bryde-by-the-Sea it is almost impossible to avoid meeting another person, however carefully you may try to avoid him. On Thursday morning, on his way to the post office to despatch the MS of an article to his agent, Fiennes bumped into John Pansel as he turned out of the

alley leading to the harbour. There was actually a
collision of bodies and as he staggered back from the
impact Dallas saw a red flush of anger spread over
the big man's face. Involuntarily he caught his
breath—the next moment would probably see an
outburst, if not an actual attack. But to his surprise,
Pansel's face cleared and he spoke in a friendly
voice.

"Terribly sorry, Fiennes", he said. "Dashed
clumsy of me. Look here, I've been wanting to meet
you. Hilary came back from the Broads yesterday ;
she's had a great time—enjoyed herself no end—and
she says we've got to be more social. It's quite true
that we're getting into a stick-in-the-mud groove. I
wondered whether you'd come and have some dinner
one night and buck us up a bit. My brain's absolutely rusting up ; I admit I'm a dull dog to talk to—
always was. It would be a kindness if you'd
come."

"I shall be delighted", murmured Fiennes, his
brain chasing round after the meaning of this
invitation. Rather like putting one's head into the
lion's den, wouldn't it be ?—injured lioness and all.

"Splendid. Come to-night."

Dash it ; one must have time to think. Was it a
trap of some kind ?

"Very sorry, but I promised to dine with a fellow
in Hunstanton to-night."

Why drag in Hunstanton, where the trouble had
begun ? The fellow was flushing up again . . .

"Oh well, to-morrow night, then ? "

Hopeless to go on dodging ; nobody in Bryde had
more than one dinner engagement a month. To go
on refusing would look like a slight—or fear ; either

way it would irritate the fellow and that was the last thing he wanted to do.

" I shall be charmed. What time ? "

" Half past seven suit you ? Unfashionably early I'm afraid, but we've got into the habit—principally because of the wireless concerts at eight."

" You don't like music while you eat ? " Dallas felt as if he were making conversation like a gauche undergraduate.

Pansel grinned.

" We generally feed in the kitchen ", he said, " and our wireless is in the living room. Awful confession, but I promise you shan't see the cabbage boiling to-morrow. Don't dress, of course ; I doubt if I could find a boiled shirt now."

The two men parted, Fiennes going on to the post office and Pansel down to the harbour. His love of sailing seemed to have returned to him and he had spent a great part of the last three days upon the creek.

Christian Madgek, swabbing out his big launch, watched John get under way and congratulated him upon his increasing skill.

" You're doing fine, Mr. Pansel ", he said.

" I'm all right, Polly, except when this damn centre-board sticks. There's the devil in it some days."

" Well, watch it doesn't turn you over, Mr. Pansel. No joke in a squall outside."

" I'll be careful. Can you let us have a crab or a lobster to-morrow, Polly ? Mr. Fiennes is coming to dinner."

" Crab, he likes. Sure to be one in the pots. I'll get you one, anyway."

John thanked him and, running easily before the
off-shore wind was soon in the little bay. He knew
the channel well now, and seldom ran aground. The
tide was running out quickly but he thought there
would be water enough to take him over the bar.
As he approached it he pulled up the centre-board,
slid over the obstacle with what looked like a few
inches to spare, and with a quick sideways jerk
dropped the centre-board back into position. There
was a grim smile on his face as the heavy piece of
iron clanged against its frame.

In the meantime Dallas Fiennes had posted his
manuscript and was returning across the saltings to
his hut. Again and again, as he walked, he turned
over in his mind the problem of this sudden change
of attitude on the part of Pansel, this apparent
friendliness, above all this invitation to dine—a
thing that had never been suggested before. Was
the fellow really a fool ? or complacent ? Was he
encouraging the affair in hope of getting a divorce ?
That would be hellishly awkward ; at all costs he
must avoid an ugly court case—the public, damned
hypocrites, did not like that, though they would
read it eagerly enough and would lap it down in a
book. If he himself were to figure as a co-respondent,
though, it would do him harm. Besides, he might
have to marry the woman—to satisfy public
opinion, and, much as she attracted him, that would
be too much of a good thing.

But there was another, more grim alternative.
Was the man subtle ? These big stupid-looking
fellows often had a streak of cunning in their make-up
that they only employed in an emergency. Was it
possible that Pansel was enticing him to the house

in order to assault him in front of his wife ? It was a nasty thought ; he would have to be very carefully on his guard and, if necessary, beat a hasty if undignified retreat.

There was really nothing more that he could make of the problem ; he must just keep his eyes open and wait on events. In the meantime he was not going to let it interfere with his work.

For the next day and a half, therefore, Dallas Fiennes hardly moved from his writing table, except to eat and sleep. All through Thursday afternoon and evening he wrote, with a furious concentration of mental energy that literally drove words from the point of his pen on to paper. On Friday morning he woke early with an uneasy feeling that something was wrong. After a hurried breakfast he returned to his writing-table, glanced at the previous day's sheets, read back, read through all that he had written, then with an angry curse tore the pages across and across and flung them into the waste paper basket. Rubbish ! Ill-written, hysterical rubbish his previous day's work appeared to him now and he was not going to put up with that. But with all his energy and determination it was infernally difficult to keep his thoughts fixed upon the story, with its created characters and imagined incidents. As was the case with nearly all his books, ' Butterfly Kiss ' relied largely upon a sex theme for its popular appeal and Dallas found it difficult to prevent his own problem from intruding upon the story which he was trying to tell.

As the day went on and attempt followed attempt, only to be discarded, Dallas found himself growing more and more irritable. A short walk in the after-

noon failed to give him an appetite for tea, and after
one more abortive attempt to write the novelist had
to admit that for the nonce his nerves had defeated
him ; he realised that while the fringe of his mind
played with the problem of *Mark* and *Ann Tassardy*,
his inner being was absorbed with the question of
what was going to happen to Dallas Fiennes that
evening. Never before, in a life of varied amorous
adventure, had he allowed himself to be drawn into
a position where bodily peril to himself became a
practical reality.

With a shrug of nervous irritation Dallas walked
across to his cupboard and took out a bottle of sherry
and a glass. He must check this ridiculous state of
nerves ; a glass of ' Amontillado style ' would soon
put that right. It was not to be supposed that any
real *danger* existed ; a black eye or a bruised back
was an unpleasant possibility, but in the twentieth
century—in England—above all, in Norfolk—
injured husbands did not apply the melodramatic
principles of the unwritten law ; the last case of that
kind that he could remember was in, or just after,
the war, and then of course everybody's moral sense,
their valuation of life, was warped and unnatural.
No, no danger, of course. No violence at all ; not
the smallest chance. The sherry was already
bringing him to his senses.

Now he felt ready to tackle *Mark Tassardy's*
trouble, but there wasn't time ; it was a mistake to
start writing when he would have to break off just
as he was getting into full swing. One more glass
and he would start for the village. · Tide was going
down, would hardly have begun to rise by the time
he came back ; he had told old Giles to leave his

boat on the saltings side of the harbour so there was
no need to flog round the long way overland. Across
Little Creek in his own boat, across the harbour in
Giles'; back the same way; it only required a little
forethought. Really it might be quite an amusing
evening; a bit awkward at first perhaps, especially
with Hilary . . . after . . . women were odd, the
way they took things . . . you never could tell
where you were with them. Well, it was all grist to
his novelist's mill—learn and laugh, that was his
motto.

Pulling on his short gum boots and slipping his
suède shoes into the pocket of his mackintosh—the
nights were cold on this coast, even in July—Dallas
turned down the lamp and opened his front door.
A third glass of sherry—just a small one—had
completed the recovery of his *moral;* he was feeling
good—definitely good.

As Fiennes walked down the shingly beach to his
boat the sun was still shining brightly, but there was
a grey haze on the horizon that would have told its
tale to an observant weather-wise man. Fiennes,
however, was not weather-wise nor, on this occasion,
observant; he gave all his attention to the manipulation of his boat, which, at this half-tide, only took
him part of the way across to his hitching-post. He
had to anchor it and walk the rest of the way over
the soft sand to the raised path. The spring tides
were running now, so that at high tide the saltings
were flooded, but the raised bank along which the
path ran was never covered. There had, however,
been heavy rain on the previous night and the path
was greasy; the smooth rubber soles of Fiennes'
gum boots gave a particularly treacherous hold on

this surface and he had not gone far before he came crashing down on his knees, giving himself a nasty jar and covering his hands and trousers with slimy mud. With a flood of curses that were lost upon that deserted waste, Fiennes picked himself up and walked on, using an exaggerated care that must have been comic to anyone who happened to see him. No more accidents happened, however; Giles Banyatt's boat was waiting for him at the end of the path, and he had soon ferried himself across to the quay and was making his way down the alley towards the Pansel's house.

He found the artist leaning against his front-doorpost, looking down the village street. Pansel smiled broadly at sight of his companion's knees.

" You've been in trouble, eh ? " he asked. " Want a wash ? "

" Thanks. I'm afraid I do rather. The path over the saltings' as greasy as butter."

Pansel put his head inside the door.

" One of our guests has crashed, Hilary ", he called. " Can he wash in the kitchen or shall I take him upstairs ? "

There was a pause ; then Hilary's voice from the kitchen :

" I'll take some hot water upstairs if you'll wait a minute."

" Oh, please don't bother, Mrs. Pansel. I can quite well wash under a tap."

Dallas Fiennes walked into the narrow hall and at the corner of the stairs almost ran into Hilary coming from the kitchen. It was the first time that they had met since Hilary's return from Norwich and both were obviously nervous, a state of mind hardly minimised by the fact that Hilary's husband was within a few feet of them and would hear everything they said, even if he did not actually see them. Hilary flushed and was thankful for the dishes of fruit that she was carrying.

"Oh, how d'you do . . . Mr. Fiennes", she gasped.

Dallas Fiennes, having his back to John, grinned.

"How do *you* do . . . Mrs. Pansel ?" he asked. "Won't you let me take those ?"

Hilary looked at his muddy hands and smiled. Dallas, following her eye, drew back his hand in disgust.

"I'm sorry ; I must wash them. Can I . . . ?"

"John, do take Mr. Fiennes up to your room", interrupted Hilary. "I must get on with dinner ; I'm behindhand."

"Trot into the kitchen, Fiennes", said Pansel. "I'm going to see what's happened to Beryl Helliott ; perhaps she's afraid of the mist."

"Mist, eh ?" Fiennes looked out of the door and saw that wisps of white vapour were drifting down the road. "I never noticed that."

"It's been coming up for some time", replied John. "Miss Helliott's supposed to be coming, but she may be afraid of being marooned. I'll walk down the road a bit and see if she's coming."

"Oh, John . . . !"

Hilary's hand fluttered nervously to her mouth as she saw her husband's big form disappear down the garden path. She found herself flushing again—idiotically nervous in a situation that was out of her depth.

" If you'll go and wash, Mr. Fiennes, I'll get on with laying the table."

" Mr. Fiennes ! "

Dallas stood in front of Hilary, his hands behind his back, a quizzical expression on his face.

" Oh, well . . . Dallas. But . . . here ? Oh, do go and wash. I must get on."

Dallas remained motionless.

" Hilary, you haven't told me what . . ."

The sound of footsteps on the road outside checked him. He walked to the door, which still stood open, and looked out.

" Only old Vokes ", he said, shutting the door. " Now, Hilary . . ."

But Hilary had taken the opportunity to slip into the living-room and was now busily laying the table. She had recovered control of herself and the situation.

" This is a dinner-party, Dallas. I'm not going to talk about myself or even about you this evening. Besides, I'm busy. Now go along and wash, and when you've done that you can get two bottles of beer out of the cupboard under the stairs and bring them in here."

Dallas Fiennes recognised the change of atmosphere. With a shrug of the shoulders he walked down the passage into the kitchen and, turning on the hot water in the sink, began to scrub the mud off his hands. In the living-room Hilary was busy arranging her modest dessert. She had been dreading this meeting, but now that it had come and the first shock was over she was going to keep control ; besides, though the party was none of her making, she was determined that it should be a success—so

150

far as her own management could make it so. The
food would be good, John was responsible for such
drinks as there might be ; it was the little details,
the trimmings, that worried her. Her best table-
cloth had got a darn in it that no arranging of
dessert dishes could hide, the dessert itself was
meagre—preserved fruit was so impossibly expensive
and cheap chocolates so obviously were cheap.
Still, the flowers looked nice and the little scrap of
silver that they had clung to shone brilliantly. In
little more than a minute Hilary had forgotten all
about Dallas Fiennes.

She was putting the finishing touches to the table
when she was startled by the sound of a crash
mingled with a stifled cry, followed by the shuffle of
uncertain footsteps in the passage outside. Running
to the door she threw it open and saw Dallas Fiennes
staggering towards her with both hands clasped to
the top of his head.

" Dallas ! " she exclaimed, her eyes wide with
consternation. " What *has* happened ? "

With a sudden lurch Fiennes dropped onto the
stairs and sat for a moment in silence, still clutching
his head. Hilary watched him in growing alarm.
Suddenly he shook himself and looked up.

" Sorry ", he said. " Afraid I've smashed at
least one bottle of beer. Hit my head the most
almighty crack on the cupboard door—it's a bit low.
I still feel quite dizzy. Terribly sorry to have made
such a fuss."

Hilary's face had miraculously cleared. She
found herself laughing light-heartedly.

" Poor thing ! " she exclaimed. " Shall I put
something on it ? Let me have a look."

Dallas bent his head and she took it between her hands and examined the injury.

" 'Tis a sair crack ", she said. " I'll put some iodine on it."

" No, no ", said Dallas. " That's really not necessary, Hilary. Your hands on my temples are the best cure of . . ."

The outer door opened suddenly and John Pansel stood on the threshold, staring at them. Hilary gave a nervous laugh.

" D . . . Mr. Fiennes hit his head on the cupboard door ", she said.

John said nothing, but hung his hat up on a peg. Dallas rose to his feet.

" I'm afraid I've wasted a lot of good beer, Pansel ", he said. " I've smashed at least one bottle."

" Never mind. There are other things to drink besides beer. No sign of Beryl, Hilary ; I'm afraid she's not coming."

" She must be afraid of the mist—as you said. She could have stayed here."

" Yes, or I could have taken her home. Never mind ; can't be helped. Dinner ready ? "

It seemed at first as if the little party would ' drag ' heavily, as Fiennes was still feeling the effects of the blow on his head and Hilary's nervousness had returned, while John Pansel was never a great talker. But it takes more than one crack on the skull to disperse permanently the effects of three glasses of sherry and Dallas was not half-way through the first tumbler of whisky which John persuaded him to drink—' to buck him up '—before his tongue was wagging freely again. He could be very amusing when he liked, especially when what he would himself have described as ' well oiled ', and Hilary was soon laughing in spite of herself while John was evidently making a determined effort to be sociable. At the end of dinner he produced a bottle of brandy with a very modest label on it. Hilary raised her eyebrows.

" Oh, John, that's not very nice, is it ? " she asked. " To drink like that, I mean—as a liqueur ? "

Her husband smiled.

" Try it and see ", he said, pouring some into a clean glass for Fiennes.

The latter sipped it, and his eyes sparkled.

" My noble host ", he exclaimed. " Where did you get this ? "

" From my wine-merchant."

John laughed at the look of astonishment on his wife's face.

" But what is it ? "

" Read the label—Macklin's Three Star Br . . ."

" Three Star nothing ! " interjected Fiennes. " This is the real stuff, or I'm a Dutchman."

" So long as you like it, that's all that matters."

" You won't tell me where you get it ? "

" I'll ask my wine-merchant to supply you, if you like ; he can decide for himself whether to extend his list of customers. Try some, Hil."

John pushed his own glass across to his wife ; she sipped it, gasped and gave a little ' Ooh ' of appreciation.

" It's lovely and warm ", she said, " but rather strong."

John laughed.

" If it had been the ordinary stuff you'd have shuddered—couldn't help yourself ", he said.

The brandy completed the work of loosening Dallas' tongue and he launched into a high-coloured but extremely witty description of the entanglements into which the characters of his new book had been drawn.   At one point in the story John Pansel gave a guffaw of laughter—and then suddenly dropped back to earth and realisation of the subject of this amusing story—the ludicrous predicament of a cuckold husband, the amorous audacities of his unfaithful wife.   A hot rush of blood rose to his face, his hands clenched under the table.   With a supreme effort he mastered his sudden burst of rage ; Hilary was looking at Fiennes and had not noticed him ; the talker himself was engrossed in his own effects and was in any case too mellow to notice anything so trivial as his host's expression.

But John could not stand any more of it ; if he was to keep control of himself—and above everything he *must* keep control of himself—this filthy story must be stopped.   He pushed back his chair.

" I'll see what the mist's doing ", he said.

His abrupt movement broke the thread of Fiennes' narrative.   He looked at his watch.

" I say, it's past ten o'clock ", he exclaimed. " I've been talking too much."

He rose to his feet and swayed slightly but steadied himself with a hand on his chair-back.

" Mist's thick as hell ", said John, coming back into the room.   " Have you got a torch, Fiennes ? "

The novelist tapped the pocket of his beautifully fitting jacket.

" I think so ", he said vaguely.   " I think so."

Hilary looked anxiously at him and then at her husband. Dallas was in no condition to find his way across the saltings in a sea mist. If it had been anyone else she would have insisted on his staying the night, but how would John take it ? would he be . . . difficult ?

Dallas, in the meantime, had put on his mackintosh and—with some difficulty—his gum boots.

" Well, good-bye, kind hostess ", he said, taking Hilary's hand and squeezing it affectionately. His speech was quite clear but too carefully deliberate. " I can't thank you enough for a most delightful evening. A really delig . . . and you, too, Pansel. Most extraordin . . . most awfully kind of you both."

He turned and walked out into the passage, stumbling over the little mat in the doorway as he did so. Hilary seized her husband's arm.

" John ", she whispered, " is it safe to let him go alone, in this ? "

A quick frown crossed John's face ; he thought for a moment, then shook off Hilary's hand and pulled his own mackintosh and hat off their peg. He picked up the suède shoes that Fiennes had left lying in the passage and thrust them into his own coat pocket.

" Half a minute, Fiennes ", he said. " I'll come with you as far as the harbour. It may be awkward getting across in this mist."

Fiennes was already half-way down the garden path and was only visible as a patch of light thrown by his torch.

" Quite all right. Quite unnecess . . . ary."

There was an ominous thickening in those few

words ; the cold air was already taking its inevitable effect.

John Pansel picked his own torch off the table by the door and took a stick from the stand.

" I'll take him back ", he said curtly and strode off into the mist.   With a look of misery on her face Hilary watched him go, then, shuddering as the cold fingers of the mist touched her, shut the outer door and turned back into the living-room.   The work of the house must be done.

Outside, John soon caught up the wavering light in front of him.   He thrust his arm through Fiennes' and walked him quickly down the road.   The apparently friendly action set the novelist's tongue wagging again.   John was too busy finding his way and keeping his companion on an even keel to pay much attention to what was being said ; in any case he was too angry to respond to it.   With some difficulty he found the end of the alley that led to the harbour and turned down it ; as they emerged into the open space which ended in the quay the light of their torches showed a dim figure crossing their front.

" Good-night ", said John automatically.

There was no reply and the figure, after a moment's hesitation, disappeared into the mist.

" Surly devil ! " said Fiennes.   " I detest a surly devil like . . . like an unfilled can."

" Here's the boat," said John curtly.   " I'll put you across."

With a good deal of stumbling Fiennes took his place on one of the thwarts and John pushed the boat off and scrambled in over the stern.   More by luck than judgment they hit the steps on the opposite side of the harbour straight away. John held on while Fiennes clumsily groped his way from the boat onto the steps At the top he slipped and came down heavily, remaining on his hands and knees.

" Most extraordinary thing ", he said deliberately, " but that's exactly what I did on the way here."

There was a plaintive note in his voice and with a shrug of the shoulders John fastened the boat's painter to the steps and climbed up to the path. It was obvious that he would have to take the drunken swine all the way and come back across the saltings alone—a prospect that he did not at all appreciate.

" Get up ", he said curtly and jerked at Fiennes' arm. Somehow the novelist scrambled to his feet and stood, gently swaying, holding on to his companion. For a moment John stood too, listening, staring into the thick blanket of mist. A deathly silence hung over the marshes. Though he knew that they were surrounded by countless birds and fishes and even beasts, there was not a splash, not a flutter of wings, not a rustle of grass or reed—none of the usual noises of the night. The mist seemed to act as a blanket to sound as well as sight ; there was a feeling of oppression, almost of dread, over everything.

With a quick shake John pulled himself together.

" Come on ", he said, taking Fiennes' arm as before.

Again the novelist broke into talk, but now there was a different note in his voice, a languorous gloating that penetrated John's inattention and made him listen with growing disgust. Fiennes began to describe some amorous midnight adventure that, he said, the mist reminded him of ; it was hardly coherent and broke off before it reached its point.

"Ah, it's a great life", exclaimed Dallas, "a great life. You know, Pansel, you're a very lucky fellow—nice little home, nice little wife waiting for you every night, but . . . but it's the *same* wife. That's my point . . . same woman every night. I couldn't do that. I want a change. Fair or dark, big or little, I love 'em all . . . but I must have change. Now last . . ."

John Pansel wrenched away his arm.

"Stop it, you damned swine!" he exclaimed harshly. "Stop it, or I'll knock your dirty face in!"

The voice stopped. Fiennes seemed to be thinking. Suddenly he burst into an unsteady laugh.

"Why, of course!" he exclaimed. "Last week! You didn't like last week, did you! Poor old fellow. Poor old . . ."

The light of Fiennes' waving torch suddenly struck upon the figure looming above him—showed him a face distorted with rage, an arm raised to strike. With a gasp, the drunken man cut off the flood of words, turned, and stumbled away into the mist.

CHAPTER XIII

SUSPENSE

JOHN PANSEL stood alone in the mist, listening. He was still trembling from the violence of his emotion. The surge of blood roared and thudded in his ears, sounding like the heavy beat of running footsteps. He strained his ears to listen, but as his pulse slackened he realised that the beat must be in his head; no other sound broke the deathly stillness of the mist-wrapped saltings. Slowly he pulled himself together, rubbed his hands upon his trousers, picked up the stick that had fallen onto the muddy path. For a moment more he stood, breathing deeply, trying to recover his sense of direction which had become confused. He could only see his feet with difficulty and the dark patch of mud on which they stood; all else was white obscurity.

Suddenly, by some freak of atmosphere—air-pocket or wind—the mist round him lifted, leaving him standing in what seemed a large white-walled room. For twenty yards all round him he could see clearly, the raised bank on which he stood, a fraction of the creek below it, the path—and on his right, almost under his feet, a black pit of slimy mud into which the tide was beginning to creep in oily trickles. John looked, shuddered violently—and the mist closed upon him again and shut out the stealthy horror from his sight.

Turning quickly on his heel John strode down the path, luck rather than sight keeping him on the bank. He had not gone far when he realised that he had not got his torch. He stopped with a jerk, trying to remember at what moment he had dropped it. Turning, he hunted slowly back along the way he had come but soon found himself wandering from side to side, getting more and more confused. A hole in the ground tripped him and he fell at full length into what was fortunately only the outer fringe of one of the many mud-holes that bordered the bank. Pulling himself out, he tried to scrape off some of the mud, but it was soon evident that nothing but water would clean him. He was uncertain, now, even of which way he was facing ; how could he possibly find . . . ? His foot, moving slightly, struck against something metallic ; stooping quickly, he picked up the torch.

With a gasp of relief, which seemed out of all proportion to such a trivial loss, John pushed the switch, but no light came—the filament had evidently been broken in the fall. Thrusting the torch into his pocket John started, more cautiously this time, to walk along the raised bank in what he imagined to be the direction of the harbour. It was slow work ; if he hurried he soon found himself off the path, stumbling over the broken ground above the creek or hovering on the verge of a mud-hole on the other side. After what seemed an hour the path swung suddenly and unmistakably to the right ; John knew that he was going in the wrong direction. With a quick intake of breath that was half-way between a curse and a sob, he turned and began to retrace his steps. He was getting more accustomed now to his task and in what seemed a surprisingly short time he pulled himself up, just in time, at the top of the steps leading down to the harbour.

The boat was riding high now, the tide rapidly approaching the full. John found that he had fastened the painter below what was now water level and he had to roll up his sleeves and grope about in the icy water before he could loose Giles Banyatt's boat. That done, it did not take him long to get across, though the tide carried him so fast that he missed the quay and landed on the shelving beach beyond. Still, that did not worry him ; he dragged the boat up as far as he could manage it, drove in the anchor at its highest reach, and strode off towards his house. This time he saw no one ; no light pierced the white blanket of mist and he had considerable difficulty in finding the alley-way. Once there, however, the rest of the way was so familiar that he felt he could have walked it with his eyes shut ; still, it was some time before he groped his way in through his little garden-gate and realised with a start that a light was still burning in the living-room. A quick frown puckered his brow, but after a moment's hesitation he opened the front door and went in. The living-room was empty, but the lamp showed him that it was nearly one o'clock— almost three hours since he had set out with Dallas Fiennes.

Taking off his mackintosh and gum boots and turning out the living-room lamp, John groped his way up the staircase. As he reached the landing he saw a streak of light under his wife's door. He did not go in nor call to her but turned into his own room ; if she were awake he knew that she would

have heard him come in. In five minutes he was in
bed.

John awoke late, to find the world still wrapped
in mist, though it seemed rather less impenetrable
than at night. Hilary had already had her modest
breakfast when he came down, and was busy—for
what appeared to him no good reason—in turning
out the living-room. John ate his boiled egg in the
kitchen, washed up his share of the breakfast things,
and lighting his pipe, went out into the garden. It
was possible now to see a few yards in front of one
and John strolled down the road into the village,
where he presently found knots of fishermen, with
an occasional visitor, lounging about, discussing the
weather. It was the general opinion that it would
clear at mid-day, though it might thicken again for
a shorter time at night.

John stopped to speak to Christian Madgek, whom
he found in conversation with a younger man, also
in blue jersey and trousers. John commiserated
with the boatman on the loss of his business—in
these holiday times the motor boat should be earning
good money carrying visitors to and from the ocean.
Christian, as usual, was philosophical.

" Others are worse off ", he said. " At least we're
not fog-bound at sea. We don't hurt here."

" Some trades thrive on a bit of obscurity ", said
the young fisherman with a sly wink at John.

Madgek took no notice. He was whittling a thole
pin and only looked up from it when he spoke to
John. The painter had the feeling that he was not
wanted and after a word or two more with the
youngster he walked on.

Back in her kitchen, Hilary Pansel worked with

nervous energy at her self-imposed task of cleaning—
as if five days' absence on the part of the house-wife
had thrown the little house into a state of squalor.
She felt oppressed and miserable, and tried to lay
the blame for at least part of her *malaise* upon the
mist. The misery was easily accounted for and she
accepted it as inevitable, but the oppression—the
sense of something hanging over her—was almost
physical, as if the damp cloak of mist was pressing
upon her. But in her heart she knew that this
feeling, too, had a mental rather than a physical
basis. The extraordinary dinner-party of the night
before, which John had sprung upon her without
explanation—indeed she and he had hardly spoken
since her return from Norwich on Wednesday—was
in itself inexplicable, but the circumstances that had
attended it—the shock of Dallas Fiennes' accident,
his drunkenness, above all the long strain of waiting
for John's return, the very length of his absence, had
all accumulated to form an atmosphere of tension
that was almost terror.

It was no use hiding from herself that she was
afraid, no use trying to disguise what she feared.
The extraordinary change that had come over John
in the last few weeks, his sullen anger, his silence,
had surprised but had not frightened her. It was the
sudden change of front, his invitation to Dallas,
that had opened her eyes to the reality of danger,
though it was only when that crash and cry had
startled her that its reality had leapt to the forefront
of her mind. Even then it had sunk into the background, obscured by surprise and disgust at Dallas'
condition, and had only gradually returned, to loom
larger and more menacing as hour followed hour

and her husband, who had gone out into the mist with the man he hated, did not return . . . did not return . . .

With a start Hilary realised that she was standing, with a dish in one hand and a cloth in the other, staring at the blank wall in front of her, visualising again the happenings of the previous night, living again the long vigil.

The sound of footsteps, which had probably broken her reverie, now reached her conscious mind. The front door opened and her husband, after hanging up his coat and hat, walked into the kitchen. His face was grey and drawn, but it seemed to Hilary that he looked more of a man than he had done for some time past ; perhaps, she thought, it was in contrast with the other upon whom her strange midsummer madness had cast so false a glamour. That freak of mind, that blindness, had lifted now with the suddenness of a fog lifting . . .

" It's clearing, I think ", said John, throwing himself onto a kitchen chair.

Hilary started, the words fitted so exactly into her thoughts.

" Jude Tasson tells me it'll clear for a couple of hours and then come down again. He's going to take Fiennes' letters across to him when he's had his dinner."

Involuntarily Hilary caught her breath. It was the first time John had spoken of Fiennes since the previous night. Why should that startle her ? She was becoming ridiculous—a bundle of nerves.

" If it does clear I'll go over to Brulcote and see that Beryl's all right. Frank seems to be away ; she must be lonely."

" Oh, do, John. I'd like to know. . . ." Hilary hesitated. " Shall I come with you ? " she added nervously.

Her husband looked at her for a moment, a flicker of light in his eyes which for so long had been dull.

" Do, if you care to ", he said.

He rose from his chair and began to lay the table.

" Better have some food now ; then we can get off the moment it clears."

They did not talk much during lunch, each seeming afraid to commit him- or herself to an advance that might not be reciprocated. But Hilary was conscious of a lifting of the cloud of dread, though the inner sense of misery remained.

Through the window they could see that the first part at least of Jude's prophecy was being fulfilled. Swathes of mist were rolling away from the house, the fence was visible, then the hedge beyond it. As the room lightened Hilary saw more clearly the ravages that had carved their mark upon her husband's face ; her heart quickened.

Their meal did not take long and Hilary ran up to her room to get her hat and coat.

" I'll leave washing up, in case it comes on again ", she called over her shoulder.

John did not answer, but stood staring out of the window. Upstairs, Hilary took out her green leather beret, pulled it onto her head, and looked into the glass. It was undoubtedly becoming, especially worn well down on one side, with a curl drawn out in front of her ear. Hilary wrenched it off and flung it on the floor. Dallas had told her that. She opened her cupboard and took out a small

felt hat that she knew John liked. It was out of
date, but . . . Certainly it *did* become her, even
if it made her look older than she had realised.
She *was* looking older. Her hand went to the lip-
stick which, in the last few weeks, had lain upon her
dressing table. She dropped it, and with one last
glance at herself—older or not, she *did* look nice—
she hurried downstairs.

John was still standing in the kitchen, staring out
of the window.

" I'm quite ready."

He did not move. She followed his glance and
saw that the hedge was no longer visible.

" Oh ! " There was misery in her voice, bitter
disappointment. " It's coming down again ! "

John nodded.

" Yes ", he said slowly, " it's coming down
again."

With the return of the mist, gloom seemed to
settle down once more upon the Pansels. John
retired to his studio, though not—Hilary imagined—
to work. She herself, after taking off the becoming
hat, returned drearily to the drudgery of her duster.
At about four o'clock she heard John come downstairs and go out ; he did not speak to her. In the
last few weeks that had happened several times and
she had become indifferent to it, but to-day after
the sudden lightening of her spirits, his silence hurt
her ; she found, to her dismay, that tears were
filling her eyes—a sign of physical and mental
weakness that brought home to her acutely the
change that had come over her in those few weeks.

John was back in time for ' high tea ' at seven
and appeared to be in better spirits. The mist, he

said, was shifting ; in places it was quite clear for a time ; evidently the wind was moving gradually round into the south-west, from which quarter it would soon clear away the chilly vapours which surrounded them. He had himself been over to Brulcote and had a talk with Beryl, who was very sorry to have missed the ' party ' on the previous night ; she had, as they had guessed, been afraid of getting lost in the mist. Frank was still away ; she had not heard from him for a week and was getting rather worried.

" I wish I'd come with you ", said Hilary. " I didn't know you were going."

" I didn't mean to, but I couldn't stick indoors any longer. When I got into the village—among the houses—it seemed to be thinner and then there were those clear bits and I thought it was lifting altogether. Besides, Jude Tasson wanted to deliver the post there and he asked me to go with him— easier for two than one."

" Had he been out to the huts ? " asked Hilary, trying to keep the nervousness out of her voice.

" Yes ; he got out in the middle of the day, when it seemed to be lifting altogether. Had a job to get back though. He didn't see Fiennes ; sleeping it off, I expect."

John helped his wife to wash up and they talked more naturally together than they had done for weeks, so that it was with a slight sense of disappointment that Hilary heard John announce his intention of going down to the ' Duck ' for a final pipe and a glass of beer. Still, she was glad that he felt like company ; he certainly seemed less morose to-night than he had been for some time past.

The mist was still hanging about when John set
out, but it was moving and seemed to have broken
up into fairly large wisps. Patches of star-lit sky
were visible from time to time and there were more
of the natural sounds of the marsh to be heard ;
sounds, indeed, seemed to travel with almost
uncanny clearness and Hilary stood for a time in the
doorway listening to the quacks and splashings of
the waterfowl. After the heavy, death-like oppression of the previous night nature seemed to be
re-awakening to normal life.

Hilary herself, however, felt tired and exhausted ;
she decided to go to bed early with a book and was
soon dozing. She was awakened by the sound of the
front door shutting and heard the familiar sound of
John kicking off his boots, lighting a candle, and
padding up the stairs in his stockinged feet. Outside
her room he stopped, then—after a pause—tapped
and put his head in.

" Good-night, Hilary ", he said with a smile, and
stumped on to his own room. With a little sigh of
relief, Hilary turned over and went to sleep.

When she awoke she found to her astonishment
that it was nearly nine o'clock ; evidently her
nervous exhaustion had been more profound than
she had realised. Unreasonably ashamed of herself,
she scrambled out of bed and hurried into her
clothes, picturing a sulky husband scratching about
in the cold kitchen for food. A glance at the window
showed her that the mist was gone, but she was too
much concerned with her domestic shortcomings
to think much of her surroundings. The kitchen
grate was cold and empty, but it was no emptier
than the kitchen itself ; John must have gone

out for a walk—perhaps with a pocketful of
biscuits.

Full of remorse, Hilary got out her emergency
spirit-stove, boiled water for tea and then two eggs,
laid the table and put her head out of the window
to look for John. There was no sign of him, nor did
he answer when she called. She went out into the
road and looked up and down it, without seeing him.
As an afterthought she went up to his room and
found him in bed, asleep. In the cold light of
morning, she was shocked to see how haggard and
old his sleeping face looked; a deeper remorse
seized her—she knew well what had caused the
change in him. She was quietly shutting the door
when he sprang up in bed with a start, staring at
her with wide eyes, as if still in the grip of a nightmare; then, as consciousness returned to him, his
face relaxed and he sank back on the pillow.

" 'Time is it ? " he asked, with a heavy yawn.

" Half past nine. I'll bring you up some breakfast."

" Half past . . . ?! Good heavens; I've over-
slept myself. I'll be down in a moment."

" No, don't, dear ", said Hilary. " It's all ready ;
I'll bring it up."

But John was obstinate. He hated breakfast in
bed—or even in a bedroom. It had always, to him,
been the hall-mark of idleness, indulged in only by
the wastrel, the parasite, or the decayed. He pushed
his wife out of the room and told her to bring him
some hot water for shaving.

Hilary took up the water that had boiled the eggs
and herself sat down to her breakfast. Her thoughts
wandered to events of the past weeks, her own

inexplicable behaviour, the climax and its disillusionment, her dread . . .

The click of a gate switched her back to the present. She looked out of the window . . . and felt her heart leap into her mouth.

A policeman was walking up the little garden path.

CHAPTER XIV

CONFESSION

HILARY knew that policeman well by sight. She had often met him on the roads when she was walking, or in Great Hayworth, where he was stationed. His name was Pentwhistle, but he was locally known as 'Stumping Tom', from a ponderous habit of gait that no rubber soles could effectually silence. Christian Madgek had been known to boast that he could hear and distinguish it a mile off, which may well have accounted for his own immunity from trouble.

Pentwhistle had always given Hilary a friendly smile and a word or two when he met her, so that the behaviour of her heart on the present occasion must have been due to that consciousness of guilt which is latent in the most innocent of mortals. She went to the front door and opened it just as a sharp rap echoed through the house.

The large blue figure almost filled the little doorway, a thick foot advanced an inch or two over the threshold. To Hilary's welcoming smile there was no response upon the heavy features of the constable ; nervousness may have contributed to their colour but solemnity struggled with self-importance for the mastery. Pentwhistle's fingers touched the peak of his helmet.

" Mr. Pansel, please, 'mm ? "

Hilary hesitated, then drew back.

" Come in, please ", she said, leading the way into the living-room. " I'll find my husband. Unless it's anything I can do ? "

The features became, if possible, more solemn.

" No, 'm. It's . . ."

Behind the constable's shoulder Hilary saw her husband appear in the doorway. His face was white and set. A trickle of blood from a razor cut ran down the angle of his jaw. His feet were in carpet slippers.

" You want me, constable ? "

Pentwhistle turned, automatically touched his forelock.

" If you please, sir. It's . . . important, sir."

He looked at Hilary.

" I'll stay, please ", she said, walking across to John and shutting the door behind him. The three remained standing. Pentwhistle looked uncomfortable but he had no instructions to argue the point. Instead, he drew a notebook from his breast-pocket.

" I understand that Mr. Fiennes was having supper with you on Friday night, sir ; is that correct ? " he asked.

Glancing at her husband's face, Hilary saw the tip of his tongue pass over his lips. His voice came harshly.

" What is it, man ? What's up ? "

Pentwhistle shifted clumsily from one foot to the other. He had been taught to ask questions, not to answer them. Still . . .

" I'm sorry to say, sir, that Mr. Fiennes has been found dead. I'm trying to trace who saw him last."

" Dead ? ! "

Hilary's gasp of horror was little more than a whisper. John was staring at the constable; his jaw set, a vein twitching in his forehead.

" Where ? In his hut ? "

Pentwhistle pulled himself together.

" Just a moment, sir, please. If you'd kindly answer my question. Was the gentleman here Friday night ? "

" He was. He had dinner with us."

" And he went back after dinner ? In that mist ? "

" Certainly he did."

" What time would that be, sir ? "

John turned to his wife.

" What time would you say it was, Hilary ? " he asked.

Still trembling from the shock, Hilary tried to collect her wits. There was a note of forced naturalness in John's voice that both puzzled and frightened her.

" About . . . about ten o'clock, I think."

" Yes, that was about it. I remember now. He said something about its being later than he expected."

Pentwhistle thought for a minute, then asked, diffidently :

" He was . . . all right, was he, sir ? "

" All right ? What d'you mean ? "

" Not . . . well . . . he hadn't had a drop too much ? "

" Good lord, no. Not in the least."

Hilary gasped. Why on earth had John said that ? If there had been an accident, wasn't that the very explanation of it ?

173

"It was pretty thick then, wasn't it, sir ? You didn't think to keep him for the night ? "

"It was thick, yes, but not so bad as all that. As a matter of fact I went down as far as the harbour with him just to see him across the water all right."

"You did, sir ? "

There was an unmistakable note of eagerness in the constable's voice.

"Yes, I went across in old Giles' boat with him and brought it back."

There was a deep flush on the constable's face as he scribbled in his note-book. When he looked up, there was a glitter in his small eyes.

"Did you go along the bank with him at all, sir ? "

"Only a few yards ; it was clearer then and he said he could manage all right."

Pentwhistle added a few words to his notes, thought a minute, then drew himself up.

"That's all I've got to ask you now, sir," he said solemnly, "but I must request you to stay about home for a bit. The Inspector'll be over any time now and he's sure to want a word with you."

He moved towards the door but John remained in front of it.

"Look here," he said, and there was a note of command in his voice that Hilary had not hear since her early acquaintance with him after the war, "you've got to tell me a bit more about this. I've answered your questions and you've told me I'm to stay where I am—under observation, I suppose. I've got a right to know what's happened. Where was Mr. Fiennes found dead, and when ? What did he die of, and who found him ? "

Again Pentwhistle went through the slow processes

of thought. He had got what he wanted—the answers to his questions—before Pansel knew what had happened—if he really didn't know. It would not be possible, or even necessary, so far as he could see, to keep the plain facts from him much longer ; other people in the village could tell him that much.

" He was found in a branch of the creek at the side of the path across the saltings, sir. This morning he was found, by Mrs. Barle what does for him. She couldn't go yesterday, which was her usual day, because of the weather, so she went this morning to tell him why and she'd come tomorrow ; she wasn't going to work on a Sunday, she said. On her way over she saw him lying there in the mud ; it was low tide."

There was silence in the little room. The significance of what Pentwhistle had said was slowly sinking into the consciousness of at least one of his hearers. Hilary felt the blood ebbing from her face ; then it surged back and beat and hammered in her ears. On the saltings ! Beside the path !—the path on which John had left him ! Dimly she heard her husband's question :

" And what did he die of ? "

Pentwhistle shrugged his shoulders.

" That's as may be, sir. He's been under the tide, anyway."

With another jab at his forelock, P.C. Pentwhistle stumped his way out of the house and down the road towards the village. John watched him till he was past the window and out of sight, then slowly turned towards his wife. She was staring at him with wide eyes, an expression of consternation—or was it fear ? horror ?—upon her face.

" Hilary! Why are you looking at me like that ? "

John's voice was still harsh, as if words came with difficulty from his throat. Hilary's reply was little more than a whisper.

" Why did you say that ? What does it mean ? "

Slowly she sank down into a chair, still watching him, her hands clasped upon her lap. John stared at her for a minute. Suddenly a strangled cry tore its way from his throat ; he flung himself on his knees before her and seized her hand.

" Hilary," he cried, " you don't believe that ? My God, if *you* believe it, what hope is there for me ? "

" But, John, why ? What does it mean ? I don't understand. Oh, I don't understand ! "

The terror in her voice unnerved him ; he buried his face in her lap and clutched at her arms. For a minute he knelt there, his shoulders convulsed with sobs. Then he looked up.

" Hilary," he whispered. " I meant to kill him ! I planned to kill him ! I can't keep it from you. Hilary, you're my wife. You're still my wife. Help me ; for God's sake help me ! "

Dumb with horror, Hilary clutched her husband's arms, drove her fingers into them, stared at him wildly ; then with a cry she flung her arms round him and pressed his head against her breast.

" John ! " she cried, " forgive me ! Oh, forgive me. It was my fault. It was all my fault ! "

For minutes the two crouched there, locked in each other's arms. Then he shook himself free, looked up at her with yearning in his eyes.

" Hilary, I must tell you. I can't keep it to myself

any longer. I've been mad with jealousy. I couldn't believe at first that you could love anyone but me. God knows why I should think that! When I saw your face light up when he came . . . when I saw that you despised me . . . I couldn't let you go, Hilary. My God, I couldn't let him have you! Not that man!''

With a cry, Hilary pressed her face against his shoulder, her own body now shaking with sobs.

'' Hilary, I loved you so! I never knew how much till I saw that I'd lost you. I knew I couldn't win you back; I knew you hated me now. But I couldn't let him have you. He wasn't fit to touch you, Hilary; he was a foul beast! I thought at first that I could drive him away from you—smash him up— terrify him. Then you went off with him and . . . I made up my mind to kill him. I'd thought it all out; I'd prepared for it. I was going to have a sailing accident. I learnt to sail that boat of Cadnall's and I let everybody think I couldn't manage the centre-board. I was going to get him to come out with me—several times; that's why I asked him to dine—to pave the way. Then, when the weather was right, I was going to capsize the boat and drag him under. Everyone knew he couldn't swim much. They might suspect me, but they couldn't prove it. And now this . . . this awful thing has happened. They're bound to think I've done it! They'll get me, Hilary. Oh, God; they'll get me.''

The agony in his voice would have melted a colder heart than Hilary's. She clasped him to her again, whispered in his ear such words of hope and encouragement as she could find.

"They shan't get you, darling. They shan't. Why should they think such a thing? John, don't, darling; don't!"

He looked up at her, wonder, hope, dawning in his eyes.

"Hilary," he whispered. "Do you still love me?"

"Love you? Of course I do! Always! Only you! Oh, John, I've been mad. I don't know what's happened to me. I suppose it's what does happen to people when they've been married some time and their lives are rather . . . monotonous. Especially if they don't have children. But it's over now. Never again, John. We'll start again, darling. We'll love each other more than ever—now that we know . . . what we mean to each other."

For a minute the two rocked in each other's arms, the pent-up emotion of the past weeks finding at last its natural outlet. Then John suddenly sprang to his feet, misery again staring from his eyes.

"But it's too late, Hilary," he cried. "They'll arrest me. They'll take me from you. It's too late."

"But why, John? Why should they arrest you?"

"Because everybody knew I hated him. He boasted . . . about you. At the inn . . . They've been laughing at me for weeks—those swine, Sarne and Vessle. On Sunday, when he came back, he . . . he was drunk then, Hilary, and he . . . oh, I can't tell you what he said . . . what they said. But I gave myself away; they all know. They must know."

White and miserable, Hilary pulled her husband

down onto the sofa beside her and took his hand in hers.

"John, you must be calm. Even if they know you hated him, that's no reason why you should have killed him. Even if you'd *said* you were going to kill him—if you'd threatened him—that would have been no proof. Don't you see, it was an accident. He lost his way, or staggered off the path into the creek. That's why I can't understand why you said he wasn't drunk. He *was* drunk. That was why you went with him."

John shook his head.

"You forget", he said, "that wound on his head!"

"Oh!" gasped Hilary. "You didn't . . . wasn't it an accident?"

"Oh, yes. It was an accident, but who's going to believe it? The man everyone knew I hated—had good reason to kill. It's known that he was here that night; it's known that I was on the saltings with him; he's found dead, with a wound on the top of his head—exactly where my stick would have hit him. What hope have I, Hilary?"

The bitterness of John's voice silenced her, as much as his words. She sat staring in front of her, trying to think.

"John", she whispered at last, "why did you tell him you had gone with Fiennes?"

John gave a short laugh.

"Because someone saw us together. At least, there was somebody down at the harbour who may have seen us. If I had kept my mouth shut and then that had come out it would have been the last nail in my coffin—only I shan't have a coffin—a blanket and quick-lime", he added with a bitter laugh.

"Besides", he went on, "when they start thinking they'll wonder why old Giles' boat was on this side of the harbour next morning and not the other, as it would have been if Fiennes had gone alone. I brought it back; they'd have guessed that. Another nail—another stitch."

"But why did you say he wasn't drunk? That explained everything."

"They wouldn't have believed me. It would have looked an obvious lie—to cover my guilt. Besides, if he was so drunk as to stagger into the creek, why did I leave him? Why didn't I see him all the way home?"

Hilary was silent for a moment. She looked curiously at her husband.

"Why didn't you, John?" she asked.

John in his turn was silent.

"I haven't told you what happened that night," he said at last. "Did you hear me come home"

Hilary nodded, not trusting herself to speak. Fear was creeping round her heart, thrusting its icy fingers through her veins.

"I didn't get back till one o'clock—three hours after we left. Someone may have seen that, too, though I don't think so. Except you, Hilary."

He looked at her strangely, but she returned his gaze steadily. After a pause, he went on:

"He was very drunk when the air got at him. I daresay he didn't know what he was saying, but he was . . . he said something that drove me mad with anger. I lifted my stick to hit him, but he ran away . . . into the mist. I was so upset, my blood was roaring in my ears, I thought I heard his feet running away—but I may have been wrong."

" And he . . . fell into the mud ? " Hilary's voice was little more than a whisper. John looked steadily at her.

" He must have " he said.

" Didn't he cry out ? "

John shook his head.

" I heard no cry."

" But why were you so late ? "

" I lost myself in the mist. I had dropped my torch and I went back to look for it. I found it at last, but the bulb was smashed. Then I lost my bearings and went the wrong way—towards the sea. It was very slippery ; I fell down several times— almost into the creek once. I had no idea how long it was till I got back."

For a time they sat in silence, Hilary still holding John's hand on her lap. He was the first to speak.

" I haven't got a hope, Hilary ", he said in a dull voice.

Hilary had been looking out of the window and for a moment it seemed as if she was not listening to him. Then, with a little shake, she pulled herself together.

" That's not true, John ", she said quietly. " If you are innocent you are in no danger, however bad things look to you now. You've only got to tell the truth. I don't suppose anybody's suspecting you at all, really. But you've got to pull yourself together. If you let people see you looking like you're looking now they *will* suspect you."

John gave an impatient shrug.

" It's easy enough to say that ", he said. " You've got nothing to worry you."

A spasm of anger crossed Hilary's face, but with

an effort she forced herself to be gentle. John had suffered horribly in the last few weeks and was in an agony of suspense now ; he wasn't really responsible for what he said. She had got to help him, to fight for him, even against himself.

" John, dear ", she said ; " I want to tell you everything—just as you've told me."

John looked up quickly.

" No, no, Hilary ", he exclaimed. " I don't want to know."

" But I want to tell you. It's all been horrible and I hate myself, but it's our only chance, to tell each other everything and then—if you're willing to try—start again."

John looked anxiously into his wife's eyes. His big hands pressed hers.

" I don't want you to tell me anything, Hilary ", he said. " I love you and I'm willing to do anything to make you love me again. It's all I want."

With a quick cry Hilary threw her arms round his neck.

" Oh, John ", she cried, " do you really love me—still ? I've been such a beast, John, but I do love you ; really, really I do. Listen, I'm going to tell you—to help myself. I should never feel happy unless I told you. Don't say anything. Just listen."

John did not speak but the pressure of his arms round her tightened. Hilary spoke in a low, expressionless voice.

" I'm not going to try and excuse myself for falling in love with Dallas. I don't even know if I did fall in love with him. But I was swept off my feet by his making love to me. It hadn't happened to me

182

for twelve years and I hadn't thought that anyone
would want to make love to me again. You don't
know what that means to a woman, John. Of
course I didn't mean to . . . to flirt with him. I
was just happy and enjoying myself and gradually
it happened—I found myself thinking all the time
about love and not caring at all—simply not bothering—about you. Then you were . . . I thought
you were rather horrid about it and I got angry
with you and that made me not try to . . . resist
him, as I knew I ought to. I suppose I really was
rather in love with him by then, but much more with
being in love."

Hilary was silent for a moment but John did not
speak, only held her closely to him. She went on :
" He urged me to go away with him. I knew he
didn't mean for good—that it would only be for a
short time and then he would get tired of me, as he
had of other women. But I didn't seem to care ; I
wanted the excitement, the adventure—something I
could look back on all the rest of my life. Every
woman, in her heart, longs for adventure, you know,
John—even if she knows it's not a very fine one.
I'm afraid I must blow my nose, John."

Surreptitiously Hilary dabbed the tears that were
filling her eyes.

" I'm afraid I didn't try very hard to resist. I
was really . . . awfully surprised at myself. I
seemed like some other woman. I just let myself
go. I'm afraid I even rather enjoyed . . . intriguing
. . . deceiving you. You remember that letter—
the second letter—I had from Gwen Farnes. Well,
it wasn't what I said it was. I had written to ask
Gwen if I could join her party after the week-end.

I meant to go on to her after . . . after being in Norwich with Dallas. I thought I could take photographs of the party and be able to describe it, so as to make you think I had really been there all the time. Oh, it was horrible of me, John ; I can't think how I could do it ! . . . She wrote back that the sailing party was off, but she would love to see me at any time ; would I come to her house in Norwich for a day or two ? That was what was in the letter that I handed to you to read. Of course I knew you wouldn't read it."

" How on earth did you know that ? " John had found himself becoming interested in the story—and hardly horrified at all.

" Because I knew you, you old silly." Hilary had caught the note in his voice—he wasn't disgusted, hardly even angry, and her courage came back to her. " You were cross and on your dignity— nothing would have induced you to touch the damn letter."

She gave a little laugh and John a rueful smile.

" Of course you didn't, but you came with me to the station, like the dear you are. I hated myself more then than at any other time and I very nearly didn't go. But I hadn't got the courage to turn back—it would have meant telling you everything. We had arranged that Dallas should go to Norwich in the car and meet me at the station. But he dug me out of the train at Fakenham and we drove the rest of the way together. I was horribly nervous, John, and not enjoying myself a bit. He gave me some wine for lunch and that made me feel reckless again. We went to a cinema and saw Adolphe Menjou making love to such a lovely girl—I can't

remember her name. He does it beautifully, John,
and I felt terribly romantic."

"My God, Menjou!" exclaimed John; women
were incomprehensible.

"We had tea in a rather jolly restaurant and went
to the hotel where Dallas had taken rooms. I felt
sleepy and said I wanted to rest till dinner—I
suppose it was the wine. I went up to my room
and put on a wrap and lay down—and actually went
to sleep. Suddenly I woke up—and Dallas was in
the room, bending over me. He kissed me and . . .
and . . . made love to me. I was horribly
frightened, partly because I wasn't properly awake.
I suddenly realised that I didn't . . . that I
couldn't . . . love him like that. I asked him to
go, and he wouldn't. He thought—or pretended to
think, that I was leading him on. He only laughed
and caught hold of me and . . . he looked horrible;
his eyes . . . I tore myself away and ran into the
bathroom and locked the door. He banged on it
but I didn't answer. After a time he said something about 'waiting till tonight' and went away.
I was afraid to come out for some time, in case he
was waiting for me, but at last I did and the room
was empty. I locked the door."

John could feel his wife trembling in his arms. He
felt no anger with her, only pity—and intense love.
He stroked her hair and whispered in her ear.

"My darling. My poor darling."

Hilary went on, the words tumbling over one
another.

"I dressed again and packed my bag and looked
out into the corridor. It was empty. I didn't dare
go down the front stairs, for fear of meeting him in

the hall. I went down the back stairs and out by the back-door. I didn't meet a soul ; it was between tea and dinner and no one was about. Out in the street I soon found a taxi and drove to Gwen's house. Fortunately she was there and alone. I told her I had made a muddle about the day or something ; I was too upset to think of a proper story. I don't know whether she believed me but she didn't ask a question. She's a darling."

John nodded.

" Yes ", he said. " Good friend."

" I stayed with her till I came back here on Wednesday. We didn't do anything special. I didn't see Dallas again. I don't know what became of him. I didn't see him till . . . Friday. It was rather dreadful being left alone with him when you said you would go and look for Beryl."

Hilary looked anxiously at her husband. He was staring out of the window and did not speak.

" John ", she said nervously ; " I don't want you to think that I think that . . . because . . . nothing actually happened, I think it's all right . . . that I haven't done anything wrong. Of course it's just as bad—worse really, because I simply ran away—funked. It was mean and cowardly, as well as beastly."

Hilary was silent. In the last few minutes John's face had grown suddenly white and haggard.

" My God ", he muttered. " And you didn't . . ."

Hilary shook her head.

CHAPTER XV

WHEN Inspector Lamming, in his office at Great
Hayworth, received Police-Constable Pentwhistle's
telephone message that the body of a well-known
resident of Bryde-by-the-Sea had been found in the
saltings, death having been evidently due to drowning, he automatically passed the information on to
his Superintendent at Dersingham. Having done so,
he proceeded to finish his breakfast, shave his blue
and bristly chin, tell his wife what he thought about
people who got drowned on a Sunday morning, and
then—still without undue haste—climbed into his
official car and drove along the winding, narrow
lanes to Bryde.

Inspector Lamming was a tall, square-shouldered
man with bushy eyebrows, clipped moustache, and a
deep cleft in his massive chin. He was a Norfolk
man but had been born, educated, and trained in
Norwich and had not yet got accustomed to the
leisurely speech and apparent dullness of the sea-
board folk ; the result was that he was in a constant
state of irritation, which did not improve his useful-
ness as an officer or his popularity with his men.
He had on the present occasion some grounds for
annoyance ; he had been up most of the last two
nights on a wild-goose chase after poachers who were
reported to be taking advantage of the thick weather
to do a little unauthorised deer-stalking in Lord

Fakenham's great park at Statcham ; a long, cold
vigil in the fog had been unrewarded even by the
sight or sound of a poacher, and Lamming had
counted on a comfortable Sunday morning in his
garden to make up for his lack of proper sleep.
However, duty was duty, and a Found Drowned,
though no matter for excitement in this part of the
world, had to be investigated and reported on as a
matter of routine.

It was no great distance to Bryde and the official
Morris was soon running between the squat, flint-
walled houses. The Inspector noticed that there
were no groups of fisher-folk hanging about, as he
would have expected, but that from most of the
doorways a head was protruding, evidently watching
something further down the road. A moment later
the explanation of this phenomenon was in sight—a
blue figure stumping ponderously down the middle
of the street ; Lamming ran his car up alongside it
and pulled up with a jerk.

" What are you doing here, Pentwhistle ? " he
asked sharply. " Why aren't you with the body ? "

Police-Constable Pentwhistle saluted.

" The body's under lock and key, sir ", he said.
" I've been investigating the circumstances."

" Under lock and key ? What the devil d'you
mean ? Why's it been moved ? "

Pentwhistle saluted again.

" The removal was carried out before my arrival,
sir. The fisher-folk brought it in. I reported the
fact of death, sir, and then proceeded . . ."

" Oh, get in the car, man ; don't stand there
jawing like an animated dummy."

The Inspector let his clutch in with a jerk.

" Where is it now, anyhow ? And why aren't you with it ? "

" When I arrived, sir, the body had been taken to the ' Anchorage ' hotel and deposited in an out-house. I cleared the public out, locked the door, and laid information by telephone, sir. Next turn on the left, sir."

" And where are you coming from now, eh ? "

" Mr. Pansel's, sir. Believed to have been last seen with the deceased."

" How d'you know that ? "

" From information received, sir. I . . . here we are, sir ; this shed on the left."

Inspector Lamming pulled up the Morris and stared at a figure in dark blue trousers and old grey flannel jacket which was standing correctly at ease in front of the shed referred to.

" Who the devil's that ? "

" Name of Tasson. He's a Special Constable, sir."

" Special Constable ! " There was an infinity of contempt in the Inspector's tone. " What's he doing, anyhow ? "

" When I proceeded on my investigations, sir, I thought it wise to leave the body under official supervision, sir. Tasson was there and after locking the door I mounted him, sir. He has the key in his possession but orders not to give it up to anyone but you, sir."

Lamming heaved himself out of the car.

" I'll have something to say to you about this later, Pentwhistle ", he said.

He approached the sentry, who came smartly to attention.

"Give me that key", Lamming said gruffly. "Now you can clear out."

Jude Tasson, who was reputed to be something of a wag, turned smartly to his right on heel and toe, executed a Guardsman's salute, and marched off in quick time. Inspector Lamming unlocked the door of the shed and pushed it open. The interior was dimly lit by a dirty window at the end ; round the walls were heaped benches, table-tops, trestles, an old bicycle, worn-out motor tyres ; in the centre, on a trestle-table lay a figure shrouded in an old sail.

Inspector Lamming brusquely pulled off the covering and looked down on the dead face of Dallas Fiennes.

"Gentleman, eh ? " he asked after a pause.

"Novelist, sir ", corrected Pentwhistle.

"What happened to him ? Lose his way in the fog and fall in ? "

Police-Constable Pentwhistle looked knowing.

"I wouldn't like to say that, sir."

"What d'you mean by that ? "

"Acting on information received, sir, I . . ."

"What the devil d'you mean by that ? " the Inspector asked irritably. "D'you mean someone told you ? "

"Not exactly, sir. I received information . . ."

"Damn it, man ; how ? "

Pentwhistle scratched his head. He liked to tell a tale in his own way, but superior authority was superior authority.

"Well, sir ", he said, "you'll likely know that these folks don't like talking—not to the police, that is. They keeps what they knows to themselves."

"Good lord, don't I know it ! " said Lamming

bitterly. " They only talk when they've got nothing to tell."

" That's right, sir. Still, in the matter of duty I passed the question round who had seen deceased last. Nobody spoke up and I didn't expect they would, so I cleared them out, locked the door, and came to telephone to you. On my return here I looked over the body and in course of doing so opened the jacket and found this bit o' paper against deceased's chest."

Pentwhistle drew from his pocket a dirty and crumpled piece of paper on which was scrawled in ill-formed letters :

He ad supper with Mtr Pansel Friday night.

Inspector Lamming turned the paper over in his fingers.

" How d'it get there ? " he asked. " It's not wet."

" No, sir. I observed that."

" Did you ! And someone put it there while you were telephoning ? "

" Oh, no, sir ; the door was locked and I had the key."

" Another key, or someone got in through the window."

" No, sir ", said Pentwhistle firmly.

" You mean that it was there before you asked the question ? Before you turned up ? "

" So I took it, sir."

For a moment the Inspector seemed interested, then shrugged his shoulders.

" What's it matter anyway ? " he said. " Tell me how the body was found, and where."

Pentwhistle told him. Mrs. Barle, going over the saltings early to explain her failure to ' do ' Mr.

Fiennes on Saturday had seen the body lying in the
muddy bottom of a branch of the creek which wound
in and out of the saltings and which at that point
ran beside the raised bank along which she was
walking. It had been nearly low tide then and the
body had been lying high and more or less dry in
the mud. Lying on its front it had been ; so much
the ' folks ' had vouchsafed ; so much indeed was
evident from the condition of the body and its
clothing.

" He lived on the sand-dunes, didn't he ? " asked
Lamming, who had heard of the odd behaviour of
this wealthy story-teller. " That path would be the
way he went to his hut, eh ? " he added.

" That's it, sir."

" Plain enough, then. He lost his way in the
thick weather. We've only to establish time and
cause of death and notify the coroner. Super's
bringing the surgeon. What was that you said about
who'd seen him last ? "

Pentwhistle had been patiently awaiting this for
the last twenty minutes. He squared his shoulders.

" Acting on information received, sir, I proceeded
to the house of Mr. John Pansel, artist, with whom
deceased took supper on Friday night. Deceased
left Mr. Pansel's house at or about ten p.m. in
company with Mr. Pansel and proceeded to the
harbour. It was very thick. Mr. Pansel saw him
across to the other side and returned home. Or so
he says."

" What d'you mean by that ? "

" We've only his word for it, sir, that he left
deceased there."

" Why ? What are you driving at ? "

" It's well known, sir . . ."

The hoot of a motor horn and a crunching of wheels on gravel interrupted him.

" There's the Super ", said Lamming, looking out of the door.

A tall, heavily-built man in uniform, with silver braid on his peaked cap, slowly extracted himself from the driving seat of yet another blue Morris ; from the near-side seat emerged a smaller man in plain clothes, carrying a bag. Inspector Lamming greeted his chief with a smart salute.

" Body's in here, sir, removed by the inhabitants before we came on the spot."

Superintendent Jett smiled.

" Yes, I was directed here ", he said. " My informant was very reluctant, though, to give even that much information away. What's the case, Lamming ? "

" Found drowned, sir ; lost his way in the fog and fell into one of those mud-holes in the saltings."

" Oh ? how d'you know that ? "

" That's where he was found, sir. Seems plain enough."

" It's not quite plain to me why a man should drown because he falls into some mud and water ", commented the Superintendent. " Still, that's purely a matter of conjecture ; we want facts. Dr. Turl here will give us the first of them."

Lamming saluted the divisional surgeon.

" It's not very light in here, sir ", he said. " Will you be able to manage ? "

" Yes, for a preliminary examination, if you shove the table nearer the window."

Dr. Turl was a quiet, grey-faced man with a

clipped moustache. He watched the table moved by the police officers and then bent over the body.

"We'll leave you in peace till you want us, doctor", said the Superintendent. "Come on, Lamming; you can tell me all about it while we're waiting."

Leaving Pentwhistle to guard the door the two officers walked slowly down the road, Superintendent Jett listening while his subordinate talked. Actually, the Inspector had not much to tell.

"Very annoying the body being moved, sir", he concluded. "People ought to know better than that by now, but these fisher-folks—well, they're a slow-witted lot, to my mind."

"I was a fisherman myself before I joined the force", said the Superintendent with a smile, "and my father before me."

Inspector Lamming blushed.

"Beg your pardon, sir, I'm sure", he said awkwardly.

"I don't mind at all, but you'll make a mistake, Lamming, if you underrate the intelligence of these people. They're slow to speak, a little slow in thought—but they've got all their wits about them. When you think they're being stupid it's generally because they mean you to; they don't give much away. Native caution, inborn in every one of them."

"Doesn't make our job any easier, sir", said Lamming.

"It doesn't. One's got to use one's eyes more than one's ears in these parts—and one's brains more still. You think it's a clear case of accident?"

"Oh, I've no information yet to form an opinion on", said the Inspector, "but it seems to me very likely. It's been very thick the last two nights; Fiennes lived on the sand-dunes and used to walk across the saltings to get to his hut—that much I've heard before. There'd be nothing odd about his meeting with an accident like this in thick weather. The mud in these side creeks is very deep and holding —if he was to fall in at low tide."

Superintendent Jett remained silent.

" Police-Constable Pentwhistle there has got some story about Fiennes having supper with a Mr. Pansel, an artist gentleman, on Friday night and their both going together to the saltings. He seems to think it's suspicious, but if you ask me it's just some old wives' gossip he's got hold of."

" Well, it's all guessing at the moment anyhow ", said the Superintendent. " Oh, there's the doctor."

Dr. Turl had emerged from the shed with his bag, which he put in the police car. Then he walked to meet the two police-officers.

" As far as one can tell at first sight, it's a case of either drowning or suffocation ", he said. " I can't tell which for certain till I've looked into his lungs. There are certain indications of suffocation—purple colouring, for instance, but the skin's so sodden that it's difficult to be sure. There's mud in the mouth and nose, which shows at any rate that he fell into mud—not water. Still, it doesn't follow that that killed him. If there's salt water in his lung he drowned. Apart from that, there is one slight abrasion on the top of the head that you'd better look at. It's nothing much, but there's been some swelling and the skin is cut."

The two police-officers followed Dr. Turl into the shed and closely examined the wound on the dead man's head. There was no blood on it and it would probably have escaped the notice of a layman.

" Difficult to say how much it bled after all the washing it's had ", said Dr. Turl, " but I should say not much."

" Would you say it would take much force to do that ? " asked Superintendent Jett. " I mean, could he have done it by a fall ? "

" Oh, yes, though that's not the place you usually fall on, except from a considerable height—and then you do more than that."

The Superintendent eyed his companion gravely.

" You think he was hit, eh ? " he asked at last.

" It's not my job to think that, one way or the other ", said the surgeon. " He *could* have been hit there ; a blow on the head from a stick might have caused that wound. That's all I'm prepared to say."

Jett nodded.

" And would you say it would take a severe blow to do that, sir ? I mean, would it have to be a deliberate, muscular blow—not just an accidental swing ? "

Dr. Turl considered before answering.

" I can see that that may be an important point ", he said. " I'd rather not answer till I've made a more thorough examination."

" Right, sir. Now, about time of death ? "

Dr. Turl shrugged his shoulders.

" Impossible to say at all accurately. There's no putrefaction or swelling. The skin's bleached, of course ; that would happen after a couple of tides. Rigor's going off, so he's probably been dead at least twenty-four hours. But that's no certainty—

so many considerations affect rigor. At the moment I'm not going to commit myself to anything closer than ' not less than 12 hours nor more than 3 days '."

Superintendent Jett made a grimace.

" That's not too helpful, doctor ", he said. " I'll not press you closer now, but if when you've made your full examination you can boil it down a bit closer, I should be grateful."

" I'll try, but I can't promise. Sorry to be so unhelpful. When'll you be going back, Mr. Jett ? "

" Well, I ought to go and have a look at the place. I arranged for the ambulance to follow us as soon as possible to take the body back. It ought to be here any minute now. If you wouldn't mind going back in that, sir, it'd give me a freer hand as to time."

" That'll do me all right. I'll get my bag out of your car."

" Then we'll get along and have a look round. You must stay in charge here, Constable. Who can show us the place ? "

" Old Giles Banyatt'll show you, sir. He's got an old tub in the harbour—ferries people across to the saltings. He'll take you across and show you the place—he's bound to know it, because he ferried the old woman over that found the body. There's not much water in yet ; you'll see it pretty much as it was when the body was found ; tide was not quite low then. You can't mistake him ; short, fat man with grey whiskers under his chin."

The description, if inaccurate, was clear enough. Superintendent Jett approached the old man, who was leaning against the stump of what had once been a cone-staff on the quay.

" Are you Giles Banyatt ? "

Giles looked at the uniformed officers, took a clay pipe from his mouth, and spat.

" That's as may be. What'll you be wanting ? "

The Superintendent smiled. The old man could have no earthly cause to conceal his identity, but Jett knew that he would part with no iota of information more than was necessary.

" We want to see where the body of this poor gentleman was found. I understand that you can show us the place and ferry us across."

Banyatt stared.

" Who'll 'ave told you that ? " he asked.

" About showing us the place ? The constable. Come on, please ; we haven't got much time."

" Tide's out ; you can walk across."

" Not without waders."

Giles glanced over his shoulder at the almost dry harbour.

" I doubt my boat's not afloat."

" A shove'll do that. Come on, Banyatt ; we'll pay your fare and something to take us to the spot."

That was too much for Giles. Slowly he waddled down the shelving beach to where his boat lay, half out of the shallow water, gave her one practised shove and held her while the two police-officers climbed aboard. There were literally only a few feet of water to be crossed, but enough to have given the two uniformed men uncomfortably wet boots and trousers. Giles led the way up the steps on to the raised bank ; slowly he waddled along it in his clumsy thigh boots, answering an occasional question monosyllabically, whenever that was possible. The day was gloriously fine, as if to make up for thirty-six hours of gloom which had preceded it ; gulls were floating gracefully in the air, terns diving swiftly into the shallow waters of the creek ; in the pool, a boat with red-brown sails was tacking from side to side—evidently its master was practising the art as he did not attempt to make out to sea and there was not enough water to take him up the creek. Jett looked about him with keen appreciation ; his work did not often bring him to this part of the coast and the peacefulness of the scene enchanted him.

*After walking about half a mile the three men came to a place where the raised bank turned sharply to the left and here Banyatt halted. It did not need any word from him to tell the police-officers that this was the spot at which the tragedy had occurred ; at their feet there opened a wide and slimy cut in the saltings, the surface of which was scored by the marks of many feet, while the bank itself showed where men had heaved themselves and their burden out onto its firm ground. There were a few inches of water in the lowest part of the cut, but the tide was still low enough n'ot to have reached this distant backwater of the winding creek.

Superintendent Jett looked down into the muddy hole and then back over his shoulder at the path along which they had come.

" Anyone coming along this path from the village in the dark or in a fog might fall straight in here, where the path turns, if he wasn't careful ", he said.

Old Giles gave a sniff, but made no comment. No native of the coast, he probably thought, would do anything so stupid, even if his legs were not under full control.

" That's what I thought, sir ", said Inspector

* See Frontispiece.

Lamming. "Clear enough case of accident, it seems—if it weren't for that . . ."

A sharp sideways kick on the ankle checked him. Superintendent Jett turned to the old fisherman.

"Did you have difficulty in walking about in that mud when you got the body out ? " he asked. "Your footmarks seem to go in pretty deep."

"Ay ; it's much as you can do to get yourself out of that mud once you're in it ", replied Giles, in the longest speech that he had yet made.

"A man who fell in there, if he fell flat, might have difficulty in getting out ? "

But this was a hypothetical question to Giles ; who would fall flat in mud ?

"I couldn't say that ", he replied.

Jett thought that the old man would be little more use and his presence would handicap them in their investigations.

"I won't keep you any longer now, Giles ", he said, "but you might tell me who was with you when you took out the body."

That, however, was asking too much—a definite question involving the movements of other people. Giles ' hadn't rightly noticed ', there were ' a many of them ', ' that Tasson ' had been one—the only one to whom Giles would give a name. Jett wondered why an exception was made in his case. Probably he was not a native and so was not covered by the protective secrecy of the others. It might be worth looking into the matter.

When the old man had gone Superintendent Jett turned to his subordinate.

"Better not say anything about that cut on the head yet ", he said.

It was a mild enough rebuke but Lamming did not like it. His swarthy face took on a sullen look—which Jett ignored.

"We shan't get much out of that mud-hole", he said. "It's too slimy to show any distinguishing marks. It might be worth looking along the path, though, in case we pick up anything of interest. You work back towards the village ; I'll go on."

The surface of the path, which had been still wet from rain when Fiennes and Pansel had walked along it on Friday night was now dry, but there were still marks of footprints to be seen in places. Most of them were indistinct but here and there the typical criss-cross markings of a rubber soled boot could be distinguished. Jett had nearly reached the point where the path takes a final turn to the right, parallel with the Little Creek, when he paused and bent down to examine carefully a footmark in what had evidently been a deeper mud-filled hollow in the path than he had yet seen. In the surface of the mud, still soft underneath though crusted over, appeared the distinct mark of a rubber boot, the heel in particular having been driven deep into the mud. What interested Jett in particular was the fact that this heel showed a distinct marking, evidently that of a patch which had been added to replace an injury.

Superintendent Jett whistled up his Inspector and showed him the mark.

"I don't know that there's any significance in it", he said, "but it's a lovely clear mark—I'd like to take a cast of it. I don't know how many people use this path—where does it lead to, d'you know ?"

"Only to that post, sir ; the people who live on

the sand-dunes use the post to hitch their boats to at high tide, but I don't fancy there are many live there now, except this Fiennes. Of course there are a fair number of people—trippers mostly—who use this path at low tide because it's the short cut to the dunes and the seashore and you can paddle across Little Creek at low tide ; otherwise you have to go round by the footpath on the grassland—over there, sir."

Lamming pointed away to the east where, three-quarters of a mile away, another high bank marked the limit of the saltings on that side.

" Do the fishermen use this path ? "

" Not much, I shouldn't say, sir, except when tide's too low for them to run their boats up the creek ; but they generally time things so as to avoid that."

Superintendent Jett shook his head.

" I'm afraid there's not much in it ", he said, " but there's just one thing about it that strikes me, Lamming : this heel mark is unnaturally deep ; it looks to me as if whoever made it was carrying something heavy."

" Or running, sir."

" No ; in that case I think there'd have been more weight on the ball of the foot. There's nothing to connect it with Fiennes' death, but we'll just keep a look-out for the owner of this boot—in case."

" It might be Fiennes'."

" In that case we'll soon know—he's got gum-boots on now—short ones. May be more in his house."

The two men strolled back along the path,

pausing as they reached the bend where the body had been found. Suddenly Inspector Lamming bent down and examined a mark on the bank where the mud joined the firm ground.

" It wasn't Fiennes' foot made that mark, sir ", he said. " Look, here it is again—this one was made this morning. The tide's been over here two or three times since Fiennes fell in."

CHAPTER XVI

INSPECTOR LAMMING ASKS QUESTIONS

SUPERINTENDENT JETT nodded in acquiescence.

" Then there should be no difficulty in tracing it ", he said. " At the moment we won't make direct enquiries for it—that would only make them shut up more like clams than ever and we haven't any reason yet for assuming that it has any significance. But if we see that mark being made by anyone we'll just note who it is ; you can tell that constable of yours to keep his eyes skinned, too."

" Pentwhistle. Very good, sir."

" Now, I think I'll go on and have a look at Mr. Fiennes' house ; I've brought his keys along. I can probably wade across that little creek ; the tide doesn't seem to be very far up yet, and I can get back by the footpath over the grassland. I think you, Lamming, might go up and see Mr. Pansel ; find out if there's anything in this story of Pentwhistle's. Anyhow, find out exactly what did happen on Friday night, where Mr. Pansel parted from Fiennes, and so on. Then cut back home, get your dinner and attend to any other work that's got to be done. Meet me again at that shed where the body is at about three o'clock. Don't let Pentwhistle leave there till I arrive because I left my despatch case in the shed with the contents of the pockets in it."

Inspector Lamming saluted and walked off down

the raised bank towards the village. When he reached the harbour the tide had risen considerably and he had some difficulty in getting across, as old Giles had disappeared, probably for the free pint which his story would earn him. At last a young, dark-eyed fisherman strolled down to the beach and paddled leisurely across to rescue the Inspector.

Lamming climbed into the boat and after a careful look at his pilot asked :

" Your name's Madgek, isn't it ? "

Christian smiled.

" Not much use my denying it, Inspector. I don't even know that I want to."

The Inspector grunted.

" I've had my eye on you for some time, young man ", he said.

" On me, Inspector ? Whatever for ? "

" You know well enough. Where were you last night and the night before ? "

Guileless innocence shone from Christian's grey eyes, fringed by their curling black lashes.

" Why, in bed, of course, Inspector. We quiet folks go to bed very early in these parts."

" Yes, and get up early too, I reckon ; damned early. I'll have more to say to you about that."

The boat grounded and Madgek, stepping into the water, gave Lamming a hand to jump ashore dry-shod. As they walked up the slope of muddy sand the Inspector glanced back at their footprints ; there was no patch on the heel of this pair of thigh boots, anyhow.

" Were you with the men that moved Fiennes' body ? " he asked sharply.

Christian's lip curled.

" Ah, you've frightened me now, Inspector ", he said. " I'm afraid to give myself away."

Lamming scowled.

" I'll find out all I want to without your telling me ", he said. " The body ought never to have been moved, anyway."

" Come to that, I suppose it ought never to have been there at all, ought it, Inspector ? "

Without bothering to answer this frivolous question Inspector Lamming left his companion and walked along the harbour front to the ' Anchorage '. Having given Pentwhistle his orders and enquired the whereabouts of Pansel's house he got into his car and drove there. As he applied his somewhat noisy brakes he noticed that the figure of a man at an upper window of the little house disappeared. Walking up the path he knocked on the door, which was presently opened by a woman whom he rightly guessed to be Mrs. Pansel.

" Mr. Pansel in, ma'am ? " he asked, instinctively touching his cap. He noticed that the woman's face, though attractive, was white and drawn.

" I . . . I'll see. Will you come in ? "

" Thank you, ma'am. I will. I'm Inspector Lamming."

In the living-room, with the door closed on him, Lamming listened carefully to the departing footsteps, which were apparently making for the kitchen. There was silence, then the creak of a stair, and a long pause.

" What's all the mystery about ? " wondered the police-officer, his interest quickening.

After an appreciable time heavier steps were heard

descending the stairs and a big man with hard eyes and a set mouth appeared in the doorway.

" Are you wanting me ? I've already told all I know to a police-constable."

" About what, sir ? "

" About what ? " The big man stared, then stammered slightly. " W-why, about Mr. Fiennes ; about his dining here on Friday night. Wasn't that what you wanted ? "

" That's quite right, sir ", returned Lamming blandly. " I understand that Mr. Fiennes supped with you on Friday night and that you walked down to the harbour with him afterwards. Is that correct, sir ? "

" Yes."

" You put him across the water onto that bank with a path along it ? "

" Yes."

" And then came back yourself ? "

" Yes."

" Straight back ? "

" Yes."

Lamming saw that the big man's eyes were fixed on him—apparently on his lips—in a stare of concentrated effort, as if he were trying to read his questions before they were uttered. His own interest deepened.

" You didn't take him all the way home—or rather, along the bank ? "

" No. I told you I came straight back from the harbour."

" Why didn't you go all the way back with him, sir ? "

" It wasn't necessary. The fog had lifted a bit."

" Had it, sir ?   I was out myself all that night and I didn't notice it lift at all."

John Pansel scowled.

" I tell you it did ", he said roughly.

" Very well, sir ; we'll leave it at that.   Had you any reason for going to the harbour at all ?   Mr. Fiennes wasn't . . . incapable, was he ? "

" No, he wasn't.   I've told your constable all this."

Lamming saw a bead of sweat run down his companion's forehead.   It was a warm day, but . . . the Inspector himself was cool enough in this airy room.

" Had he not drunk anything at all for supper ? "

" Oh, yes, a little, of course."

" What, sir ? "

" Oh, whisky I think."

" That all, sir ? "

To Lamming's surprise, a flicker of a smile crossed Pansel's face.

" That's positively all, Inspector ", he said lightly.

Hilary Pansel, listening at the door, wondered why her husband so carefully refrained from mentioning the wonderful brandy that they had all drunk that night.   There must, she thought, be something odd about that brandy.

Inside the room Inspector Lamming was cogitating his next line of enquiry.   A vital question had yet to be asked and the Superintendent had not told him whether to ask it or not ; he had only told him not to talk about it.   On the whole, Lamming decided that he was here to find out what he could and that covered this point ; if he went about it carefully he need give nothing away.

"Can you tell me, sir ", he asked, " whether Mr. Fiennes met with any accident on the night of his . . . that's to say, on the night he supped with you, Friday night ? "

John Pansel's eyes narrowed. There was an appreciable pause before he answered.

"What sort of accident do you mean ? " he asked.

"Well, any sort of accident, sir."

"You don't mean . . . well, he fell into a mud-hole in the saltings, didn't he ? I don't know when that happened, of course ", he added hastily.

Inspector Lamming looked at him curiously.

"I wasn't referring to his being drowned, sir," he said. "Did he receive any kind of injury ? "

Pansel's face cleared.

"Oh, you mean that crack on the head ? " he said with a laugh. "Yes, he got a knock when he was fetching some beer from the cupboard under the stairs."

Inspector Lamming's face expressed surprise. It seemed to him improbable that a guest would fetch beer from a cupboard under the stairs.

"Did you see the accident, sir ? " he asked.

Pansel shook his head.

"No ", he said ; "as a matter of fact I wasn't here at the time."

Surprise gave place to incredulity. Not here ? ! the host ? Suddenly a thought occurred to him. He leaned forward.

"This wasn't a tête-à-tête dinner by any chance, sir ? " he asked sharply.

John Pansel shot him an angry look.

"Certainly not. I went down the road to see if I could meet Miss Helliott, who was supposed to be

209

coming to supper too. She didn't come, because of
the fog, so I came back."

The sudden burst of anger had given John Pansel
assurance. He was speaking now in a more confident
voice. Inspector Lamming glanced back over the
pages of his notebook ; suddenly he looked up.

" I thought you said you drank whisky that night,
sir ? "

" So I did ; what about it ? "

" Then why was he fetching beer ? "

Lamming's voice had a ring of eagerness in it ;
had he trapped this careful witness ?

" The last bottles of beer we had were broken
when Mr. Fiennes hurt himself."

A pat answer—too pat, thought the Inspector.
Still, he was in no position to refute it.

" This accident, sir," he asked ; " did it seem to
injure Mr. Fiennes much ? "

" Oh, no ; made him feel a bit silly for a minute
as one does when one gets a crack on the head ;
never had one, Inspector ? "

There was a glint in John Pansel's eye as he asked
the question. Inspector Lamming ignored it.

" He wasn't still feeling the effects when he went
home ? "

Pansel hesitated for a moment ; then :

" He might have been, of course. He didn't say
anything to me about it."

Lamming closed his note-book and stood up.
He saw Pansel's face clear, evidently at the prospect
of an end to his interrogation.

" I suppose, sir, you can't suggest any explanation
of Mr. Fiennes' death ? " Lamming's voice was
almost casual as he asked his last question.

Pansel shook his head.

" Only the obvious one," he said. " It looks as if he had stumbled into the mud in the fog and hadn't been able to get out."

Lamming nodded.

" Yes, sir ", he said ; " it does . . . look like that."

He walked to the door.

" And now I'd like a word with Mrs. Pansel ", he said.

Instantly the artist's face clouded. Lamming saw his fist clench convulsively.

" Surely that's not necessary ", he exclaimed. " I've told you all we know about the matter."

Inspector Lamming raised his eyebrows.

" All *you* know, you mean, don't you, sir ? "

" All *we* know. We were together all the time Mr. Fiennes was with us."

" Were you ? I thought you said you were out of the house when the . . . alleged accident happened."

" Only for a minute or two. And what do you mean by ' alleged ' ? "

" Only that I haven't yet had direct evidence of it, sir. Your evidence, of course, is only hearsay—if you were out of the house at the time."

John Pansel shifted his feet. After a moment's hesitation he said :

" Very well ; I'll fetch my wife. You've no objection to my being present ? "

Inspector Lamming smiled.

" Oh, every objection, sir. That would be quite irregular."

With a shrug of the shoulders John Pansel turned

and opened the door. Neither man had heard the
quick patter of feet as Hilary disappeared towards
the kitchen at mention of her name. At John's call
she re-appeared.

"The Inspector wants to ask you a question or
two", said her husband gruffly.

"That's right, ma'am; just one or two. And
I'm sure, sir. that Mrs. Pansel'll be able to answer
much more easily if I have her undivided attention.
It's your house, but . . ." (he looked significantly
at the front door) ". . . if you *would* be so obliging?"

With a last movement of hesitation and another
shrug, John Pansel left the house, giving Hilary one
quick, anxious glance as he disappeared.

"Now, madam", said Lamming cheerfully,
"while we're out in the passage perhaps you'll tell
me just what did happen to Mr. Fiennes on Friday
night."

Hilary's eyes widened with alarm.

"I . . . I don't know", she stammered.

"I mean about that little accident he had . . .
to his head."

"Oh, that." She could not quite keep the relief
from her voice and Lamming could not fail to notice
it. "He hit his head on that cupboard; he was
getting something out for me."

"Getting what, ma'am?"

"Some bottles of beer; he dropped them both—
broke them."

"Were there any more?"

"No."

Pat again. But perhaps immaterial.

"You saw the accident?"

"No, I was in the living-room, laying the table."

"Oh . . . h." There was significance in the Inspector's exclamation. "So you didn't see the accident yourself?"

"No."

Lamming leaned towards her.

"Then how do you know there was an accident?" he asked deliberately.

Involuntarily Hilary shrank back.

"I . . . he told me. I heard a crash and a . . . a cry, and I ran out to see what had happened. Mr. Fiennes was holding his head and the bottles were on the floor, broken."

"I see. And your husband; where was he?"

"He'd gone down the road to meet Miss Helliott."

"And how d'you know that, ma'am?"

"He told me."

Inspector Lamming nodded slowly.

"I see," he said again, deliberately. "He told you and Mr. Fiennes told you. And you yourself . . . know nothing about it?"

"Oh, yes I do. I've told you that I came out at once and saw Mr. Fiennes standing there . . . and the broken bottles."

Hilary's face was white, her eyes fixed anxiously upon the aggressive face of the police-officer. Lamming enjoyed the sensation of power which her looks gave him.

"And you bandaged him up, ma'am?"

"Not bandaged. I put some iodine on the place."

"It was a bad cut?"

"Oh, no; it raised a bit of a lump and the skin was cut, but that was all."

"Not enough to make him feel bad when he left here—stagger and that like?"

" Oh, no."

" Ah ; now Mr. Pansel thought it might."

Hilary bit her lip. She did not know what John had said. He had been so odd about the drinking—making light of it to the constable. Now it seemed . . . Oh, why couldn't he just tell the exact truth.

" Now, perhaps you'll just show me the cupboard where this accident happened, ma'am."

Relieved at being able to do anything so simple, Hilary led Lamming the few steps to the cupboard under the stairs and opened it. The Inspector took a small torch from his pocket and examined the lintel.

" No sign of anything here, ma'am. No blood or hairs."

" There wouldn't be, would there ? "

Lamming shrugged his shoulders.

" There aren't, anyhow."

He knelt down and examined the floor, which was made of tiles, as was the floor of the passage.

" No broken glass." He put his head down and sniffed. " No smell of beer."

" But I swept up the glass and washed the floor yesterday morning."

Hilary's voice was plaintive. Her own word was being doubted now ; that was intolerable.

Lamming rose to his feet.

" Perhaps you'll show me what you put on the gentleman's head ? " he asked.

Hilary turned quickly on her heel and ran up the stairs, returning almost at once with a small bottle of iodine.

" There," she exclaimed, thrusting it into Lamming's hand.

The Inspector smiled and calmly pocketed the bottle.

"I'll keep it for a day or two if I may, ma'am. Just confirmation. I think you've told me all I want to know."

He walked down the little passage towards the front door, but stopped beside the coat pegs and picking up the skirt of John's mackintosh which hung there, examined it carefully. Hilary watched him with ill-concealed anxiety.

"This Mr. Pansel's mac, ma'am?" the Inspector asked.

Hilary nodded.

"Keeps it very clean, doesn't he?"

Lamming's hand felt the lining of the skirt, then of the sleeve.

"It's all damp. Has he been in the water lately?"

Hilary felt her heart throbbing violently. What was she to say? What had John said? What did they know?

"I . . . I don't know. He may have."

"Or has it been washed?"

Lamming's face was thrust forward towards hers. She stared, almost hypnotised, at the fierce grey eyes. She did not answer. She *could* not answer.

The Inspector took a quick step to the front door and threw it open. John Pansel was at the garden gate, watching the house.

"Will you come in a minute, sir, please?"

Automatically John obeyed. Lamming pointed at the mackintosh.

"Have you been washing that mac?"

John shot a quick glance, over the policeman's shoulder, at his wife. Her eyes signalled dismay.

" Yes, I have," he said. " What of it ? "

" Why have you washed it ? "

" Because it was muddy. As a matter of fact I got it muddy on Friday night. I slipped as I was getting out of the boat and fell in the mud."

" Mud ? It's sand in the harbour, isn't it ? "

" Very muddy sand. My coat was dirty anyhow, so I took the opportunity of washing it."

Inspector Lamming frowned. Always the man had an answer. But he felt that there was something wrong, something he ought, by skilful questioning, to expose. He racked his brains for the vital question. Suddenly a thought struck him.

" What time did you get back here on Friday night ? "

John Pansel felt the blood slowly drain from his face, drain—it seemed—from his heart. It was the one question of all others he had dreaded. *He did not know whether his return at* 1 *a.m. had been seen.* The police evidently knew a good deal. Somebody might have followed him—that figure in the mist that Fiennes and he had seen on the quay. He dared not be caught out in a lie about so vital a matter.

" I don't know exactly," he said, " but it was pretty late. I lost my way in the mist."

" Lost your way ? I thought you said the mist had cleared."

" It did, but only for a time. Then it came down again thicker than ever."

" You found your way down to the harbour all right, with Mr. Fiennes."

" Yes, but I had a torch. When I fell getting out

of the boat my torch hit something and the bulb broke."

Inspector Lamming was looking past him at a little shelf above the umbrella-stand. On it lay a nickel torch.

" Is that it ? "

" Yes. But I . . ."

Lamming took a quick step forward, picked up the torch and slid forward the button. A gleam of light stabbed the shadow behind the door.

" . . . but I put a new bulb in yesterday."

The Inspector looked steadily at John Pansel, then slipped the torch into his pocket.

" I shall have to take this with me, sir," he said.

CHAPTER XVII

WHEN Lamming left him, Superintendent Jett stood for a few minutes looking down at the expanse of mud, scored with the marks of plunging feet, where for two nights and a day Dallas Fiennes' body had lain at the mercy of the rising and falling tide—lain within a few feet of the path along which at ordinary times people daily passed—may even have passed in those two days, but passed blinded by the shroud of mist which had hung over the sea-coast night and day. Had he lain there struggling, calling for help, unable to tear himself from the clinging, clutching mud ? Or had he fallen, stunned by a blow on the head, a helpless victim to the creeping waters ? Lifting his eyes Jett looked at one of the reaches of the creek, winding in and out through the saltings ; a trickle of water was moving slowly up it, creeping stealthily over the mud, stretching out fingers to one side and the other, rising steadily, remorselessly . . .

The big policeman gave an involuntary shudder. What a horrible death, trapped in the mud, to feel the water gradually creeping round and over your body, up to your craning neck, to your mouth, your nostrils . . . a gurgle, a choke, one last desperate effort, and then . . . darkness and oblivion.

" I'm getting imaginative," said the Superintendent aloud. " I'd better get looking for facts."

Walking back along the raised bank to the post at the end, he saw that since he had been here fifteen minutes ago ' Little Creek ' had spread into a considerable channel ; he doubted if he would even be able to wade across it. He noticed, however, that lying on the sand between him and the rising tide was a small boat ; if it had oars in it he would, he decided, take the liberty of borrowing it.

A minute's walk took him to the boat, a blue and white, flat-bottomed affair which would not require many inches of water to float it. There were a pair of oars, carefully shipped, and Jett, after lifting in the anchor, sat down in the boat and waited for the tide to float it. As he sat, his eyes instinctively ran over the boat and soon rested upon a strip of tin tacked to the stern ; a closer scrutiny showed him that it was a strip from a penny-in-the-slot machine and was stamped with the name ' Dallas Fiennes '.

Superintendent Jett whistled.

" His own boat. Wonder if this ought to tell me anything ? Yes, it ought. It could only get here when the tide was at least two hours before or after low tide—perhaps three hours. If Fiennes was the last man to use it, it ought to give one two pretty accurate alternatives as to when that was. That might be useful ; I'll jot it down."

By the time that the note had been taken and the note-book tucked back into a capacious breast-pocket the water was lapping round the boat. If Jett had known enough to wade and push for a bit he would soon have been in water deep enough to carry him ; as it was he had to wait another quarter of an hour before he felt the boat ride free. After that it was only a matter of five minutes before he was across to the other side, anchoring his borrowed vessel to the sloping beach of the sand dunes.

Drawing a bunch of keys from his pocket Superintendent Jett approached the hut which, from a distance, Giles Banyatt had pointed out to him as the novelist's. It was a more substantial building than the rest and stood apart from them. In its only door was a Yale lock, as well as an ordinary knob. Slipping the thin key into the lock Jett turned it and pushed open the door. It gave on to a large, light room, evidently the main living-room of the hut.

Crossing the threshold, Jett looked about him. The remains of a meal lay upon the table in the centre of the room ; in one of the windows another table was covered with sheets of manuscript and one or two reference books. On the floor lay a couple of envelopes and in the waste-paper basket a crumpled bill. The three latter Jett put in his pocket. Opening one of the two inner doors he found himself in a fair-sized bedroom, the bed of which had been roughly made. A pair of silk pyjamas hung over a chair, fur-lined slippers peered from underneath ; for the rest, the room was comparatively tidy. On a chair beside the bed lay a book and an electric torch, beside a candlestick with a short length of candle. The second door from the living-room led into a small kitchen ; the range showed a burnt-out fire, the table a litter of pots and pans in one of which were scrapings of the scrambled egg that Jett had already identified in the next room. Returning to the living-room, Jett gave another look round.

" Nothing to pick on here," he said. " I'll lock the place up and then if anything suspicious does crop up I can come back and look over his papers.

Personally I think he fell in and couldn't get out."

Superintendent Jett returned to his boat none too soon ; in the short time he had been away the tide had lifted it to the full stretch of its anchor cable which he had omitted to carry up the bank. The water now stretched right across the expanse of sand between the sand dunes and the raised bank ; Jett rowed across, tied his boat to the post and walked back along the path. Reaching the harbour, he too had to wait for a ferry across—Giles being still, presumably, engaged in gossip—and during his wait it dawned upon him that he was hungry. A glance at his watch told him the reason—it was nearly two o'clock. Fortunately for him a young man in a sailing boat presently appeared and, lowering his sail, ferried Jett across to the quay, from which a few minutes' walk took him to ' The Anchorage.' The body, he found, had been removed. Pentwhistle was still mounting guard over his Superintendent's despatch case. Jett dismissed him to get his belated dinner and himself sought the hospitality of Mr. Cadnall.

The proprietor of ' The Anchorage ' was a tall, florid man, who had more irons than one in the fire. A shrewd judge of the stock market, he was able to provide himself with enough money to lose in comfort on the turf. In addition, he was always ready to further, and to profit by, any of the little transactions beneath the rose in which sundry inhabitants of Bryde from time to time indulged. As a matter of policy, therefore, he was only too willing to oblige Superintendent Jett with a meal, a first. rate meal, too, at this late hour and tried his

best, though unsuccessfully, to refuse payment
for it.

Having the dining-room to himself, Jett invited
his host to take a glass of port with him and to give
him in return an outline of the affairs of the ' foreign
colony ' at Bryde.   John Pansel had always been
friendly with Cadnall, as well as with his two boys—
his mentors in the art of sailing—but Dallas Fiennes,
Sarne, and Vessle, having conferred most of their
patronage upon Sam Pete of ' The Virgin Duck ',
were not in Cadnall's best books.   He knew all about
the story of the novelist and Pansel's wife, but he
was not going to give his friend away for the sake of
a conceited fellow like Fiennes ; he painted a glowing
picture of the artist's moral character, pooh-poohed
the idea of any ground of quarrel between the two,
and overdid his advocacy to such an extent that
Superintendent Jett came away with the definite
impression that there was something to hide.

His next interview did nothing to dispel this.
Mrs. Barle, who not only looked after Fiennes' house
but had actually found the body, had obviously got
to be questioned, though if she were a typical native
Jett was not sanguine as to the information he would
get.   The sea-board folk were intensely secretive
about themselves and their doings, even in the most
trivial matters, and if obliged to give information
would always say whatever they thought most convenient, without any regard to its accuracy.   Mrs.
Barle, however, evidently did not consider her
employer's affairs needed this elaborate protection ;
she talked freely and—Jett thought—truthfully.
Her arrangement with Mr. Fiennes, she said, was to
' do his house out ' twice a week, on Tuesdays and

Saturdays, clean his cooking utensils, change his sheets on Saturdays, and attend to his washing. For these services she was paid the handsome sum of ten shillings a week.

Jett questioned her as to the days on which she did not attend and learnt that the novelist made his own bed, gave some sort of wash-up to his crockery, and on the whole was not quite so untidy as most men would be. Mrs. Barle explained, what Jett already knew, that owing to the fog she had not been over as usual on Saturday but had popped over early on Sunday morning to explain her absence and to promise a special visit on Monday ; work on the Holy Day she would not—not outside her own home, that was. It was in the course of this promissory visit that she had gone along the raised bank across the saltings, just before low tide, and had seen the poor gentleman's body stuck fast in the mud. Yes, face down he had been, and quite a job the men had had, she heard, to get him out. No, she had not seen the body removed—she didn't hold with corpses and had come home quick and taken a dish of tea to steady her nerves, after telling old Giles Banyatt of what she had found. No, to the hut she had not gone, not after seeing the poor gentleman lying there in the mud, past any help from her ; so that made it five days since she herself had been at Mr. Fiennes' hut.

On the question of Fiennes' relations with the other ' foreigners ' Mrs. Barle was loquacious and gave Jett the significant information that she had on more than one occasion carried a note from Mrs. Pansel to Mr. Fiennes, and *vice versa*. The last occasion on which she had done this was Tuesday week—yes, it would be the 12th. of July if the Superintendent said so. She had not, of course, seen the contents of any of these notes, such not being her way, but she had formed the opinion that the two persons concerned were carrying on in a way that was not right nor proper. She had had serious doubts as to whether she ought not herself to refuse to carry the notes but had feared to lose her job and she a widow with six.

Thanking Mrs. Barle for her help, Superintendent Jett made his way back towards 'The Anchorage', where he knew that Inspector Lamming—a punctual man—would be awaiting him. So far as he himself was concerned Jett saw very little reason to doubt that Dallas Fiennes' death was due to an accident. In his experience the simple, normal explanation of these affairs was usually the correct one. In this case there was a perfectly normal explanation; Fiennes might easily have lost his direction in the fog, stumbled into the creek, and been unable to free himself from the clinging mud. It was, perhaps, curious that no cries for help had been heard, but fisher-folk were early-bedders and heavy sleepers; alternatively, Fiennes, falling headlong, might have got his mouth choked with mud and been unable to shout. The one really questionable point was the wound on the dead man's head; that would have to be explained before all doubt could be dismissed.

The conversations which he had had with Vaughan Cadnall and Mrs. Barle certainly suggested that there had been 'something up' between Fiennes and Mrs. Pansel, but that was a long way from proving, or even suggesting, that Pansel was a murderer. It was quite enough, though, to set tongues wagging in this back-water—enough to account for that note that had been found on the body, some mischief-maker's contribution to the mystery. Long experience of the curiosity-ridden coast-folk taught Jett to discount evidence of this kind. No; unless Lamming had dug out something fresh or unless Dr. Turl's report opened up a new line of suggestion, Jett felt that a few more hours would see him through the police part of the investigation; he could then report to the coroner and the latter with his jury would no doubt bring in one or other of the common alternative verdicts: 'Found drowned' or 'Death by misadventure'.

Five minutes' conversation with the impatiently waiting Inspector, however, blew all this comfortable imagining to the winds. Still hot with suspicion, Lamming was able to paint such a vivid picture of the suspicious behaviour of the Pansels as, taken with the actual information which he had elicited, made it quite clear to Superintendent Jett that a really serious investigation of their relations with Fiennes would have to be made. For a moment he thought of going straight off and interviewing them himself but, after a little further thought, decided that precipitate action might do more harm than good. There were plenty of other enquiries to be made and, now that his suspicions had been seriously aroused, Superintendent Jett went about them with a will.

In the first place he set his Inspector the task of compiling a list of all the people who had been present when the body was removed. That point of the patched boot heel must be followed up; it might be—probably was—quite irrelevant to the enquiry, but it would be unwise to ignore it. For himself, after a quarter of an hour's reflection in the back seat of his car, he drew up a list of people to be questioned : Pete, the landlord of 'The Virgin Duck' at which—Cadnall had told him—both Fiennes and Pansel spent a good deal of their time ; Mr. Sarne and Mr. Vessle, the two 'foreigners' most commonly seen in their company ; young Mr. Helliott of Brulcote, who appeared to know the two principals ; the postman, Tasson, perhaps—about whom Jett's curiosity had been aroused. That would do for the moment ; no doubt other names would suggest themselves as the enquiry proceeded.

As it happened, the last name on the list was the first to be dealt with. If the truth were told, Jude Tasson had been hanging about most of the day in the vicinity of the 'Anchorage' in the hope of getting a word with the most important of the police officials. Jude was fond of attention, even of publicity, from which it may be gathered, as Superintendent Jett had guessed, that he was no native of Bryde-by-the-Sea, nor even of Norfolk. He was, in fact, a Londoner, and his presence and position in Bryde were due to his having married—or rather, been married by—the widowed post-mistress, for whom he now acted as supernumerary postman.

Jude Tasson, though a Londoner, was no cockney. The son of a successful small shopkeeper in Clapham he had been a sufficiently bright boy to win a scholarship at the local Secondary School, but this he had forfeited after a year by his incurable idleness, and he had then been set to work in his father's grocery store. This had been a failure from the first and the exasperated Mr. Tasson had drafted him

into a big warehouse owned by a friend, wherein
Jude, though still idle, was not allowed to display
his talent for impertinence and insubordination with
which, by the aid of a glib tongue, he had driven his
father to despair. The patience of the warehouse,
however, after a time wore thin and young Tasson
soon began to drift—was drifting definitely towards
trouble when war broke out in 1914. Jude enlisted
at once and was greatly improved by his five years'
service in the R.A.M.C., in which as an orderly his
nimble wit made him a favourite with the patients if
not with the senior staff. An attempt on the part
of an optimistic young Commandant to promote him
to a position of greater responsibility had ended after
six weeks with the ignominious removal of his short-
lived chevron. After the war Jude got a job at a
hospital, lost it, and had begun to drift again when
an ill-earned holiday jaunt with a friend had taken
him to Bryde-by-the-Sea ; here his light-hearted
spirits, shining in bright contrast to the guarded
solemnity of the natives, captured the heart of Mary
Lewison, widowed in the war and allowed by a
benevolent P.M.G. to keep on her husband's old
charge, which she had successfully controlled since
his departure to the recruiting-office.

Though he had lived in Bryde some thirteen years,
Jude Tasson was still regarded as a ' foreigner ', an
object of suspicion to the other folk, if also of considerable popularity among the young. For both
opinions there were good grounds ; his popularity
was easily accounted for by his high spirits, his
humour, and his friendliness ; but he was a ' talker ',
he could not keep his mouth shut, and this was a
source of positive danger to such of his associates as

engaged in minor activities not approved by the law—to them and to their relations, and that covered the greater part of the population. So while the children adored Jude the adults laughed at his pranks but kept their mouths shut in his presence—a practice which did not prevent him from knowing the greater part of what went on in the dark o' the moon.

Though itching with impatience to take the lime-light Jude had not dared to interrupt the big police officer, either during his conversation with the Inspector or while he sat pondering and writing in the back of the car. When, however, the great man emerged, looking for the moment—as he picked up the cap knocked off his greying head by the hood of the car—slightly less formidable, the Special-Constable-cum-Postman stepped forward and gave a smart salute.

" Eh, my lad ; what can I do for you ? "

" Beg your pardon, Mr. Superintendent, but I thought you might like to take my evidence."

" And what's your name ? "

" Tasson, sir—Jude Tasson. I'm the postman here and Special Constable ", Jude added with pride.

Jett smiled.

" Oh, yes. I heard that you had been on duty this morning ; very glad of your help."

" Thank you, sir. But I've got some evidence to give."

Jett nodded. He expected nothing of interest ; a glance had shown him what type of man Tasson was, explained why his name was not included in the local conspiracy of silence.

" You were one of the men who moved the body."

Jude looked slightly disappointed—he would have liked to announce his own importance himself ; then he looked slightly pleased—the police were evidently interested in him.

" That's right, Mr. Superintendent ; I was there ", he said, " and what's more, I used my eyes."

He paused, to give weight to his words.

" You did ? "

" I did, sir. Have any of these other chaps told you how he was lying ? "

Superintendent Jett smiled.

" Nobody's told me anything very much about him yet ", he said.

" Well, now I'll tell you, Colonel. He was lying on his face and his arms and legs were pushed down into the mud—stuck tight in it ; so was his face. Now what does that mean ? "

Jude stepped back a pace and looked up at his companion, his perky face alight with intelligence. Stepping forward again he pointed his finger at the policeman's chest and only just refrained from prodding him as he made his point.

" It means that the tide was out when he fell in. He fell into mud and not into water. Water's been over 'im, of course, but it's my belief you'll find he died of suffocation and not of drowning—smothered in the mud. If he'd fallen into water we should have found him lying *on* the mud and there'd have been no difficulty in getting him out, but he fell into mud and as he tried to get up he drove his legs and arms deep into the mud—there was no resistance, you see—nothing to give him a push. He'd have tried to keep his head out but he'd soon get tired and have to drop it forward and each time he did that he'd get more mud in his eyes and mouth and nose. Not a nice way o' dying, Mr. Superintendent, and I've seen some."

Jett looked at his companion thoughtfully. This was important news. He knew, of course, about the probability of suffocation, as opposed to drowning, but the point about the legs and arms being driven into the mud was new to him—though he might have guessed it from the state of the clothes. There was just this one significant point about it : if Fiennes had been hit on the back of the head and had fallen, stunned, into the mud, his limbs would probably have remained more or less on the surface. *If* he was stunned ; and surely no murderer would strike a blow, under such circumstances, with less than stunning force, especially if he were as powerful a man as Lamming reported this Pansel to be. It was an interesting side-light.

But all he said to Jude Tasson was :

" And if he did fall into the mud, what of it ? "

Jude's face fell. These country policemen were all alike—no imagination.

" Oh, well ; I don't know. It gives you a line on the time, anyhow. It's not low tide all round the clock. About how long's he been dead, d'you think ? "

Disappointment could not for long suppress Jude's curiosity.

" Why d'you ask ? "

" Well, I'm just wondering whether he was dead when I went over yesterday. If I'd gone my usual way I'd 'ave found 'im myself, likely enough."

" What's that ? You went over where yesterday ? "

" To 'is hut—with 'is letters, you know."

" You did that ? What time ? Across the saltings, did you go ? "

There was no doubt about the interest in the big police-officer's face now. Jude responded to it.

" Not across the saltings I didn't—not yesterday. If I had, I suppose I'd 'ave found 'im—if he was there then, eh ? " He looked enquiringly at the Superintendent but getting no answer continued. " Of course the Post Office isn't bound to deliver to those huts, but I've got a private arrangement with Mr. Fiennes to take his letters to 'im. At low tide I used to go, so that I could get across the harbour and Little Creek without a boat—he wasn't particular to time. But yesterday the weather was that thick I didn't mean to go at all. But about mid-day it looked like clearing so I had my bit of dinner and went round by the footpath."

" What footpath ? "

" There's one runs over dry land round the east side of the saltings ; it's a mile or more further than the other way but it's the only way of getting across Little Creek when tide's in, unless you've got a boat. It was half tide when I went yesterday, so I went round. It got thicker again before I got to the dunes but I thought I'd go on. I had a job to find my way back, though."

" But you got to the house ? "

" The hut ? Yes, I got there all right."

Pride of service ; His Majesty's Mails always get there.

" But Mr. Fiennes wasn't there ? "

Jude shook his head.

"Not unless he was still asleep", he said. "My orders were to shove the letters in the box and if the door was open to go in and take any that he'd put ready for me—if he wasn't there himself, that is. If he was going to be away from the hut for long he usually locked the door—'cept, that is, on the days old Mother Barle was coming. Matter of fact I was surprised to find the door locked yesterday ; I thought he'd be sure to be in on a day like that. But then, I thought, he might have been asleep ; sometimes, he told me, he used to work all night and sleep all day, and that's what I thought he must be doing yesterday. It wasn't my job to wake 'im, though I knew old Mother Barle would if she came along and found the door shut—it was her day, Saturday. But there, it wasn't likely she'd come in all that fog, and as a fact she didn't."

For a minute or more Superintendent Jett stood in silence, turning over in his mind what the postman had told him, wondering if there was anything of significance to be drawn from it. Suddenly a thought struck him ; he thrust a hand into the pocket of his tunic.

"You say you took over some letters to Mr. Fiennes yesterday. Did you happen to look at them ? " he asked.

Jude grinned.

"I hope I'm 'uman ", he said. "I don't open letters, of course, but I look at the envelopes—to people like Mr. Fiennes, that is—and I read the postcards. Makes a bit of interest in a stick-in-the-mud place like this. There were two letters for Mr. Fiennes yesterday, one was a bill, I should think, and the other was from 'is girl."

" His girl ?   D'you mean . . . ? "

Jett checked himself abruptly, but not in time to conceal his meaning from the acute Jude.

" No, I don't mean her ", he said with a wink. " I should per'aps have said ' one of his girls '.   I 'appened to know that hand-writing—he'd had a lot of it and it didn't take much guessing to tell it was a girl.   That's one reason why I made a point of taking his letters over yesterday—might 'ave been something important."

Jett drew from his pocket the two torn envelopes that, an hour or two ago, he had picked up off the floor of the dead man's hut.

" Seen those before ? " he asked.

A glance was enough for Jude.

" Why, yes ", he said, " those are the two I took over yesterday morning."

CHAPTER XVIII

THE WIND SHIFTS

SUPERINTENDENT JETT and Inspector Lamming were sitting in the latter's small office in the police-station at Great Hayworth. Against the mantelpiece leaned a thin, soldierly-looking man of middle age, wearing a grey flannel suit, flannel shirt and faded Forester tie. This was Major Fennell, Chief Constable of the County, who had motored over from Norwich for a conference on the case which Superintendent Jett had reported to him over the telephone earlier in the evening. The hour's wait involved by the Chief Constable's journey was occupied by Superintendent Jett in having a cup of tea and some cheese at ' The Comely Ram ', licensee Sam Dallington, and in running over his notes and generally putting the story, so far as he knew it, in order. The Chief Constable had arrived at eight o'clock and for three-quarters of an hour had leaned against the mantelpiece listening to the tale unfolded, first by Inspector Lamming and then by Superintendent Jett.

" So you see, sir ", the Superintendent concluded, " that washes out the idea of Pansel having killed him on Friday night. Those letters were only delivered mid-day yesterday and Fiennes opened them after that. He must have gone out again after that, thinking perhaps—like other people did— that the weather was going to clear ; then when it

thickened again I suppose he must have turned
back, lost his way, and stumbled into the mud."

" Why do you say ' turned back ' ? " asked Major
Fennell, relighting his pipe, which, in the interest
of the story, he had allowed to go out.

" Because his body was lying head towards the
sea, sir. Besides, there's a bend in the path there ;
it's the very place he would fall in on his way back
towards the sand-dunes."

The Chief Constable nodded.

" You think it was an accident ? "

Jett shrugged his shoulders.

" At the moment I do, sir. I don't see that we've
anything definite to go on—in any other direction.
Of course we must go on looking about."

Inspector Lamming had been for some time
showing obvious signs of disagreement. Now he
could curb his impatience no longer.

" Begging your pardon, sir ", he said, " but I
don't see that this letter business lets out Pansel.
What's to stop him having gone there last night and
killed Fiennes, carried his body along the bank and
dropped it into the creek ? "

Major Fennell took his pipe from his mouth and
blew a cloud of smoke at a blue-bottle that had
settled on his shoulder. The disconcerted insect
beat a hasty retreat through the window.

" Ingenious ", he said, " but surely cutting it a
bit fine. When was low tide last night ? "

Lamming looked at a small calendar on his desk.

" Roughly 10 p.m., sir."

" And the body was found at . . . ? or rather,
you saw it at . . . ? "

" 11 a.m., sir ", answered Superintendent Jett.

" Rigor ? "

" Passing off, sir, Dr. Turl said."

The Chief Constable shook his head.

" After only thirteen hours ? Not likely."

" Dr. Turl put twelve hours as the minimum, sir ", interjected Lamming eagerly, " and there'd be no water in that part of the creek two hours each side of low tide ; we know that from what we saw this morning. That might make it fifteen hours."

Major Fennell smiled.

" Special pleading ", he said. " What was the skin like ? "

" Sodden, sir, very sodden ", answered Jett. " Palms of the hands like wash-leather."

" Then I bet it had had more than one tide over it. Any inflation ? "

" No, sir ; not visible to the layman, anyhow. Dr. Turl didn't mention it. But he did say twelve hours."

" Twelve hours to three days, wasn't it ? Two absolute extremes, both damned unlikely. Still, I mustn't put my opinion against his. I believe it is a fact that water shortens the period of rigor ; warm weather, too."

" Thank you, sir ", said Lamming, as if a point in the game had been conceded to him.

" But why fix on Pansel ? The only suspicious point against him is that he was on the saltings with Fiennes on the day he was last seen, but now we know he was alive after that—Fiennes, I mean."

" Oh, no, sir, begging your pardon. There's a lot more against him than that. If you'd seen him

236

yourself. . . . That man's got something on his conscience all right."

Inspector Lamming was of the bull-dog breed; if he once got his teeth into an idea it took more than a word to dislodge him.

" Why had he washed his mac, sir ? Who washes a mac in midsummer—unless he wants to get rid of something ? Why did he lie about a broken bulb ? Why was he so pat with his answers to everything—that knock on the head—a pretty story, that ; no sign of broken glass or beer on the floor, no . . ."

" Half a minute, Inspector ", interrupted the Chief Constable, " we can check that point. What's Dr. Turl's number ? "

In a few minutes the connection was made and the police-surgeon's voice answered.

" That you, Turl ? D'you recognize my voice ? "

" Major Fennell, isn't it ? "

" Good for you ; then you'll be able to answer a question or two. I'm speaking from Great Hayworth, about that case you were over to this morning. I don't want any details over the 'phone—only two points. Have you had a good look at that abrasion ? "

" I have, Major."

" Was there anything on it—anything medicinal, I mean ? "

" Not a thing."

" Sure ? "

" Perfectly."

" If anything had been put on, you'd have been able to tell ? "

" That depends on what it was and when it was put on."

" Iodine, on Friday night."

" Then I can't say, one way or the other. Iodine is soluble in salt water ; all trace of it would have disappeared by now."

" Thanks. Just one other point. Was it drowning or the other alternative ? "

" The other."

" Right ; you'll let us have your report as soon as possible ? "

" I'm writing it now. Superintendent Jett said he'd call for it."

" I'll tell him. Good-night, doctor."

Major Fennell hung up the receiver.

" No help there ", he said, and repeated what Dr. Turl had said. There was silence for some minutes, each man busy with his thoughts.

" Well, what are you going to do about it, Jett ? " asked the Chief Constable at last.

The big Superintendent came out of his brown study.

" I thought I'd get London to look up Mr. Fiennes' history, sir ", he said. " There's more than one story about him, I fancy."

Major Fennell nodded acquiescence.

" And I thought I'd send them this letter, though I don't believe there's anything to be made of it."

He took from his despatch-case a single sheet of common notepaper, folded in four ; it had evidently been sodden with water and mud, though it was dry now. At first sight it appeared to bear no writing, but closer inspection showed faint, undecipherable marks."

" Written in pencil, sir ; not a mark left worth talking about."

Major Fennell took the paper and held it up to the light.

" I shouldn't be too sure ", he said. " Written in pencil means pressure as a rule ; that'll probably show up under a microscope—to an expert, anyhow. Look, this looks like the signature—a single name I should say. Isn't that a capital N ? "

Superintendent Jett looked over his superior officer's shoulder.

" It might be, sir. Anyhow, I'll send it them. Tasson, the postman, thought it was from what he called ' one of his girls '."

Major Fennell nodded.

" Worth looking up—his career ", he said. " Old sins have long shadows. What else ? "

" I agree with Inspector Lamming, sir, that we can't ignore Mr. Pansel just because of these letters. We haven't had the advantage of seeing him, sir ; that seems to have made a strong impression on Inspector Lamming—his manner, sir, I mean, rather than what he actually said, which doesn't really amount to much."

The Chief Constable smiled. He liked his officers to support their subordinates ; Jett would not carry it too far.

" I don't think I'll see him myself just yet, sir. If there's anything wrong he'll be well on his guard by now—recovered his balance. Better take him by surprise later on, if things point that way. I don't think we shall get much more by asking questions ; they're like clams, these people. Not only the natives ; there are one or two gentlemen living more

or less permanently in the village, who used to mix
with the deceased and Mr. Pansel—a Mr. Vessle, a
singer, I believe, and Mr. Sarne, an engineer. They
talked, of course, but they didn't say anything—
' nothing at all wrong between Fiennes and Pansel,
best of friends, must have been a pure accident '—
all that sort of thing."

Major Fennell nodded.

" I know," he said. " Public School spirit. Only
means they liked Pansel better than Fiennes."

" I should be glad of your help there, sir ", continued Superintendent Jett. " If you'd let me have
one of your plain-clothes men from Headquarters we
could plant him in the village as a visitor. Any of
our divisional men might be spotted."

" Good idea. I'll send Sergeant Voles over first
thing to-morrow—by train to Fakenham. You'd
better see him there and give him his orders. Then
he can come on by train or bus like a good little
holiday-maker."

The Chief Constable was pleased. He had recently
organized a detective-branch of the County Constabulary, under the control of Headquarters—an
innovation adding not a little to the Police expenses
of an already heavily-rated County. He had, of
course, the full support of his Standing Joint Com-
mittee, but . . . he was glad of an opportunity to
justify the experiment.

" Then I thought, sir, that we'd keep a look-out
for the owner of that patched boot-heel ; it's the
only foot-mark of any possible significance near the
spot. I've got a list of the men who moved the body
and it belongs to one of them. I got the list from
Jude Tasson—the only talker in Bryde. I didn't ask

him if he knew the owner of the boot because I don't want it known that we're interested in it. It ought not to be hard to spot it for ourselves."

" Let's see the list, Superintendent, may I ? "

Major Fennell read aloud from the page in Superintendent Jett's note-book :

" Giles Banyatt—that's the old ferryman ? Joseph Soller, Albert Soller, William Soller ; brothers ? "

" Three generations, I understand, sir. Live on the quay, more or less."

" Christian Madgek—that's a good name."

" And a bad hat ", muttered Inspector Lamming.

" Oh ? what's his trouble ? "

" Poacher, sir. Gambler, too, I fancy."

" Dear, dear. Well, we can't hang him on his reputation. Barney Pewter—delicious—and Ted Costing. No, as you say, you oughtn't to have much difficulty in picking the needle out of that haystack. Well, if that's all I'll be getting back. If there's anything I can do for you, Superintendent, let me know."

When the Chief Constable had gone, Superintendent Jett spent another ten minutes with Inspector Lamming, discussing the morrow's plans and then set off home in his car. On the way he called in on Dr. Turl at Hunstanton and received the latter's report. The autopsy had revealed nothing startling. There had been no salt water in the lung, which showed that the man had been dead before the tide reached him. Death was due to suffocation, and the presence of mud far back in the mouth and nose suggested that that substance had been the cause of the suffocation. The abrasion on the head was fairly severe, but Dr. Turl did not think it would have had a stunning effect ; he was not, however, prepared to assert this definitely. There was no trace of alcohol in the stomach, but even with the ' bottling ' effect of the mud it was unlikely that any trace would be left after twelve hours ; the suggestion, therefore, that excessive drinking played some part in the tragedy was neither proved nor disproved. As to the time of death, Dr. Turl was as guarded as ever ; the absence of any sign of inflation, however, enabled him to reduce the outside limit to ' three days, probably two ' ; the inside limit remained at ' 12 hours but more probably 18 '.

Thanking Dr. Turl for his report and promising to send a copy to the coroner, Superintendent Jett continued on his way to Dersingham. The choice of this small village as the headquarters of the Divisional Superintendent was due to its proximity to Sandringham and the expressed wish of King Edward VII, who had given the land on which the station was built. During the winter months it was Superintendent Jett's privilege upon many occasions to stand behind his Monarch at the big covert shoots and admire the neatness and precision of his shooting ; at such times extra police were drafted to Sandringham and extra wrinkles of care appeared upon Superintendent Jett's usually placid face, but at this time of year his duties dwindled to the gentle ebb and flow of a summer sea. To-night was the first for months on which he had had a problem to take to bed with him.

It did not keep him long awake, however. Jett believed in working while you are at work and resting in between—and in rest he included recreation. After a late supper and a game of halma with his daughter to promote digestion he went to bed, told his wife what was on, and fell into the sleep of perfect health and an easy conscience.

On the following morning he put in a couple of hours' hard work on routine matters and was on the point of starting for Fakenham, where he was to meet Major Fennell's detective-sergeant, when a telephone message informed him that, if he could make it convenient to call, the Manager of the Eastern Counties Bank at Hunstanton had some information which he thought might be of interest to the police. A nod being as good as a wink to Superintendent Jett, it was not long before he was sitting in a small office faced by a neat, black-coated figure.

"It was good of you to call so promptly, Superintendent", said Mr. Dench. "I hope I am not going to waste your time—or rather, in a sense, perhaps I hope I am. That is not very clear, I am afraid, but you will see my point. I read with regret in the papers this morning of the death of one of our clients, Mr. Dallas Fiennes, of Bryde-by-the-Sea. As the circumstances of his death are, I understand, the subject of police enquiry, I thought it my duty to place at your disposal some information which might conceivably have some bearing on the matter. That is pre-supposing foul play, and for that reason I said that, in one sense, I hoped I was wasting your time."

Superintendent Jett bowed. It was no good getting impatient with these fussy little men; they would put things in their own way; to try and short-circuit them only meant more delay in the long run.

"About a fortnight ago"—Mr. Dench consulted a pad in front of him—"on Tuesday, 12th July, to

be exact—Mr. Fiennes cashed a cheque for £50.
That is, I think I am at liberty to inform you, a
larger amount than Mr. Fiennes was in the habit of
drawing in cash. He took it in the form of thirty £1
notes and four £5 notes ; it is the latter fact that I
felt might be of interest to you. I know nothing
about the circumstances of the case ; you may be
satisfied that death was due to an accident (that is
not clear from the newspaper account), or even
supposing you are not so satisfied, you may have no
reason to suppose that money plays any part in the
case ; but if it does, if there is any question of
robbery as a motive for . . . I say, *if* this is the case,
then I feel that it may be of assistance to you to have
the numbers of the notes which we issued to him on
12th July. That refers, of course, only to the £5
notes ; we keep no tally of the notes of smaller
denomination except under special circumstances.
Here is a list of the numbers of the £5 notes . . ."
Mr. Dench handed across a typewritten slip, " and I
trust that they may be of assistance to you in tracing
the dastardly . . . that is to say, *if* . . ."

Superintendent Jett rose slowly to his feet, tucking
the slip away in his pocket-book.

" I am very much obliged to you, sir ", he said ;
" it's just possible that the question of these notes
may arise. I needn't say that I will treat what you
have told me as confidential."

Back in his car he wrenched the gear in with an
impatient jerk.

" Gosh ", he said to himself, " all that talk. . . .
Two minutes and twenty words would have done
the whole thing. Well, I'd better try and trace these
notes."

There had been no £5 notes in the case which he had taken from the dead man's pocket. A £1 and a 10/- note there had been; that did not suggest robbery as a motive—unless it was a clever ' cover ' to the extraction of a considerably larger sum. There might be money in the hut—he must look; or the notes might have been paid away—in which case they could probably be traced.

The visit to Hunstanton had made Superintendent Jett nearly an hour late for his rendezvous with Detective-Sergeant Voles, but he had no anxiety about that. Soon after he had pulled up in a quiet corner of the station-yard at Fakenham a clean-shaven young man in a light grey suit, who had been leaning against the booking-office door, reading a newspaper, detached himself from his suit-case, strolled down to the closed car, and asked for a light. After ten minutes of apparently casual conversation the young man strolled back to his luggage and the police-car slid off in the direction of the sea.

At Inspector Lamming's office Jett was handed a telegram, which had arrived a short time before. It ran :

" *Police Station. Great Hayworth, Norfolk.*
Ref. death Mr. Fiennes our representative arrives Great Hayworth 3.48 to-day Please give information and facilities Granton and Pard Solicitors."

" No moss growing on that firm. They may be useful ", was the Superintendent's comment.

The tide, half an hour later than on the previous day, was still low when the two police officers arrived at Bryde. Equipped now with gum-boots they were more or less independent, and wading across the trickle of water in the harbour they made their way along the raised bank, past the scene of the tragedy, to the post to which Dallas Fiennes' boat was still tied as Jett had left it yesterday. It was no use to them now and the two men walked across the wide stretch of quivering sand, waded through Little Creek, and soon found themselves in Fiennes' hut. Already there was a deserted, tragic look about the place. Dust and sand were accumulating, flies buzzed out of a stained jam-pot on the table. Jett glanced at the windows.

" I wonder if he shut those shutters at night ", he said. " The point didn't strike me yesterday, but the place was light when I came in."

"Not much to go by, sir, anyway ", said Lamming. " He probably didn't shut the shutters when he went out on Friday evening—sun still shining— no, probably not, because 'it was beginning to get thick in the evening—but daylight, anyhow."

Jett nodded.

" And he'd have opened them when he got up and opened his post. We might ask Tasson if they were open when he brought the letters."

" He's had a meal of some kind, sir, I see."

" Yes, that ought to have told me. Scrambled eggs suggests breakfast—or high tea. He wouldn't have had high tea before going out to dinner with the Pansels, so that also means a meal on Saturday. How blind one can be."

Inspector Lamming thought it wiser to make no comment.

It did not take long to search the hut or to realise that the small safe in the cupboard by the fireplace was the only place in which a normal man would be likely to keep money. It opened to one of the keys on Fiennes' bunch and contained an account book, pass-book, insurance policies, and literary contracts. In a small drawer was a bag containing £2.7.0 in silver and a £1 note. Nowhere was there any trace of private correspondence.

" Well, if he was a philanderer he was a wise one ", said Jett. " Kept nothing in writing—and I'll bet that means he didn't commit himself much in writing. Anyhow, we shall have to try and trace those notes, Lamming, His solicitor may be able to help us there and we'll go through his accounts. Then we'll notify banks and local tradesmen ; shouldn't be difficult."

Little Creek had risen and spread considerably during their search of the hut, but thanks to their gum-boots they were able to get across dry-shod. As they approached the raised bank Superintendent Jett said :

" Keep a look out for that boot mark, Lamming, I meant to have another look at it as I came along but I suppose we were talking and I missed it."

" Funny thing, sir, but I missed it too ", answered Lamming. " It shouldn't be hard to find—can't have been far from the bend."

But it was hard to find. Hunt as they would, between the post and the scene of the tragedy, there was not a trace of the heel-mark that had attracted their attention on the previous day.

" That's odd ", said Superintendent Jett. " The tide must have been over the bank and washed it away."

Lamming shook his head.

" No, sir. The tide never covers this bank—I

asked about that. Besides, you can see by the flotsam where it reached last high tide."

The two men stared at each other in silence.

" Then somebody's trodden it out ", said Superintendent Jett, slowly.

CHAPTER XIX

It was Wednesday morning and John and Hilary
Pansel were working off some of the evil vapours of
the past week in a vigorous walk over the hills
behind the village. It was a scorching hot day but
with the sweat of their bodies they felt that they
were ridding themselves of some of the noxious
influences—jealousy, anger, suspicion, fear—that
for the last week had poisoned their minds.

For the first time since that terrible morning—
only three days ago, though it seemed an age—when
the first blue-coated figure had walked up their
garden-path to announce the death of Dallas
Fiennes, they felt they could breathe more freely.
The inquest was over and to their intense relief—to
the disappointment, too, of the whole, or nearly the
whole neighbourhood—the jury had returned a
verdict which removed from the tragedy the
suspicion that it concealed a crime. The Coroner, a
doctor and a man of independent character, had been
completely unconvinced by the police suggestion
that an adjournment was desirable for the purpose of
allowing time for further investigation. What
grounds, asked the Coroner, were there for a suggestion of foul play ? An abrasion on the head ? As a
medical man he was confident that this abrasion was
not made by a blow of stunning force—and nothing
less would suffice to connect it with the death ;

moreover it had been accounted for, and—in his opinion—quite satisfactorily accounted for, by the Pansels' story. A suggestion of motive? Based on what? Where was the proof? Based on fishwives' gossip, was his contemptuous comment. Missing bank-notes? Why missing? Why not paid away in the normal course of such commodities? What more could Superintendent Jett urge? His Inspector's instinct? A missing heel-mark? No; by themselves they were negligible.

Mr. Gerald Pelly, junior partner in the firm of Granton and Pard, representing the dead man's executors—there were no relatives—being far from satisfied, had protested; being young and over-confident had tried to browbeat the Coroner and had been politely but firmly squashed. The enquiry had been carried to a conclusion and the jury, without undue delay, had returned a verdict of ' Found drowned '; on the Coroner pointing out, with some acerbity, that such a verdict could hardly be applied to a man who had *not* been drowned, they had amended it to ' Death by Misadventure ', whereupon Dr. Crandle had dismissed them with his blessing.

It was an enormous, an almost unbelievable relief. Last night, for the first time for many weeks, Hilary had lain in John's arms and, from very happiness and the exhaustion of reaction, had cried herself to sleep. Not so easily was the load to pass from John's mind; the iron had entered too deeply into his soul. Moreover he knew, though he did not tell Hilary, that a verdict of ' Misadventure ' from a Coroner's jury did not necessarily mean a dropping of the case by the police. The outlook was lighter, undoubtedly, but it would be long before he could rid himself of the terrible dread that had taken possession of his mind.

As they paused for breath at the top of the hill Hilary slipped her warm hand into her husband's.

" John ", she said, " you're looking terribly tired and drawn. Somehow or other, in a few days, I'm going to take you away somewhere for a change of air and scene."

" But Hilary, we . . ."

She squeezed his arm.

" No, John dear, you're not to say it. I know we can't afford it. I know all that. But this isn't a moment to be careful. It's too big, too vital a moment in our lives. We'll manage somehow ; I'll think out a way of making it possible. But we've got to go . . . and start afresh. It shall be a new honeymoon for us, John dear—a real one. Wouldn't you like that ? "

John looked for a long moment into her eyes, as if trying to read what was in her mind. Then suddenly he seized her in his arms and crushed her to him.

" Oh, Hilary ! " His voice was stifled with emotion. " Oh, my darling ! My darling ! "

For a minute they clung together ; then Hilary gently released herself.

" Come on ", she said, " I'm enjoying this walk."

For an hour more they strode on under the burning sun, following quiet lanes or skirting, by beaten tracks, the shimmering acres of corn. As they bore left-handed towards the sea again they suddenly ran into Beryl Helliott, who was standing in a gate-way talking to a sun-burnt labourer. She greeted them shyly; for all the remoteness of her life she knew most of what was done—and said—in Bryde-by-the-Sea. The labourer, with a touch of his battered hat and a polite 'good-morning', moved off down the lane.

"Oh, Beryl", exclaimed Hilary impetuously, "isn't it a relief that it's over!"

Quick to respond to her friend's lightened spirits, Beryl kissed her affectionately.

"Darling, I'm so glad", she said. "It must have been awful for you having those dreadful policemen asking you questions. Poor Mr. Fiennes; I don't wonder he lost his way. *I* didn't dare go out in that thick weather, and I was born in the place. What a terrible death—in that awful mud."

Hilary, catching sight of John's haggard face, quickly changed the subject.

"But how are you, Beryl? I haven't seen you for days—it seems more like weeks."

"Oh, I'm monotonously well . . . only rather lonely."

"Lonely? Isn't Frank back yet?"

"Not a sign of him. Pennyweather's getting worried about the crops—he thinks we ought to start cutting the barley. I told him that if Frank's not home tomorrow he must start without him."

"But what's he up to?"

"Goodness knows. He said he'd got some business to attend to. He's always been very old-fashioned about women not knowing anything about business. I've wondered whether he might be selling Brulcote. I thought he was only going to be away a day or two but he's been away a fortnight now. I can't understand it."

"Doesn't he write?"

"One postcard—last week—to say he'd be back this week. No address even, so I can't write to him or anything."

"No postmark?" asked John.

"S.W., that's all. I'm really getting rather worried."

"Poor dear." Hilary squeezed her friend's arm. "Men are so silly about business; they always think it necessary to make mysteries and mountains out of molehills. I expect some lawyers have got hold of him and are simply wasting time so as to make money."

"Have you thought of writing to his solicitors?"

John's deep voice, his slow, commonplace words, seemed to Hilary to act like balm on the rather highly-strung nerves of herself and Beryl. What a comfort a good, slow, stolid man could be at times.

"I hadn't thought of it."

"Well, if you want to get hold of him, send them a letter and ask them to forward it to Frank if they know where he is."

"I think I will. Thank you, John."

They were not far now from Brulcote and Beryl had little difficulty in persuading them to stay to lunch. Sweaty clothes, she said, were an everyday affair in a farmer's home. The lunch itself was simple, but their long walk in the sun had given the Pansels a healthier appetite than they had known for weeks. In the afternoon they took garden chairs out into the orchard and while Hilary and Beryl twittered away over the agreeable nothings that women have the happy faculty of finding to discuss, John puffed at his pipe and, with one ear to their gentle murmurs, the other to the drone of bees and coo of doves around and above him, gradually slipped off into blessed oblivion. The lines of care melted from his face and Hilary found herself looking at the man she had married and for twelve years loved, the man whom for three nightmare weeks she had forgotten and so nearly lost.

As they walked home in the late afternoon they said little, but Hilary had slipped her hand through her husband's arm and John pressed it to his side as if afraid to let it go. Their way took them past Hugh Fallaran's cottage. The barrister was in his garden, pipe in mouth, picking superfluous shoots from mammoth sweet peas which climbed up wires to record-breaking heights. He waved a welcoming hand.

" Come and see me win the *Daily Mail* prize ", he said, and plucking a magnificent five-blossomed specimen, handed it to Hilary.

" ' Queen of my Heart ' ", he said. " Name of the flower, though Pansel knows how appropriate it is. Come on, tea-time."

Hilary glanced quickly at her husband and was happy when she saw the cheerful smile on his face.

" We can't rush in on you at a moment's notice ", he said.

" True, you won't find any éclairs or Buzzard luxuries. But fresh lettuce and yellow butter and brown bread are no mean substitute—and a perfectly good china tea. Come on ; don't stand there bickering."

He led the way into the little sitting-room, lined

with books, which he had contrived to make so comfortable and individual. Tea was soon ready and Hilary, leaning towards Hugh and speaking in not much more than her normal voice, managed to make him hear as he had never thought to hear again. The happiness that this meant for him was reflected in his rising spirits, and the little party was as wonderful a success as only impromptu parties can be. John so far departed from his natural reserve as to say :

" This has been a happy day for us, Fallaran. You know the Coroner's jury brought in a verdict of ' Death by Misadventure ' ? "

" Yes, I heard that. But why . . . ? " He glanced from one to the other.

" Hadn't you h . . . didn't you know ? We . . . I was under suspicion."

" Suspicion ? "

Fallaran stared at John.

" Yes. Fiennes dined with us the night he died. I took him back as far as the saltings—it was thick, you remember. I left him quite close to the place where his body was found."

" I heard he'd dined with you but he was found two days after that, wasn't he ? "

" Yes, but . . . the police put me through it pretty closely."

Fallaran smiled.

" Oh, well, they would. Partly routine, partly the fun of the thing—for them. But they can't possibly have thought you'd had anything to do with his death. What possible motive could you have ? "

Hilary slipped her hand into John's under the

table-cloth. For a moment there was silence ; the two men looking into each other's eyes.

"Fiennes had the reputation of being a lady-killer", said John slowly.

Hugh Fallaran turned his eyes to Hilary. A slow smile broke over his face.

"Not this lady", he said, laying his hand lightly for a moment on her arm.

Hilary felt a flush of colour slowly spreading over her whole body. She turned quickly to John.

"Mr. Fallaran must think we're a couple of idiots, John. And so we are—imagining things."

She rose to her feet.

"It was a lovely tea. Thank you ever so much."

"Thank you for coming. It's a long time since I've been so . . . enjoyed myself so much. But look here, John Pansel, if these policemen really do bother you, for goodness' sake come to me. I can still tackle a policeman, even after twenty years of Admiralty, Probate and Divorce. And you know", he turned his smiling eyes upon Hilary, "I'd like to be a sort of auxiliary defence force."

"You might have . . ." began John, then checked himself. "I'll count on you", he finished awkwardly.

Fallaran escorted them out of 'the policies', as he liked to call his half acre of garden. At the gate they shook hands.

"Good-night, Mr. Fallaran", said Hilary, "and thank you, most awfully."

"Night", echoed John, already shy at the slight expression of feeling he had displayed.

"Good-night, Mr. and Mrs. Pansel", said their

host. "Some day I'm hoping that you'll feel able to use my Christian name—if you ever discover what it is."

"Why, of course", said Hilary, with a smile. "Good-night, Hugh."

CHAPTER XX

ON Thursday morning, 28th. July, Superintendent Jett received a telephone message from the Fakenham police station to the effect that a chemist in that town, Domnel by name, had reported himself to be in possession of a bank-note which might have some bearing upon the case. Picking up Inspector Lamming in his car, Superintendent Jett reached Fakenham just as Mr. Domnel was closing his one-man-and-a-boy business for the mid-day break.

" Yes, sir ; Domnel is my name ", said the little man in a black alpaca jacket, leading the way into an inner room. " Two o'clock sharp, George ; not three minutes past, mind, nor yet five. Derived, my old father used to tell me, and he had it from *his* father, from the words Doom and Knell—a very unfortunate derivation for people of our calling—and we have been chymists in Fakenham since the year 1721. But sit you down, gentlemen. May I offer you a glass of anything—ginger wine, perhaps ? or a cordial ? No ; well no doubt you want to get down to business. Now I don't know whether what I have to show you will be of any interest. The note in question is not one of those for which you are enquiring—I received, of course, the confidential memorandum from our local police in that connection. No, this is not a £5 note. It is a £1 note—a bank-note, it is true, though one still finds it

difficult not to refer to them as Treasury Notes.
Here it is."

Mr. Domnel produced a black pocket-book and
from it extracted an envelope, which he handed
across to Superintendent Jett. The envelope contained a £1 note, limp and smudged with some
brown substance. Jett turned it over and looked
enquiringly at the chemist. The little man rubbed
his hands.

" Not convey anything to you ? " he asked.
" Just a dirty note ? So it would naturally appear
to most laymen. But to me, sir, it says more than
that." He lowered his voice. " That note, Superintendent, has been soaked in sea-water ! Not just
wetted, but saturated."

" Oh ? How can you tell that ? " Polite interest,
not much more, coloured the Superintendent's
enquiry.

" Well, sir, that is just a bit of luck. Although
my business is almost entirely of a dispensing
character, small but regular, I'm thankful to say, I
make a hobby of analytical work—always was
fascinated by it and regret that it no longer comes
my way in the matter of business. Now when that
note came into my hands I thought by the feel of it,
as well as by the look and the taste, that it had been
in the sea. I carefully extracted . . . but I won't
go into technical details ; it is sufficient for your
purpose—for the moment, that is ; unless you
require me to give evidence upon oath—it is sufficient
for your purpose for me to inform you that that note
is, as I expected, impregnated with salt and that the
dirt which you see upon it is a smear of mud of the
type which is found in the saltings along this coast—

mud of a character compounded of loam and sand which is constantly soaked by sea water."

"That's very interesting, Mr.—er—Domnel, but there may, of course, be many such notes in circulation in a sea-faring neighbourhood."

"True, sir, though Fakenham is hardly a sea-faring town. I merely offer you the information for what it is worth." There was a touch of huffiness in Mr. Domnel's tone. "I received your enquiry for certain bank-notes. I read at the same time a report of the death of a gentleman, in what appeared to me suspicious circumstances, in the saltings not twenty miles from here. I receive this note and, having analysed it, I offer you the information for what it is worth. I may be quite mistaken. I . . ."

"Very good of you indeed, Mr. Domnel", hastily interposed the Superintendent, "and may be of decided help to us. May I ask where you got the note from ?"

This display of proper interest mollified the little chemist.

"I cannot tell you the man's name", he said, "but I can describe him. He came in yesterday evening, just before closing time, and asked for a bottle of iodine, as he had cut his foot. I offered to bandage it for him, but he declined my assistance. He was a small man, smaller than myself, not much more than five feet, I should say. Thin-boned, too, but not ill-nourished. He had colour in his cheeks and light in his eyes, but his teeth were shocking—terrible. I'd know him again, if you wanted me to pick him out."

Inspector Lamming, who had shown increasing

interest as the description developed, now spoke for the first time.

" Had this chap got a finger missing ? " he asked.

Mr. Domnel frowned in concentration of thought.

" Now you mention it ", he said slowly, " I think perhaps he may have. I remember now noticing something odd about his hand—I thought at the time he'd got his finger tucked away. The first finger of his left hand."

" That's the chap. I know him, Mr. Jett ; he's . . ."

But Superintendent Jett had risen to his feet and was holding out his hand.

" Very grateful to you for your help, Mr. Domnel ", he said blandly. " I don't know whether there's anything in this, but if there is I'll let you know. I'll keep this note, if you'll allow me ; here's another in place of it."

Out in the street, the two police officers got back into their car and drove off towards Great Hayworth.

" Well, who is he ? "'asked Superintendent Jett, as soon as his attention was released from traffic worries.

" Name of Fardell, sir ; Simeon Fardell, a pedlar— and then some. Well-known character in 'these parts. He has the reputation of being a money-lender and I've my own suspicions that he's a receiver of stolen goods—or at any rate of poached game."

" Ah, yes ; I've heard of him ", said Jett, " though I don't think I've ever set eyes on him. Interesting character ; I'd like to get to know him. You'd better pull him in, Lamming. . . . No, don't do

that ; it might frighten him and shut his mouth.
Let me know where to find him and I'll have a talk
with him. Not that I expect there's any connection with Fiennes—must be hundreds of salt-
water notes about the coast."

" I'm not so sure about that, sir ", said Lamming,
doubtfully. " Fishy notes, yes ; dirty notes, yes.
But I don't fancy these chaps carry their notes
about them when they go to sea—they're too scarce
to be risked. Straight into the biscuit box and the
bank on Friday, I should say. Of course, it depends
just how much salt water there is on this note ; if
it's been held in a wet hand it's one thing ; if it's
been thoroughly soaked it's another."

Superintendent Jett looked at his companion and
smiled.

" Wish father to the thought, eh, Lamming ? "

" Beg pardon, sir ? "

" You don't want this case to peter out into
Misadventure."

Inspector Lamming's sturdy jaw advanced a
millimetre.

" It's not misadventure, sir—and that . . .
Coroner's going to eat his words."

Jett laughed.

" He was a bit tiresome, wasn't he. But this
doesn't exactly point to your man, you know,
Lamming."

" Perhaps not, sir, . . . but I'm keeping my eye
on him."

It does not take the Norfolk County Constabulary
long to find an itinerant pedlar and on the following
Friday morning, Mr. Simeon Fardell was surprised
to see a neat, dark car pull up behind his cart as he

sat in a shady lane eating his mid-day bread and cheese. A large man in a blue serge jacket, white collar, Sam-Browne belt, and silver-braided cap slowly emerged from the car and walked towards him.

" Holy Jake ", murmured the pedlar to himself, " what's this outfit ? "

" Good-morning, Fardell ", said the uniformed figure. " I'm Superintendent Jett, County Constabulary, and I'd like a word with you. No, don't get up ; I'll take a seat beside you."

Jett lowered himself slowly onto the bank.

" Go on with your lunch. I want to ask you about a bank-note that you paid over to Mr. Domnel, the Fakenham chemist, on Wednesday evening."

Fardell squinted at his companion out of the corner of his eye, but the big man was busy filling a pipe.

" You don't happen to remember, I suppose, how that note came into your possession ? "

" Well, there, mister, how should I remember a thing like that ? I don't keep no accounts, I don't. Money comes and money goes with me ; here to-day and gone to-morrow."

" Bank-notes common in the pedling business ? " asked Jett blandly.

" Ah, that wasn't a bank-note ; just an ordinary green Fisher."

Jett shook his head.

" You're not very observant, Mr. Fardell. Fishers and Bradburys are out of date ; that note was signed by Mr. Catterus, Chief Cashier of the Bank of England. But that's a detail ; the point is, where did you get it from ? "

"But I've told you, Colonel, I don't know where I got it. Notes come into my hands sometimes, though not as often as I'd like, and then generally I have to give back fifteen bob in change. I've no more idea where that note came from than I . . . than I . . ."

"Than you know why I'm asking about it, eh? Well, I'll tell you, Fardell, and then perhaps you'll be able to remember. That note was taken from the pocket of a dead man. Did you take it?"

Superintendent Jett thrust his face close up against his companion's and glared at him with accusing eyes. The pedlar shrank back.

"So help me, Jake, I didn't. You know I didn't, mister. Not been near a stiff, I haven't, not for . . . not for . . ."

"That'll do", said Jett sternly. "I've said enough, Fardell, to show you that you'd better come across with it. It'll go no further unless there's a case of murder for the court, and if there is—and you've kept anything back—you'll be for it as an accessory, if not as a principal."

Simeon Fardell was in a quandary. It was against all his instincts, against his business principles, to talk to the police, especially to mention names. But murder!

"Now, Fardell, who have you had pound notes from in the last week?"

Superintendent Jett was not going to give the pedlar time to think; he must get what he wanted before the effect of shock had worn off.

"But, mister, dozens of people, I have!" The little man's voice was plaintive. "Money goes through my hands . . ."

264

" Yes, I know all about that—and a bit more besides. You can't afford to play with me, Fardell. Come, I'll help you. Who've you had money from in Bryde ? "

A quick intake of breath told Jett that he was warm.

" Bryde, sir ? Well, I was through Bryde o' Monday. Mr. Pete, at the ' Virgin Duck ', he took a couple o' saucepans off me and paid for them in paper. But Mr. Pete, you wouldn't think wrong o' . . ."

" I don't want any thinking, Fardell, I want facts."

The pedlar hesitated. Jett fired his last cartridge.

" Who have you been lending money to in Bryde ? "

Fardell stared at him in astonishment—not unmixed with admiration.

" Jake, you busies . . . ! "

" Come on, Fardell. It's murder, mind."

" I . . . I don't . . . Holy J . . . you won't give me away, mister ? They'd wring my neck if they thought I'd squeaked."

He looked anxiously about him, but the lane was deserted save for themselves and the shaggy pony quietly cropping the grass a yard or two away.

" I've told you it won't go any further unless it comes to trial—even then I may not need your evidence."

Fardell leant close up against the massive blue figure and whispered. Jett listened and nodded.

" How much ? " he asked.

" Twenty-five ; on account that was. I've been waiting a long time for it and I'd given him till next

week—Tuesday—but when he paid up that much I
gave him another month for the rest. No good
pressin' 'em too hard ", the money-lender added
philosophical.y.

" And he paid you that money on Tuesday?
This Tuesday? "

Fardell nodded.

" Let's see it."

The pedlar looked at him in innocent surprise.

" But, Colonel, you don't think I carry all that
money about with me? Any little dough I get
goes into my bank account to pay my debts."

" And how d'you lend money if you don't carry
it about with you? "

" Aw, come. It's only once in a way I oblige a
friend—all in the way of trade. I've got none on
me, Colonel; may I sink if I have."

" How was the money paid? Notes? "

Fardell nodded.

" Fives and ones? "

The pedlar shook his head, smiling to himself as
he did so. What mutton-headed fools policemen
were—as if he would accept bank-notes!

" All ones and halfs ", he said. " And mighty
dirty at that."

Jett pricked up his ears.

" Been in the water, eh? "

Fardell shrugged his shoulders.

" How can I say? They were a dirty lot, same
as a lot as pass through my hands ", he said, with
unconscious irony; " that's all I can say."

" Tell me where you banked them, and when."

After more hesitation, Simeon Fardell parted
with all the information about the notes that he

was in a position to give, and Superintendent Jett, thanking him, drove away. The method he had employed to get it was not one that he cared for, or often used, but he felt convinced that nothing else would have made the money-lending pedlar speak. And it was worth having, for the name that Fardell had whispered in his ear was that of one of the men who had moved the body of Dallas Fiennes —and one of those men was wearing the boot with the patched heel.

CHAPTER XXI

WEATHERCOCK

" AND the theory now ? " asked Major Fennell.

Superintendent Jett pondered his answer.

" I wouldn't say there was a definite theory yet, sir ", he said slowly. " A suggestion, perhaps. This man Madgek seems to have been badly in need of money—I got that impression from Fardell, though not in so many words. Why he should have needed it I can't make out and I haven't been able to find out. There's not much money in fishing now, of course—not from these little places, that is—but he makes quite a good thing out of his motor-boat and his odd jobs of building . . ."

" And his poaching ", muttered Inspector Lamming.

Jett smiled.

" But what does he spend it on ? He's a single man, living alone. Tasson thinks he's got a girl somewhere over this way but he doesn't know who it is and in any case one would imagine that a few pairs of stockings and a cheap ring would be all he'd buy for her ; these sea-board folk don't usually spend much on their women."

" And he paid Fardell twenty-five pounds ? "

" Yes, sir ; out of a total debt of forty. Twenty-five, of course, is rather a significant figure. Fiennes drew out fifty, but twenty of them were in bank-notes—fivers—which anyone in these days knows

can be traced. That left thirty in small notes, and
there was a pound or two left about—on the body
and in the safe. Twenty-five seems exactly the
round sum that would be paid out of that haul."

"But if he knew the fivers could be traced why
should he take them ? "

Jett shrugged his shoulders.

"Greed perhaps—or he may think that he'll be
able to plant them quietly when it's all blown over.
That coroner's verdict, you know, sir ; may be very
useful to us yet."

"False security ? M'm. Well, go on ; how was it
done—and when ? "

"That's not so easy, sir. He may have lain for
him—knowing his habits—that he always used that
path. Knocked him on the head, flung him
into . . ."

"Hold hard a minute ! " interrupted the Chief
Constable. "If you're suspecting Madgek of the
murder, you can't suspect Pansel too. And if you
don't suspect Pansel then you must accept his
story of how that knock on the head happened.
Madgek can't have done it."

Superintendent Jett looked crestfallen.

"That's so, sir ; stupid of me. Well, I must
leave aside for the moment just how he killed him,
but he either took his money then, if he had it on
him, or took his keys and got the money out of the
safe. The difficulty is, when did he do it ? It was
done at low tide, or an hour or so each side of it.
That means either round about nine o'clock on
Friday night, or half-past nine on Saturday morning,
or ten o'clock on Saturday night ; both the first
are a wash-out because we know now that he was in

his hut after Tasson took the letters there at mid-
day on Saturday and we know he had breakfast on
Saturday morning, which doubly washes out Friday
night. But ten o'clock on Saturday night brings
it terribly close to the time when he was found;
even if you put it at eight p.m., that's only fifteen
hours before Dr. Turl looked at him and he thinks
he'd been dead at least eighteen hours then. It's
a puzzle."

Major Fennell sat at the office table and drew
aimless geometrical figures on the blotting paper.
The blue smoke of his pipe curled up towards the
ceiling.

" It is a puzzle ", he said at last. " Would you
like a theory ? "

" Very much, sir."

" I know one oughtn't to theorize; one's tempted
to make the facts fit in. But . . . well, it's rather
fun. I wouldn't be too much worried about tides
if I were you; it may blind you to other possibilities. There's no doubt that Fiennes went into
the creek at low tide, but was he killed then ? Not
necessarily, I think. There are more ways than one
of smothering a man, you know. And it's much
more likely that he was attacked at his house than
on the saltings; I don't believe in the ' laying for
him ' theory—much too chancy; though he might,
of course, have been followed. But after all, the
whole significance of that heel-mark that you found
was the fact that it was so deep—at least, that's
how it struck me. The suggestion is that the
wearer of it was carrying something heavy. What
does that suggest ? Lamming here touched it the
other day."

The Inspector blushed with pride.

" He said : ' What's to stop him having gone there last night ' (that was Saturday night) ' and killed Fiennes and carried his body along the bank and dropped it into the creek ? ' He was referring to Pansel, of course, but it might equally well apply to Madgek. That can't, by the way, have been Pansel's boot-mark because he wasn't there when the body was moved—and you found the same mark there, didn't you ? "

" Yes, sir, made since last high tide, too."

" Quite. Say for a moment that it was Madgek's boot, how's this for a theory : he kills Fiennes at his hut sometime after mid-day on Saturday— after Tasson delivered the post—say one or two o'clock ; that's a good twenty hours or more before Dr. Turl saw him. Then it occurs to him to make it look like an accident. But it's high tide, more or less, then, and he knows enough about death at sea to realise that it can't be made to look like drowning, so he waits—or comes back—when the tide's down, carries the body across to the saltings and shoves it into the mud, so that it looks as if the mud had done the smothering. He knows that the next tide will wash away all trace of his own foot-marks in the mud of the creek and he probably thought the path on the bank wouldn't show anything—it was practically dry except in one or two hollows. That covers your time difficulties, Jett, and explains the foot-mark. The fact of that foot-mark being deliberately wiped out afterwards is the most significant fact we've had up-to-date ; it *must* mean a guilty conscience."

Inspector Lamming's eyes glistened with excite-

ment ; the scent was hot now, the hunt was up.
Even the placid Superintendnent was impressed.

"That's a very ingenious theory, sir ; I don't see
a hole in it."

Major Fennell laughed.

"Don't you, Jett ? " he said. "I do. A damn
big one. How was the killing done ? That'll take
some explaining. In any case you've got a long
way to go before you can fix it on Madgek.
You've got definitely to connect the money with
him ; it *looks* as if what he gave Fardell was Fiennes'
money, but it's not certain. You've got to prove
that he knew, or had good reason to suppose, that
Fiennes had got money. You've got to prove that
that mark was made by his boot. You've got to
satisfy yourself that he *could* have been there at
that time—that he hasn't got an alibi. You've
got your work cut out."

Superintendent Jett rose to his feet.

"We have, sir, but we've got something to bite
on now. So far I haven't made any direct enquiries
about those boots, because I didn't want to start
people talking and in any case there was nothing
definite to connect them with the death. Now
there is. I'll find them. And I'll find out where
young Madgek was at the relevant times."

"That should all help. By the way, I suppose
you haven't made any more of that note that was
found on the body—the one about his having supper
with Pansel, I mean ? "

Superintendent Jett shook his head.

"No, sir, and I doubt we never shall. It was
common paper and might have been written by
anyone—no recognizable finger-prints. My view is

that it was put there by the murderer to divert attention from himself."

The Chief Constable frowned.

" You know, I almost doubt that ", he said. " It would be an awfully risky business ; if someone had seen him do it—and there were a lot of people about —it would be sure to point suspicion at him. My own impression is that it was simply a mischief-maker who'd heard these stories about Fiennes and Pansel and was out to make trouble without having to show his own nose. It's typical of these people."

Superintendent Jett gave a wry smile.

" Some of them, sir ", he said. " Anyway, I'm afraid it'll remain guesswork."

" You've heard no more from Scotland Yard ? They weren't very helpful, I'm afraid."

" No, sir ; only that string of women he was supposed to have had affairs with. There was one name among them that connected with what his solicitor told me—Mr. Pelly. He'd come down with instructions to reveal the outline of the will if it was wanted. The bulk of his money goes to the Authors' Society to found a bursarship or a scholarship or something . . ."

" Aha. Perpetuate the illustrious name of Fiennes ", murmured Major Fennell.

" But there was an annuity of a hundred a year to Jane Beldart—a child of two, I understand. And one of the names on the Yard's list is Beldart—Miss Norah Beldart, an authoress in poor circumstances. I don't know whether . . ."

There was a knock at the door and a voice asked for the Inspector. In a minute he was back.

" That's a message from Detective-Sergeant Voles, sir ", he said. " We arranged that he should telephone to my brother-in-law, who's a chemist here, if he wanted to say anything. The Superintendent thought he'd better not ring up the station. Just a code-message—' please send me another bottle of that medicine as soon as possible '. That means he'll be at a place that the Superintendent fixed up with him."

" Going now, Jett ? " asked the Chief Constable.

" Better, sir, I think. I don't want him to have to hang about in a suspicious manner. It's up on the hill above the village—quiet place."

" I'll drive you over ; my car's not so well known as yours."

Ten minutes later Major Fennell pulled his car up alongside a young man in a grey suit who was evidently out for a Sunday morning walk through the quiet lanes.

" Can I give you a lift ? " he asked quietly.

The young man hesitated, looked at his watch . . .

" Well, I am a bit late. Thank you, sir, I'm making for Walsingham, lunching with some friends of my sister's."

" Jump in."

The car drove off. Nobody, as it happened, had seen this careful pantomime.

" Never saw such cautious chaps ", said Detective-Sergeant Voles. " Not one word have I got out of any of the inhabitants, not even out of my landlord, Pete. Sometimes he and one of those two gentlemen, Mr. Sarne and Mr. Vessle, have a gossip across the bar counter but never so that I can hear anything. But last night a chap came in who was here a fortnight ago—a commercial. He was very excited about Fiennes' death—said he was sure he'd seen him there last time he was in—Sunday night, a fortnight ago that was.''

" That was the 17th ", said Superintendent Jett, consulting his diary; " the Sunday before it happened.''

" That's right, sir. He tried to pump the landlord about it—last night, I mean—but Pete shut him up—or rather, he wouldn't talk. This chap, Salomon, his name is, came over to the table where I was sitting and was soon telling me all about it. Won't cost the County more than one and ninepence, either ", added Sergeant Voles with a grin.

" I'll pass that ", said the Chief Constable.

" It seems that there was the hell of a row that night. Sarne was there and a little pompous fellow who sounds like Vessle and another chap I can't identify. After a bit Fiennes came in. He'd just got back from Norwich—motoring; Salomon heard that. Then they got talking together in whispers and chuckling a good deal. Fiennes called for a bottle of his special sherry and they lapped that down and ordered another. That loosened their tongues a bit and Salomon gathered that they were talking about some adventure that Fiennes had had in Norwich—a woman, he thought, but he didn't pay particular attention because he was having a game of draughts with another commercial. They got very noisy, and then suddenly the door opened and a big man came in and stood there staring at Fiennes. They all seemed a bit startled and awkward and then Fiennes called to the big man to

have a drink ; ' My merry Pansel ', he called him.
The chap did drink with them, but he didn't seem
to like it much ; awkward, Salomon thought, and
not very fond of any of them. But he still wasn't
paying much attention—Salomon wasn't."

"Half a minute, Voles ", said the Chief Constable.
"Your friend didn't hear the woman's name that
they were talking about ? "

"Not her name, sir, no, but . . . you'll see, sir."

"Sorry. Go on."

"All of a sudden the little man that I think was
Vessle jumped to his feet and started singing.
Something about a horn and a deer—Shakespeare,
he said it was. Salomon said he had a good voice
but was rather tight. They all stared at him and
then Sarne burst out : ' Now you've said it. You'll
get your neck broken ! '—or something like that, and
roared with laughter. Fiennes and Pansel stared at
each other and Fiennes said ' Do they fit ? ' and
Pansel suddenly turned round and rushed out of the
room. The others all stared at each other for a bit
and seemed rather uncomfortable ; then they
started drinking again and cheered up and started
pulling Fiennes' leg about this woman and what he'd
been up to in Norwich and what was going to
happen to him now. Then it was closing time and
they all cleared off, pretty noisy and tight. Salomon
said that when he read about Fiennes being dead he
put two and two together and made sure that it was
this man Pansel's wife that they'd been talking about
and that he'd done him in."

The Chief Constable and Superintendent Jett
looked at each other in thoughtful silence.

"Perhaps I'd better get back now, sir ", said

Detective-Sergeant Voles; "my sister hasn't really got any friends in Walsingham."

Major Fennell cast an appreciative eye at his protégé.

"Useful work, Voles", he said. "Cultivate your friend Mr. Salomon and see if you can't get the landlord, Pete, to talk. But don't give yourself away. It won't do for you to tackle Sarne or Vessle. You'll have to try again, Jett."

"You think he was week-ending with Mrs. Pansel, sir?"

"Sounds like it. I'll ask the Norwich City Police to have a hunt round; it's their job. Got a photograph of either of them?"

"Mr. Fiennes, sir, yes. The Yard got one for me through a Press Agency. I've nothing of Mrs. Pansel."

"Pity. Still, she's not a common type. I can give them a pretty clear description."

"You want us still to go on with the other line, sir?"

"By all means, yes. Weathercock's shifting about a bit, that's all."

CHAPTER XXII

N O R W I C H   C I T Y

A YOUNG man dressed in a blue serge suit and wearing a grey soft hat walked up to the reception window of The Gables Hotel, Norwich, and asked if he could see the manager. The Gables was a large and popular hotel, not far from the Castle, much frequented by motorists and by well-to-do visitors to the Cathedral City. At the present moment, half-past three on a Sunday afternoon, it was unusually quiet, the luncheon rush being over and most of its clients being either asleep or out enjoying the sunny afternoon. The young lady in the office, quiet and serene, replied that the manager was out and was there anything which she could do.

" It's a confidential matter ", replied the young man, with a slight frown.

" I expect I can deal with it ", replied the young lady. " I am the deputy-manager—and Mr. Bagnet's daughter ", she added with a smile. The Gables was a privately owned hotel and its proprietor, Mr. James Bagnet, a considerable figure in the City.

The young man still appeared to hesitate but Miss Bagnet, being naturally curious, soon had him inside the manager's office while the hall porter took over the duties of reception.

" I do that job on Sundays as well as my own ", explained Miss Bagnet, " it gives Miss Hoole a day off and we've had to cut down our staff to a minimum in these hard times. You're not staying here, are you ? "

The young man shook his head.

" I'm Detective-Sergeant Hack of the City Police ", he said, showing his warrant-card. " I'm trying to trace a gentleman who is believed to have stayed in an hotel in Norwich on Saturday and Sunday, 16th and 17th July. There is believed to have been a lady with him but it's not known whether he would have registered under his own name. I have a photograph of him which may help . . ."

Miss Bagnet looked carefully at the photograph which Sergeant Hack handed to her.

" Oh, yes ", she said ; " I remember him. I was in the hall when he arrived. A very good-looking man—interesting-looking. Striking grey eyes—I wondered who he was."

" Did you hear his name ? "

" No, but I looked it up after he'd signed ", replied Miss Bagnet with a smile. " I've forgotten it now, but I'll soon tell you."

She left the room and presently returned with the registration book. Flicking over the pages to Saturday, 16th. July, she ran her fingers down the column.

" Here you are. ' Mr. and Mrs. Douglas Finch, British, Grosvenor Hotel, London '. They came by car, I think. George could tell you."

" Did you see his . . . Mrs. Finch ? " enquired Sergeant Hack.

" Yes, I saw her ; I didn't notice her particularly." There was a note of indifference in Miss Bagnet's

voice. " Rather tall, decent figure, frumpish, not
bad-looking. I should think she *was* his wife."

" About five foot eight, blue eyes, fair hair,
clear complexion, slim figure ? " quoted Sergeant
Hack.

" That's about it ", replied Miss Bagnet.

" And how long did they stay ? "

Miss Bagnet glanced at the book.

" Only the one night. George can probably tell
you what time they left on Sunday. Gallett, our
head-porter, is off every other Sunday ; he is to-day."

George, summoned from temporary duty in the
reception office, remembered Mr. Finch's departure
quite well. The gentleman had a very nice Baroda
coupé—George was a connoisseur—and had brought
it round himself a little before eleven. They had
driven off, as far as he could tell, in the direction of
Newmarket.

Well satisfied with the prompt success of his
mission, Detective-Sergeant Hack thanked Miss
Bagnet and took his leave. George, ushering him
out, confided that in his opinion Mrs. Finch had
been ' a bit of all right '. Back at City Police headquarters the detective heard that Major Fennell
would like to be rung up at his house, which was
three miles out of Norwich on the Cromer road, as
soon as any definite information came in. The call
was soon through and Hack made his discreet
report.

" Gables Hotel, sir, with the lady as described.
Left eleven a.m. Sunday, by car—a Baroda coupé—
apparently in the direction of Newmarket."

Major Fennell hung up the receiver and lit his
inevitable pipe. Pacing up and down his study, he

thought over the problem which this new development presented. There was no getting away from the fact that a quite definite motive now existed for the removal of Mr. Dallas Fiennes by an injured husband. Taken in conjunction with the other known circumstances of the case it simply could not be ignored. An extremely unpleasant job would have to be done and one which, Fennell realised, could be better done by himself than anyone else. With a shrug of his shoulders the Chief Constable resigned himself to the call of duty. He looked at his watch. If an unpleasant job must be done, the sooner the better. But he could not well go at once; he had guests playing tennis and staying to early supper. He would run over to Bryde directly after that; it would, in any case, create less talk if he arrived at Bryde after dark; for everybody's sake he did not want to advertise his visit.

It was, therefore, some time after nine when his quiet-looking 30–60 Pancras glided up to the garden-gate of John Pansel's little house on the outskirts of Bryde-by-the-Sea. With a heavy heart Fennell walked up the short stretch of path and knocked at the door. It was opened almost at once by a big man, who peered at him in the half-light.

" Can I come in a minute, Mr. Pansel ? "

At the sound of the quiet voice, John Pansel stepped back and made way for his visitor to enter, looking at him with what seemed nervous curiosity as he did so.

" I'd like a word with you alone ", said Fennell in a low voice. " My name's Fennell ; I'm Chief Constable of the County."

He saw the blood ebb out of his host's face,

leaving it deathly white. The man's hand trembled as he shut the door.

"Come into the kitchen then—if you don't mind."

He led the way down the passage and, lighting a lamp in the little kitchen, shut the door behind his visitor.

"My wife's in the living-room", he said. "Sit down, won't you?"

"Thanks. I've got an unpleasant subject to talk about, Mr. Pansel, but I won't beat about the bush. We're still making enquiries into the circumstances connected with Mr. Fiennes' death and I'm bound to tell you it's come to my knowledge that you had grounds for being on anything but good terms with him—in fact, that he had done you a very great wrong. Under the circumstances I think you'll understand that I'm compelled to enquire as closely as I can into the report. You're not obliged to say anything, but it's my duty to give you an opportunity of doing so."

While he was speaking Major Fennell saw the colour come slowly back into Pansel's face, which now bore a very angry look. He saw, too, with some disquiet, that the man's hands were clenched into two very formidable fists.

"What grounds are you talking about? What wrong?"

The Chief Constable tried to pick words that would gloss over the crudeness of what he had to say, but it wasn't easy. Better be blunt, he decided.

"We have learnt that Mrs. Pansel spent a week-end in Norwich with Mr. Fiennes."

The artist sprang to his feet, his face flushed

with anger, his eyes flashing. He towered above his visitor. Suddenly he turned on his heel and, striding across to the window, looked out into the night. When he turned round again his face and voice were both more nearly normal.

"You're doing your duty, I expect", he said. "But it's a bit difficult to listen to that sort of thing and keep one's temper. It amazes me that you should believe such a story on the strength of a lot of old fish-wives' gossip. I know it's been going about that my wife was flirting with Fiennes. She *was* friends with him—liked him very much, I believe—may even have flirted with him a bit in a mild sort of way. It's deadly dull for her here and I don't blame her much if she did. But as for doing what you say—giving me 'grounds for' . . . whatever it was—'a great wrong'—and that sort of thing; it's absolutely preposterous . . . and untrue."

He paced up and down the little kitchen, trying to control his temper. The Chief Constable sat in silence, a horrible feeling of discomfort at the pit of his stomach. Poor devil; he evidently believed in his wife. Now he'd got to smash that belief.

"I'm sorry, Pansel", he said quietly, "but unfortunately we've got definite proof that your wife spent the week-end—or rather, the night of Saturday, 16th. July, with Fiennes at the Gables Hotel in Norwich."

"What ? !"

John Pansel stared at his visitor, a look of agonized doubt creeping into his eyes.

"That's not true ! That's not true ! She was with a friend in Norwich—a girl friend."

Slowly Fennell shook his head.

" She was ! She . . . I . . ."

The door opened and Mrs. Pansel walked in.

" I heard what you said. In fact, I've been listening ", she said, with a quiet smile. " I think I've a right to take part in this talk—as it's all about me."

Major Fennell had risen to his feet and was staring at her in embarrassed silence.

" I expect you're the Chief Constable, aren't you ? " said Hilary Pansel. " I didn't hear that, but I don't see who else you can be."

Fennell nodded.

" Yes ", he said. " I'm very sorry, Mrs. Pansel . . ."

" It's quite all right ", she interrupted him. " It's much better to clear things up. I know there's been talk. But please come into the other room—this smells of stale dinner."

She led the way into the living-room, telling John to bring the whisky.

" It's quite true ", she said, when they were all seated and Major Fennell uncomfortably fingering his glass ; " it's quite true that Dallas Fiennes and I were about together a good deal during the weeks before he died, and that seems to have made people talk a lot. Perhaps it's natural that they should. But it's not true that I stayed with him in Norwich or anywhere else. You talked about Saturday, 16th. July. That was when I went to Gwen Farnes, John ", she went on, turning to her husband. " It's only a fortnight ago—though it seems longer."

" I know ", said her husband. " I really think, Major Fennell, that you might have taken a bit more trouble to investigate your story before you come talking to me about ' great wrongs '." John Pansel seemed to have taken a particular dislike to that expression. " I knew all about my wife going to Norwich ; why, I even walked to the station at Great Hayworth with her myself—carried her bag. Sounds as if she was eloping with another fellow, doesn't it, or do you take me for a *mari complaisant ?* "

There was a sneering note in John's voice that distressed Hilary. But he was being pretty highly tried ; she realised that.

Major Fennell put down his glass, shifted uncomfortably on his chair. It was all very well, but what was to stop Fiennes meeting her at the other end even if her husband did put her in at this ?

" I'd better tell you all I did ", said Hilary Pansel, who seemed to read his thought. " I left Great Hayworth by the 9.40 and reached Norwich at about twelve. I did some shopping, had lunch at a Gater restaurant in one of the big streets, and in the afternoon went to a film I'd specially wanted to see. It was an Adolphe Menjou film called ' Paris loves ' and it was at a big cinema near the station. I don't remember the name, but you can't miss it. I can't prove I was there of course, but at least you can check that that film was on there then. The commissionaire's got a *Médaille Militaire*, by the way, if that's any help to you ", she added with a laugh.

Major Fennell looked surprised.

" Clever of you to know that ribbon, Mrs. Pansel ", he said, " they aren't very common."

" There was one at the hospital I was in in the

war. D'you remember him, John? Captain Rashworth; he'd been a sergeant-major in the Coldstream before he got a commission."

"I should think I do", said John, his face softening. "A 'stout fellow', if ever there was one."

Noticing the Chief Constable's expression, he added:

"My wife nursed me in the war, Major Fennell, and married me afterwards. I was a bit of a wreck after the war and she got me going again."

Good heavens! thought Fennell, this doesn't sound like a 'faithless wife' story—which was exactly what Hilary had intended him to think when she started that train of thought.

"Then I took a taxi out to my friend's house on the outskirts of Norwich, just off the Ipswich road. I got there some time before seven, I think. Miss Farnes, her name is, Major Fennell. I stayed with her till Wednesday. She'll be able to tell you that I'm telling the truth."

The Chief Constable rose to his feet.

"I don't know what to say", he said, hesitatingly. "I'm *sure* you're telling me the truth, Mrs. Pansel. I needn't assure you that I shouldn't have said what I did to your husband if I hadn't had what I thought was convincing proof . . . someone must have made a pretty bad blunder." He stopped; looked at the big man who was standing now with his hand on his wife's shoulder. "But Pansel, you don't deny, do you, that something happened at that inn in the village—the 'Virgin Duck', isn't it?—on Sunday evening? Fiennes was offensive, wasn't he ? Wait—you needn't answer if you don't want to."

Major Fennell had for a moment forgotten his official position in the interest of the story.

"He was, indeed", said Pansel grimly. "He was drunk. He was always boasting of what he thought were his conquests. I'm not at all sure he wasn't trying to make his congenial friends think something like what you've evidently been told— by them, I suppose. I cleared out. I might have made a mess of them if I hadn't."

"I see", said Major Fennell slowly. "Thank you. "Well, I'm afraid it will be my duty, Mrs. Pansel, to check your . . . what you've told me. I wish you . . . I think I should tell you that somebody is by way of having identified you. I can hardly ask you to come to the hotel with me and . . ."

"And ask them to say whether I broke the seventh commandment with Mr. Fiennes ? " asked Hilary with a wry smile. "Well, I think that is asking rather a lot."

The Chief Constable's eyes had strayed to the mantelpiece, where stood a photograph of Hilary taken a year or two after her marriage.

"You wouldn't let me take that photograph, would you ? I know I'm being rather irregular, but it would be the quickest and easiest way of clearing the whole thing up."

For a second Hilary hesitated, holding John's arm to stop him speaking. Then :

"All right", she said. "Don't publish it in the *Police Gazette* unless you must."

"Oh, no ! " Major Fennell's voice was

shocked. "And of course nobody shall know who this is."

"Thank you. You'll let me have it back. It's the only one . . . John's got."

Again Geoffrey Fennell felt the certainty creep over him that this woman could not be an adulteress. Still, he must do his job. He said good-bye and drove off into the night. Back in the living-room, John Pansel stared at his wife.

"Hilary! What does it mean?"

Hilary laughed.

"Oh, it doesn't mean I've been deceiving you after all, you old silly. It's quite true—what I told him—except the part that you know isn't true."

"But that photograph . . ." The slower-witted John stumbled over his words. "It's a frightful risk to tell all those lies."

Hilary shrugged her shoulders.

"I know", she said. "I always wanted to tell the whole truth, but you began it. That was why I came in. When I heard you beginning to say: 'It isn't true!' I thought I'd better come in. If we've got to lie, let's lie convincingly."

"But all those places you said you went to—shops and restaurants—did you go there?"

"No, of course I didn't."

"But he'll find out you didn't!"

Hilary laughed.

"Not he!" she said. "Do you know Gater's restaurants? They're always cram-full. What hope has he of finding out that a perfectly ordinary-looking woman *hasn't* been there?"

"But the hotel?"

288

" Yes, that's the risk. But he already thinks
they've identified me there. But I don't believe
they can really identify me. I was only in the hall
a minute and then we were taken upstairs by a
porter and shown our rooms. Porters don't notice
anything. I never saw the chambermaid—I was
only there about an hour, remember. And when I
slipped out by the back-stairs I didn't see anybody
either. What I can't understand is why they say I
stayed there—when I didn't ! "

" But Hilary ", John persisted, " why on earth
did you let him have the photograph ? They'll
identify you by that."

Hilary laughed.

" I believe that was a brain-wave ", she said. " It
was a shock for a second ; it would have looked
frightfully guilty to refuse. But don't you see, it's
the very thing that'll prevent them identifying me.
It was taken nearly twelve years ago ! Of course,
looking at me in this light and then looking at the
photograph—well it's obviously me. But only a
man would be so blind as not to realise that it's
useless for getting me identified by someone who
only saw me for a few minutes. When I went there,
in a modern hat, I must have looked completely
different—frightfully older. If anyone noticed my
appearance at all it was a woman, and she'll have
thought I looked middle-aged and plain."

" Rubbish ! " said John hotly.

Hilary put her hand to his cheek.

" Dear John ; I do—to young women, anyhow.
No, I'm sure that photograph won't help him and
he's feeling all embarrassed and *wanting* to believe
me. It'll be all right, I'm quite sure, John."

CHAPTER XXIII

MISTAKEN IDENTITY

A DAMNED awkward business, the whole thing, thought Major Fennell, as he drove home. Walking into a fellow's house and telling him his wife had been deceiving him with another fellow, when all the time she hadn't ; and he felt sure she hadn't—a nice-looking, straightforward girl who had evidently been a good wife to him for years ; decent-looking fellow, too—knocked about in the war and nursed back to health by his wife. What on earth had the Norwich City Police been up to, making a mess of that identification ? That was an awkward business too ; he had no jurisdiction in Norwich and absolutely no right to criticise or shove his own oar in. And yet he could not now be satisfied with any identification other than his own. He would have to go and see Staddart and be tactful. The trouble was that Staddart had not had the job long and he didn't know him well ; these promoted Superintendents were sometimes very touchy.

Major Fennell need not have worried. Mr. Staddart had only one idea in life and that was to get a job done in the best and quickest manner. He at once suggested that the Chief Constable of Norfolk should detail one of his own men to go into the matter again, either alone or in company with Sergeant Hack. Fennell jumped at this, thanked his opposite number and in five minutes was out on

the job with Detective-Sergeant Hack. It was
Bank Holiday, but that means no holiday to the
police—not to the Detective branch, anyhow, if
there is work to be done ; nor was the holiday likely
to interfere with the investigation. Shops would be
shut, but Major Fennell did not expect anything
from them anyhow ; on the other hand, Gater's
Restaurant, the Cinema and the Gables Hotel would
all be open ; Miss Farnes might or might not be at
home.

Gater's Restaurant was a wash-out. An over-
worked manager, struggling to conceal his annoyance
at being interrupted to-day of all days, summoned
one or two vague-looking young ladies who could get
no further than : ' I'm sure I couldn't say ', or ' Well,
she might have been '. Major Fennell soon gave it
up and made for the Pandamonic Cinema near the
station. Here he was easily able to check the fact
that ' Paris Loves ' had been in the bill on 16th. July,
but the bemedalled Commissionaire could give him
no more than a smile and a shake of the head.

" Saturday afternoon, sir ? And a fortnight back ?
Not a hope. Hundreds of young women and
middle-aged women and old women and their gents
I get past me every hour. Now if it had been
yesterday and the lady had spoke to me or something. No, I'm afraid I can't help you, sir, much
as I'd like to."

Obviously hopeless. Well, he hadn't expected
anything. After all, the hotel was the crux of the
matter—and Miss Farnes. Getting back into his
car, he drove up to the ' Gables '. As a matter of
etiquette Major Fennell had asked Sergeant Hack to
take the lead in each enquiry, giving his own name

and official position ; he (Fennell) could then chip
in with any questions he wanted to ask, without
disclosing his identity. This method was followed
at the Gables Hotel and the two police officers were
soon interviewing in the manager's office the various
servants who might be expected to identify Dallas
Fiennes and his lady friend. Sergeant Hack, who
had begun the day on the defensive, thinking that
he was being criticised for a suspected blunder, had
soon thawed under Major Fennell's simple and
friendly manner. He asked first to see Miss Bagnet
and, without saying anything about a mistake,
showed her half-a-dozen photographs of young and
youngish women, including Hilary Pansel's, and
asked her if she could pick out Mrs. Finch. The
girl looked them through casually and shook her
head.

" I shouldn't say any of these were her ", she said,
" but then, I didn't pay much attention to her—only
a glance."

Sergeant Hack frowned involuntarily. He wanted,
naturally, to have his first report confirmed.

" The lady I described to you is one of those ", he
said. " Would you mind looking again—rather
carefully ? "

Miss Bagnet did so and gradually eliminated all
except the photograph of Mrs. Pansel.

" This might be her ", she said, " but she was a
lot older than this. It's an old photo, isn't it ? "

Sergeant Hack looked relieved and glanced at the
Chief Constable.

" It may be ", said the latter, horrid doubt
stealing over him again. " Do you definitely
identify it ? "

" Oh, no, I can't say that, but it's the only one of those that might be her—or so I should say. But you'd much better ask the chambermaid. She'll have had a much better look at her than I did."

Miss Bagnet returned to her duties, sending the appropriate chambermaid to take her place.

Emma Golling was a plump, middle-aged body, whom Fennell at once put down as an excellent witness. She answered quietly that she remembered, not the name Finch, but the lady who occupied Room 27 on Saturday, 16th. July. No, she had no particular reason to do so, but she had a good memory. Handed the photographs, she looked through them dispassionately and shook her head.

" You're sure ? "

" Quite sure, sir."

A final, clinching question occurred to Major Fennell.

" Look here ", he said, " did the lady look a . . . a *fast* sort of person ? Was she made up, I mean—scent, and all that ? You can speak frankly ; that won't go any further."

The corners of Emma Golling's mouth gave a slight downward twitch—the only sign of feeling she had given throughout the interview.

" They're all about the same ", she said,—" these week-enders."

It was enough for Geoffrey Fennell. No one in their senses would describe Mrs. Pansel as ' a week-ender '. He religiously completed his task, interviewing the head-waiter, who assured him that though the gentleman had breakfasted he had not seen any lady ; the head-porter, who remembered vaguely a gentleman that might be the one in the photograph but could not put a face to the lady; the under-porter, who had assisted at the departure on Sunday morning but to whom, apparently, all young ladies were alike—' nice legs and smelt lovely ' was his illuminating comment. No, it had not been Mrs. Pansel who stayed at the Gables with Dallas Fiennes that Saturday night, thought Major Fennell, whoever it may have been.

So much for the negative; now for the proof positive. The address given him by Mrs. Pansel was on the outskirts of the city, just off the Ipswich road. It did not take the Pancras long to get there and as it was now nearly one o'clock Miss Gwen Farnes was at home. This time Major Fennell left Sergeant Hack in the car and was presently ushered into a small drawing-room, looking out onto a pretty garden. The room was overcrowded with fussy Victorian furniture and knick-knacks, probably inherited from a more spacious home. Miss Farnes, who presently came in from the garden by the French window, was a woman of about thirty-six, good-looking and well-built, but wearing the air of masculine independence that is so unattractive to a man. She greeted her visitor as if he were exactly the person she was expecting and wanting to see; the word ' hearty ' passed uncomfortably across the back of Fennell's mind.

" I'm Major Fennell. I'm the Chief Constable of the County—not the City ", he explained. " It's been my duty to ask various people to account for their movements on Saturday and Sunday, 16th. and 17th. July—a fortnight ago roughly, among them Mrs. John Pansel. She sent me to you to confirm her story. I think perhaps, if you'll allow me, I'll leave

it to Mrs. Pansel to give you the reason for this
enquiry, but I shall be grateful if you will tell me
what you know of Mrs. Pansel's movements on those
days."

Miss Farnes looked at her visitor in silence for
half a minute, the frankness of her stare causing
Major Fennell some embarrassment. Then she
seemed to make up her mind.

"I can tell you that in a few words", she said.
"Hilary Pansel arrived here a little before seven on
that Saturday. We had dinner together, sat out in
the garden afterwards, talking, and went to bed at
about half-past ten. On Sunday we had breakfast
at nine and sat in the garden all day, talking and
reading, till after tea and then we changed and went
to the evening service at the Cathedral. After that
we . . ."

Major Fennell raised his hand.

"You needn't go on, Miss Farnes", he said.
"That covers the ground. I am sure I can accept
your word . . ."

"You needn't accept my word alone", said Miss
Farnes, with intelligent anticipation. "My maid
knows Mrs. Pansel well; she has been with me for
ten years. I'll ring for her and then you can ask
her anything you like. She won't gossip."

She tugged the long silken bell-pull and almost at
once the little maid who had admitted Fennell
appeared.

"Kitty, will you tell Major Fennell what time
Mrs. Pansel arrived here on Saturday about a fortnight ago—and anything else he asks you. I'll be
out in the garden, Major Fennell."

The maid's account bore out in every particular

the story told by her mistress. Shown the photographs, she at once picked out Mrs. Pansel. The
Chief Constable was completely satisfied. He
thanked her, took leave of Miss Farnes, and rejoined
Sergeant Hack. It had been his intention to go up
to the Lakenham ground in the afternoon and watch
Norfolk playing their annual match with Hertford-
shire in the Minor Counties Championship, but
Fennell had sufficient imagination to realise the
anxiety that Mrs. Pansel must be suffering. So he
gave up his plan, dropped Sergeant Hack—with
many thanks for his help—stopped at his home for
a late lunch, and motored over to Bryde. On his
way, as a matter of form, he called in at Great Hayworth Station and obtained confirmation of Mrs.
Pansel's story that she had been seen off from there
by her husband and had travelled by the morning
train to Norwich on the Saturday in question. That
done, he continued his journey to Bryde. As he
expected, both Hilary Pansel and her husband were
at home ; the look of anxious anticipation in their
eyes sufficiently rewarded him for his unselfishness.

" I've brought your photograph back, Mrs.
Pansel ", he said. " It has been a real help in clearing up a bad blunder. I'm absolutely satisfied that
everything you told me is true and I apologise very
sincerely for having even for an instant believed
anything else."

Hilary blushed and for a moment her eyes
wavered.

" Thank you, Major Fennell ", she said, " it was
very good of you to come and tell me so promptly."

" I think I should say that the officer who made
the first enquiry was badly misled by a very careless

296

bit of identification by someone who ought to have known better. He didn't get it as fully checked as he ought to have done, but I think that was partly because of the unmistakable identification of Mr. Fiennes by more than one person ; he then accepted the identification of you by one witness as enough. It shows how dangerous it is to work on description without a photograph and I must take the blame for that."

"You mean ", said John Pansel slowly, " that there *was* some one—some woman—with Fiennes ? "

"Yes, there was. They left on Sunday morning. They went towards Newmarket, I believe."

After a few more exchanges of polite apology and thanks the Chief Constable took his leave. The Pansels, husband and wife, remained staring at each other.

"What on earth does it mean ? " asked John at last.

Hilary gave a little shudder.

"I've been thinking about it, John ", she said. " I think that when he found I was gone he . . . he was very angry . . . naturally . . . and went out and . . . got somebody else to take my place."

John glared.

"You mean some woman off the streets ? "

Hilary flushed with shame.

"Perhaps not that," she said. " He may have known someone at the theatre . . . in a touring company. He knew a lot of theatrical people. He may have found some . . . old friend there and persuaded her to go and stay with him. Probably he got her to cut the evening performance—send a note to say she was ill. Then, if the touring

297

company was moving on somewhere next day he probably motored her over. Major Fennell said they went towards Newmarket—that probably means Cambridge. If you were to enquire you'd probably find that the company that was at Norwich that week was at Cambridge the next."

The dull light of anger still smouldered in John Pansel's eyes.

"My God!" he muttered, "and he came back here and made those fellows think that he had been with you!" He clenched his hands, rage shaking him. "The damned swine. I'm glad! My God, I'm glad . . ."

Hilary seized his arm.

"John! John, dear, don't! It's all awful but . . . he is dead."

CHAPTER XXIV

THE ATTACK LAUNCHED

IN the meantime, Superintendent Jett had not been letting the grass grow under his feet. He had decided that the time had arrived to abandon veiled enquiries and to come out into the open, even at the risk of exciting curiosity and of putting the murderer—if murderer there were—on his guard. His first move was to draft—with the approval of the Chief Constable—a notice to appear in the press :

> " *The Police are anxious to trace four £5 Bank of England notes, Nos...................... which are known to have been in the possession of Mr. Dallas Fiennes shortly before he was found dead in the saltings at Bryde-by-the-Sea, Norfolk, on Sunday, 24th. July. Anyone able to give information on this point is requested to communicate with the Chief Constable, Norfolk Constabulary, Norwich.*"

That, thought Superintendent Jett, would give a pretty clear indication of what was in the wind without too directly flouting the finding of the Coroner's jury. The notice would be in the local daily papers the next day, Monday, and possibly in the big dailies as well.

The next thing was to interrogate the fisherman, Madgek, and this would have to be very carefully done. Superintendent Jett spent nearly an hour thinking over his line of approach, but he realised that a good deal would depend upon how Madgek responded. Jett decided in any case not to take Lamming with him to this interview as it was quite evident that the Inspector was on bad terms with Madgek, and this would be liable to check any confidences that the latter might otherwise feel inclined to make.

It was, as it happened, no easy matter to get a word with the boatman. The bank-holiday week-end was the cream of the harvest season for the owners of motor-boats, and Christian Madgek spent his whole day in rushing backwards and forwards between the harbour and the sea. The whole day, that is, except at low tide, and as that had been at just before noon—before, that is, Superintendent Jett came to his decision—there would be no further break until the holiday-makers tired of their fun. Jett did not, of course, want to interrupt Madgek in the middle of his profitable activities ; to do that would be to excite unnecessary talk, besides doing the fisherman serious financial harm and putting his back up. Fortunately, the most tireless of holiday-makers cannot resist the call of supper, and at eight o'clock Jett saw Madgek anchor his boat and make his way to the tiny house which was his home. A few minutes later the big Superintendent approached it.

The door was open and, looking into the little room, Jett saw that the table was laid with a cheerful red and white cloth, on which were a loaf of bread, a piece of cheese, a jug and some crockery. Madgek himself was standing in front of the fireplace, stirring something in a saucepan, his back to the door. At the Superintendent's knock the man's body stiffened and remained for a moment still ; then slowly he turned round and looked towards the door with an expressionless face.

" Good-evening. Can I come in a minute ? " asked Jett.

Madgek nodded.

" Mind your head ", he said, automatically.

" I'm Superintendent Jett of the County Constabulary. I've some questions to ask you on an important matter."

He glanced at the open door and Madgek walked across the room and shut it.

" Will you take a chair ? "

Superintendent Jett lowered himself on to the small Windsor chair which stood against the window. Madgek sat down by the table, his face illuminated by the evening glow. Jett was struck by the beauty of the man's face, the steel grey eyes with their heavy fringe of lashes, the fineness of the nose. Without being in any way shifty or sly, the face gave an impression of secretiveness ; an unusual and interesting type.

" I'm making enquiries ", began the Superintendent, " about some money—bank-notes—that were known to be in the possession of Mr. Fiennes just before his death. You know, of course, about the circumstances in which his body was found."

Madgek evidently did not take this as a question, as he sat silent, his eyes fixed steadily upon the police-officer's face.

" It's come to our knowledge, Madgek, that a few days after Mr. Fiennes' death you were in a position to repay a considerable sum of money in the form of a debt, which a short time previously you had said you were quite unable to pay. I want to ask you whether you are prepared to make a statement as to how you suddenly came to possess this money. I should tell you that you're not bound to answer that question if you don't want to."

As he talked, Jett saw a very faint expression of surprise come into the grey eyes, deepening almost to consternation. It was very faint ; the man's features remained unchanged, and when he spoke his voice was calm enough.

" I've got a trade, Superintendent. I make money, especially in holiday time. You'll likely have seen me to-day."

" How much have you taken to-day ? "

It was an acute question. No Norfolk fisherman likes to admit that he is doing well—that he is anything but a poor man. And yet, Madgek had got to account for his last remark. For a moment his eyes flickered from side to side ; he was calculating, Jett thought.

" Four or five pounds, perhaps."

" And the same yesterday ? "

" Likely enough."

" And you earn that all through the summer ? You must be a rich man."

" Oh, no, I don't ! " the answer shot out, almost automatically. " Bank-holiday week-end, this is."

" And what do you earn on an ordinary week-end ? "

" Two or three pounds perhaps—sometimes more, sometimes less, according to the weather."

" And on week-days ? "

" Perhaps a pound, in holiday time."

" If you earn all that, Madgek, why do you have to borrow money ? "

A frown wrinkled the man's forehead ; a muscle moved in his jaw.

" I have to live. And I had to borrow to buy my boat. It takes a long time to pay off."

" How long have you had it ? "

" Four years."

" You pay off in small instalments ? "

" Yes ; that's right."

" How much at a time ? "

But the fisherman saw the trap.

" I don't pay in regular instalments. The man that obliged me lets me pay as I can. Sometimes a pound or two, sometimes more."

" And this time you suddenly paid . . . how much ? "

A bead of sweat detached itself from the dark curls and ran slowly down Madgek's nose. Unconsciously he brushed it away.

" You'll have been told that, I'm thinking."

" Perhaps. But I want to know if I've been told right."

A very slight pause.

" I paid twenty-five pounds. This is the holiday season and I saved all I could to get square."

" You were able to pay that, in spite of the fact that the week-end before you paid it was spoilt by the weather ? "

" I'd have paid it all off if it hadn't been for that."

" Ah, you still owe some money ? "

" Another fifteen."

" I see ; thank you, Madgek. I'm bound to ask

you some more questions, though. Will you tell me where you were on the night of Friday, 22nd.—that's Friday week—the night the weather was thick ? "

Madgek gave a short laugh.

" Why, Superintendent, I was in bed. We're early folk here."

" In bed when—to when ? "

" Directly after closing. I had a glass in the tap-room at the ' Anchorage ' ; I was in bed by a quarter past ten and wasn't up till five."

" And the next night ? Saturday ? "

" About the same. Up a bit earlier to get my boat ready if the weather cleared."

" I see. I suppose you've no way of proving you were in bed all those two nights ? I advise you, Madgek, to think very carefully before you give me any false information. This is a very serious matter, as you'll no doubt understand, and I shouldn't be questioning you if I hadn't got very solid reasons for connecting you with the disappearance of those notes."

Again that look of consternation leapt into the man's eyes.

" But I . . . I don't know anything about that money ! I didn't know the man was dead till Sunday morning ! "

Superintendent Jett leaned forward.

" What time on Sunday morning ? " he asked. " Or was it Saturday night ? "

" No, I swear it wasn't ! I knew nothing about it till Giles Banyatt told us on Sunday morning and we went and fetched in his body."

" It's a pity, Madgek, that you can't prove to me

where you were on Saturday night—and Friday night too."

There was a pause, while the two men stared at each other, trying to read each other's thoughts. Then Madgek seemed to take a decision.

" All right ", he said, " I'll tell you where I was. And I can prove it. I was after rabbits in Statcham Park."

Superintendent Jett's lip curled.

" All that secrecy about a few rabbits ? " he asked.

" Inspector's got his knife into me ", replied Madgek, sullenly. " I won't say we wouldn't have taken something else if we got the chance."

" I see. And who were ' we ' ? "

" You're not going to bring this up against them ? "

" Not this time—if they tell me the truth."

" I was with Ben Gedge and Jo Fletting. Young William Soller was out too. We went out soon after ten and got back at dawn."

Superintendent Jett rose to his feet.

" All right, Madgek ", he said, " I'll check your story. I should have been readier to have believed it if you'd told me the truth straight away. Good-night."

He left the cottage and Christian Madgek stood staring after him. Slowly the fisherman walked across to the door and shut it, then sank down into his chair and stared into the dying fire. The little clock on the mantelpiece ticked away in the silence ; in the saucepan the stew of vegetables gradually grew cold.

* * * * *

Superintendent Jett had left his most important

question unasked. He had been greatly impressed
by the Chief Constable's theory that the murder
might have been committed at mid-day on Saturday
and the body dumped in the creek at low tide that
night. The vital question, then, was : where was
Madgek at—or about—mid-day on Saturday ? He
had not asked the question because he thought he
would first check up the man's other statements and
then, perhaps, when returning confidence had put
him off his guard, would fire it as a surprise shot.
Madgek must now think that the police were only
concerned with the two nights ; he would be the
less likely to concoct an alibi for mid-day on
Saturday.

In one way the questioning of Madgek had thrown
away an important point ; there would be little
chance now of finding the £5 notes if the man had
got them. Jett would have liked to have gone
there with a search warrant before putting Madgek
on his guard, but he knew that no magistrate would
have granted one on the flimsy evidence at present
in his possession. That must wait till something
more definite had been collected ; even then, with
the known unwillingness of criminals to part with
their spoil, it might not be too late. In the meantime there was a lot of spadework to be done.

It was too late to do any more that night, but
Jett told Inspector Lamming to get to work first
thing next morning, questioning Gedge, Fletting,
and young Soller about the Friday and Saturday
nights on which Madgek had said he was out poaching with them. The Superintendent himself had
some other work to attend to in the morning but he
promised to come over in the afternoon. Lamming

was none too well pleased at hearing Madgek's story ; he had himself been out the greater part of both those nights on a report of poaching, and had not succeeded in finding even a trace of the misdemeanants.

However, when Superintendent Jett arrived at Great Hayworth police station shortly before two the following, Monday, afternoon, he found his subordinate on very good terms with himself. He had rounded up and extracted confessions from all three men—Soller, as a matter of fact, was little more than a boy—and was bitterly disappointed when the Superintendent told him of his promise not to proceed against them if they told the truth.

Superintendent Jett listened thoughtfully to Lamming's account of his interviews. It occurred to him that the Inspector had had a suspiciously easy task in extracting these confessions. It was not the habit of the natives of this coast to admit anything, either about themselves or about their neighbours ; if they spoke they had an object in speaking—in this case, their object might be the substantiating of an alibi for Christian Madgek.

" Lamming ", he said, " I'm a bit suspicious of these confessions. What I want you to do now is to get hold of each of those fellows in turn, run him over to Statcham in your car, and get him to show you exactly where they were working those two nights. They may contradict each other or you may know, from your own movements that night, that they're lying."

It was not a job that appealed to Inspector Lamming, but orders were orders and he departed upon it with as good a grace as possible. Super-

intendent Jett followed him in his own car but
instead of stopping in Bryde, ran on along the coast
to the little town of Wells. On the previous night,
after leaving Madgek, he had gone down to the
harbour and examined the big motor-boat by means
of which the fisherman had said that he earned the
money to repay Fardell ; he was now on his way to
interview the maker, whose name he had found in
the stern.

Jabez Holyman was able to give him a good deal
of very useful information. In the first place Jett
learnt that the boat had not been paid for cash down.
The arrangement had been for one substantial cash
payment on delivery, followed by monthly instalments of £10 during the summer months and £2
during the winter. The payments had been completed by the end of the previous summer. It did
not look, therefore, as if Madgek had had to borrow
from Fardell in order to pay for the boat. Superintendent Jett further questioned the boat-builder
as to the likelihood of Madgek having been able to
earn £25 during the last three weeks, including the
week-end ruined by thick weather. Holyman
smiled and said that if he had thought that, he
would not himself have been content to wait three
years for his money by accepting monthly instalments of £10. He thought that £15 was the outside
limit of what Madgek could have earned during the
period referred to—probably not so much.

Superintendent Jett, who had been to some
extent impressed by the fisherman's story, returned
to his task with renewed eagerness. One problem
was still puzzling him : how to trace the patched
boots. If he made any sort of broadcast enquiry

for them the owner would certainly hear of it and might very well destroy the boots ; on the other hand, the method of ' keeping their eyes open ' had failed. After careful thought Jett decided to take a risk and to question the postman, Jude Tasson. Although he had been one of the men who brought the body in, there appeared to be no possible grounds for suspecting him. He was an intelligent, observant man and—he was the one inhabitant of Bryde who seemed willing to talk.

It was no difficult matter to find the postman. When not on his rounds he was generally down at the harbour watching the holiday-makers and picking up an occasional sixpence for an odd job. There he was this morning, and Jett—who was in plain clothes—sent a small boy to tell him that a gentleman would like to see him outside the ' Anchorage '. Tasson soon appeared and as there was still just time for a drink they had one in the private bar. As it happened, there was no one else there, and the Superintendent explained his problem. Tasson listened, a look of shrewd interest on his face. To Jett's disappointment, however, he declared that he had never noticed the patched boot-heel and did not know who it belonged to. He could, of course, if the Superintendent liked, enquire, but . . . he doubted if anyone in Bryde would tell him even if they knew.

" D'you know, Mr. Jett, what they're saying about this money that's missing ? " he asked with a smile.

" Oh, they know about that ? "

" Yes, they know. Somebody brought in an *East Coast Courier* by the bus this morning

There's not a soul in Bryde doesn't know about it now and they've all decided who took the money."

" Who ? "

Tasson laughed.

" Old Mother Barle ! "

" Nonsense ! "

" Nothing'll persuade 'em she didn't. She found the body and she took the money ; that's their way of looking at it. But wild horses wouldn't drag that from them if you were to go round asking questions."

" Well, keep your eyes open for those boots, Tasson, but don't ask anyone—and above all don't talk about what I've told you."

The postman promised and Superintendent Jett re-entered his car and drove off to the rendez-vous which he had arranged with Detective-Sergeant Voles. The plain-clothes man had picked up nothing more since his talk with the commercial traveller at the ' Virgin Duck ', but Jett thought he could now make use of him in another way. The flannel-clad figure emerged from behind a gate as the police-car drove up.

" Well ; heard anything fresh ? " asked Jett as they drove off.

" A lot of talk about your advertisement, sir. They don't know what to make of it at the ' Duck '— I can see that, though they don't talk much. Pete and the two gentlemen think Pansel did it, I'm sure, but naturally they don't think he'd have taken the money."

" Of course not. Well, go on listening, Voles, but I've got another job for you. I've been talking to Tasson, the postman, about those boots. He swears he doesn't know who they belong to, but I'm not satisfied ; it's just the sort of thing he'd be likely to know. It occurs to me he's afraid of giving one of these fellows away to the police—too definitely, I mean. They're a fairly tough lot ; I don't think they'd be over-gentle with a squeaker. But Tasson likes talking, and he likes a drink. Get to know him, give him a drink or two—not too obvious—get him to talk ; you know."

Voles nodded.

" And one other thing. Keep an eye on Madgek. He's on his guard with me and Inspector Lamming. But you might catch sight of something. Particularly watch him after closing time at night ; that seems to be his moment for starting off on surreptitious expeditions."

Having primed the detective with these instructions, Superintendent Jett dropped him not far from where he had picked him up and continued on his way to the police-station at Great Hayworth, where he put a call through to the Chief Constable's office in Norwich. He did not expect to find his Chief in the office on a Bank Holiday, but he wanted to make an appointment with him for the next day. The constable on duty in the office answered the call.

" The Chief Constable's not in now, sir. I believe he was going over to Bryde this afternoon. But there's a call just come through from Ipswich that I think is about your case. Superintendent Willey was trying to get you at Dersingham ; I'll put you through to him, sir."

A moment later Jett heard the voice of the Chief Clerk.

" That you, Jett ? We've just had a call through from Ipswich. A chap walked into headquarters there this morning at lunch time and said he'd read your advertisement about the notes missing from Fiennes' body and he thought he could tell you something interesting. It seems he was holiday-making at Bryde about three weeks ago and one day—Tuesday, 12th July he fixes it at—he was going on a trip in a motor-boat when a gentleman came on board and as he got on he tripped and fell. A fat pocket-book fell onto the bottom of the boat, open, and this chap says it was stuffed with notes ; everyone must have seen it, including the boatman. The point is, he gives a description of the boatman and it strikes me that it's that chap the Chief was telling me about—black curly hair, very good-looking, black eyelashes. That your chap ? "

"Sounds like him ", said Jett. " But how does the Ipswich fellow know it was Fiennes who came aboard ? "

"Saw his photograph in the papers at the time of the inquest, but as the jury found that verdict he didn't think it worth while to report what he'd seen. Ipswich have taken a statement from him and they're sending it up at once, but I thought I'd give you the outline in advance."

"Thanks, Willey ; thanks."

Jett hung up the receiver and stood looking out of the window, thinking over what he had heard. A sparkle came into his eyes.

"By Jove ", he said to Inspector Lamming, who didn't know what he was talking about, " that fits one of the points the Chief said I'd got to prove— that Madgek knew, or had good reason to suppose that Fiennes had got money. That was the day Fiennes cashed his cheque at the bank—Madgek saw the pocket book when it was dropped. That definitely links him up! Lord, Lamming, I wish I could get hold of the Chief. I want that search warrant!"

The door opened and Major Fennell walked in.

CHAPTER XXV

ARREST

THE Chief Constable, who had just come from his interview with the Pansels, listened carefully to Superintendent Jett's account of the development of his case against Madgek and agreed that there were now sufficient grounds for applying for a search warrant. If either the notes or the tell-tale boot were found, especially the former, and if Madgek failed to satisfy the police as to his movements on the Saturday while the coast was still wrapped in mist, then a further step of applying for a warrant for arrest could probably also be taken.

Superintendent Jett was never a man to waste time once a line of action was decided on. Before he went to bed that night he had got his search warrant signed by a magistrate, and soon after 5 a.m. the next morning he, together with Inspector Lamming and Police-Constable Pentwhistle were knocking at the door of Madgek's cottage. The fisherman was shaving and the look of astonishment on his lathered face would have been comic under other circumstances. Jett produced his warrant.

" I hold a warrant authorising me to search your house and premises, Madgek. You'd better look at it."

Madgek stared from the Superintendent to the folded paper and back again.

" Search my house ? ! "

Blank amazement changed slowly to a concentrated stare of thought ; slowly the man's face cleared but he did not move out of the doorway.

" What right have you got to come breaking into a man's house at this time of day ? " he asked stubbornly.

" There's my right. I told you to read it. And I must caution you not to interfere with me or my officers in the execution of our duty."

He put his hand on the man's arm and pushed him sharply aside. For a moment Madgek's body stiffened, anger flashed into his eyes ; it looked as though there would be ugly trouble—an open razor is no pleasant weapon to face. But he controlled himself and going across to the window, on which a small mirror was fixed, started again to shave himself. At a sign from the Superintendent, P.C. Pentwhistle remained with the occupier of the house while Jett and Lamming went into the little backroom in which he slept.

Superintendent Jett had had some experience of searching when he was a young constable in Norwich. It took him more than an hour to go through the bedroom and living-room, but by the end of that time he was satisfied that not even the flimsy banknotes were hidden inside the house. He made his way out into the little yard which Madgek used for his building materials and saw at once that here was a much more formidable proposition ; small stacks of timber and bricks, heaps of sand and shingle, tiles, ladders, a carpenter's shop with its tools and paint-pots—here was a haystack in which something a good deal larger than a needle might well be hidden; but Superintendent Jett was undismayed. He had arrived early for this very reason. Every heap of sand or shingle was shifted, every brick and plank moved. Inspector Lamming rummaged among the tools in the shop. At a quarter to seven Jett came to the last corner in the yard—a heap of junk. Lifting a rusty iron cowl he uncovered a pair of gumboots on one of which the heel had been roughly patched.

Replacing the cowl and leaving Inspector Lamming to watch it, Jett returned to the cottage, where Madgek was now calmly breakfasting and paying no attention to the hungry Pentwhistle.

" How many pairs of gum-boots have you got, Madgek ? "

" Only these I've got on."

" I'm looking for a pair with a patched heel. Have you got a pair like that ? "

Madgek scowled at his questioner.

" I've told you these are all I've got."

" Come out into the yard, please."

Reluctantly the fisherman followed. Jett removed the cowl.

" Whose boots are these ? "

Madgek stared at them.

" Those aren't mine ", he said. " I never put them there. Someone's planted them. Mayhap you did yourself."

Jett eyed him thoughtfully.

" I'll give you one more chance, Madgek ", he said. " Whose boots are these ? "

" I tell you I don't know."

" Very well. I'm going to take a cast of these and of the ones you've got on. Pentwhistle, spread

316

that heap of sand out flat. Mr. Lamming, will you run over in your car, please, and get some plaster of Paris."

Half an hour later the cast had been taken ; it left no doubt in Jett's mind as to the ownership of the patched boots, though he knew that a jury might be less easily satisfied. He led the way back into the little house, and sat down opposite the fisherman.

" I'm going to ask you some questions, Madgek ", he said. " You needn't answer them if you don't want to."

The fisherman stared at him in silence. Superintendent Jett leaned forward.

" Here's the first one ; were you out on the sand-dunes by Mr. Fiennes' hut at any time between sunset on Friday 22nd and sunrise on Sunday 24th ? "

For a fraction of a second Madgek hesitated. His eyes searched the Superintendent's face.

" I've told you where I, was on Friday and Saturday night ", he answered.

" That doesn't answer my question. I said *any time* in those thirty-six hours."

The tip of Madgek's tongue moistened his lips.

" How can I answer that ? " he demanded sullenly. " A man can't remember everywhere he went a fortnight ago. Sometimes I have to leave my boat down at the pool at low water and walk back across the saltings."

" And did you that Saturday ? The Saturday of the fog ? "

The Superintendent's voice was very quiet, but there was a deadly intensity in its tone. Madgek's eyes shifted from face to face. Again a trickle of moisture ran down his forehead.

" No ", he said, " I didn't. I never went near the huts that day."

" Then where were you on that foggy day ? "

" I was about the village or mending my gear. There's many saw me. Young Soller was helping me with my gear. Mr. Pansel came and talked to us."

" What time was that ? "

" Before noon—ten to eleven perhaps."

" Soller was the lad you say was out poaching with you ? "

Madgek did not answer. His thumbs moved over and over the surface of this thick blue trousers. Jett rose to his feet.

" Stay about the place, Madgek ", he said. " I may want to ask you some more questions."

The fisherman remained silent and did not move as the police-officers left the house. People were moving about the village now and many eyed the police-officers curiously.

" Stop in Bryde to-day, Pentwhistle ", said the Superintendent. " Don't watch Madgek too obviously but he mustn't get away. He won't try in daylight, I don't think. We must get word to Voles, Inspector ; I don't want anyone to see him talking to a policeman ; your nephew might take a message. And I'll get through to the Chief and ask for another of his plain-clothes men ; it's at night we shall have to watch him. I've not got quite enough yet, but by God, I'm going to."

All the way back to Dersingham Jett puzzled over his next line of action. It was all very well to feel sure himself, but he knew that one vital link was missing from his case. Either he must prove that the murder was done at the hut during the afternoon of Saturday—when Madgek had no alibi, or he must prove that Madgek was near the hut at that time and so could have done the murder in the manner in which the police believed that it had been done.

Jett ran over the theory—the Chief Constable's theory—in his mind, filling out the bare bones with material since gathered from witnesses or culled from his own imagination. Madgek, badly in need of money, had seen Fiennes' bulging pocket-book. A week or so later the blanket of fog had given him—perhaps suggested to him—an opportunity. Knowing, as he did, every inch of the saltings and sand-dunes, he had made his way through the mist to Fiennes' hut, some time after noon—after Tasson had delivered the mail. Fiennes by that time was up—had read his letters and pocketed them. Possibly he had left his hut ; Madgek, anyhow, had killed him, perhaps tripped him up, ' locked ' him and smothered him—pushed his face into the soft sand, perhaps (this, realised Jett, was still conjecture, but Madgek was powerful enough to do what he liked with Fiennes). He had then taken the money, either from pocket-book or safe, and returned to Bryde to establish as much of an alibi as possible. Later, perhaps, he had conceived the idea of making the whole thing look like an accident, had gone back to the hut, carried the body across Little Creek and along the raised bank, finally throwing it face downwards in the creek where it was found next morning ; this part of the business

might have been done any time within two hours
either side of low tide—say between 8 p.m. and
midnight. As Madgek's reputed alibi began with
a drink at the ' Anchorage ' before 10 p.m., it was
probable that the frame-up had taken place between
that hour and 8 p.m.

At the end of his review Jett felt less comfortable
than he had done before it ; the method of killing
was so uncertain, and he had not yet connected
Madgek with the hut during the afternoon. There
was much still to be done ; after putting through
his request to the Chief Constable for another plain-
clothes man he turned to other work, hoping to
come back to the case later with a mind cleared
and refreshed.

He was not destined to have much rest ; soon
after three that afternoon Inspector Lamming rang
up from Great Hayworth to say that Detective-
Sergeant Voles had just come in with important
information. Jett realised that it must indeed be
important to make the detective disobey the
instructions that had been given him. Getting rid
of the rest of his work as quickly as possible, Jett
climbed into his car and drove back to Great
Hayworth.

In the charge-room sat Jude Tasson, looking
nervous and ill at ease, and a young constable ; in
the small inner office were Inspector Lamming and
Detective-Sergeant Voles. Without wasting time
on excuses, Sergeant Voles started his story.

" I got hold of Tasson after his dinner, sir, and
stood him some port in the private bar of the
' Duck '—port often makes 'em talk ; they aren't
accustomed to it and don't realise what a small glass

or two can do. We got onto Fiennes' death and
your advertisement. I saw he wanted to talk but
was nervous, so I didn't urge him. Presently it
came. He knew you were after Madgek and hinted
that he knew something important. But he wouldn't
come across with it, and at last I took a risk and
told him who I was—threatened him that he'd said
too much to go back—was in danger as an accessory.
He broke down then and talked. It's important,
sir ; I thought you'd better hear it from him, so I
brought him straight along."

Superintendent Jett looked thoughtfully at the
young detective.

" You certainly have taken a risk, Sergeant ",
he said. " It'll be justified by results—not otherwise. Bring him in, Inspector."

Jude Tasson, now miserably sobering down,
shivered with nervousness as he sat on the hard office
chair in front of the three police-officers. His tale
was quickly told ; he had not told it before, at first
because he had not realised its significance and later
because he was afraid of the vengeance of the
fishermen on a 'squeaker' ; only the wine, he
declared, had loosened his tongue. What he had to
tell was simply this : when he took the letters to
Mr. Fiennes' hut that Saturday he had seen, during
a momentary lifting of the mist, a figure ahead of
him which he recognized as Madgek's ; he had
called to him but apparently Madgek had not
heard ; almost at once the mist thickened again
and he had seen no more of him. No, he had not
seen Madgek near Fiennes' hut, but among some
other huts beyond it. That had been at about
1.30 p.m. He admitted now that he knew Madgek

to be the owner of the patched boot; his reasons for denying that knowledge previously had been, as he had stated, fear of the fishermen.

Jett carefully questioned Tasson but could not shake him in his story. He was certain of the day, the time, the place, and the man. Had Madgek heard that call? Jett wondered; if so, it would account for his hesitation when asked whether he had been out to the huts that day—he had not known whether he had been recognized; to deny his presence there had been a risk only less great than admitting it.

"Wait in the other room, Tasson", said Superintendent Jett curtly. As the door closed he turned to his colleagues. "That's what we wanted, Lamming; we'll go for that warrant now and pull him in. You were right, Sergeant; the news justifies the risk—as it turns out. But I think you were lucky."

He returned to the charge-room and, taking a 10/- note from his case, gave it to Tasson.

"You'd better keep away from Bryde this evening, young fellow", he said. "Run along and amuse yourself in Hunstanton or where you like, but don't come back till late. Bewd, see him on to the Hunstanton bus."

The obtaining of the warrant took a great deal longer than Jett had anticipated. To make sure of getting it he asked the Chief Constable to come and support his application to the Chairman of the Bench, Sir John Helborough. Sir John, however, was difficult to locate, and when located still more difficult to persuade. It was nearly eleven o'clock that night when the two police-officers parked their car in a quiet corner of Bryde and walked down towards Madgek's house. A figure detached itself from the deeper shadows of a shed and joined them. It was Detective-Constable Glease, who had arrived from Norwich late that afternoon and been posted by Inspector Lamming.

" He's taken a walk, sir ", the man murmured. " Sergeant Voles is after him. I went along as far as the cross-road to see which road he took ; then Sergeant Voles sent me back in case you turned up."

" Which way did he go ? "

" The Great Hayworth road, sir."

" Damn. How did we miss him ? When did he go ? "

" Nearly an hour ago, sir."

Jett tugged at his moustache.

" How shall we find either of them now ? Must be somewhere in Great Hayworth. Come on, Lamming ; we must go back. Wait here, Glease, in case he doubles. Don't leave him."

They drove slowly back towards Great Hayworth. The moon was rising, throwing heavy shadows across the white ribbon of road. Suddenly Jett pulled up the car with a jerk. A dark figure had jumped almost in front of it.

" Beg your pardon, sir. Only recognized you at the last moment. He's down there. Sergeant Voles is with 'im."

Police-Constable Pentwhistle, in plain clothes, pointed at the dark mass of a barn standing some hundred yards from the road.

" How did you get here ? "

" I'd just had my supper, sir, and gone out for a breath of air before turning in when Sergeant Voles bumped into me. He told me that Madgek was round the back of the 'Comely Ram'; he told me to keep an eye on him and follow if he went after Madgek. I slipped across the road into a doorway. Presently Madgek came out and a girl with him— Dallington's daughter, what keeps the 'Ram'. They walked off back this way, the Sergeant followin'. He's down there now. I missed you as you went past first time; didn't recognize the car in time."

"Wait here with it then. Come on, Lamming."

Very cautiously the two officers made their way down the shady side of the hedge till they reached the barn. At one corner stood Sergeant Voles, watching the big double-doors.

"He's in there with the girl, sir. I've not looked in—he'd hear me. But there's no other way out."

"What's he up to?"

Sergeant Voles shrugged his shoulders.

"Well, if he's not out soon I'm going in to fetch him."

Only a few minutes had passed, however, when with a ponderous creak, the black door swung open; a man and girl came out into the moonlight. For a moment they stood hand in hand, looking into each other's faces; then the girl flung her arms round the man's neck and they clung together passionately.

"Chris. Oh, Chris, my darling."

The words, whispered though they were, came clearly to the watchers.

"There, my girl, there; don't you take on."

Gently Madgek disengaged the girl's arms. With a sob she turned and stumbled away, passing close to the police-officers without seeing them. Madgek stood watching her, the moon shining on his face and bare head, making it—Jett thought—almost unbelievably beautiful. When the girl had disappeared down the road Madgek turned to shut the barn door. Superintendent Jett, coming quietly up behind, touched his shoulder. With a gasp Madgek spun round, his face white and horrified.

" Christian Madgek ", said Jett quietly, " I hold a warrant for your arrest on a charge of killing and murdering Dallas Fiennes on or about the 22nd. of July. It is my duty to warn you . . ."

CHAPTER XXVI

"THE HAPPY PILGRIM"

CHRISTIAN MADGEK appeared before Sir John Helborough the following morning and was remanded in custody till the following Monday. He made no statement but asked if he might see Mr. John Pansel to consult him about his defence, and this was granted on the understanding that a police-officer would be present throughout the interview. John Pansel reached the police-station within an hour of the adjournment and was at once admitted to Madgek's cell. He shook hands with the fisherman and gave him a friendly, nervous smile.

" What's the trouble, Polly ? " he asked. " We've heard nothing in Bryde and the constable who fetched me was mysterious."

" They've got me for murder, Mr. Pansel."

" Murder ? ! "

John's jaw dropped. He stared at the fisherman in consternation.

" They say I killed Mr. Fiennes and took his money and dropped his body in the crik to make it look like an accident. They say I knew he'd got money because I saw a fat pocket-book drop in my boat—and that's true. They say I was badly in need of money—and that's true. They say they can trace some of the money to me—and that's a lie, because I never touched it. I never knew the man was dead till old Giles came and told us and then

we all lifted him out together and brought him along
home. But I *was* near his hut when they say he was
killed and I denied it, and that's where I'm in
trouble. I don't know what best to do, Mr. Pansel,
and I thought mayhap, as you'd been friendly with
me, you might give me a word of advice. I don't
know who else to ask."

John Pansel sat down on the bed beside Madgek
and put his hand on the man's knee.

" Yes, tell me all about it, Polly ", he said gravely.
" I'll help you if you'll tell me the truth."

Christian Madgek glanced uneasily at Police-
Constable Pentwhistle who was seated in a corner
of the cell. Pentwhistle was there to see that
nothing passed from the visitor to the prisoner, but
Christian did not want any policeman to hear what
he was going to say. He dropped his voice hope-
fully.

" Well, Mr. Pansel, it's like this. As you know
there's nothing in the fishing now. I make a bit by
my boat and a bit by my building, but it's not much.
I get a few rabbits and duck that don't belong to me
and an occasional deer from the Park, but there's
little in that. A few months ago I got to hear that
they were going to try and run brandy in here, duty
free, and it seemed a good way of earning a bit extra
and getting a bit of fun. I'd better not tell you who
else is in it but you may guess one or two."

John Pansel nodded.

" I was given a bottle of that brandy ", he said.
" Wonderful stuff."

" Well, sir, this is what happened that time when
the weather was thick. They were going to land a
cargo at the pool as soon as the tide was high enough

for their boat to get in—sometime between eleven and midnight. Then I was to ship it into my boat and run it back into Bryde and stow it in my yard. Sim Fardell was to come along the next night and do the distributing with his cart. It had gone easy enough before. But this Friday we're talking of it came over thick, as you know, and I never thought they'd make it, but they did; the lugger came in close in the evening under cover of the weather, and they ran their boat into the pool almost on time. But I was afraid of running up the crik in that fog; if I'd run aground I could never have cleared my boat before daylight and there I'd have been found with the goods—in *my* boat. No getting away from it. I didn't even take my boat down to the pool."

John Pansel was staring at his companion.

" Were you at the harbour at about ten o'clock that evening ? " he asked.

" Yes, Mr. Pansel, I was ; and I saw you and Mr. Fiennes come down and you called ' Good-night ', but I knew you hadn't seen who I was because you didn't say my name. I thought I'd better not be seen about there just then, so I faded out."

Pansel nodded slowly.

" If I'd known that before . . ." he said. " Well, go on ; what did you do ? "

" I dumped the stuff in an empty hut on the sand-dunes. Nobody ever goes into it—it's a dirty old place. I covered the kegs up as best I could with some old planks, but it had taken me a terrible time to do and by the time I'd finished it was long past daybreak. But the weather was still thick and I thought I'd carry one of the kegs back with me, so as to save time next night. The tide was going down again by then and I waded Little Creek and went along the raised bank. I could just make out the track, but that was all. I didn't see a soul and I stowed the keg away in my yard."

" You didn't see Mr. Fiennes' body in the creek as you came along ? "

" Not a thing ; it was all I could do to see where I was going. The police say it wasn't there then. They say I dumped it in the next evening at low tide."

John Pansel stared at the fisherman, but said no more.

" During the morning, as you know, Mr. Pansel, it looked like clearing and I got nervous about whether I'd left any tracks round that hut to make people curious. So I slipped over there somewhere about one and had a good look round. The police asked me if I was over there in the day and I lost my head and said I wasn't. Now they say I was seen there and that'll hang me like enough."

Pansel put his hand on the man's arm and gripped it.

" No, it won't ", he said. " Not if you're an innocent man. Go on."

" Next night—Saturday night—it wasn't nearly so thick and I slipped down in my boat and got the stuff away and stowed in my yard. Sim Fardell was there and we took a keg across to . . . well, we did the local distribution, and then he took another away in his cart. He got the last of them cleared two or three nights ago, just before the police came along and searched my place ; he didn't like to come every night for fear of somebody noticing. I was well paid for my share in the landing and that's where I got the money from to repay Fardell—that and what I earned. The police talk about my having given Fardell a note that had been soaked in sea-water; likely enough it had—I got it from a seaman. When that Superintendent came to see me I thought he was after the brandy; I had to tell one or two lies that I needn't have done and that's got me into trouble."

John Pansel nodded.

"I know, Polly; it generally does", he said gloomily.

"But I thought I was safe enough because I'd fixed up with some men to swear I'd been out after game in Statcham Park both nights; I'm to pay them if any trouble comes of it. Of course they know what I was really up to, but they won't talk. As a matter of fact, Fardell and I had fixed up a story beforehand for the police to hear there was going to be poaching in the Park that night; we wanted to draw 'em away from the coast. I believe that Inspector fellow spent most of those nights crawling round Statcham in the fog."

Christian was unable to resist a sly glance at Pentwhistle.

"But it was the boots that were my big mistake."

"Boots?"

"Yes; it was like this. On Sunday morning when the police-officers were messing about round where the body was found I saw them looking at the path further along, where it bends towards the post. In the evening I went along, as a matter of curiosity, to see what they'd been looking at and there I saw a mark made by one of my boots—it had got a patch on the heel; that keg I carried was dashed heavy and at one place where there was some soft mud my heel had made a deep mark. I thought they might trace me back to the hut where I'd stowed the brandy, and like a fool I stamped out the mark and went back and hid my boots. I ought to have cut 'em up but I don't like parting with good stuff. Of course I'd got another pair. When the police came yesterday they found those boots and now they say that deep mark was made by me carrying the body. Lord, I was a fool!''

"But, Polly", said John, "you've only got to tell the truth about this smuggling and they can't hang you. You may get something for smuggling, but not much.''

Madgek shook his head.

"I can't prove I didn't kill him, sir. I was near there when they say it was done.''

"But it may not have been done then. That's only their idea.''

"But I've told so many lies, Mr. Pansel", said Christian gloomily. "And . . . it's not only hanging I'm afraid of.''

John Pansel raised his eyebrows.

"What d'you mean?''

Madgek was silent for a minute, as if wondering how to frame his answer.

"I've been courting a girl in Great Hayworth—daughter of Dallington of the 'Comely Ram'. He's a warm man and she'll come in for a lot of money. I knew he wouldn't let her marry a fisherman with no money so I've been making out I'd got a lot put by. I've given her expensive presents. That's how I've got into debt with Fardell. If Dallington finds out I've been smuggling—if I'm jugged for it, anyhow, he'll never let her marry me—though the old hypocrite's had some of the brandy, I'm prepared to bet. I've lost her now, you see, Mr. Pansel, whether I hang or not."

John Pansel looked steadily at his companion.

"Or is it her money you've lost, Madgek?" he asked curtly.

Christian drew back, then sank his chin on to his hand.

"I reckon I've deserved that, Mr. Pansel", he said. "I've thought too much of the money. But last night I told her all about it and she . . . she was fine, Mr. Pansel. She'd stick to me if she could, but her father'll stop her. And I found I didn't want to lose her, money or no money; I think last night we both really loved each other for the first time. And now I'm going to lose her."

With a sigh that was almost a sob, Christian Madgek sank his head between his hands. John Pansel watched him, his own face reflecting the misery and pain of the other's. There was silence in the little cell, each man deep in his own thoughts. At last Pansel rose and, dropping his hand on to Madgek's shoulder, said:

"Don't worry, Polly. We'll get you out of this. I'll see about your defence. I can't promise to keep what you've just told me quiet, but if you're an innocent man you'll not hang; I promise you that."

He held out his hand and Christian Madgek gripped it tightly.

"You've been very good to me, Mr. Pansel. I don't know why you should help me or why you should believe I'm not a murderer."

John Pansel smiled.

" Cheer up, Polly ", he said. " There may be good reasons for killing a man like Fiennes, but I can't believe that twenty quid is one of them."

* * * * *

While her husband was with Christian Madgek, Hilary Pansel walked over to Brulcote to see Beryl Helliott. She found her friend in a state of some excitement, as her brother had returned late the previous night, after nearly three weeks' absence ; he was at present about the farm, talking to his foreman, and his sister took Hilary out into the garden to tell her, ' in confidence ', all about it. Poor Frank, apparently, had got tangled up with some girl and—well, the fact was, he thought he ought to marry her—he was so quixotic ; he had been running about between her and her family and his solicitors, trying to arrange things and not liking to tell Beryl—but she had got it out of him last night. The girl's parents, of course, were all for the marriage but *most fortunately* the girl herself didn't seem to want to marry Frank, and in the end he had come to some arrangement about money which would probably mean selling or borrowing or something dreadful that Beryl couldn't understand. But at least it was better than his tying himself up with some dreadful little . . .

At this point Frank himself appeared, carrying a bundle of letters and a waste-paper basket. He shook hands rather shamefacedly with Hilary, probably guessing that ' confidences ' were in the air.

" It's so stuffy indoors ", he said, " and I've got

to plough through all these letters and things that
have come while I've been away."

He sank down into a garden chair beside them and
ripped open a long buff envelope.

" Oh, Lord ", he groaned, and picked up the
next.

The two women discussed the affairs of Bryde in
gentle murmurs which were suddenly interrupted
by an exclamation from Frank. He was sitting up,
staring at a thick envelope which he had just
opened and from which he had drawn a wad of bank-
notes. Slowly he counted them—four £5 notes and
a number of smaller ones.

" Fifty pounds ! "

He looked inside the envelope ; it contained no
letter. The envelope itself was addressed in block
letters. It was not registered.

" Frank ! Where did all that money come from ? "
exclaimed Beryl excitedly.

Frank looked at his sister and back at the notes.
A flush of colour spread over his cheeks.

" I . . . I believe Fiennes must have sent them ",
he said. " I asked him to lend me some money just
before I went away but he turned me down flat.
He was rather offensive about it. But . . . I don't
know who else . . ."

His voice trailed into silence. Hilary was staring
at the flimsy sheets of paper.

" But those notes ", she said ; " they must be
the ones the police are advertising for ! I don't
remember the numbers but there were four £5
notes and . . . oh ! "

" What is it, Hilary ? "

" Why, the police arrested Christian Madgek last

night. John's gone over to see him this morning.
Can it be about these notes ? "

"They don't think he killed Mr. Fiennes, do
they ? " asked Beryl.

Hilary stared aghast at her friend. Was that
awful nightmare still hanging over Bryde ? Surely
the jury had said it was an accident ?

"I must go and see John ", she said resolutely.
"Can I have the numbers of the notes, please,
Frank ? "

She jotted them down and hurried off back
towards Bryde. When she reached her home she
was surprised to find that John had not come back.
It was nearly time for tea, so she stirred up the fire,
put on the kettle and went upstairs to tidy her hair.
On her dressing-table was an envelope addressed to
her in John's writing. She tore it open and after
reading a line or two her heart seemed to stop
beating.

HILARY (he wrote),

     Christian Madgek has been charged with the
murder of Fiennes. I don't think he is in any
danger but it shows they don't believe it was an
accident. They will go on now till they find out
who did kill him. I can't face the awful strain of it
and all the trials. I'm going to write down what
happened and when you've read it I want you to
send it to Major Fennell. I only told you part of
the truth, Hilary ; I was so dreadfully afraid of
losing you. And now I have lied to you and lost
you too. I told you that I meant to kill Fiennes—
planned carefully to kill him so that it looked like
an accident—a boating accident. Then this hap-

pened and I killed him in a blind rage and could only struggle afterwards to hide what I had done. I shan't see you again, Hilary; I couldn't bear to say good-bye to you. The only way is to go now, quickly. I love you so much, more now than ever in my life.

JOHN.

If you want help, go to Hugh Fallaran. I've written him a note.

On separate sheets of paper was John Pansel's statement.

On Friday, 22nd. July, Mr. Fiennes dined with us. He had had rather a lot to drink before he came and when he left, as it was foggy, I thought I had better see him back across the saltings. We were on bad terms and when we were on the path across the saltings he said something, perhaps because he was drunk, that was more than I could stand. I lifted my stick to hit him and he ran off into the fog. Almost at once I heard him give a cry and then there was a smacking thud. I went forward and saw that he had fallen into the muddy creek and was floundering on his face in the mud. I scrambled down and pushed his face into the mud till he stopped moving. Then I got back onto the path and tried to get home, but I had lost my torch and when I found it the bulb had gone. I took a long time to get home; once I fell into the mud myself and once I found I had been going in the wrong direction and had to go back. I got home at about one and I didn't think anyone had seen me, but I couldn't be sure.

Next day I waited for the body to be found. There was just a chance it might be taken for an accident but it would be known that he had been dining with me and that I had gone as far as the saltings with him—and that I hated him. My mackintosh and trousers were filthy from being in the mud. I washed the mac. and hid the trousers. And I put a new bulb in my torch, which seemed to excite the Inspector the day he came. I'd had Fiennes' shoes in my pocket all the time and they had got wet through, so I had to bury them.

The mist was still thick on Saturday but Jude Tasson told me he was going to try and get the mail out to Fiennes' hut. In the afternoon I saw him again and he told me that he had been out to the hut and it was locked; he thought Fiennes was asleep, as he sometimes was when he had been working all night. Tasson had put the letters in the box and come away. That put a wonderful idea into my head; if I could make it look as if Fiennes had got home that night there would be nothing to connect me with his death.

I went down to the inn that evening for a drink and stayed there till ten; then I went home, said good-night to my wife, who was already in bed, and as soon as I thought she was asleep I slipped out again. It was still thick but not as bad as the night before. It was low tide at ten that night and I had no difficulty in getting across the harbour on to the raised bank. I found Fiennes just as I had left him, except that the tide had been over him twice and he was soaking wet. His torch was still in his hand and I took it; he would hardly have had it with him in daylight, even in a fog. I got the keys out of his pockets and went along to his hut. I found the letters in the box, opened them, threw a bill in the waste-paper basket, crumpled up the envelopes and threw them on the floor, and pocketed the

*private letter. Then I had another idea. To make it
look as if he'd had breakfast I lit the oil-stove and made
some scrambled eggs and ate them. I cleaned his torch
and left it beside his bed. Then I locked the hut and
went back to the body and shoved the keys in his trouser
pocket and the private letter in his jacket. The tide
was just beginning to cover him and I had a job to get
across the harbour, but again I got home without
meeting anyone.*

*I don't think I need say any more, except that of
course Madgek had absolutely nothing to do with the
man's death and I hope he will be released at
once.*

JOHN PANSEL.

Hilary tried to read what John had written, but
she was dazed and faint with the shock and the
words meant very little to her. She only realised
that John thought he should be punished and not
Christian Madgek. He must have killed Dallas
after all ; she couldn't understand it, after what he
had told her . . . perhaps later she would be able
to. But Christian was not in danger now . . . the
notes he was supposed to have taken had turned up
. . . there was no need now for John to say anything. Where was John ? If only she could find
him . . .

Staring out of her bedroom window with unseeing
eyes Hilary gradually became aware of what she was
looking at. The saltings were before her, the creek
winding towards the sea. The tide was falling and a
small sailing boat had got stuck on a bank of sand ;
the occupant of it had got out and was trying to
push it off into deeper water. Something familiar

about the figure, distant as it was, suddenly penetrated to Hilary's conscious mind ; with a start she leaned out of the window and stared at it.

"It's John !" she exclaimed, and dashing downstairs, ran out into the road and down towards the harbour. In the village people watched curiously the hurrying, panting woman, her face drawn, her eyes staring but seeming to see nothing about her. On the quay old Giles Banyatt was leaning against a post. Hilary ran up to him.

"Mr. Pansel", she gasped ; "is that him in the sailing boat ? "

"That's him, Miss", replied Giles, who had known her for twelve years as a married woman. "And what he thinks he's doing trying to sail down the crik on a falling tide is more than I can tell."

"But can I catch him ? Can you take me ? "

Giles shook his head.

"You'd catch him best by running across the saltings to the point. I doubt he'll get across the bar, anyhow. Slip into my boat, miss ; I'll put you across."

In half a minute she was across the harbour, flying down the raised bank. Away to her left she could see the little boat moving slowly down towards the sea. Panting and dizzy she staggered on, her legs trembling but her will keeping them somehow in motion. Waving frantically she splashed through Little Creek, but the boat was now in the pool and slipping over the deeper water towards the shallow bar. Two or three fishermen were on the sloping beach beside the pool, laying out a net. They, too, were watching John Pansel, who was tugging at his centre-board to raise it in order that he might slip across the bar.

"Awkward, that boat of Cadnall's", said one of them. "Look, he can't get that centre-board down again. It's always sticking, unless you know the trick. I've seen the boys capsize with that."

"If he doesn't get it down he'll have trouble", said another. "Wind'll catch him once he's clear of the headland."

Hilary, staggering with exhaustion but still waving as best she could, came up to the little group.

"Oh, stop him", she gasped, "can't you stop him ?"

They looked at her in surprise but seeing that she was in earnest—in trouble—they raised their arms, waving and shouting with a will. The figure in the little boat, still struggling with the recalcitrant centre-board, paid no heed to them. The off-shore wind was carrying him swiftly out to sea, the boat leaning over dangerously as a cross-current of air caught it. The men looked significantly at each other. At that moment the boat lurched violently, heeled over, and flattened out on the water, the waves—small though they were—breaking over the sail.

"Hope he can swim."

"Tide'll carry him out."

"Oh", cried Hilary. "Can't you get to him ? Oh, quick, quick."

The men ran clumsily down to their heavy boat and tried to heave it into the water, but the tide had fallen too low. Not till it turned could they put to sea. The men left it and hurried along to the shore, but they knew that only the strongest swimmer could beat back against tide and current in clothes and boots. But no figure struck out for the shore, nor clung to the rocking hull. The *Happy Pilgrim* floated alone upon the face of the sea.

THE PERENNIAL LIBRARY MYSTERY SERIES

Ted Allbeury

THE OTHER SIDE OF SILENCE   P 669, $2.84
"In the best le Carré tradition . . . an ingenious and readable book."
              —*New York Times Book Review*

PALOMINO BLONDE   P 670, $2.84
"Fast-moving, splendidly technocratic intercontinental espionage tale
. . . you'll love it."   —*The Times* (London)

SNOWBALL   P 671, $2.84
"A novel of byzantine intrigue. . . ."—*New York Times Book Review*

Delano Ames

CORPSE DIPLOMATIQUE   P 637, $2.84
"Sprightly and intelligent."
          —*New York Herald Tribune Book Review*

FOR OLD CRIME'S SAKE   P 629, $2.84

MURDER, MAESTRO, PLEASE   P 630, $2.84
"If there is a more engaging couple in modern fiction than Jane and
Dagobert Brown, we have not met them."   —*Scotsman*

SHE SHALL HAVE MURDER   P 638, $2.84
"Combines the merit of both the English and American schools in the
new mystery. It's as breezy as the best of the American ones, and has
the sophistication and wit of any top-notch Britisher."
          —*New York Herald Tribune Book Review*

E. C. Bentley

TRENT'S LAST CASE   P 440, $2.50
"One of the three best detective stories ever written."
          —Agatha Christie

TRENT'S OWN CASE   P 516, $2.25
"I won't waste time saying that the plot is sound and the detection
satisfying. Trent has not altered a scrap and reappears with all his old
humor and charm."   —Dorothy L. Sayers

Andrew Bergman

THE BIG KISS-OFF OF 1944 P 673, $2.84
"It is without doubt the nearest thing to genuine Chandler I've ever come across. . . . Tough, witty—very witty—and a beautiful eye for period detail. . . ." —Jack Higgins

HOLLYWOOD AND LEVINE P 674, $2.84
"Fast-paced private-eye fiction." —San Francisco Chronicle

Gavin Black

A DRAGON FOR CHRISTMAS P 473, $1.95
"Potent excitement!" —New York Herald Tribune

THE EYES AROUND ME P 485, $1.95
"I stayed up until all hours last night reading *The Eyes Around Me,* which is something I do not do very often, but I was so intrigued by the ingeniousness of Mr. Black's plotting and the witty way in which he spins his mystery. I can only say that I enjoyed the book enormously."
—F. van Wyck Mason

YOU WANT TO DIE, JOHNNY? P 472, $1.95
"Gavin Black doesn't just develop a pressure plot in suspense, he adds uninfected wit, character, charm, and sharp knowledge of the Far East to make rereading as keen as the first race-through." —Book Week

Nicholas Blake

THE CORPSE IN THE SNOWMAN P 427, $1.95
"If there is a distinction between the novel and the detective story (which we do not admit), then this book deserves a high place in both categories." —New York Times

END OF CHAPTER P 397, $1.95
". . . admirably solid . . . an adroit formal detective puzzle backed up by firm characterization and a knowing picture of London publishing."
—New York Times

HEAD OF A TRAVELER P 398, $2.25
"Another grade A detective story of the right old jigsaw persuasion."
—New York Herald Tribune Book Review

MINUTE FOR MURDER P 419, $1.95
"An outstanding mystery novel. Mr. Blake's writing is a delight in itself." —New York Times

THE MORNING AFTER DEATH P 520, $1.95
"One of Blake's best." —Rex Warner

Nicholas Blake (cont'd)

A PENKNIFE IN MY HEART P 521, $2.25
"Style brilliant . . . and suspenseful." —*San Francisco Chronicle*

THE PRIVATE WOUND P 531, $2.25
"[Blake's] best novel in a dozen years . . . . An intensely penetrating study of sexual passion. . . . A powerful story of murder and its aftermath."
—Anthony Boucher, *New York Times*

A QUESTION OF PROOF P 494, $1.95
"The characters in this story are unusually well drawn, and the suspense is well sustained." —*New York Times*

THE SAD VARIETY P 495, $2.25
"It is a stunner. I read it instead of eating, instead of sleeping."
—Dorothy Salisbury Davis

THERE'S TROUBLE BREWING P 569, $3.37
"Nigel Strangeways is a puzzling mixture of simplicity and penetration, but all the more real for that."
—*The Times* (London) *Literary Supplement*

THOU SHELL OF DEATH P 428, $1.95
"It has all the virtues of culture, intelligence and sensibility that the most exacting connoisseur could ask of detective fiction."
—*The Times* (London) *Literary Supplement*

THE WIDOW'S CRUISE P 399, $2.25
"A stirring suspense. . . . The thrilling tale leaves nothing to be desired."
—*Springfield Republican*

Oliver Bleeck

THE BRASS GO-BETWEEN P 645, $2.84
"Fiction with a flair, well above the norm for thrillers."
—*Associated Press*

THE PROCANE CHRONICLE P 647, $2.84
"Without peer in American suspense." —*Los Angeles Times*

PROTOCOL FOR A KIDNAPPING P 646, $2.84
"The zigzags of plot are electric; the characters sharp; but it is the wit and irony and touches of plain fun which make the whole a standout."
—*Los Angeles Times*

John & Emery Bonett

A BANNER FOR PEGASUS   P 554, $2.40
"A gem! Beautifully plotted and set. . . . Not only is the murder adroit
and deserved, and the detection competent, but the love story is charming."
        —Jacques Barzun and Wendell Hertig Taylor

DEAD LION   P 563, $2.40
"A clever plot, authentic background and interesting characters highly
recommended this one."   *—New Republic*

THE SOUND OF MURDER   P 642, $2.84
The suspects are many, the clues few, but the gentle Inspector ferrets out
the truth and pursues the case to its bitter and shocking end.

Christianna Brand

GREEN FOR DANGER   P 551, $2.50
"You have to reach for the greatest of Great Names (Christie, Carr,
Queen . . .) to find Brand's rivals in the devious subtleties of the trade."
        —Anthony Boucher

TOUR DE FORCE   P 572, $2.40
"Complete with traps for the over-ingenious, a double-reverse surprise
ending and a key clue planted so fairly and obviously that you completely
overlook it. If that's your idea of perfect entertainment, then seize at once
upon *Tour de Force.*"   —Anthony Boucher, *New York Times*

James Byrom

OR BE HE DEAD   P 585, $2.84
"A very original tale . . . Well written and steadily entertaining."
—Jacques Barzun and Wendell Hertig Taylor, *A Catalogue of Crime*

Henry Calvin

IT'S DIFFERENT ABROAD   P 640, $2.84
"What is remarkable and delightful, Mr. Calvin imparts a flavor of satire
to what he renovates and compels us to take straight."
        —Jacques Barzun

Marjorie Carleton

VANISHED   P 559, $2.40
"Exceptional . . . a minor triumph."
—Jacques Barzun and Wendell Hertig Taylor, *A Catalogue of Crime*

George Harmon Coxe

MURDER WITH PICTURES P 527, $2.25

"[Coxe] has hit the bull's-eye with his first shot."

—*New York Times*

Edmund Crispin

BURIED FOR PLEASURE P 506, $2.50

"Absolute and unalloyed delight."

—Anthony Boucher, *New York Times*

Lionel Davidson

THE MENORAH MEN P 592, $2.84

"Of his fellow thriller writers, only John Le Carré shows the same instinct for the viscera." —*Chicago Tribune*

NIGHT OF WENCESLAS P 595, $2.84

"A most ingenious thriller, so enriched with style, wit, and a sense of serious comedy that it all but transcends its kind."

—*The New Yorker*

THE ROSE OF TIBET P 593, $2.84

"I hadn't realized how much I missed the genuine Adventure story . . . until I read *The Rose of Tibet*." —Graham Greene

D. M. Devine

MY BROTHER'S KILLER P 558, $2.40

"A most enjoyable crime story which I enjoyed reading down to the last moment." —Agatha Christie

Kenneth Fearing

THE BIG CLOCK P 500, $1.95

"It will be some time before chill-hungry clients meet again so rare a compound of irony, satire, and icy-fingered narrative. *The Big Clock* is . . . a psychothriller you won't put down." —*Weekly Book Review*

Andrew Garve

THE ASHES OF LODA P 430, $1.50

"Garve . . . embellishes a fine fast adventure story with a more credible picture of the U.S.S.R. than is offered in most thrillers."

—*New York Times Book Review*

THE CUCKOO LINE AFFAIR P 451, $1.95

". . . an agreeable and ingenious piece of work." —*The New Yorker*

A HERO FOR LEANDA P 429, $1.50

"One can trust Mr. Garve to put a fresh twist to any situation, and the ending is really a lovely surprise." —*Manchester Guardian*

MURDER THROUGH THE LOOKING GLASS P 449, $1.95

". . . refreshingly out-of-the-way and enjoyable . . . highly recommended to all comers." —*Saturday Review*

NO TEARS FOR HILDA P 441, $1.95

"It starts fine and finishes finer. I got behind on breathing watching Max get not only his man but his woman, too." —*Rex Stout*

THE RIDDLE OF SAMSON P 450, $1.95

"The story is an excellent one, the people are quite likable, and the writing is superior." —*Springfield Republican*

Michael Gilbert

BLOOD AND JUDGMENT P 446, $1.95

"Gilbert readers need scarcely be told that the characters all come alive at first sight, and that his surpassing talent for narration enhances any plot. . . . Don't miss." —*San Francisco Chronicle*

THE BODY OF A GIRL P 459, $1.95

"Does what a good mystery should do: open up into all kinds of ramifications, with untold menace behind the action. At the end, there is a bang-up climax, and it is a pleasure to see how skilfully Gilbert wraps everything up." —*New York Times Book Review*

FEAR TO TREAD P 458, $1.95

"Merits serious consideration as a work of art." —*New York Times*

Joe Gores

HAMMETT P 631, $2.84

"Joe Gores at his very best. Terse, powerful writing—with the master, Dashiell Hammett, as the protagonist in a novel I think he would have been proud to call his own." —*Robert Ludlum*

C. W. Grafton

BEYOND A REASONABLE DOUBT P 519, $1.95

"A very ingenious tale of murder . . . a brilliant and gripping narrative." —*Jacques Barzun and Wendell Hertig Taylor*

C. W. Grafton (cont'd)

THE RAT BEGAN TO GNAW THE ROPE   P 639, $2.84
"Fast, humorous story with flashes of brilliance."

—*The New Yorker*

Edward Grierson

THE SECOND MAN   P 528, $2.25
"One of the best trial-testimony books to have come along in quite a while."   —*The New Yorker*

Bruce Hamilton

TOO MUCH OF WATER   P 635, $2.84
"A superb sea mystery. . . . The prose is excellent."
—Jacques Barzun and Wendell Hertig Taylor, *A Catalogue of Crime*

Cyril Hare

DEATH IS NO SPORTSMAN   P 555, $2.40
"You will be thrilled because it succeeds in placing an ingenious story in a new and refreshing setting. . . . The identity of the murderer is really a surprise."   —*Daily Mirror*

DEATH WALKS THE WOODS   P 556, $2.40
"Here is a fine formal detective story, with a technically brilliant solution demanding the attention of all connoisseurs of construction."
—Anthony Boucher, *New York Times Book Review*

AN ENGLISH MURDER   P 455, $2.50
"By a long shot, the best crime story I have read for a long time. Everything is traditional, but originality does not suffer. The setting is perfect. Full marks to Mr. Hare."   —*Irish Press*

SUICIDE EXCEPTED   P 636, $2.84
"Adroit in its manipulation . . . and distinguished by a plot-twister which I'll wager Christie wishes she'd thought of."   —*New York Times*

TENANT FOR DEATH   P 570, $2.84
"The way in which an air of probability is combined both with clear, terse narrative and with a good deal of subtle suburban atmosphere, proves the extreme skill of the writer."   —*The Spectator*

TRAGEDY AT LAW   P 522, $2.25
"An extremely urbane and well-written detective story."

—*New York Times*

UNTIMELY DEATH P 514, $2.25

"The English detective story at its quiet best, meticulously underplayed, rich in perceivings of the droll human animal and ready at the last with a neat surprise which has been there all the while had we but wits to see it." —*New York Herald Tribune Book Review*

THE WIND BLOWS DEATH P 589, $2.84

"A plot compounded of musical knowledge, a Dickens allusion, and a subtle point in law is related with delightfully unobtrusive wit, warmth, and style." —*New York Times*

WITH A BARE BODKIN P 523, $2.25

"One of the best detective stories published for a long time."
—*The Spectator*

Robert Harling

THE ENORMOUS SHADOW P 545, $2.50

"In some ways the best spy story of the modern period. . . . The writing is terse and vivid . . . the ending full of action . . . altogether first-rate." —Jacques Barzun and Wendell Hertig Taylor, *A Catalogue of Crime*

Matthew Head

THE CABINDA AFFAIR P 541, $2.25

"An absorbing whodunit and a distinguished novel of atmosphere."
—Anthony Boucher, *New York Times*

THE CONGO VENUS P 597, $2.84

"Terrific. The dialogue is just plain wonderful." —*Boston Globe*

MURDER AT THE FLEA CLUB P 542, $2.50

"The true delight is in Head's style, its limpid ease combined with humor and an awesome precision of phrase." —*San Francisco Chronicle*

M. V. Heberden

ENGAGED TO MURDER P 533, $2.25

"Smooth plotting." —*New York Times*

James Hilton

WAS IT MURDER? P 501, $1.95

"The story is well planned and well written." —*New York Times*

S. B. Hough

DEAR DAUGHTER DEAD P 661, $2.84
"A highly intelligent and sophisticated story of police detection . . . not to be missed on any account." —Francis Iles, *The Guardian*

SWEET SISTER SEDUCED P 662, $2.84
In the course of a nightlong conversation between the Inspector and the suspect, the complex emotions of a very strange marriage are revealed.

P. M. Hubbard

HIGH TIDE P 571, $2.40
"A smooth elaboration of mounting horror and danger."
—*Library Journal*

Elspeth Huxley

THE AFRICAN POISON MURDERS P 540, $2.25
"Obscure venom, manical mutilations, deadly bush fire, thrilling climax compose major opus.... Top-flight."
—*Saturday Review of Literature*

MURDER ON SAFARI P 587, $2.84
"Right now we'd call Mrs. Huxley a dangerous rival to Agatha Christie." —*Books*

Francis Iles

BEFORE THE FACT P 517, $2.50
"Not many 'serious' novelists have produced character studies to compare with Iles's internally terrifying portrait of the murderer in *Before the Fact,* his masterpiece and a work truly deserving the appellation of unique and beyond price." —Howard Haycraft

MALICE AFORETHOUGHT P 532, $1.95
"It is a long time since I have read anything so good as *Malice Aforethought,* with its cynical humour, acute criminology, plausible detail and rapid movement. It makes you hug yourself with pleasure."
—H. C. Harwood, *Saturday Review*

Michael Innes

APPLEBY ON ARARAT P 648, $2.84
"Superbly plotted and humorously written." —*The New Yorker*

APPLEBY'S END P 649, $2.84
"Most amusing." —*Boston Globe*

THE CASE OF THE JOURNEYING BOY   P 632, $3.12
"I could see no faults in it. There is no one to compare with him."
                           —Illustrated London News

DEATH ON A QUIET DAY   P 677, $2.84
"Delightfully witty."   *—Chicago Sunday Tribune*

DEATH BY WATER   P 574, $2.40
"The amount of ironic social criticism and deft characterization of scenes and people would serve another author for six books."
         —Jacques Barzun and Wendell Hertig Taylor

HARE SITTING UP   P 590, $2.84
"There is hardly anyone (in mysteries or mainstream) more exquisitely literate, allusive and Jamesian—and hardly anyone with a firmer sense of melodramatic plot or a more vigorous gift of storytelling."
         —Anthony Boucher, New York Times

THE LONG FAREWELL   P 575, $2.40
"A model of the deft, classic detective story, told in the most wittily diverting prose."   *—New York Times*

THE MAN FROM THE SEA   P 591, $2.84
"The pace is brisk, the adventures exciting and excitingly told, and above all he keeps to the very end the interesting ambiguity of the man from the sea."   *—New Statesman*

ONE MAN SHOW   P 672, $2.84
"Exciting, amusingly written . . . very good enjoyment it is."
         —The Spectator

THE SECRET VANGUARD   P 584, $2.84
"Innes . . . has mastered the art of swift, exciting and well-organized narrative."   *—New York Times*

THE WEIGHT OF THE EVIDENCE   P 633, $2.84
"First-class puzzle, deftly solved. University background interesting and amusing."   *—Saturday Review of Literature*

Mary Kelly

THE SPOILT KILL   P 565, $2.40
"Mary Kelly is a new Dorothy Sayers. . . . [An] exciting new novel."
         —Evening News

Lange Lewis

THE BIRTHDAY MURDER P 518, $1.95

"Almost perfect in its playlike purity and delightful prose."

—Jacques Barzun and Wendell Hertig Taylor

Allan MacKinnon

HOUSE OF DARKNESS P 582, $2.84

"His best . . . a perfect compendium."

—Jacques Barzun and Wendell Hertig Taylor, *A Catalogue of Crime*

Frank Parrish

FIRE IN THE BARLEY P 651, $2.84

"A remarkable and brilliant first novel. . . . entrancing."

—*The Spectator*

SNARE IN THE DARK P 650, $2.84

The wily English poacher Dan Mallett is framed for murder and has to confront unknown enemies to clear himself.

STING OF THE HONEYBEE P 652, $2.84

"Terrorism and murder visit a sleepy English village in this witty, offbeat thriller." —*Chicago Sun-Times*

Austin Ripley

MINUTE MYSTERIES P 387, $2.50

More than one hundred of the world's shortest detective stories. Only one possible solution to each case!

Thomas Sterling

THE EVIL OF THE DAY P 529, $2.50

"Prose as witty and subtle as it is sharp and clear. . .characters unconventionally conceived and richly bodied forth . . . . In short, a novel to be treasured." —Anthony Boucher, *New York Times*

Julian Symons

THE BELTING INHERITANCE P 468, $1.95

"A superb whodunit in the best tradition of the detective story."

—August Derleth, *Madison Capital Times*

BOGUE'S FORTUNE P 481, $1.95

"There's a touch of the old sardonic humour, and more than a touch of style." —*The Spectator*

Julian Symons (cont'd)

THE COLOR OF MURDER   P 461, $1.95
"A singularly unostentatious and memorably brilliant detective story."
                        —*New York Herald Tribune Book Review*

Dorothy Stockbridge Tillet
(John Stephen Strange)

THE MAN WHO KILLED FORTESCUE   P 536, $2.25
"Better than average."   —*Saturday Review of Literature*

Simon Troy

THE ROAD TO RHUINE   P 583, $2.84
"Unusual and agreeably told."   —*San Francisco Chronicle*

SWIFT TO ITS CLOSE   P 546, $2.40
"A nicely literate British mystery . . . the atmosphere and the plot are
exceptionally well wrought, the dialogue excellent."   —*Best Sellers*

Henry Wade

THE DUKE OF YORK'S STEPS   P 588, $2.84
"A classic of the golden age."
          —Jacques Barzun and Wendell Hertig Taylor, *A Catalogue of Crime*

A DYING FALL   P 543, $2.50
"One of those expert British suspense jobs . . . it crackles with undercur-
rents of blackmail, violent passion and murder. Topnotch in its class."
                                                        —*Time*

THE HANGING CAPTAIN   P 548, $2.50
"This is a detective story for connoisseurs, for those who value clear
thinking and good writing above mere ingenuity and easy thrills."
—*The Times* (London) *Literary Supplement*

Hillary Waugh

LAST SEEN WEARING . . .   P 552, $2.40
"A brilliant tour de force."   —Julian Symons

THE MISSING MAN   P 553, $2.40
"The quiet detailed police work of Chief Fred C. Fellows, Stockford,
Conn., is at its best in *The Missing Man* . . . one of the Chief's toughest
cases and one of the best handled."
          —Anthony Boucher, *New York Times Book Review*

Henry Kitchell Webster

WHO IS THE NEXT?   P 539, $2.25
"A double murder, private-plane piloting, a neat impersonation, and a delicate courtship are adroitly combined by a writer who knows how to use the language."   —Jacques Barzun and Wendell Hertig Taylor

John Welcome

GO FOR BROKE   P 663, $2.84
A rich financier chases Richard Graham half 'round Europe in a desperate attempt to prevent the truth getting out.

RUN FOR COVER   P 664, $2.84
"I can think of few writers in the international intrigue game with such a gift for fast and vivid storytelling."
                    —*New York Times Book Review*

STOP AT NOTHING   P 665, $2.84
"Mr. Welcome is lively, vivid and highly readable."
                    —*New York Times Book Review*

Anna Mary Wells

MURDERER'S CHOICE   P 534, $2.50
"Good writing, ample action, and excellent character work."
                    —*Saturday Review of Literature*

A TALENT FOR MURDER   P 535, $2.25
"The discovery of the villain is a decided shock."   —*Books*

Charles Williams

DEAD CALM   P 655, $2.84
"A brilliant tour de force of inventive plotting, fine manipulation of a small cast and breathtaking sequences of spectacular navigation."
                    —*New York Times Book Review*

THE SAILCLOTH SHROUD   P 654, $2.84
"A fine novel of excitement, spirited, fresh and satisfying."
                    —*New York Times*

THE WRONG VENUS   P 656, $2.84
Swindler Lawrence Colby and the lovely Martine create a story of romance, larceny, and very blunt homicide.

Edward Young

THE FIFTH PASSENGER   P 544, $2.25
"Clever and adroit . . . excellent thriller. . . ."   —*Library Journal*

If you enjoyed this book you'll want to know about THE PERENNIAL LIBRARY MYSTERY SERIES

Buy them at your local bookstore or use this coupon for ordering:

Qty	P number	Price

postage and handling charge	$1.00
_____ book(s) @ $0.25	_____
TOTAL	

Prices contained in this coupon are Harper & Row invoice prices only. They are subject to change without notice, and in no way reflect the prices at which these books may be sold by other suppliers.

HARPER & ROW, Mail Order Dept. #PMS, 10 East 53rd St., New York, N.Y. 10022.

Please send me the books I have checked above. I am enclosing $_____ which includes a postage and handling charge of $1.00 for the first book and 25¢ for each additional book. Send check or money order. No cash or C.O.D.s please

Name_____

Address_____

City_____ State_____ Zip_____

Please allow 4 weeks for delivery. USA only. This offer expires 8/31/86
Please add applicable sales tax.